THE DEVIL YOU KNEW

MIKE COBB

THE DEVIL YOU KNEW BY MIKE COBB

This book is a work of fiction. Any references to historical events, real people, or real places are used fictitiously. Other names, characters, places, and events are products of the author's imagination, and any resemblance to actual events or places or persons, living or dead, is entirely coincidental. Characters' actions and motives, incident details, and dialogue are drawn from the author's imagination and are not to be construed as real.

ISBN: 978-0-578-37143-6 (pbk.)

MG Cobb Books LLC
www.mgcobb.com

First Edition, September 2022

Cover design by Kian Sadri, Mandy Rahiya, and Laura Sadri

Interior design by Awadhesh Yadav

A Word of Caution

IN A WORK OF PERIOD FICTION, THERE IS OFTEN TENSION between fidelity to the time period and the risk of offending the reader. Certain offensive words and cultural norms, which are unacceptable today, are used in this work. While the decision to use them was not taken lightly, their presence is important to the accuracy and integrity of the period. It is hoped that their incorporation will, at the very least, shed light on a time in our history when attitudes and mores that are taboo today were commonplace. Their use is not intended in any way to disrespect the reader or any group of people.

"You have to quit confusing a madness with a mission."
Flannery O'Connor

PART ONE

Chapter One
I, Billy Tarwater

1963

"WON'T YOU COME."

The Reverend Virlyn Kilgallon's baritone reverberated in a thunderous cannonade, his voice at once magisterial and dark. The altar call always came at the end, when the congregants were sufficiently energized by his twenty-five minutes of prophecy and supplication. The sermon was timed with precision. I know because I clocked it with my Caravelle self-winding, a gift from my Granddaddy Parker.

The year was 1963. I was a tow-headed eleven year old, not quite ready to make the lonely walk to the chancel rail, but old enough to feel pangs of guilt, accompanied by a generous dollop of fear. Looking back, I now understand that my anxiety was borne of both a dread of the curtain-cloaked water vessel behind the choir loft and a sense that I was missing out on something big.

Was there some great, liberating secret lurking behind the curtain—a secret shared only by members of the club, manifest in a covert handshake or a knowing back-channel glance—a secret that I dared not ponder until I made The Walk myself? The Walk. The dreaded Walk. Each Sunday I would steel myself and stand on the edge of the precipice. But every time, I would throttle. Back away. No, not yet. Not ready. Not today. Maybe next week.

What lies behind the curtain carries great weight, conjuring all sorts of images, both good and bad, hopeful and foreboding. But more often than not, when the curtain is finally drawn back, the ordinary, the mundane, dispels any notion of mystery. *Pay no attention to that man behind the curtain*, the Wizard said. A part of me yearned to ignore the Wizard—to throw open the faux velvet. But another part of me reveled in the impenetrable mystery.

My *ignore-the-Wizard* self would sometimes conjure memories of the fourth grade experience at the Nathan B. Forrest Elementary School, a two-story red brick on the edge of my neighborhood, around the corner from the public library and Fire Station No. 13, and a block away from the A&P. Downstairs were K through 3, upstairs 4 through 7 (we didn't have middle school back then). In '60, as a third grader, I had never been upstairs. We of the lower classes were forbidden to make the journey to the upper reaches—our day would come, we were told. The two fourth grade teachers, Misses Throckmorton and Sexton, both spinsters, looked—to my eight-year-old eyes—to have been at least a hundred, maybe a hundred and one. In the minds of all of us third graders, they were the oldest, meanest creatures we'd ever known. We feared what lay ahead for us next year. And believe me, the images we concocted were not pretty. But then, when we finally made it to the top, we learned that upstairs was really no different from downstairs—

just a little more worldly, a little more challenging. And Miss Throckmorton, my teacher, was an innocent compared to the ogre I had imagined. I should have learned a lesson from that.

The liturgical plunging into the depths at the hand of the reverend—there wasn't much to it, really, as I would later find out.

* * *

"Won't you come."

We always sat in the second pew from the front, in the very center, facing the reverend head-on so that, when he proclaimed the inerrant word of God, we would be assured he was speaking directly to us, as if we were the only souls in the room. I would be flanked by Grandmother Tarwater on my left and my mother on my right. My brother Chester would be somewhere in the balcony, where the teenagers sat, surely to enjoy some semblance of privacy for *whatever-they-did-up-there*. It was only on the rarest occasion that my father would grace us with his presence, even though it was *his* mother who sat beside me and who would, on occasion, retrieve a stick of Doublemint gum from her purse and slip it to me when her daughter-in-law wasn't looking. I can still remember the pear green packaging with its dark green and white logo. Her beam of diabolical satisfaction as she surreptitiously passed it. The double-strength peppermint juice coated my tongue and drifted down my throat. Somehow, that seemingly simple indulgence allayed the discomfort of my bony frame against the hard mahogany surface (I was skinny back then—would that I could recapture that aspect of my youth), the cold clime of the sanctuary, the jarring from the sermon that, as it went on, bore more opprobrium than good news.

* * *

I wasn't Billy back then. I was Binky. Not a nickname I would have enthusiastically chosen. But it was given to me when I was much younger and, to my abiding chagrin, it stuck. The name had nothing to do with pacifiers, by the way—I'm told I would puff my cheeks and eject the tasteless abomination, formed of rubber and plastic, across the room whenever my mother tried to force it on me—a poor excuse for the real thing, I must have thought. Rather, the moniker had derived from my odd habit as a tot, hopping restlessly, doing a little twist, and sticking my backside in the air like a lapine doe in heat. Anyway, the nickname stuck, and I lived with it until the age of twelve-and-a-half, at which time Binky left home for good and Billy arrived, standing at the door, shuffling back and forth, raring to be let in.

* * *

"Raise a hand. I see your hand…and your hand…and your hand."

I would sit on that cold, hard bench and watch the hands go up throughout the congregation. Some old and wrinkled. Some young and firm. Some worn and calloused. Some pale and smooth like mine. Within minutes, most of the fold would have both hands in the air, waving them back and forth and beckoning the firmament.

"Now rise before God."

My grandmother would reach down and pull me up by my bony elbow as she leapt from her seat. My mother followed suit. The entire congregation stood before the reverend and swayed like a mighty wind casting back and forth on a restless sea.

"Won't you come. Your name was written in the Lamb's Book of Life. Show Him you love Him. Confess before all." He swept his hand across the room in a wide arc. "And you. You who have not found Him. Will this be the day you cross the line of faith?"

The choir would open up with the invitational hymn, their sotto voce voices gradually rising to a crescendo that rattled the twelve-station stained glass windows along the side walls of the sanctuary. *On Christ the solid Rock I stand. All other ground is sinking sand.*

One by one, damned near half the flock would leave their rows, sidle gingerly in front of their more reluctant pewmates to the aisle, and promenade to the chancel rail, their hands clasped before them or, on occasion, still raised in the air. One or two of the petitioners my age or a year or so older would profess his or her lust to be gulfed in that big, awesome tank of water. The occasional adult, finding himself having reached maturity without knowing God's salvation, would plea for the gift of immersion, tears streaming down his cheeks.

My grandmother would sashay to the front of the sanctuary, a queen pink lace handkerchief held tight in her hand. My mother would follow. I would sit alone, with my palms flat against the seat, my thumbs and forefingers slightly under my scrawny thighs, wondering when I would be ready to make The Walk, stand before the congregants who would have chosen on that particular Sunday to remain in the pews, and profess my love of the Almighty, praise be.

At the time, I reckoned that all Southern Baptist churches behaved like my grandmother's. I would later learn that some preachers assumed God didn't require multiple trips to the rail—one profession of faith, followed shortly thereafter by the dunk in the tub, was sufficient. But not Virlyn Kilgallon. He expected it every Sunday—I once heard him refer to it as "hitting the sawdust trail," something about a reference to tent revivals. But thank God he didn't require multiple dips in the bath. Otherwise, we would have been in church all day on baptism Sundays.

* * *

When the altar call was not afoot, I amused myself in assorted ways, some harmless, some not so much. My diversions of the latter kind shall remain, at least for the time being, unadvertised. But they often involved some clandestine desecration of the hymnal pages. As for the former, my favorite distraction involved carefully examining the odd members of that motley group that called themselves a choir, for whom I made up aliases. There was No Neck Nancy—the woman (she must have been in her early thirties) whose head literally sat smack-dab on her shoulders with nothing in between. Whenever she wanted to look to the right or the left she had to turn her entire body. I now know the malady for what it is, or was (I have no idea where she is today or, for that matter, whether she is *anywhere*)—Klippel-Feil syndrome. But at the time, she was just one more freak, likely having escaped from a carnival midway somewhere. And there was See Me Sylvia. My grandmother claimed she came to church primarily for one reason—to show off her fancy hats and jewelry—but there didn't seem to be much there worth flaunting. Launchpad Leonard would, out of the blue, produce the loudest, most explosive belch you'd ever heard—so loud, in fact, that it sounded like one of those Atlas rockets blasting off from Cape Canaveral. And whenever I saw him do it outside the choir loft without his robe, his quaking beer belly spilling over his belt buckle, my first instinct was to run for my life.

How would I have survived Sunday mornings without diversions? My brother, perched high above the sanctuary floor in the balcony with his friends, no doubt had his own amusements. More than once, I suspected him of sneaking out of the church just as the service began, sitting in the back seat of the Brookwood Wagon reading *Mad* Magazine, only to scurry back in a few minutes prior to the service's ending so he could walk out with the rest of the assembly and my mother would be none the wiser.

* * *

Almost every Sunday, Reverend Kilgallon's mien and comportment would take a bleak and sinister turn about halfway through the sermon. It was as if he became a different man altogether. Not the paternalistic pastor calling his flock to salvation, but, rather, a demonic, truculent savage condemning all in his presence to a life of eternal damnation.

I would always see it coming. He would remove his wire-rimmed bifocals and whack them onto the lectern—I awaited some Sunday when he would send shards flying across the room. His face would redden. The veins in his temples would pulse. A curious tic would come upon him—an emergent twitching around his right eye. Then he would let loose, pointing to the balcony and setting free a stentorian roar. "Sinners all. The whole vile lot of you. You will roast in Hell—like sizzling bacon at the men's fellowship breakfast." (Okay, he didn't really say that last part about the bacon—I made that up—but the thought may have crossed his mind.) Then he would turn on the assembly at large, sweeping his finger across the room and damning every single one of us.

An electric charge would run down my spine as if I had been sitting on metal, rather than mahogany, and the Almighty Himself had let loose a bolt of lightning onto the church. I would give a little shake and look back at the balcony.

Is my brother up there? Or is he in the station wagon, reading The Lighter Side *or* Spy vs. Spy, *oblivious to the judgment, the condemnation, that has just been leveled on him?*

On all of us.

Chapter Two
Virlyn Kilgallon

Summer 1963

"WHY, MISS HUDSPETH, YOU'VE DEVELOPED INTO QUITE the young woman. How old are you now, fourteen?" Cut to the chase, the reverend thought.

"Thirteen, sir." She averted her gaze. Looked at her lap. Ran her index finger along the folds of her powder blue linen skirt. Her Peter Pan collar, her chestnut fringe bangs ending a good two-and-a-half inches above her brow ridge, the trace of baby fat lingering in her cheeks, these all made her look younger and purer than she surely was. And those gawd-awful cat-eye glasses didn't do her any favors. But he knew that behind the façade of propriety befitting an adolescent Sunday schooler, behind her upswept spectacles, there lurked a hormone-fueled teenage passion yearning to break out. He could see it in her imploring hazel eyes. The way she ran the tip of her tongue between her lips and pursed them ever so slightly. He knew something had to give, lest the archfiend himself should grab hold of her and never let her go.

"Miss Hudspeth, do you have any idea why I asked your mama to send you back here?"

"No, sir," she said, not looking up. "She just said you were anxious to see me,".

"And where is she right now—your mama, I mean?"

"I suppose she's in the sanctuary waiting for me. Or maybe the fellowship hall. She can't leave 'less I do, seeing as it's a thirty-minute walk home. And it must be ninety degrees out. And I'm not allowed to hitchhike."

"I'm worried about you, missy." Upon his utterance of missy, she looked up. Glared at him. He took a deep breath. "I've noticed that lately you've retreated to the balcony with those…boys." It was all he could do to spit out the word. *Boys. Teenage satyrs* would be more fitting. But he knew well enough to ration his words. In time she'd learn their true import, and hopefully not the hard way.

"There's nothing but trouble up there. I guarantee you that."

"Reverend, I didn't mean any harm. None at all. I promise. It's just that—"

"I understand. I was your age once. It's just that what?"

"Well, please don't take this the wrong way, Reverend. It's just that, being as there aren't that many people my own age down in the bottom pews, it's more…well…it's more interesting up there."

He felt the slightest spasm come over his right eyelid. His hands began to sweat. "What you really mean is you don't have to listen to dusty old Reverend Kilgallon's yawn-inducing sermon if you're up there with the boys, indulging in their sport. That's what you really mean, isn't it?"

"It's not just the boys. It's the girls, too."

"But that *is* what you mean, isn't it? Tell me something, Cynthia. What was my lesson about today?"

Whatever coloring there had been drained from her face. She looked to her lap again. Fiddled with the linen. "I don't know, sir."

"Cynthia, do you remember a girl, not much older than you at the time, by the name of Jean Williams?"

She nodded.

"Did you ever wonder why she just up and disappeared?"

Again, she nodded.

"Do you know where she ended up?"

"No, sir."

"They shipped her off to the Florence Crittenton Home for unwed mothers. Have you heard of it?"

"Yes, sir."

"Cynthia!" He shot his hand in the air. Pointed to where the ceiling met the wall, in the direction of the sanctuary. "Cynthia. Listen to me. Satan himself, through one of those satyrs. Those debauchers. Up in that gallery of sin. Do you really want to wallow in that den of iniquity?" A numbness came over him. He felt the blood rush to his head. His temples throbbed. "*He* did it. He planted the seed in that poor girl. He sent her away. He made sure she'd never come back." He leveled his eyes on Cynthia Hudspeth. "Be careful, Cynthia. It could happen to you."

"I'd never want that for anybody, sir. Not even my worst enemy."

“Cynthia, you’re thirteen and you’ve still not been anointed with the living water. Have you?”

She shook her head, never looking up.

“Do you know, if you die tomorrow, you will spend eternity in Satan’s grasp?”

Tears welled up and ran down her face. She sobbed and fell into herself.

He lurched to her side. The spasm over his eyelid grew. His knees quivered. He placed his weeping, palsied palms on her forehead, pressing hard to keep from collapsing at her feet. And just as he did—just as flesh touched flesh—it came over him. The essence of the divine entered his tongue.

“…neema lash sovah amin tolah …”

He jerked away. Jammed his fist into his mouth. Backed off.

She regained her composure, jumped from her chair, and dashed out of his office, calling out for her mother.

* * *

Confederate Avenue Baptist Church, a mile south of I-20 and a stone’s throw from the Old Soldiers’ Home, was the second church to call the Reverend Virlyn Kilgallon to the pulpit. He had arrived in Atlanta, with a steamer trunk and a suitcase bursting at the seams, from Irondale Missionary Baptist, just east of Birmingham. When he first laid eyes on the Confederate Avenue building, he was struck by the simplicity of its brick façade. Its smallish acorn-pedimented center door. Flanked by two single side doors topped with simple triangular pediments. Its humble wooden steeple.

At the age of thirty-four, he had come to an assembly filled with the Spirit but largely bereft of able-bodied men. He had arrived a year, to the day, after a fleet of 360 Japanese warplanes leveled a fusillade of bombs on Pearl Harbor, and he had been here ever since. Twenty years was a long time to stay in one place. At times he wondered how long it would be before the congregation tired of him and ran him off *on the next train out of town*, as they had his predecessor.

He didn't remember how, when, or why the glossolalian spirit had first visited him. He just knew it had. He was convinced that, should the tongued phantasm ever come upon him in the pulpit or at the Sunday School lectern (which, in either case, it never had), the deacons would surely rush to his side, believing that some sort of Tourettian affliction had suddenly befallen him, and secrete him away to the ninth floor of Grady Hospital. Or they would simply assume he had run off the rails and joined the ranks of the charismatics, a frightful prospect for the proper Christian ladies of East Atlanta, and send him packing on that train he sometimes worried about. Or they would throw a burlap sack over his head, tie it around his neck, and ferry him off to the nearest Pentecostal church.

* * *

He bolted from his office, down the hallway, first to the fellowship hall, then to the sanctuary. The Hudspeths, mother and daughter, were nowhere. He searched the parking lot. He knew their car, a Silvertone Green Fairlane, late fifties. He had seen them leave in it before—Mrs. Hudspeth, Cynthia, and Mr. Hudspeth (on the rare occasion he saw fit to show up).

Virlyn Kilgallon reentered the church through the side door, the one that faced the parking lot. He plodded to the sanctuary and eased himself into the front pew, dead center before the pulpit. There was an eerie quiet. He buried his head in his palms, resting his elbows on his knees, and petitioned deliverance for that poor gamine.

For a fleeting moment, he thought he heard a wisp of breath coursing through the organ pipes, letting out a hushed dulcet strain. The pipes flanked the curtained baptistry behind the pulpit, above and behind the choir loft.

He rose, walked past the chancel rail, and climbed the three steps to the pulpit. He stood before an empty room. Raised his hands to the heavens.

To the left, just past the upright piano, was the door that led the one flight up to the baptistry. He eased open the door and ascended the stairs.

The water was cold, limpid. He broke the still surface with his hand. Ripples spread across the tank. He removed his hand and wiped the hallowed water across his face. The sacramental elixir tasted sweet on his lips.

Chapter Three

Billy Tarwater

Summer 1963

ONE SUMMER SUNDAY AFTERNOON, AS EVERY SUNDAY afternoon, we went to my grandmother's house—the Doublemint grandmother. We left the church around twelve fifteen. Her house is a five-minute drive from the church. We wouldn't eat dinner until close to one thirty.

She somehow managed to pack us all into her tiny dining room—Mom and Dad, my brother and me, Uncle Newell (my dad's brother) and Aunt Lottie, and my dead grandfather's cousin, Loreen—and, of course, Granny Tarwater. Eight people in a shoebox.

Dovey Mae always ate by herself at the porcelain enamel kitchen table—but only after everyone in the dining room had dug in. It's funny how we remember little things from decades past; there was a black spot where the white porcelain had chipped off. An inch across. Amoeba-like. Right where the edge of Dovey Mae's plate would have been. I fretted something awful over that spot.

I looked over at the swinging door that separated the dining room from the kitchen. It was closed. I knew Dovey Mae was sitting just on the other side of the door. "Granny T, why can't Dovey Mae eat with us?" I asked, knowing the answer before the words left my mouth. I did it to provoke the predictable icy stare from my mother, but I wouldn't have admitted that at the time.

"Why, Dovey Mae's the help, Binky," my grandmother replied. "She'd be uncomfortable sitting in here with us. She's not one of us. And we're not her people. And besides, it's crowded in here already." Granny Tarwater looked around the table to five knowing nods. My brother, staring out the window, likely cooking up yet another scheme to torment me the next chance he got, paid no mind to anything being said. "She's just fine where she is," Granny Tarwater said. "Now you tend to your own affairs. Eat your food and don't worry about her."

In fifth grade just ended, we had studied ancient history. Dinner at my grandmother's reminded me of a picture, in my textbook, of one of those Roman food orgies. She and Dovey Mae would have spent early Sunday morning, before church, cooking enough food for a Roman army. And Dovey Mae would have stayed behind while we were at church, making final preparations—cubing the Idahos for potato salad, baking the biscuits to a golden brown and setting them aside for warming just before the meal, nursing the Butterball with a slow and patient baste. Two things struck me as odd, but I never broached them to my grandmother. Why was Dovey Mae allowed to be alone in Granny Tarwater's house, even though she wasn't *one of us*? Did my grandmother really trust her with the silver—and with the wad of cash I knew she kept stuffed in a Mason jar in the refrigerator? And didn't Dovey Mae want to go to *her* church instead of drudging over a hot stove? I assumed she had a church. I knew she was a woman of God.

* * *

Once, in the middle of summer, I sauntered into my parents' bedroom, a room that I rarely entered even though the door was usually open. I must have been looking for something. Maybe my mother had sent me to find her pampered Mexican apology for a dog, yappy Sissy, the Chihuahua. *She's not my dog, no way.* Or perhaps I went in there to turn on the big, boxy beige exhaust fan, strategically placed in the bedroom window to pull air through the entire house—it could get downright stifling in the summer without air conditioning. But, all these years later, I can't remember why I happened in there. What I do remember, though, is that I encountered Dovey Mae, who cleaned house for my mother on Wednesdays, on her hands and knees beside the bed. At first I thought she might have gone and died right there, on all fours. I was frightened. I didn't want Dovey Mae to die. After all, she and I had known each other for my entire life—all eleven years of it. Then I saw her left leg fidget. And I heard faint mumbling. *She's OK. She's just cleaning the dust from under the bed,* I thought. *But it sounds like she's praying. Or maybe she's just muttering boozy nonsense.* I knew she had a problem with the bottle—even on the job. My mother made sure to comment on it every chance she got. "That Dovey Mae's at it again," she would say, or something like that. Then again, maybe Dovey Mae was just occupying herself in conversation to ease the tedium.

* * *

The other day, I ran across a photograph of Granny Tarwater and Dovey Mae standing in the kitchen. The venetian blinds on the rear door window are open, and if I look hard, I can see the fig tree in the back yard. My grandmother is holding a basket of scratch biscuits in both hands, presenting them to the camera like some sacrificial offering. Dovey Mae is standing beside her, her chocolate brown arm bent ninety degrees at the elbow, her hand on her hip. She's in a crisp white uniform and her hair is wrapped in a gingham head rag. She has a strained smile. She doesn't look happy. Come to think of it, my grandmother doesn't look that happy, either. My uncle had forced the camera on them on a Sunday afternoon, right in the midst of dinner preparation. Of that I was certain. The nerve!

But I've gotten ahead of myself.

Alcohol, for as long as I can remember, was taboo in my grandmother's house. But each family member on my father's side had had the awkward misfortune, at one time or another, of catching Granny Tarwater sneaking a nip of brandy (strictly for medicinal purposes, she would attest when confronted). In my case, it happened before dinner one Sunday afternoon—in the root cellar. She went down there, she said, to fetch a jar of canned fig preserves. Unbeknownst to her, I had descended the wooden stairs into the dark, partially excavated basement a few minutes earlier. My grandmother's house straddled a Confederate fortification from the Atlanta Campaign of 1864. The battlement ran from the northeastern corner of the back yard to the southwestern corner of the front. I knew that because I had seen it on a map at the library. I dreamed of one day finding a trove of Minié balls and bayonets in the unexcavated part of the cellar. *If I root around enough*, I thought. My grandmother, on the other hand, cared nothing about such frivolities. When I heard her coming, I hid in the corner behind a stack of Juicy Gold produce crates filled with empty Mason jars and lids. She crossed the cellar to within a few feet of me, slipped her hand behind a double-stacked row of canned peaches, and retrieved a half-drunk bottle of brandy. I peered through the crate, between the jars, straining to read the label on the bottle. It said Christian Brothers. Did she buy that brand because of its name? And did she buy it herself—right out in the open—with witnesses? Or did she have an accomplice? I wondered. She took a healthy swig, wiped her mouth with the hem of her apron, and headed to the stairs. When her foot hit the first tread, she must have remembered what she claimed to have come down for. She pirouetted, grabbed a jar of fig preserves, and proceeded up the stairs. I never looked at my grandmother the same after that. I was impressed that she had a bit of a mischievous streak, unbeknownst to me until that afternoon in the cellar.

From that point on, I would have an occasional dream that my worldlier-than-I'd-realized grandmother and her maid would engage in barking-at-the-moon drunken debauchery when no one else was around. I would awaken to the realization that my imaginings were about as far from real as the prospect of Dovey Mae dining at the table with us.

* * *

Growing up, I didn't know many black people. Sure, I'd see them downtown on shopping trips with my mother to Rich's or Davison's, but I had explicit instructions not to interact with them. Not to look them in the eye. And, by all means, not to get within touching distance.

One time, Mom and I were sitting in the Rich's restaurant, the one on the multi-level glass bridge—the Crystal Bridge—that spanned Forsyth Street and connected the main store with the Store for Homes. We had just finished my favorite shopping-trip snack, a slather of cream cheese sandwiched between two slices of date nut bread. And a Coca-Cola, of course—or, as I called it back then, a Cocola. A black woman came over to take away the dirty dishes. When she reached across to get my glass, her arm brushed against mine. She recoiled. I thought my mother was going to go apoplectic. *Why is Mom reacting like that? It's just an arm.* As soon as the bill had been paid, I was whisked to the nearest restroom to wash up.

I had direct dealings with only three blacks—Dovey Mae, Shorty the shoeshine boy, and the old Negro, with the wagon and half-dead mule, who used to come around the neighborhood looking for day work. That was it. Three in a city of two hundred thousand *not-one-of-us*es.

* * *

After an hour of gorging on dinner, we of the Roman army—having succumbed to Granny Tarwater's insistence that a single helping was clearly not enough—lumbered to the screened porch, sweet iced teas in hand. My brother scurried out the back door. Dovey Mae set about clearing the table, putting away leftovers, hand washing the dishes, and wet mopping the floor.

Uncle Newell, squeezed between Aunt Lottie and Cousin Loreen on the glider, loosened his belt, sighed deeply, and proceeded to regale us with stories from the war, to my dad's arresting eye rolls and my mother's under-the-breath rebuke—"now Herman, mind your manners." Uncle Newell, it seems, had "seen action," as he called it, in the Ardennes. My father, on the other hand, never left the confines of the stores facility at Mayport Naval Base. He would sometimes quip that he had bravely fought in the Battle of the Mosquitoes.

I gazed through the screen and down the street, my eyes peeled for the like-clockwork arrival of Mrs. Hudspeth. But I wasn't really watching for the mother. My eager adolescent self hoped against hope that Cynthia, two years my senior, would accompany her. Cynthia Hudspeth had a habit of wearing tight denim cutoffs––I would later hear them called Daisy Dukes. Lord only knows how she got away with it, with her mother the way she was, and especially on a Sunday after church. But I was grateful that she did.

Sure enough, here came Mrs. Hudspeth, flouncing along the sidewalk in our direction. She wore dungarees, like the ones my Aunt Etta from South Georgia wore. *Etta from Metter*, I thought with a chuckle. A ring of two dozen keys dangled at Mrs. Hudspeth's side. *What could all those keys be for?* She would tell us on more than one occasion that they were the keys to God's Kingdom. She would adopt a defiant stance, feet at shoulder width, hands on hips, and proclaim that she was "reborned again."

But where's Cynthia?

"Good afternoon, Mrs. Hudspeth," my grandmother called out.

Mrs. Hudspeth—Adele was her name—swung to face the porch, adopted her *reborned again* stance, and jangled her keys. She looked up and over the pitched roof. "Mighty fine day. Not a cloud in the sky."

I so wanted to ask Mrs. Hudspeth about her daughter, but I thought the better of it. As soon as I realized Cynthia would not soon be traipsing up the street to join her mother, my attention shifted elsewhere. The adult back-and-forth became a muted trombone, like the wah-wah in a *Peanuts* TV special. But on that summer Sunday in '63, the first of those specials, "You're In Love, Charlie Brown," was still four years away.

The adult wah-wah was broken by the mention of Cynthia's name. "That Cynthia Jane. I'll swan, I don't know what I'm going to do with that girl. I caught her at the window again."

In time, I would learn what Mrs. Hudspeth meant by catching Cynthia at the window. But on that Sunday afternoon, I didn't have a clue.

* * *

At the end of the day, as dusk began to set in, we piled into the Brookwood—Dad behind the wheel, Mom beside him, my brother and me in the seat behind them, and Dovey Mae in the wayback.

Dovey Mae lived with her husband in the Fourth Ward, in a shantytown called Buttermilk Bottom. Some say it got its name from the water that backed up in the sewers, which gave off a sour buttermilk smell. But Dovey Mae swore to me that it was because they ate a lot corn bread with buttermilk poured over it. The roads were unpaved. Electricity was scarce, even in the sixties. The houses were dilapidated hovels of unpainted wood and broken windows. But I never saw Dovey Mae arrive for work in anything other than a crisp white uniform. How she managed that, living under such conditions, I'll never know.

A year and a half later, developers would level Buttermilk Bottom to make way for the new Civic Center, slated to open in '67, the same year the *Peanuts* TV special debuted. Dovey Mae would be forced to relocate to Mechanicsville, in the Second Ward. But this afternoon, she was living in the same house on Currier Street where she had lived for over a decade.

I think back to those times we took Dovey Mae home. I wonder what ran through her mind when, somewhere just past the corner at Edgewood and Boulevard, my father would order us to lock the doors. Once, the clicking of the locks, one-by-one, thumbs against the lock posts, elicited from me an ill-conceived remark. "Dovey Mae, why, Buttermilk Bottom's nothing but a dangerous, run-down slum."

She promptly put me in my place. "We may have streets that has gravels on 'em. Or dirt. And it may be run down, but it's because of the slam-slum landlords. The folk that own they homes do the best they can when they's working day and night. The ones that's rented out, they's only run down because the landlords don't keep 'em up. Everybody love on everybody in the Bottom. Nice people. And we go to church...when we can."

Chapter Four

Ruby Jepperson

September 3rd, 1963

"LOOK WHAT YOU'VE GONE AND DONE, RUFUS." RUBY Jepperson glared at her deer-in-the-headlights son. "If I didn't know better, I'd swear you was raised in a barnyard with sows for friendlies. When your daddy gets home..."

The boy swung around, looked down, pondered his meandering muddy footprints charting a course across the linoleum, from the front door halfway to the kitchen.

"...he'll show you what's what. Man says there's a hair's breadth between a egghead and a featherhead. I know that's right." She pointed to the kitchen door.

Rufus Jepperson turned back around and faced the kitchen.

"Take your shoes off, boy. 'Less you want twice the mess to clean up."

Rufus bent down and untied his PF Flyers. He slipped his socked feet from his shoes, careful to avoid the mud. He picked his shoes up by the strings and tied them together. Off he minced to the kitchen in his socked feet, his muddy shoes dangling from his finger.

"The mop's behind the kitchen door. So's the pail. Put some soapy water in it. Hot," she said. *They say the boy's smart for eleven years. But sometimes I wonder.*

Ruby looked across the room. Rufus's book bag lay higgledy-piggledy next to the front door, right where he had plopped it when he entered the apartment. Her eyes fell on the sewing table along the adjacent wall, the wall that butted up to the unit next door. The stack of cuttings eight inches high. The McCall's sewing patterns folded beside the cuttings. Tacked to the wall, just above the sewing machine, the East Atlanta Pharmacy calendar. The square for Friday, one week away, was outlined with a bold black marker. And inside the square, scrawled diagonally across the date in the same bold black, MRS. HALLMAN.

Sam—he was Shorty at work, but she couldn't bring herself to call him by anything other than the name his mama'd given him—wouldn't be home for another two-and-a-half hours. Eight-year-old Recy had gone home with a classmate to spend the night. And Rufus? He had come back into the living room, pail and mop in hand. He had a big scowl on his face and was swabbing the floor with soapy water, fanning the mop back and forth with little care.

* * *

Ruby still remembered when she had first laid eyes on Sam. It seemed like yesterday. *What was it, twelve years ago?* She had walked into the Busy Bee Café and there he was, behind the counter slapping a hamburger patty onto the grill.

At the time, he was an old man, twenty-eight to her seventeen. And he had already been married and divorced, with two kids and an ex-wife living in Birmingham. What was it about him that she had found so attractive? He wasn't the manliest man she'd ever met, short and stocky, with nappy hair and a big round pumpkin face, black as pitch. And it sure wasn't his money. He didn't have any. Maybe it was his age. He had seemed streetwise and worldly, a far cry from the boys she hung out with on the south side. Sam, she had been told more than once, had left his family home on the St. John's River, just outside of Chaseville, where the water took a hairpin at Reddie Point and continued down to the Atlantic, and shipped off with the 92nd Infantry Division—the Negro division—in '42. Came back with a gimp leg and an out-of-kilter swagger. Got married. Stayed that way long enough to father two children. Flew the coop when he caught her straying a little too far from the bedroom.

Ruby and Sam got married four months after they met. Six months after that, he left the Busy Bee and took a job shining shoes at the East Atlanta Barber Shop. With tips, the pay was equally meager. But now he came home every day smelling like Kiwi polish instead of cooking grease. With Ruby's job as the cleanup woman at Edna's Cut-n-Curl and seamstressing at night, they scraped by. Living in the projects helped stretch the money.

* * *

Ruby heard the front door creak. She looked at the clock on the kitchen wall. It was a little after six thirty. "Sam?" she called out.

"Ooh, dat smell from de kitchen. You're puttin' your foot in it again, Baby."

She'd recognize that Lowcountry Gullah baritone anywhere—the dats and the dems and the duhs. She and Sam were might near married a whole year before she would stop asking him to repeat half the words that came out of his mouth. Still, to this day, she sometimes had trouble making them out.

"Where're the young'uns?" Sam stood in the kitchen doorway.

"Rufus is in the bedroom. He better be studying. Otherwise, he's gonna be cruisin' for a bruisin'."

"Now, Ruby. You need to go light on the boy."

"Go light! You should have been here earlier. He tracked mud halfway across the room."

"He's a boy, Ruby. Dat's what boys do. I did when I was his age. You made him clean it up, didn't you?"

Ruby planted her hands on her hips and glared at Sam. "Of course I made him clean it up. But I told him you'd show him what's what when you got home. There's a hickory switch in the closet, you know."

"And Recy?"

Ruby looked up. Ran her hands down her apron front. Shook her head. "She's down at that little girl Annie Turner's. Staying the night. You go wash up. And get your boy. Supper'll be ready in ten minutes."

Sam reached into his pocket, pulled out a generous handful of change. Plopped it all down on the table. "Day's tips, Baby. Ain't much, but it's better'n a poke in the eye."

"Sam," she scolded. "How many times have I told you not to dump the money where we eat. No telling who's hands been touching it."

Sam picked up the coins one by one, stuffed them back into his pocket, and trudged out of the room.

Sometimes I think I'm raising three sprats. Where'd the man I knew twelve years ago run off to?

After supper, Rufus returned to the bedroom to finish his homework. Ruby turned her attention to Mrs. Hallman's cuttings and settled before the Singer Portable, where she would likely remain until well past midnight. And Sam flumped onto the front stoop, fired up the first of several Old Golds, and would linger there in solitude until his own bedtime, closer to ten. Not much changed, night after night. He would just sit there, staring across the Carver Homes commons.

Her mind wandered to the monotonous chucka chucka of the needle punching through the teal broadcloth, the feed dog popping up and down, the bobbin spinning.

That Sam, he tries, she thought. *He's a good man. With a good heart. A family man. Good to his children, even if he* hasn't *picked up that switch in months. And good to me. I love it when he calls me Baby and all. But he keeps to himself. I wish I knew what's inside that head of his. What's he thinking about, sitting out there on the stoop for hours on end?*

She knew the days had to be hard on him. A grown man. A forty-year-old bootblack shining shoes at the barbershop for minimum wage and a dime here, a quarter there. *Who cares that he gives the best spit-shine in the city. There he is, polishing the shoes of men half his age. And they still call him a shoe shine* boy. *Shorty the Shoe Shine Boy.*

Chapter Five

Billy Tarwater

September 3rd, 1963

IN SEPTEMBER OF '63 I STARTED SIXTH GRADE. I WAS assigned to Miss Bramlet's class. She was old as dirt, just like Miss Throckmorton. She wore black lace-up army boots with big, blocky heels and stomped around like the WAC training sergeant she supposedly had been in a past life. And whenever she wanted us to be quiet, she would hiss at us like a pine snake instead of shushing like any normal person. Terrifying.

I lumbered down the dark, dingy hallway at Nathan B. Forrest Elementary, with its drab green walls and the ever present waft of pink sawdust sprinkled on upchuck. Things just weren't the same as last year. I felt an odd sense of detachment. Like I shouldn't be there. Then it hit me. Cynthia Hudspeth had moved on. She was at Murphy High now. I yearned for the day, two years out, when I could break away and join her where the big people went. The good news was that I'd still see her at church. And I always held out hope of spotting her trailing behind her mother on one of Adele Hudspeth's Sunday afternoon parades past my grandmother's porch.

Cynthia and her mother—and her father, whom I rarely laid eyes on—lived two doors down from Granny Tarwater, to the right when I stood on the front porch looking out. Sandwiched between the Hudspeth house and my grandmother's house was a one-story whitewashed bungalow surrounded by a five-foot chain-link fence. That's where Leonard Seymour lived. Launchpad Leonard. The Atlas rocket launcher. He kept to himself. Rumor had it that his wife of twenty years had run off with the Fuller Brush salesman, taking their brood of three children and the bank account with her. They say Leonard had been a mean-spirited man ever since, soured on the world, although he did continue to sing in the choir. Looking back, I wonder if his eructations may have driven his wife to the brush man.

* * *

A lot had happened in the news over the late spring and summer. Most of it had to do with what my father called the "Negro problem." A month or so before summer break, a judge had made Mayor Allen tear down the Peyton Wall, a wood and steel barricade that the city had erected across the road to keep the blacks on the western edge of town from infiltrating the white neighborhood next door. The mayor said it was to stop residential race mixing. The judge said it was unconstitutional. Mayor Allen would see the light and go on to became a champion of civil rights and desegregation. I imagine he came to regret putting up that barricade.

Then, on a single day in June, Governor Wallace stood on the steps at the University of Alabama and tried to block two black girls from going to class, and next door in Mississippi, a black man named Medgar Evers was killed by a member of the White Citizens' Council.

I didn't learn about those things in school or from my parents, though. While I got a smattering from Walter Cronkite's nightly news, it was Dovey Mae who told me all about them. She knew the backstory, things they didn't cover on TV. Personal things. She told me about the time she took the Greyhound to Jackson to visit kinfolk and got to meet Medgar Evers at the Mississippi State Fair. About how handsome he was, with an infectious smile and a gentle manner. About how, on the morning he was gunned down, the police escort that usually followed him home was nowhere to be found. About how people said the police were in the Klan. She told me about how her neighbors, hired onto an all-black Atlanta construction crew at minimum wage, toiled at hard labor to build the very wall meant to block them from the whites. About how she felt betrayed by the mayor. When she got to talking, especially if she had a little hooch in her, she'd go on and on. I learned things from her that I never would have learned from my own family. "My people been livin' this every day," she would say.

* * *

Adele Hudspeth idolized George Wallace. She said he was a gift from God, sent down here to "rid the US of A of infidels, nigger lovers, and Commonists." I never understood how she could look up to a man like that. I hoped Cynthia didn't understand it either, but I didn't know for sure. Infidels and Communists were one thing, but for the life of me, I couldn't see why anybody should have it out for the blacks, with all they'd been through. At the time, I gave my father the benefit of the doubt and assumed that was what he meant by the Negro problem—all they'd been through—but over time I came to realize his sentiments were closer to Mrs. Hudspeth's than to the seen-the-light mayor's. To make Dovey Mae eat in the kitchen was bad enough. Or to hasten me to the Rich's restroom to wash up, as my mother had done. But that man Wallace just seemed downright mean-spirited to me. And to kill that black man in Mississippi, in his driveway? It just wasn't right.

* * *

The first weekend after school had started back, my buddies and I had other things on our minds. We rode our Schwinns to the Madison Theater, half a block up the street from the East Atlanta Barber Shop and next door to the Nibble Nook Luncheonette and Ice Cream Parlor. The movie house, with its Moorish Revival façade and concrete gargoyles, had begun to show signs of wear after thirty-five years. "Down-at-heels" my mother called it. But we didn't care that the seats were torn and the aisle carpeting was tatty and forever sticky on the soles of our shoes. The Saturday matinee was one of our two year-round rituals, even through the dead of winter. The other was donning our ten pounds of army gear and spending the afternoon traipsing through the neighborhood like a ragtag infantry platoon.

The feature that Saturday was a B-grade science fiction movie called the *Last Woman on Earth*. The gist of the film, as I recall, is that a mysterious apocalypse sucks all the oxygen out of the air, and the world's population suffocates to death, except for three people who had been on a scuba diving trip off the coast of Puerto

Rico. Most of the movies we saw on Saturdays were of a similar ilk, and they fueled my keen imagination. Still do.

We settled into the back row after we had loaded up on concessions. We sat back there so we could watch the teenagers make out, all kissy-kissy like, which was as entertaining as the movie itself. I had bought my usual Zero candy bar and a large Cocola. Gary Alford, my best friend at the time—the pudge to my scrag, the butterball to my bones—always got the same thing I did. I have no idea why; it was just the way he was. Jimmy Coleman claimed he was allergic to white chocolate—one of his many professed allergies—and got a box of Milk Duds instead. And Nick Papadapoulos, the troublemaker among the four of us, ordered the biggest container of Mr. Dee-lish popcorn they had. I feared that, before the movie ended, he would have lobbed damned near half of it, one piece at a time, over the heads of the other theatergoers and gotten us tossed out—if it happened once, it could happen again.

* * *

The following Saturday, the 14th, we decided to execute an infantry assault on the imaginary enemy army stationed along the creek down the street from my house. It was at the bottom of a wooded hollow that went by various names depending on the nature of our adventure on the given day. Sometimes Dead Man's Gulch. Sometimes The Deep Jungle. This morning, it was The Siegfried Line, inspired by the recently-released *Hell is for Heroes.* We were sure from the start that it would be a stupefyingly successful foray, with Krauts' dead bodies splayed along the creek bed before it was over. My gear was World War II issue, purchased secondhand from Harry's Army Surplus and Sporting Goods.

Helmet. Canteen. Bolt-action Enfield rifle, nonfunctional, of course. My Uncle Newell's Ardennes field jacket—size XL—hung on me like a rumpled full-size spread on an unmade twin bed, and with the sleeves rolled up halfway and fastened with safety pins. My mother had dutifully sewed service patches onto the shoulders and front panels of my uniform—the one item not from Harry's or my uncle but, rather, purchased out of the Sears catalog. And, best of all, I had a canister gas mask. No risk of asphyxiation for me.

We tramped down the middle of the street in eager anticipation of what lay ahead. The no-name stream—not much more than a muddy trickle—ran south-to-north through a large culvert under the street to the spot where the attack would occur. It then meandered roughly north-northeasterly—I knew that, thanks to my vintage military pocket compass—and eventually connected with its larger counterpart named Sugar Creek. We speculated how far downstream the trickle would run crimson once our task at hand had been completed.

We stood at the creek's edge and peered across. But there was no sign of the enemy. *They must be hiding behind the trees.* Nick was about to step into the creek bed when Jimmy yelled, "Watch for quicksand. It'll suck you in. You'll drown." We imagined there was quicksand all around. The reports back from the advance scouts had told us as much. Plus, we knew all about quicksand from *The Mongols*, another Saturday matinee movie.

"What are you, nuts? I ain't scared of no quicksand," Nick shot back, and proceeded to trudge across the muddy creek bed.

Gary and I followed, stepping gingerly onto the flat stones that lay about. *No need to take chances.* When we had made it across, we looked back. Jimmy was still standing on the far edge of the creek, pale as a wraith. With a lot of coaxing, and a little shaming on Nick's part, Jimmy finally decided to inch across and join us on the enemy side.

We stormed the enemy lines, routed the Germans from behind the trees, and took them down with ease. Mission accomplished.

Gary, Jimmy, and Nick—big grins on their faces—crossed back over the creek. I lingered behind to pay last respects to the fallen. I was about to step into the creek bed when I noticed something out of place, in a briar thicket about halfway between the culvert and where I stood. I couldn't make out what it was. As I approached the thicket, I saw a pair of girl's panties, pale pink with fringe around the edge, hanging precariously from a long thorn. My heart throbbed with excitement. I reached out, grabbed the panties, and stuffed them into Uncle Newell's coat pocket. I debated whether to tell the others about my find. I would surely be a hero if I did. But I decided not to. Maybe later. *For now, it's my little secret.* I marveled at my self-restraint.

"Hey guys, wait up," I yelled.

We suffered no apparent casualties, although Jimmy feigned a limp that drew skeptical glances from the three of us. We marched back to my house in victory, Jimmy pulling up the rear with a decided hobble.

We crowded inside the pup tent in my back yard for a post-battle assessment, celebrated by half-crumbled Oreos retrieved from Gary's backpack. Then we went our separate ways. It had been a long, hard-fought struggle, but we prevailed.

After what we'd been through, a hearty dinner and a good night's sleep were in order. Morning would come sooner than we wished, when we would dress in our finest and be hauled off to Sunday services. Jimmy would go to the Methodist church next door to our school. Nick to the Greek Orthodox church on Pryor Street. Gary didn't go to church, and oh, how I envied him most Sundays!

For me, a good night's sleep was not to be. For one thing, I couldn't get those panties off my mind. I slipped out of bed in the dark of my room, slithered over to the field jacket, draped across the chair, and retrieved my find from the side pocket. I lay in bed, holding the panties tight. My thoughts were going a mile a minute. It never occurred to me to wonder how a girl's undergarments had ended up in a thicket by the creek bed. I had something else on my mind. *I wonder if Cynthia wears panties like this.*

But there was something more disturbing that kept me up. Fall hadn't set in yet. It was eighty-plus degrees out and even warmer inside. The big beige exhaust fan was running—I could hear its dull rumble from down the hall—but my door was closed. I had cracked my window and opened the blinds for some air. The wind was blowing hard. The little acorn at the end of the lift cord knocked against the wall with a rhythmic clank, clank, clank. The cadence would have otherwise lulled me to sleep, were it not for the next door neighbors. They were at it again. I could hear him bellowing, cursing at her and calling her names. "Lervene, you're nothing but a goddamned slut," I heard him say. And "I have a good mind to lay you out right here and now." Then a loud thwack. And a scream. I couldn't make out anything she said. I knew the next time I saw her hanging the wash on the line, lifting her arms above her head, they would be covered with black and blue splotches. I'd seen them too many times. Even at eleven, I knew something was bad wrong. Sometimes, when I was in the back yard and the fighting would begin, my mother would make me come inside. She probably had no idea how many times I lay awake at night listening to it.

* * *

Sunday morning I was back in the pew, wedged between Granny Tarwater and my mother. Between White Shoulders and Estée Lauder. *They're especially smelly this morning,* I thought. *Did they both somehow manage to spill the bottles all over themselves?* I feared, with so many odors coming at me from right and left—gardenia and lilac and bay leaf and God only knows what else—I would surely smell like the Rich's perfume counter before it was over. What would Cynthia think if she caught a whiff of me?

Other than the olfactory overload, it was a typical Sunday. That is, until the service was over and we piled out of the church. Reverend Kilgallon would always stand just outside the door and acknowledge each of us with a nod or a handshake. But this morning was different. He was standing off to the side, away from the main door. He was in deep conversation with Cynthia and Mrs. Hudspeth. The reverend was pointing his finger at the daughter, her head hung low. The mother was in her military *reborned again* pose. Nobody seemed happy.

"What are they talking about?" I asked my mother.

"They're talking about her," my brother chimed in.

"Cynthia?"

"Of course Cynthia. They're talking about The Walk. When she's gonna do it. Don't you know anything?"

Chapter Six
Cynthia Hudspeth

September 6th, 1963

THE FIRST FOOTBALL GAME OF THE SEASON, THE 6TH OF September at Cheney Stadium, had been a blowout. The Murphy Eagles drubbed the Southwest Wolves 21 to 0.

Cynthia had never been to a high school game. It was exhilarating, especially watching that boy Marvin Darby—the cute one she'd heard so much about. But he was sixteen. She doubted he would pay her any mind. She looked forward to next summer when she could try out for freshman cheerleading. Best way to meet boys, she'd heard. She had wanted to go out for the eighth grade squad, but Mama had said no—"Wait 'til next year." Cynthia wondered if, when next summer rolled around, it would be the same old story. Wait 'til next year. And another year. Until, finally, she would graduate without ever having waved a pompom.

Cynthia had gotten a ride to the game with Martha Ann Dullums. She didn't know her well, since Martha Ann was three years her senior, same as the Darby boy. But Cynthia and Martha Ann both went to the same church, and Martha Ann had shown her around Murphy High the first week of class. The big old high school was daunting enough with Martha Ann's help; Cynthia couldn't imagine what it would have been like if she had been on her own.

"Don't let anybody sell you an elevator pass," Martha Ann had said. "The school doesn't have an elevator. That joke's as old as my granny's knickers, but every year, half the eighth grade class seems to fall for it. And oh, one other thing. Don't eat the fish sticks on Fridays. They're downright dreadful."

"What's so bad about them?" Cynthia had asked.

"They look like brown dog turds, they taste like cat food, and they leave a greasy film in your mouth. And don't make beet poop with your straw. It's disgusting."

"What's beet poop?"

"Mainly the boys do it. I've seen some girls do it, too, but not the type you'd probably hang out with. We have sliced beets once a week—out of a can, I'm sure. They make little holes in the beets with their straws until the stuff oozes out the other end, like poop."

Cynthia had vowed not to fall for the elevator thing, to avoid the fish sticks at all cost, and to look away if the boys started playing with their food.

* * *

The following Friday, the Eagles would go up against the Grady Knights. It was an away game. Given that the stadium was halfway across town and Cynthia had no other way to get there,

Martha Ann had offered her a ride again. They were to meet at the East Atlanta Pharmacy for shakes an hour before game time. Cynthia's mother trusted Martha Ann. After all, she seemed a good Christian girl and was in church most Sundays, even if she did sit in the balcony. It drove Cynthia crazy, though, when her mother referred to Martha Ann as her chaperone. She was thirteen. She didn't need a chaperone.

Cynthia rode the school bus home. She changed clothes, told her mother bye, and walked the three blocks from her house to the drug store, arriving fifteen minutes before the agreed meetup time. She hoisted herself onto the stool closest to the front door and ordered a vanilla shake with a teaspoon of malt sprinkled on top. She waited for Martha Ann. But when thirty minutes rolled by and she hadn't turned up, Cynthia began to worry. She had written Martha Ann's phone number on a piece of notebook paper, which she had folded and slipped into her purse. There was a phone booth inside the drug store, to the left of the rear door and next to the RCA tube testing station. She inserted a dime and dialed. There was no answer. Maybe Martha Ann forgot they were to meet. Or maybe she ended up having to do something with her parents and couldn't reach Cynthia to let her know.

What do I do now? She wanted, more than anything, to go to the game, even if she arrived late. She didn't have enough money for a cab. She could go back home to see if Mama would give her a ride. Or she could mosey nonchalant-like over to McKnight's Garage, where her Daddy was probably settling up his weekly parlay card bet with his friends. But in either case, she probably could kiss the idea of going to the game goodbye. *I'll hitchhike,* she thought. But she had been strictly forbidden from ever getting in the car with a stranger. *Mama will never know.*

She moused down Glenwood past Harry's Army Surplus to Moreland Avenue, two blocks away, looking in every direction for fear someone would see her and ask her where she was going. When she reached the Moreland Avenue intersection, she extended her right arm with her thumb pointed upward, as she had seen others do. *If they catch me—Mama and Daddy—I'm dead.* She was so nervous, she held her right bicep with her left hand to try to keep her arm and thumb from shaking. At least ten cars passed without even slowing down. The light changed, bringing the Moreland Avenue traffic to a halt. She lowered her arm and moved away from the street. She didn't want to be standing there with all those stopped cars. Somebody sitting at the intersection, with time to look closely, might recognize her with her arm out. *Too risky.* As soon as the light changed, her thumb was back up. Two more cars passed. Then an old, rusty car—she thought it might be a Hudson—slowed at the intersection. The driver turned onto Glenwood, pulled over and stopped just past where Cynthia was standing. She approached slowly. She could make out in the side mirror that the driver was a black man. There was no one else inside, as far as she could tell. Her first instinct was to turn and walk away. She wouldn't dream of getting in the car with a colored man, let alone one she didn't know. But she decided to walk up to the driver's window anyway. No harm in talking and, besides, it'd be rude to ignore the man after he had stopped for her. When she reached the car, she recognized the driver. She would occasionally go to the barbershop with her father. This nice old Negro was always there, shining shoes. He had a big round face. And he always had a smile. He and her father would sometimes talk about baseball. She remembered he favored the Birmingham Black Barons. She liked the name.

"Where are you going?"

She hesitated. Shifted on her feet. She felt a lump swell up in her throat. *Should I? He seems harmless. And besides, I'll miss the kickoff.* "Grady Stadium." She barely got out the words. *Mama and Daddy can never know what I'm about to do.*

She slid into the back seat and slumped down so no one would see her.

He pulled into the Texaco station, made a U-turn, and headed back to Moreland Avenue. He took a right at the intersection and drove north toward Virginia-Highland.

The radio was blaring, with some guy named Alley Pat Patrick calling out between songs, "WAOK, your home for cool jive and the best rhythm and blues this side of Chicago." She hadn't heard that kind of music before, but she liked it.

"I mighta not stopped if I hadn't recognized you from de barbershop," he said. "Don't you come in with your daddy? Real quiet man with de mustache? Why, I shine his shoes all de time."

The man had a funny way of talking. She strained to make out what he said.

"That's my Daddy, alright."

"I shouldn't be doin' this," he said. "You know how much trouble we both'd be in if somebody caught you in the car with me? And what are you doin' anyway, out on a night like this thumbin' a ride? Does your daddy know?"

"No. And please don't tell him." She explained about Martha Ann. About how she had waited for her, but she never showed up.

He paused for a long time. She wondered if he had understood what she had just told him, about Martha Ann and all.

"I won't tell nobody. Best for both of us that I don't. But you better be careful. A young girl like you out by yourself. How old are you, anyway?"

"Thirteen, but I'll be fourteen in December." She sat up, confident they were far enough past East Atlanta that no one would recognize her.

"I got a son not much younger than you. If I caught him out hitchhikin'…I don't know what I'd do. But it's even worse for a girl." He hesitated. "How're you gonna get home? After the game, I mean."

"I'll find somebody to give me a ride. There'll be a lot of people there from my school. This is a big game. Second one of the season. They say we may have a champion team this year."

She looked up at the rearview mirror. Their eyes met. That's when she noticed the thing dangling on a string from the mirror mount. Little sticks, like hickory switches, were tied together in an X to form arms and legs, sorta like on a School Manners Stick Figure poster. Tiny feathers hung from one arm. Some kind of dried bean pods or something drooped from the other. A third stick, straight as an arrow, shot up from the middle of the X, with a white skull-like head on top of it. The skull had hollowed-out eyes, nostrils, and a turned-down mouth—all jet black. Black yarn was sticking out of the top every which way for hair. Somebody had taken blue paint and dabbed smudges on all three sticks. It looked like a wooden version of a voodoo doll.

"What's that?" She gasped.

"What's what?"

"That voodoo thing."

“Voodoo thing? No voodoo. It’s called a hoodoo haint. Keeps evil spirits away.”

“A hoodoo ain’t?”

“Not ain’t. Haint.” He let out a deep breath with the h. “It’s Gullah Geechee, child. From the low country. Them’s my people.”

“What’s the low country?”

“Means different things to different people. For me, it’s down Jacksonville way. You been to Jacksonville?”

“Can’t say as I have. It looks scary.”

“Nothin’ to be scared of. It’s a good thing. Keeps me safe. Not like voodoo.”

She caught a whiff of the faint smell of Clorox, like what her mother used for bleaching the whites on laundry day. Strange, she thought. *Maybe he spilled shoe polish and had to clean it up. Or maybe it’s another way to ward off evil spirits—like wacky Aunt Maggie and the bag of moth balls she carries everywhere for the same reason.*

* * *

He stopped at the corner of Tenth and Monroe. She dug through her purse and pulled out a dime.

“This is all I’ve got for a tip,” she said.

“I don’t want a tip. I did this ’cause I like your daddy. He’s a good man. And you seem like a good girl.” He reached into his shirt pocket and pulled out a card. He wrote something on the back. “Here, take this. Number on the front’s the barbershop. The one on the back’s where I stay. If my wife answers, her name’s Ruby. She’ll understand.”

Cynthia took the card.

SAM "SHORTY" JEPPERSON
EAST ATLANTA BARBER SHOP
MA7-4592
"BEST SHINE IN TOWN"

On the back was a scribbled phone number. She put the card in her purse.

"Listen, you be careful," he said. "And don't be hitchhikin'. If I'm not working or if I'm close to get'n off, and you need somebody to give you a ride, I'll do it. It'll be our little secret, 'cept for Ruby."

Cynthia waved to Shorty as he drove away.

The Eagles weren't as lucky as they had been the week before. They lost to Grady High 35 to 7. Cynthia looked for Martha Ann. She asked around. No one at the game had seen her. She got a ride home with a classmate of Martha Ann's who hadn't seen her either, not since earlier that day at school.

I'll call her tomorrow, Cynthia thought. *I hope she's OK.*

* * *

The next morning, Cynthia tried Martha Ann's house again. Still no answer. She decided to go over there. It wasn't that far away, maybe a fifteen-minute walk.

She passed with swift steps down Flat Shoals Avenue and turned left at Van Epps Street. Just as she did, a police car sped by in the same direction. She kept walking. Martha Ann lived in a ranch at the end of a long, steep driveway at the corner of Van Epps and Blake Avenue. As Cynthia approached the ranch, she looked up to see the police car in the driveway, its rotating light bathing the surrounding houses and trees in red. Her first inclination was to keep walking. But she just couldn't do that.

Something must be bad wrong. *What if something happened to Martha Ann on her way to meet me last night?* she thought.

She climbed the steps to the front door. It was open. The officer and the girl's parents were standing in the living room. Mrs. Dullums was sobbing. Mr. Dullums' head was buried in his hands. The officer was writing on his notepad. Just as Cynthia cleared the threshold, Martha Ann's mother looked up with a quizzical gaze.

"I'm sorry to barge in," Cynthia said. "I'm a friend of Martha Ann's. She was supposed to meet me at the drug store after school yesterday. She was gonna give me a ride to the game. But she never showed up."

"I know you. From church," Mrs. Dullums replied.

Cynthia learned that Martha Ann didn't get off the school bus when it rolled down Blake Avenue and stopped at the corner. She didn't get off because she never made it on when the bus driver loaded up at the high school. Martha Ann's parents and the police were piecing together disparate fragments of information. The bus driver had confirmed to Mr. Dullums that his daughter was a no-show. And so far, her parents had not turned up anyone who had seen her leave the school.

* * *

The next morning at church, Cynthia sat with her mother in the pew instead of escaping to the balcony. She looked around. The was no sign of Martha Ann's mother or father. Or of their daughter. She could have been in the balcony where she usually sat, but it was unlikely that she would have been there if her parents weren't at church.

Reverend Kilgallon preached on II Thessalonians 1:9 and "Hell Is Everlasting." For the first time in months, Cynthia paid attention to the sermon. If she hadn't, she would surely have caught her own hell from her mother, sitting right there beside her. The reverend made no mention of Martha Ann. Cynthia had expected him to say something like "Holy Spirit everlasting, bring Martha Ann back home to her parents. They're worried sick." Then there would be more than the usual amens from the pews. If he *had* said that, Cynthia would have wondered why he felt the need to tell God that Martha Ann's parents were distraught—wouldn't God know that already? But none of that happened. The reverend didn't say a word about her. Was she still missing? And if so, did he not know? Cynthia assumed her mother wasn't aware of it, because the subject of Friday night and how Cynthia had gotten to the game never came up. Were Martha Ann's parents lying low, keeping quiet until they knew more? Cynthia felt an uncommon tenseness, but she didn't know whether it was from the reverend's dreadful sermon or from her fretting over Martha Ann, or both. Or maybe it was because she sat next to her mother rather than in the balcony.

However tense things were in the sanctuary, they were doubly so once Cynthia and her mother found themselves in serious conversation with the reverend after church. He took both of them aside and proceeded to give Cynthia what she could only describe as a good old-fashioned tongue lashing. And Mama did nothing but just stand there and nod her head. Maybe he *did* know about Martha Ann after all; maybe it was the girl's disappearance that prompted him to lay into Cynthia like he did. Or maybe it was the recent talk they'd had in his office, when he started getting all weird and glassy-eyed and speaking funny, and she ran out of the room.

Chapter Seven

Billy Tarwater

September 15th, 1963

WE HAD NO SOONER GOTTEN HOME FROM SUNDAY dinner at Granny Tarwater's than there was a rhythmic knock on the door—two-three-one. It has to be Gary, I thought.

I flipped on the porch light and peered through the sidelight. Sure enough, Gary stood there all anxious like. I opened the door.

"Hey, did you hear about that girl that never made it home from school and they can't find her?" he said.

"What girl?"

"Martha Ann Dullums. The one that lives around the corner."

I didn't know what he was talking about, but Gary would sometimes hear about things like that before anybody else. His father was a police detective. Homicide.

"My Daddy told me. Said an APB came through yesterday afternoon." Gary got this goofy grin on his face. He liked to use police terms like APB and DOA. "I bet one of them Krauts—one that got away before we had a chance to gun him down—kidnapped her," he continued.

I ignored his comment and told him I knew of her, but I didn't really know her. And besides, I didn't have time to talk about it. I had my homework to do. I played it cool, like a missing girl from the neighborhood was no big deal. Told him he'd best leave, that we'd talk tomorrow. But as soon as Gary's feet had hit the curb in front of my house, I sneaked into my brother's room and looked her up in the Azuwur, the high school yearbook. There she was, real pretty like, almost as pretty as Cynthia Hudspeth. She was in my brother's class. And I wasn't positive, but I thought she went to my church.

Early the next morning before sunup, the 16th of September, I opened the front door and peered into a black void. *The delivery boy should have thrown the newspaper by now.* I stepped onto the front stoop in my bathrobe and slippers and looked right, then left, searching for a patch of white poking through the darkness somewhere. Then I saw it, perched atop one of the hawthorns that ran the length of the front of the house. I shook my head. *Even I could throw better than that, and I'm the one never allowed to be the pitcher.*

I grabbed a chair at the kitchen table. The others were still asleep. I snapped the rubber band from around the paper. I unfolded the fifty-or-so-page tome, hoping to find something about Martha Ann Dullums' disappearance. But what I saw, staring at me from the top of Page 1, was more shocking than I expected. More than the Peyton Wall. More than the Alabama governor and those two girls at the university. More than that man Evers. More than a high school girl gone missing.

BOMB KILLS 4 CHILDREN, INJURES 20 AT NEGRO CHURCH IN BIRMINGHAM

Somebody had set off a dozen dynamite sticks, killing four girls while they were in Sunday school. One of them was my age. Governor Wallace—Mrs. Hudspeth's Governor Wallace—posted a $5,000 reward for information about whoever did it. That was real thoughtful of him, seeing as how he had treated those two black girls at the university so badly. The police were looking for two men in a 1960-model sedan. Reverend King arrived in Birmingham late Sunday—I knew all about him from Dovey Mae. President Kennedy sent the FBI in. I knew I had to talk to Dovey Mae about this when I saw her next Sunday. She had kin in Alabama. She may have known the dead girls—or some of the others. I wanted to call her before Sunday, but she didn't have a phone. I'd have to wait a whole week.

After I had finished the church bombing story, I scoured each page. Most of the other headlines seemed boring compared to what had happened in Birmingham. An anti-Castro mob in New York. Vice President Johnson in Denmark. The Bears upset the Packers. Finally, near the bottom of Page 18, in a square no bigger than the length of my little finger, there it was: MISSING GIRL. The article said Martha Ann, the sixteen-year-old daughter of Mr. and Mrs. Albert Dullums of East Atlanta, was last seen Friday at school and had gone missing. It described her as 5'3", 110 pounds, brown hair, hazel eyes. She had left for school Friday morning wearing a maroon box pleat skirt, white blouse, and black and white saddle oxfords. I didn't know what a box pleat was, but I could guess.

Anyone having information as to her whereabouts should contact the police. I stopped reading the paper at that point.

By then my mother, father, and brother were stirring around, preparing for the day. For reasons that I still don't understand, I didn't say a word to any of them—about the bombing or the missing girl. Perhaps I was too distraught to bring any of it up.

After having used up most of the morning reading through the paper, I was running late. I dressed and scarfed down a bowl of Cheerios. I rushed to the corner to await the arrival of the school bus. I saw it approach from a block down the street.

* * *

I was sure that, by midday, a pall would have fallen over her school, and my school, and all of East Atlanta for that matter. It took a while for the news to reach my school, but by the afternoon recess, everybody was talking about the missing high school girl. And, as sixth graders sometimes do, my classmates conjured up every story, every angle imaginable, no matter how outlandish. She was abducted by an out-of-town degenerate in a trench coat—what somebody said they'd heard called stranger danger. She ran away to join the Ringling Brothers trapeze team. She got pregnant and her parents swept her away in the still of the night to a home, claiming for cover that she had gone missing. An axe-wielding murderer, straight out of *Dementia 13*, had gotten hold of her. A hornet-eyed Martian swooped her into his UFO and took her away. *So much for a pall falling over the school*, I thought. *Could it be, just maybe, that somebody closer to home has done her harm and here we are fantasizing about circuses and Martians?*

* * *

That evening at supper, the subject of Martha Ann came up, as I expected it would. I asked my brother about her. He said she was one of the balcony teenagers at church. He put up a brave front, but his face was drained of color and his voice trembled. I knew he was scared. So were my parents. It isn't every day that a kid from the neighborhood disappears. My classmates' musings notwithstanding, serious thoughts of *who's next* inevitably creep in. People become preoccupied with concern for the missing and a dread that there may be something more sinister and serial going on, a *when will the next shoe drop* anxiety. While my parents didn't come right out and say it, I was sure that was what they were thinking.

The days passed...Tuesday...Wednesday...Thursday. The end of the week came and she was still missing. Notices had gone up all over town. Stapled to telephone poles. Taped on the wall at the A&P. At the library. The post office. The barbershop. Everywhere you went, that was about all you heard people talking about. The Page 1 story from Monday had been relegated to the deep recesses of people's minds. When something hits close to home, everything else seems minor. The Dullums, thanks to pledges collected throughout the neighborhood, had posted a $1,500 reward. The mix of gloom and panic that I knew would eventually set in had finally arrived, boasting to all within earshot, "you can't get rid of me now."

* * *

On Sunday we piled into the Brookwood. For the first time in months, at my mother's insistence, my father was accompanying us to church. *Will the reverend mention Martha Ann from the pulpit today?* I thought as we pulled into the lot. We parked next to my grandmother's decade-old black Bel Air, the one she drove three times a week, tops—to church for Sunday services and Wednesday night supper, and to the grocery store. She would usually arrive before us, her eyes barely clearing the dashboard, even with a 6-inch-thick pillow on the seat. She would stake out our spot in row two and await our arrival. I was certain that, on this day, she would be shocked when she looked up and saw her son sidling into the pew.

As usual, I didn't pay much attention to the reverend's fire and bluster, but from the little I heard, his sermon was a continuation of the week before. It seemed the reverend had more to say about the everlasting damnation of those who don't know God, as told by that guy named Paul he always talked about, than he could cover in a week. But I focused more on the characters in the choir loft. No Neck Nancy sat rigid like a stone statue. Launchpad Leonard would nod off, his chin falling to his chest, then suddenly jerk his head up, his eyes as big as a giant squid's. Then he would do it all over again. *He usually stays awake*, I thought. *Not getting enough sleep lately? Maybe his burping keeps him up at night.* I let out a muffled guffaw. Granny Tarwater poked me between my ribs.

Although I wasn't listening to the sermon, I kept my ears peeled for mention of Martha Ann. Halfway through, I was jolted from my woolgathering by her name. I snapped to attention. The reverend's demeanor was more sullen than usual. Like a looming fog under a slate-dark sky. He spoke in a basso monotone, never looking up from the lectern. "This girl, this helpless waif of a girl. Lord deliver her." Amens resonated through the sanctuary. I wondered why he chose to call her a waif. Was she really a waif? Would her parents call her a waif?

The reverend eased over to his green leather-seated throne, the one he usually sat in when the choir was doing their thing. He plopped into it as if it were his nest. He motioned with a *come here* gesture to somebody in the congregation—somebody sitting in the side section to my right. A man and a woman rose from the pew and faltered to the front of the church. She wore a brimless hat—my mother called them pill boxes—with a veil like a black spider web that reached the bridge of her nose. He lumbered hunch-shouldered beside her. It occurred to me, as they walked down the aisle, that he was the spitting image of Henry Wilson, Dennis the Menace's father. But I knew this was not the time or place to be thinking such things. Not with everything all somber and sullen. They climbed the steps to the pulpit and stood at the lectern. She lifted her veil. Then it occurred to me who they were—Martha Ann's parents. They pleaded for the return of their daughter—first to God, and then to anyone in the pews who may have seen something, heard something. "Please bring her home," Mr. Dullums begged. His wife let out a heavy sob.

The reverend sat stone-faced with eyes of cut glass. He held his bifocals in his lap. He was concentrating hard on something. On what, I wondered.

* * *

That afternoon at Granny Tarwater's would be my first opportunity to speak with Dovey Mae about the Birmingham church girls, but I knew Martha Ann would be on everybody else's minds. The two of us would need to get away from the others so we could talk one-on-one. I hatched a plan. It wasn't a great plan. Unfortunately, it involved contriving a little accident in the root cellar. But I knew it would work.

Throughout dinner, I was filled with impatience. So much so that I must have unconsciously kept looking at my Caravelle, because at one point my mother glared at me and tapped her left wrist. As soon as everyone had risen from the table and headed to the porch, I scurried down the stairs. I found the nearest jar of fig preserves. I held it at arms-length, shoulder height, closed my eyes, mouthed a *please forgive me*, and released it. Nick would have been proud of what I had just done. The impact sent broken glass and reddish purple goo flying across the floor in all directions. It just missed my shoes and pant cuffs. I was lucky, I guess. I went running up the stairs, through the living room and onto the porch. "Granny T, I broke a jar of preserves."

My mother was surprisingly calm. And my father didn't say a word. He rarely did. Granny Tarwater sent Dovey Mae to clean up the product of my *accident*, as I knew she would. I felt bad for Dovey Mae, since I had created the mess in the first place. But I offered to help her clean it up. After all, it was the least I could do.

"Dovey Mae, did you hear about those little girls in Alabama?" I reached down, gingerly picked up a shard of glass between my fingers, and placed it in the trash can she had brought from upstairs, accompanied by a pail of soapy water and a big sponge the size of my head.

She was on her hands and knees, absorbing the sugary glop into the wet, soapy sponge and retrieving the pieces of glass as she went. "May need a mop to finish the job," she said.

Did she not hear my question?

"Dovey Mae, did you hear—"

"I heard you the first time, Binky." She stood up, wiped a smear of soap and purple across her apron panel. Shook her head. "Them innocent little girls was killed for no reason 'cept they's hated for who they is." A tear meandered down her cheek. "Pure evil. That's all it is. Pure evil."

"Did you know any of them, Dovey Mae?"

"I knew them, Binky. I mean, I didn't *know* those four little girls by name. But I see them every day, everywhere I go. Why, I was one of those little girls once, too. So yes, I knew them." She fixed her eyes on mine. "You can't know what it's like. It's not possible. I don't fault you for that. But it's just not possible."

"Why are they hated so much, Dovey Mae? They were so young."

She fiddled with her apron strings. Looked down at the floor. "We better get this mess cleaned up. Otherwise, your grandmama's gonna come down here and we'll both find ourselves in a heap of trouble."

We finished cleaning up the fig mess. I raced up the stairs. *I hope I haven't missed the Hudspeth strut*, I thought.

* * *

I could have sworn I heard Martha Ann's name mentioned as I approached the door to the porch. But when I crossed the threshold, the room got quiet. Uncle Newell, Aunt Lottie and Cousin Loreen had assumed their usual, creature-of-habit positions on the glider. The others—Granny Tarwater, my mother and my father, sat in the three matching metal chairs facing the glider. Uncle Newell had already loosened his belt and had settled in. I assumed his war stories were over for the day, undoubtedly to my father's great relief.

"Has Mrs. Hudspeth come by yet?"

"No, but why do you ask, Binky?" my grandmother replied.

"Oh, I don't know. Just curious, I guess."

The conversation on the porch started back up, with every conceivable topic touched on except Martha Ann's disappearance. That seemed odd to me, but I decided not to bring it up if nobody else was going to.

* * *

Nightfall arrived and we all prepared to leave. Cynthia's mother had not blessed us with her bounding sidewalk presence. Come to think of it, I hadn't seen mother or daughter in church that day either. Perhaps the mother was keeping the daughter under lock and key—with one of those that dangled from her side—for fear there really *was* a serial degenerate in a trench coat out there…or the *Dementia 13* axe murderer come back to life. *Fishy, fishy, in a brook, Daddy caught you on a hook.*

Chapter Eight

Cynthia Hudspeth

September 21st, 1963

I BOUND TO THE DRUG STORE IN GIANT LEAPS, LIKE A gargantuan grasshopper. Eight-foot vaults. I sail through the cool night air between footfalls. I'm wearing my Murphy High white and royal blue gym shorts. And a letter sweater—Marvin Darby's sweater. And under the shorts and sweater, my one-piece bathing suit—the one with the ruffle arm holes. I'm on my way to meet Martha Ann. We're going to the Grant Park pool for a swim. I'm on cloud nine. But when I near the parking lot behind the pharmacy, that's when I see the police cars. The flashing lights. The people huddled in a circle. As I get closer, my euphoria turns to dread. There's Martha Ann, sprawled on the asphalt. Her eyes are bloodshot slits. Her mouth is agape, dried spittle caked at its corners. Her skin is blue—Murphy High blue. Her…

Cynthia awoke in a sweat. She squinted. Rubbed her eyes. Looked around her room. A solitary beam from the streetlight shone through the window, insinuating itself into the otherwise pitch black bedroom. *It was just a dream*, she thought.

* * *

The last week had been hard, maybe the hardest of her short life. Martha Ann hadn't been seen in over a week. The whole town was in a panic. But the source of Cynthia's anxiety was not just fear. The fear was there alright, but there was also a nagging worry that, somehow, she was responsible for Martha Ann's disappearance. *If I hadn't asked her for a ride. If she hadn't said she'd meet me at the soda fountain.* But then Cynthia remembered hearing that Martha Ann had not even made it onto the bus Friday afternoon. Whatever happened, it must have happened right after school.

And then there was the window thing. It blew up over the weekend, so much so that her mother had even kept her home from church. Cynthia thought back to the conversation on Saturday. They had gone to the A&P together. They were on their way home. She couldn't remember exactly how it had come up, just that it had. Her mother was all over the place. One minute she was talking about the Southeastern Fair, scheduled to open in five days. The next minute, Martha Ann. Then—bam—the window. Just like that.

"Mama, I can't help it. Sometimes, when I'm getting ready for bed, he's just there. Staring at me from his bedroom."

"Can't help it?" Adele Hudspeth brought the Fairlane to a slow crawl. Pulled over and stopped at the curb halfway down Gresham Avenue. She glared at her daughter. "You do realize, Cynthia, that if you weren't standing in the window half-naked, he wouldn't have any reason to be gawking at you. You do realize that, don't you?"

"Mama, I don't think he means any harm by it."

"Cynthia, you're thirteen years old. He's a grown man." Her mother hesitated. Took a deep breath. "I'm not saying he would do you harm, but there are bad people out there. Really bad people. You know that. Your friend's been missing for a good week. Her parents are out of their wits. I pray the Lord will deliver her back into their arms soon. But if the Evil's got hold of her…I don't even want to think about it."

For the first time Cynthia could remember, her mother got that same glassy-eyed look that the reverend sometimes had.

"I'll tell you one thing. If I catch you one more time in that window, I'm going straight to your father. Then, when next Sunday comes, he'll drag you down to the front of the sanctuary, even if he has to do it with you kicking and screaming bloody murder. You'll stand in front of the whole congregation and tell them what you've done. Then the reverend, he'll cast the demon spirit out of you. If you're lucky, you'll learn your lesson and the only thing you'll have to face is every God-fearing member of the church taking you for a temptress."

"And if I'm *not* so lucky?"

Cynthia's mother shook her head. "Don't bait me, Cynthia. Try me too much and you'll see. I'll go out to the shed myself and get some plywood and a hammer and some tenpennies. I'll board your window tight. Is that you want, Cynthia?"

"But what about Mr. Seymour? He's the one doing all the ogling. Not me."

"Leonard Seymour…he'll face his own reckoning. You're the one I'm worried about right now. And another thing, any man I know, your Daddy included, if you tempt him, he'll look. He's just a red-blooded man."

Adele Hudspeth pulled away from the curb and continued south. Not a word was spoken the rest of the way home.

Cynthia was not allowed to leave her room all day Sunday except to eat and use the bathroom.

* * *

It was Monday, the 23rd of September. That morning, the police showed up at school.

Cynthia was sitting in English class, reading Chapter 3 of *The Scarlet Letter*, when her teacher called her to the front of the room. "There's someone here to see you—in the principal's office," her teacher said.

On the one hand, she was grateful to get pulled out of class. She wasn't keen on reading about Hester and the scaffold anyway. But on the other hand, getting called to the principal's office was not her idea of the best way to get out of her scarlet misery.

She shambled down the front hall. As she approached the office, she saw two police officers standing just inside the doorway. The principal, Admiral Atwood—everybody called him that because, rumor had it, he had been a rear admiral or something in the war—was talking to the taller of the two officers, who was nodding. The other officer was writing something on a notepad.

Cynthia entered the front office. All three men looked up. Admiral Atwood spoke first. "Cynthia, these gentlemen are from the police department. They're here to speak with you about Martha Ann Dullums." He motioned Cynthia and the police through the doorway into his office. "You can sit in here. I'll shut the door so you can have privacy. Mrs. Sadler, my secretary, is right outside the door if you need anything."

The two officers said Martha Ann's parents had told them their daughter had made plans to meet Cynthia late in the afternoon on the day she disappeared.

When had Cynthia last seen the missing girl? She couldn't remember for sure, but she thought it had been earlier in the day on Friday, between first and second periods, when they had firmed up plans to meet at the drug store.

How well did Cynthia know her? Not well, really.

Had Martha Ann said anything that would have indicated she was in some kind of trouble or had planned something out of the ordinary before the two girls were to meet? She hadn't.

Could Cynthia confirm what Martha Ann had been wearing that day? She couldn't.

Did Martha Ann have a boyfriend? Cynthia had no idea; she hadn't noticed her hanging out with any boy in particular, but seeing as they were three years apart, their paths didn't cross much, in or out of school. Martha Ann hadn't mentioned a boyfriend, and if she had one, wouldn't she have gone to the football game with him instead of Cynthia? That is, unless he played on the team.

She tried to tell the officers about her dream. They weren't interested.

Cynthia left the office feeling like she hadn't been much help. By the time she walked into the hallway, her English class had ended. She breathed a sigh of relief. Poor Hester, with her big red A, could wait. She made a beeline to Algebra ten minutes late.

For the rest of the day and on the bus ride home, Cynthia couldn't get Martha Ann Dullums off her mind.

* * *

She stepped off the bus and walked the block to her house. As she neared her driveway, she saw her mother and Mr. Seymour in their front yards, engaged in what appeared to be heated conversation across the chain-link fence. Cynthia shuffled backwards and hid behind an oakleaf hydrangea, its white flowers beginning their Autumn pink-to-red journey, its leaves to a palette of yellow, oranges and browns. *A good camouflage*, she thought. The hydrangea stood near the sidewalk between the Seymour and Tarwater yards. From her vantage point, she could see her mother and Mr. Seymour, but she couldn't make out what they were saying.

"Hey, Cynthia," a voice called from behind. It was that Tarwater boy, Binky.

"Be quiet. Can't you see I'm hiding?" she said in a whisper. *What's he doing here on a weekday?* she thought. *Why isn't he at home?* Forrest Elementary was only seven blocks away. Maybe he decided to walk to his grandmother's house instead of taking the school bus to his own neighborhood.

He just stood there on his grandmother's front stoop, taking in her every move. She tried to ignore him, but it was hard, knowing two eyes were fixed on her like a bobcat tracking its prey. Finally, her mother and Mr. Seymour finished whatever conversation they were having and went their separate ways.

Cynthia stood up and swung around to face Binky. "Binky, what are you doing staring at me like that?"

"I'm not staring," he said. His eyes found the tops of his shoes.

She walked halfway to the stoop. "It looked like you were staring."

"I didn't mean to," he said, never looking up. "Hey, where were you yesterday…in church, I mean?"

"Mama made me stay home."

"Is it because of that Martha Ann girl? The one that's missing?"

"No, not directly. But Mama's worried just like everybody else."

"Are you worried? About you, I mean. I know everybody's worried about Martha Ann, but are you worried about yourself? My mother said if it happened to one, it could happen to others."

"A little. You?"

"Yeah. It's scary."

"Listen, Binky, I gotta go. You take care of yourself, OK?"

Chapter Nine

Billy Tarwater

September 23rd, 1963

ON MONDAY AFTERNOON, RATHER THAN TAKE THE BUS home from school, I legged it the seven blocks to Granny Tarwater's. I was careful every step not to make eye contact with any stranger I might encounter, as my mother had instructed—"… what with an abductor on the loose," she had said. The good news was that, in East Atlanta anyway, strangers were rare.

My mother was running errands and said she'd pick me up after her trips to the A&P and the bank. Ever since Martha Ann had gone missing, I was not allowed to stay at home by myself. It seemed the whole town had gotten flat-out het up, as Dovey Mae would say. And my mother was no exception. I understood why, but I didn't like my style being cramped. I was surprised she even allowed me to ride the bus home, seeing as Martha Ann had disappeared somewhere between her school's exit and the place where the buses lined up. Or to walk to Granny Tarwater's, for that matter. At least I was still allowed to roam my neighborhood with my friends—before sundown, anyway.

I entered Granny T's through the back door. *I'll have to get on to her for leaving the door unlocked*, I thought. Halfway through the kitchen, I heard a voice coming from the living room. It was a woman—not my grandmother.

"Peter, is Susan still angry at me? And where has she run off to?"

Who's Peter? I thought. *And who's Susan? And who is that woman doing the talking? And why is Susan angry at her? And has this Susan person run away from home or something?* As I passed into the living room, I saw Granny Tarwater sitting at rapt attention in front of the black-and-white glow from the Zenith. Watching *The Secret Storm*. With the volume cranked up so high it blasted my ears.

My first inclination was to ask her who all these people were and what the deal was with Susan. But the last thing I wanted to do was get all tangled up in some stupid soap opera, so I breezed past her, uttered a brief "Hi, Granny T," and stepped out the door and onto the front stoop.

That's when I saw Cynthia. *What's she doing hunched down by that bush?* I thought. *The one with the ugly cone-shaped flowers—old people's flowers.* She was too old to be playing hide-and-seek. Maybe she was spying on somebody. Or hiding from the *Dementia 13* axe man.

Then I spotted Cynthia's mother and Launchpad Leonard standing across the fence from each other. Mrs. Hudspeth was wagging her finger in his face. He had his hands on his hips and was shaking his head. *What are they talking about? And why is Cynthia hiding from them?*

I called out to Cynthia. She shushed me. I just stayed there on the stoop, watching her but not saying a word. Then Mrs. Hudspeth and Leonard Seymour left. Cynthia stood and stepped toward me. Any concern about what her mother and Launchpad Leonard had been saying to each other, or why Cynthia was hiding behind the bush, disappeared. There she was, talking to me. She turned and walked away, but not before telling me to be careful.

She just told me, Binky Tarwater, to take care of myself. Cynthia Hudspeth, the prettiest girl I know, just told me to take care of myself.

* * *

That night, secure in the confines of my bedroom, I slipped my hand into the pocket of Uncle Newell's field jacket. I fished around inside, running my fingers along the edge and bottom, until I felt the fringe. I pulled the pink panties out.

Ever since I found them hanging on the long thorn, I had debated where to hide them. In the depths of my sock drawer? Nope. My mother would surely find them there. Between my box springs and mattress? Nope again. Dovey Mae turned the mattress too frequently, or at least too unexpectedly, for them to be safe there. Maybe in the bed springs themselves? There was a tear in the fabric on the bottom that let me hide things in there. But that just didn't seem to be an appropriate place to hide something so special, so delicate. After all, the springs were sort of rusty and sharp. Fine for candy and comic books. Not for panties. Hidden in the shoe box beneath my baseball cards? My brother rummaged through my things too often for that to be a good place. And no matter how many times I protested—"My things are my things. Stay away."—he never listened.

The safest refuge, as far as I could tell, was where I had kept them hidden in the first place, in the field jacket. I wondered, however, whether General Patton would ever have been caught dead with pink panties in *his* field jacket.

I fell asleep holding them, thinking of Cynthia and wondering if hers were pink. If hers had fringe. I slept well that night.

* * *

Two nights later, it would be another story altogether, at least as far as getting a good night's sleep was concerned.

Early Thursday morning, I was awakened to a loud banging. I sprang military straight, kicking the sheets away. *What was that?* I rubbed my eyes. I fumbled for the alarm clock on my bedside table. The radium hands glowed 10 after 3. I heard a rustling that began down the hall and wended to the living room.

The banging continued.

My bedroom was midway along the center hall that ran the length of our house. I crept into the hallway. The door to the living room was across the hall to my left. The kitchen to my right. I went right, away from the noise. My plan was to enter the living room from the dining room instead of the hall—a bypass attack. I creaked toward the kitchen. The solitary night-light at the end of the hall behind me was of little help as I stumbled through the dark. I opened the kitchen drawer and felt around for the biggest knife I could find, my mother's 12-inch butcher knife. I proceeded from the kitchen into the dining room, knife in hand. I got on my hands and knees, crawled into the living room with my right hand balled in a fist around the knife handle, and hid behind the sofa. The living room was dark, illuminated by only the faint light from the hallway. My mother and father entered the room.

The noise was coming from the front door. I clenched the butcher knife tight. My heart raced. Visions of *Dementia 13* beset me. My first inclination was to race into the living room brandishing my weapon, ready to slash the axe murderer as soon as the door was opened. But then I had second thoughts. *Stay where you are, ready to charge if backup is needed*, I told myself.

My father approached the door slowly. He gripped a Louisville Slugger in his right hand. My mother followed closely. My father held his left hand behind him, palm out, motioning for her to leave the room. She didn't. My brother, eyes half shut, stood in the doorway from the hall.

My father squinted through the sidelight. Shook his head. As an aspiring astronomer, I had been following the moon phases. And I knew that, this morning, it was a waxing crescent. Not much more than a sliver. I don't know why he didn't flip on the porch light, but he didn't. Maybe it was because it would have shone through the sidelight and into the room.

"Who's there?" my father said.

"Open up," a woman's voice called out. "Please."

"Who is it?"

"Lervene. Culpepper. Please let me in."

He unlatched the deadbolt and threw open the door. My mother flipped the living room light switch. Our next-door neighbor rushed into the room. Her left eye was dark and shiny, like the back of a bluebottle fly. She was pressing a bloody cloth or handkerchief or something tightly to her mouth. Her arms were covered with the same black and blue bruises I was used to seeing when she was at the clothesline. She had cuts on her forearms. Her hair was a tangled mess. She was in a terrycloth bathrobe that reached her ankles. She was shoeless, not even wearing socks.

Dad pointed to the wingback chair near the door. She sank into the cushion. Mom rushed to the bathroom and returned with a wet washcloth, a roll of gauze, first aid tape, and a bottle of Mercurochrome. "In God's name what happened, Lervene?" she asked, as she wiped Mrs. Culpepper's mouth with the washcloth, dabbed Mercurochrome on her cuts.

"Ben's at it again. This time worse than ever. He went into one of his rages. I swear, if I hadn't run, I think he'd have killed me." She looked at her lap, then at my mother. "I couldn't ask for a better man when he's sober. But when he gets into the bottle, he's a monster."

Dad closed the curtains and engaged the deadbolt. "Where is he now?" he asked.

"He's inside the house, I'm sure. He wouldn't be able to stumble halfway across the yard without falling flat on his kisser and ending up with a mouth full of centipede—the shape he's in."

Dad headed to the kitchen. "I'm calling the police."

She leapt from the chair. "Please don't. Don't get them involved. It'll be OK. He just needs to sleep it off. Come morning time, he'll be back to the good Ben—but with a bad hangover, I'm sure."

"But Lervene, look at yourself. Look at what he's done to you."

"Herman, you don't know the half of it. This is the way we live. The way I live. If the police get involved, they'll take his side. I've seen that before. Or they'll haul him away and lock him up. Then what will I do? Please, I beg you, don't call the police. He'll settle down by morning. He'll call in sick to the car lot, I'm sure, and by afternoon everything will be forgotten."

"Lervene, this isn't normal."

"Herman, it may not be normal to you…please don't call."

My father gave in.

"You can sleep here tonight, on the sofa," my mother said. She got a pillow and a blanket from the hall closet.

I slinked out of the room. I couldn't sleep the rest of the night, fearful that drunken Ben Culpepper would come looking for his wife, show up at the door with a machete, and chop us all to bits.

* * *

Later that day at school, the librarian visited our classroom. We moved desks out of the way so she could set up the filmstrip projector in the middle of the room. She projected a picture onto the wall. I don't remember exactly what it said, but it was something like "How to Protect Yourself from Perverts and Kidnappers," with a picture below it of kids on a playground. I could read the title fine, except for one place where the picture got sort of distorted by the clock on the wall. Where the writing fell on the clock, the letters looked like they were crawling up the bottom edge between the 5 and the 7. Otherwise, it was fine.

Nick, who was sitting next to me, leaned over. "I don't need to learn nothin' about no preeverts," he whispered, emphasizing the pree. "We got enough of them right here in school."

"Shut up, Nick," I replied. "Just watch the filmstrip. You may learn something for a change."

About ten minutes into what we had been told would be a thirty-minute presentation, on a slightly blurred image of a little girl being grabbed by an ice cream vendor, a brownish burning hulk with ragged edges began creeping across the picture from the upper right corner. It reminded me of the creature from *The Blob*. The filmstrip was melting before our eyes. The librarian turned off the projector, uttered something under her breath, packed up and left. I wondered how we could possibly protect ourselves, having seen only a third of the filmstrip. And what about the poor souls in the other classes who didn't at all get to see it? And another thing—would I ever again feel safe buying a hunky from the Ice Cream Man?

* * *

The last Saturday in September came. There was still no sign of Martha Ann Dullums. It had been two weeks since she disappeared. More notices had gone up all over town. The reward had been upped to $2,000. A BOLO—another of Gary's fancy police terms—had been issued throughout the state and beyond, as far away as Chattanooga, Greenville, Birmingham. The police were going door to door seeking clues.

We had plans that day for another campaign along the banks of the no-name stream. This time we wouldn't be taking the Germans. We'd take the Japs along the River Kwai. We were sure it would be another resounding victory. But our mothers, especially Gary's and mine, insisted that the foray be over and done with, and that we be secure at home, before five-thirty. We could do that, but it would take hard work and determination. "Blood and guts," as General Patton would say.

"Too bad we're undermanned," Nick said. "That Jimmy. I swear. Scared to leave his chain-linked backyard."

"It's not Jimmy," I replied. "It's his mother." But right after I said that, I realized my defense of him was off base—and Nick knew it. It wasn't his mother who confined him to the yard. It was Jimmy himself. *Some dogface he is,* I thought. *General Patton would have thrown an AWOL court-martial at him.*

The three of us, Gary, Nick, and I, stomped down the street, singing a dreadful little ditty Nick claimed he created just for the occasion, but I suspected his older brother had composed it. It went something like: "Grounded banzai kamikaze. Ship him off to Nagasaki. In a beat-up wooden casket. The dead nip's head lay in a basket." I have no idea why, after all these years, I still remember such grim doggerel. But I do. And when the earworm makes its nest, I have a hell of a time getting rid of it.

Nick had fashioned a cloth band that ran around his helmet just above the rim. It was light blue with tiny grey checks. It looked like it had been made from an old shirt or something. Surely his mother had sewn the ends together. I couldn't imagine Nick doing that himself. It read Kill The Japs Or Bust in Magic Marker black, with a little smudge on the dot over the i.

This may just be the crown jewel of our military careers, I thought. *Poor Jimmy. Sorry he has to miss it.*

Chapter Ten

Adele Hudspeth

September 28th, 1963

ADELE HUDSPETH PULLED THE FAIRLANE INTO THE church lot. She brought it to a stop in the space next to the one marked Pastor. Where the mud-spattered silver Valiant sat. She assumed it was Virlyn Kilgallon's. She put the car in Park. The engine assumed a rough idle and gave off a blue-grey haze in the rearview. She wondered if the car had been smoking all along and she just hadn't noticed it. I'll swing by McKnight's when I leave here. Get Mac to check it out.

She gripped the wheel so hard that her knuckles turned white. She rehearsed what she would say to the reverend. She was usually not at a loss for words. But bringing up something so close to home—church home—was not easy. Would he hear what she had to say? Would he understand? Or would he shut her down altogether? She knew he could be volatile, a scold at times. But even with his flaws, he was a man of God. And if anybody could help her sort through the mess she was in—Cynthia was in—he was the one. She turned off the ignition. The engine chugged, spewed out one final cloud, and went quiet.

The side entrance to the church had been held open by a broken broomstick wedged between the door and the frame. *Should I remove it or leave it?* She left it where it was. Inside, the windowless hallway was illuminated by a solitary fluorescent light on one end, where the hall branched into a T—sanctuary to the left, everything else to the right—and the small window in the entry door behind her. She breathed in the familiar odor of must, the result, she assumed, of stagnant air. The building was hushed, save for a dull, distant hum. Perhaps it was the refrigerator or the chest freezer in the kitchen off the Fellowship Hall. Or the ballast in the fluorescent fixture. Or maybe it was one of those noises that old buildings just make—the ones nobody can ever pinpoint, but they're always there.

She broke the silence. "Reverend Kilgallon." She called out again. No response. When she reached the T, she saw a light shining from beneath the door at the far end to the right. It was the reverend's office. She inched down the hall, mulling over how to break the ice.

A light tap on the door. "Reverend Kilgallon."

"Who is it?"

"It's Adele Hudspeth."

"Come on in, Mrs. Hudspeth."

Papers were scattered over his desk like a funnel cloud had passed through. He motioned to a splat back chair against the wall across from where he sat, beneath the framed black-and-white photograph of a dozen or so people, all dressed in white, waist deep in a river. Another group of people, in suits and Sunday dresses, stood on the river bank. A man in a suit and tie stood in the water facing the ones in white. He cradled the back of one of the people, a woman who looked to be seconds away from an immersion. Adele Hudspeth strained to make out whether the suited man was a younger Virlyn Kilgallon, but the image was slightly blurred, and she didn't want to stare too hard. The caption under the photograph: CALLED DOWN TO THE RIVER.

"Have a seat." He cleared his throat with a guttural hork.

It wasn't until she sat down that she took a good look at him. He looked different. He was pale. His face was furrowed and gaunt. The circles under his eyes darkened by the minute. He stared past her, as if he were somewhere else. "Reverend, thank you for meeting on a Saturday. I…I just—"

"I assume you're here to talk about that missing girl, Martha Ann Dullums, and the regrettable pall that's fallen over the town."

"No. That's not why I'm here. Reverend, it's abou—."

"It's your daughter, isn't it? The fact that she hasn't seen fit to purify her soul. She's old enough to know better. But she doesn't seem to realize the danger she places herself in."

"It's not that either, Reverend."

"Then what is it, Mrs. Hudspeth?"

"It's about Leonard Seymour."

He grimaced. "Leonard Seymour? Why Leonard Seymour? What's he done?"

She took a deep breath. *Here it comes.* "Mr. Seymour has been… how can I say politely?"

"Just say it, Mrs. Hudspeth."

"Well…he's been spying on Cynthia through her bedroom window. From his window."

"Spying? What do you mean, spying?"

"At night. He watches her through the window when she gets ready for bed."

"How many times has this happened, Mrs. Hudspeth?"

"Five or six that I know of. The first time I saw it, I was fixing to go to bed myself. I passed by her bedroom. The door was cracked. That's when I saw it. For all I know, it's been going on for a long time. Cynthia doesn't want to talk about it. I used to could talk to her about anything, but these days, she just shuts up."

"When he…when he spies on her, as you say, Mrs. Hudspeth, is she—"

"Is she undressed? Is that what you're asking, Reverend?"

"Well…yes."

"Let's just say she's not in any condition for a man to see her. 'Cept her Daddy."

He stood up. Walked around his desk. Placed his hand on her shoulder. "Mrs. Hudspeth, who is in the wrong here? The seducer or the seducee? Don't you see the fallacy of your coming here this morning, telling me there's a problem with Leonard Seymour, a worshipful believer, but a mere mortal nevertheless, who did what any man would do."

"Any red-blooded man? That's what I said to Cynthia. But I wasn't excusing what he did, mind you."

"The problem's not with him. The problem's with her." Virlyn Kilgallon raised his arms. Looked to the ceiling. "She took of the fruit thereof, and did eat, and gave also unto him; and he did eat."

"But what can I do, Reverend? How can I stop it?"

His right eyelid twitched. His hands were trembling and sweaty. He steadied himself with one hand on the edge of his desk. He buried his other fist in his mouth. Bit tight as if to keep some mighty beast from letting loose. Finally, after a minute or two, he freed his fist and spoke. "Mrs. Hudspeth, don't you see. It's not just about the window. A good thwacking on the backside can put a stop to that. But why is she doing it in the first place? It's more than the window. These teenagers. I don't know what's got into them, but it wasn't like this when I was their age."

She recalled what she had told her daughter. *Every God-fearing member of the church will take you for a temptress…any man I know, your Daddy included, if you tempt him, he'll look.*

* * *

Virlyn Kilgallon followed Adele Hudspeth through the door leading to the parking lot. He removed the broken broomstick and tossed it to the edge of the bushes.

"You're leaving, too, Reverend?"

"House calls, Mrs. Hudspeth. The Good Lord can't forget the homebound."

She got into her car, rolled the window down, and turned the key in the ignition.

"Mrs. Hudspeth, your car's smoking something awful. And it sounds like a panzer. You need to have that checked out."

"That's where I'm headed now. To McKnight's. I've got a whole afternoon of errands to run and I want to make sure old smokey here will get me where I need to go."

Reverend Kilgallon placed his hand on the edge of her open window. "Adele—may I call you Adele?—I'll pray for you and your daughter. If there's anything at all that I can do for you, or her, let me know."

In all these years, he's never called me by my first name, Adele thought. Somehow, it eased her angst.

* * *

She drove out of the church lot and onto Confederate Avenue, turning left onto Moreland…right at Glenwood…right at Gresham. Half a block past the Glenwood-Gresham intersection, she turned onto the alley that ran to McKnight's Garage. She pulled in front of the second bay, the one that said Oil and Lube, put the car in Park and got out without turning off the engine. She could see four darkened figures huddled in the far corner of the garage. She could tell right off that one of them was her husband. As she came closer, she saw one of the men—she thought it was Harry, from the army surplus store—blow into his cupped hand. He shook his hand and threw something toward the wall. She assumed it was dice. Mac was there, too. She didn't recognize the fourth man.

"Cecil, can I talk to you?" she called out.

Her husband turned and walked to where she stood. Kicked the gravel. "What is it, Adele?"

"I can see you're making good use of the weekend. Have you looked at the grass lately?"

"Sorry. I'll be home later. Where've you been?"

Cecil didn't know about Cynthia and the window, at least as far as Adele knew. And she wasn't about to tell him about it, standing there outside Mac McKnight's garage. "Errands. And I still have more to do. But I need to have Mac look at the car first. It's shaking when I put it in Park and it's spitting out smoke."

She looked on as Mac cut the engine. He opened the hood. Took a tool from his box and removed a spark plug. Then another. And another. He held one in the air between his thumb and index finger. "See this, ma'am. It's covered with black soot. Spark plugs are fouled." He looked at her husband and smirked. "Cecil, don't you know how to take care of a car?"

Cecil Hudspeth walked away without saying a word.

She left McKnight's with a new set of plugs and $8 poorer. From there she went to the five-and-dime, then the A&P, then the shoe store to pick up a pair of resoled peep-toes. One more stop at the bank drive-thru and she could head home.

* * *

She pulled into the driveway and put the car in Park. The engine purred like new. The dashboard clock read 4:45.

Leonard Seymour came out of his house holding a can of Schlitz in one hand and a half-smoked cigar in the other. He wore a faded and cracked Atlanta Crackers T-shirt, stretched in the midriff so the baseball was an oval. She hadn't said a word to him since Monday. She had gotten out of the car and turned toward her house when he spoke. *Should I ignore him?* she thought.

"Mrs. Hudspeth, do you have a minute?"

She swung to face him. "That depends, Leonard. Have you thought about what we talked about? Are you ready to apologize? Are you ready to stop preying on my daughter? Otherwise, I have nothing to say."

"Mrs. Hudspeth, let me explain. It's not like I'm creeping around her window. If your daughter continues to undress right before my eyes, what do you exp—"

"This conversation is over, Leonard." She stormed into the house.

It was quiet inside. She called out for her daughter. Cynthia's bedroom light was on, but she was not there. There was an opened Skippy jar on the kitchen counter. She stepped onto the back stoop and scanned the backyard. No sign of Cynthia.

Chapter Eleven

Billy Tarwater

September 28th, 1963

Halfway between my house and the River Kwai, the tune changed from Nick's little ditty to the Colonel Bogey March—*da da…dadada deet deet da…da da…dadada deet deet da*. Back then we didn't know the name of the tune. We called it something else, thanks to Nick's father.

"My Daddy says it's called Hitler's Only Got One Ball," Nick said with a grin.

Gary drew together in a hunch and let out a spittle-laden guffaw. "Haha. Why is it called that? Did he really have just one ball?"

"How would I know?" Nick replied.

We approached the clearing in the jungle. We could see Jap POW Camp 16 just across the stream. Our first mission would be to ambush the camp, kill Commander Saito, and free the prisoners.

We hadn't quite made it to the crossing when Gary pointed to the culvert. "Over there. That's The Oven."

"The Oven? What's that?" I asked.

"Don't you remember? From the movie. That dark sweat box where they put Colonel Nickerson."

"Oh yeah. I remember now."

"It's not Nickerson, like me, you dumbass," Nick interjected. "It's Nicholson."

"Whatever, Nick. Let's head that way. Free the colonel." Off Gary dashed.

Nick and I followed, our canteens jouncing on our belts, my gas mask flailing from the hook on my backpack. We were still a good distance behind Gary when he reached the culvert. He came barging back toward us in a flailing gallop, slightly bent over, shaking his head and holding his nose.

"What is it, Gary?" Nick asked.

"It smells awful. There's something rotten in there. Maybe a dead dog."

"Aw, Gary," Nick replied. "It's probably nothing. I bet it's just a rat or a possum. You're as bad as Jimmy. A couple of sissies if you ask me." He looked at me. "Binky, give me that mask."

"Nobody calls me a sissy and gets away with it," Gary shot back, and got into his two-fisted Sonny Liston pose.

"Aw, get over it. I was just kidding, Gary. Binky, let me have that mask. I'll go into The Oven by myself."

I unclipped the gas mask and handed it to Nick. "I'm not sure the cannister's any good, Nick. Harry had a box of 'em and I bought three for a dollar. But seeing as they're probably twenty years old, who knows?"

Nick placed the mask over his head. He looked a little like the *Creature from the Black Lagoon*. Or maybe one of the *Invaders from Mars*. And his voice was so muffled, I had to strain to understand him.

"I'm going in. Back me up, men," Nick muttered. He headed toward the culvert.

"Do you have a flashlight, Nick?" Gary yelled.

Nick swung to face Gary. "Of course, I have a flashlight. I ain't goin' in no cave unprepared."

* * *

I remember that day as if it were yesterday. September was coming to an end. The leaves on the oaks and ashes and tulip poplars would soon embark on their yearly passage from green to red to yellow to dead brown. The night's chill would begin to set in, presaging winter's gloom. Save for the occasional gambol in the snow, life would slow to a near crawl. Short-sleeve shirts and Bermuda shorts would be stowed away, replaced by flannel shirts and blue jeans, heavy coats and gloves.

Winter would never stop us from engaging in our regular forays into enemy territory. It just meant that we would have to bundle up. But I would soon learn, on that last Saturday in September, that our innocent diversions, our weekend recreations, would never be the same again. They say the passing of time smooths the wrinkles, eases the pain so it's little more than a pinprick. By and large, that may be true, but September 28th, 1963 is indelibly seared in my mind like a scar that will never fade.

* * *

From where we stood, we had a good view of the entrance to the culvert. It was big. So big, in fact, that Nick could stand up straight with at least a foot of headroom. Nick shined his flashlight into the void. He turned to face us, pointed to the mask, and gave a thumbs-up. I assumed that meant the two-decades-old cannister still worked.

Nick wasn't inside the culvert very long. He dashed out, flapping one hand and tugging at the gas mask with the other. When he was halfway to where we stood, he jerked the mask off.

"There's a body in there. We gotta call the police."

"Do you think it's Martha Ann?" I asked.

"I don't know. But it is a girl alright. And she's nekkid!"

We took off up the street toward my house. But when we got to my front yard, Gary kept running.

"Where are you going, Gary?" I yelled.

"To get my Daddy."

Nick and I barreled into the house. My mother was in the kitchen.

"Quick," I shouted. "Call the police."

"What's happened? Where's Gary?"

"Gary's OK. He went home. But there's a body in the culvert. We just found it."

"No, I found it," Nick interjected.

"OK, Nick, *you* found it. Does it really matter?"

"A body?" My mother gasped.

"Yes, a body."

She dialed the operator. There was a tremble in her voice.

"They're sending the police," she said when she had hung up. "Oh, I wish your father was here."

"Where is he?" I asked.

"He's at Gray-Y with Chester." She looked at the clock over the sink. "It's 10:15. They probably won't be home for another two or three hours."

"We're going back down there," I said.

"Binky, you don't want to get mixed up in all that."

"But Mother, we found the body—*Nick* found the body. He has to be there, and I need to be there with him. Right, Nick?"

Nick nodded.

* * *

We beat the police there. We sat on the ground near the briar thicket and waited for them to arrive. My Caravelle said 10:35. *Why aren't they here yet?*

About that time, Gary showed up. "It's my Daddy's day off, but he's coming. He called HQ. Said he'd meet 'em down here. He just needs to get all suited up."

"Suited up?"

"Yeah, dressed. Like in a coat and tie."

"On a Saturday?" I asked.

"Yes, Binky." Gary had the exasperated look on his face that he sometimes got when he thought somebody had asked a stupid question. "That's what detectives wear when they're on the job."

"The police are so slow. He'll probably beat 'em here just like we did," I said.

At 10:47, I saw a black and white sedan rocketing down the street, siren blaring, red light flashing. It took me back to when the police cars were in front of Martha Ann's house.

"Shit." Gary said. "Did they have to come all the way from Decatur Street?"

I glared at him. "Don't ever use that word in front of my mother. She'll tan your booty."

"It's just a word, Binky," Nick interjected. Then he looked at Gary. "Mama'll tan your snow white ass, mama'll tan your snow white ass," he said in a singsong.

"Cool it, Nick," I said.

The car swerved to the curb just above the culvert. Two policemen got out. They climbed down the embankment and approached the culvert. One of them looked over at us. "You boys need to get home. Go ahead on, now. You don't need to be here."

Gary stood. Poked out his chest. "Gus Alford's my daddy. Homicide."

"I don't care who your daddy is. He could be the mayor, for all I care. You don't need to be here."

We scooted behind the briar thicket and crouched. There was no way we were leaving.

Both officers ran into the culvert. Pretty soon, another squad car came. Then another. Then an unmarked car without a red light on top. Two men with coats and ties got out of that car and slid down the bank. They had to be detectives.

"Where's your Daddy?" I asked Gary.

"He'll be here in a minute."

Gary's father parked behind the detectives' car. He joined them outside the culvert.

"Daddy, I'm ov—"

"Shut up, Gary," Nick whispered and put his finger to his lips. "You wanna get run off?"

The two officers came out of the culvert. They both held handkerchiefs to their faces. We watched as they stood at the entrance, talking to Mr. Alford and the other two. They shined their flashlights into the dark tunnel. The other four men remained on the street near the embankment. One of them was standing next to the open driver's-side door of his squad car. He had one foot planted on the running board and was talking on the radio. Another guy—I assumed it was his partner—was standing next to him, writing on a notepad. One was looking up and down the street like he was waiting for somebody. The fourth guy dropped a cigarette to the pavement and squashed it with his shoe.

Nick pointed to the detectives. "Are they scared to go in?"

"Of course not," Gary said. "Are you crazy? They're checking things out first. And they can't all go in together anyway. There's not enough room in there."

"What's there to check out? The body's inside," Nick replied.

I heard another vehicle approach. It was an unmarked, black-and-white paddy wagon-like panel truck with a red light on top. It stopped behind Mr. Alford's car. Two men got out. They weren't in police uniforms or coats and ties. They wore khaki pants and work shirts. They both carried little boxlike suitcases, sort of like my mother's train case, but bigger. And a camera dangled from one man's neck. They set their cases at the top of the embankment.

The one without the camera slid partway down the bank. The other man handed him the cases and then slid down the bank himself. They joined the five other men standing around the culvert entrance. Then they both went inside, accompanied by Mr. Alford and one of the other detectives.

"What are the cases for?" I asked.

"They're for evidence," Gary replied. "They'll lift fingerprints. Pictures. Look for clues. Put things in little plastic bags. Stuff like that. I learned that from my Daddy."

The detective—not Mr. Alford, but the other one—came out, climbed up the embankment to the street, and said something to the policeman talking on the radio.

By then, the whole place was crawling with newspaper reporters, WSB and WAGA vans, and gawkers from all over the neighborhood. But the police made them stay up on the street. We were the only ones with front-row seats, thanks to the briar thicket.

At 12:05, a long, dark green ambulance or hearse or something pulled up. It had no windows on the sides, except in the front. The word CORONER was across the door in white. Two men stepped out and pulled a stretcher from the back. They carried it down the embankment and into the culvert.

At 12:35, the men hauled the stretcher out. The body was on it. Covered with a sheet.

My stomach lurched.

Mr. Alford and one of the other detectives began walking in our direction, paying close attention to something on the ground. As they came closer, I realized they were following a track in the dirt—two faint parallel lines that ran from roughly where we were to the edge of the culvert. I hadn't noticed it before, and I assumed Gary, Nick, and Jimmy hadn't either. Otherwise, they would have said something.

Mr. Alford saw us first. "Gary, go home. You, too, boys. You don't need to be here."

"But—"

"You heard me. Get on home. Now."

"But Nick here foun—"

"You don't want me to tell you again, Gary."

* * *

Back at the house, I shut my bedroom door. Turned on my crystal set, put on my headphones, and dialed in 750 WSB, hoping to hear something about the body. Nothing. I tried 920 WGST. Nothing. The local news wouldn't be on TV 'til six. I called Gary at home from the kitchen phone. "Has your father said anything?" Not a thing. But he couldn't have. Gary said his father hadn't even been home, that he must have gone straight to police headquarters.

* * *

I unfolded a lawn chair in the front yard and waited anxiously for the evening *Journal*. I had my Mickey Mantle mitt ready so I could bag the folded, rubber-banded paper when the boy lobbed it across the yard. He was older, and a much better throw, than the kid who delivered the *Constitution* in the mornings. People passing by—and there were a lot of them because of what had happened down the street just a few hours earlier—must have wondered what I was doing, sitting there in a lawn chair with a mitt and nobody to throw a ball to me.

Sure enough, at 4:45 like clockwork, here he came. He hurled the paper. Pop fly to center field. I jumped from my chair. Held my shaking gloved hand high in the air. Caught that sucker. Just like that.

There it was, at the bottom of the front page—no Page 18 this time—the headline: MISSING GIRL'S BODY FOUND. My heart pounded like a pile driver. I skimmed the article, picking up words here and there. Martha Ann Dullums. Sixteen. Only child. Daughter. Mr. and Mrs. Albert Dullums. East Atlanta. Missing since the 13th. Found in a culvert. That was it. Nothing about her being naked. Nothing about how she died. Nothing about a suspect. Nothing I didn't know already. Maybe they were keeping the details out of the paper because they didn't want to give anything away. Maybe they had a suspect in mind.

I dropped the paper onto the lawn chair and ran into the house. I made a bee line to my room and locked the door.

Who would have wanted Martha Ann dead? And why?

Chapter Twelve

Cynthia Hudspeth

September 28th, 1963

SATURDAY MORNING, CYNTHIA SLEPT IN AFTER STAYING up way too late playing 45s and reading *Teen Life*. Mama wouldn't let her buy the magazine—said they were smutty. She had to borrow copies from girls at school. And if she ever got caught with one in her room? The thought sent a little shiver through her every time she thought about it.

By the time she managed to drag her drowsy self out of bed, the house was empty. She stumbled into the kitchen, taking in huge breaths with each gaping yawn and wiping the sleepy-seeds from her eyes. The clock over the stove said 9:43. There was a note on the table—well, not completely on the table—half on it and half hanging off the edge. From Mama. It was as if she just sort of threw it down there and didn't pay much attention to where it landed. The note didn't say where she was going, just that she wouldn't be home 'til late in the afternoon. And Daddy? *Who knows? Probably at McKnight's or hanging out at the cab stand.*

She opened the refrigerator door. A quick shelf-by-shelf survey told her there was nothing worth eating that didn't have to be cooked. She grabbed a Coke from the top shelf and shut the door. She instinctively turned the bottle upside down to see the name of the city molded into the bottom. Most of the time it was Atlanta, but sometimes it was Birmingham, Chattanooga, Knoxville. *A cold Cocola and a glob of peanut butter on Ritz crackers. It'll have to do.* Actually, come to think of it, that probably was her breakfast of choice most weekends—at least when she was the one responsible.

She slipped into her favorite pair of denims and a Murphy High sweatshirt. By the time she stepped out the front door, it was almost 11:30. Leonard Seymour was huffing and puffing as he pushed the reel mower across his front yard. When she first noticed him, he was walking away from her, toward Mrs. Tarwater's. But as soon as he made the U-turn at the yard's edge and headed back her way, he settled his gaze on her. The rotary blades sent tiny snips of grass flying every which way. She had a fleeting image of the man's big toe caught in the blades—*I can dream, can't I?*—followed by a slight, but only slight, pang of guilt. She looked away, turned, and quickened her pace to the sidewalk that ran along the street. She normally would have walked past Mrs. Tarwater's house and turned left onto Gresham, but this time she would walk down the street the other way, toward Moreland Avenue and away from Leonard Seymour. *What a creep*, she thought. *He's got me in so much trouble. At first, I thought nothing of it. But the more I think about it... he's a creep. Why would I want to take off my clothes in front of him? A fat old belch of a man.* She turned right at Moreland Avenue. *Now,*

Marvin Darby, that's a whole 'nother colored horse—or however the saying goes.

When she reached Glenwood Avenue, she thought back to the day Shorty Jepperson picked her up right on that very corner and took her to Grady Stadium. It was also the last day anybody remembered seeing Martha Ann Dullums.

What's happening? she thought. *Craziness all around. Everything's weird. Martha Ann gone missing. Two weeks and not even a clue. That Peeping Tom Seymour creeping me out. The reverend telling me I'm going right to you-know-where if I don't straighten up. Straighten up? From what? And then that kid Billy Tarwater studying me. I'm sure* he'd *like to see me pull my britches down.* She stifled a laugh. *But I don't blame him. He's just being a boy. A red-blooded boy.*

Just then, a long green ambulance with CORONER on the side careened off of Moreland and onto Glenwood, its red light flashing. It sped down the street and took a right on Flat Shoals. She watched it until it was out of sight.

* * *

Just before she entered the drug store through the back door, she looked down the alleyway across the street, where McKnight's was, just to make sure her Daddy didn't see her—in case he was there. She plopped onto the stool. Her feet dangled a full six inches above the footrest.

"What can I getcha?"

She fumbled through her purse. She quickly realized she had no money. She knew Weldon, the weekend fountain guy, about as well as anybody in any of the shops in East Atlanta. But he was on the job. She was sure he'd get in trouble if he gave her a free drink.

A boy from Murphy was sitting by himself at the other end of the fountain. She'd seen him around, but she didn't know him. *If I give him a big smile, I wonder.* But he was at least a junior. What interest would he have in a thirteen-year-old? *Worth a try, though.* She hopped down and moved to one stool away from him. Struck up a conversation. His name was Tommy.

"Hey, Weldon," Tommy called out. "This girl here wants a white cow. My treat. And spit on it."

"Spit on it? I don't want him spitting in my shake. And what's a white cow, anyway? That's not what I asked for."

"Don't worry," Tommy said with a sly grin. "That's soda jerk lingo. A white cow's a vanilla shake. That *is* what you wanted, isn't it? And spit on it means add raspberries on top. That's my little extra gift to you."

"How do you know that stuff?" Cynthia asked.

"'Cause I work over at the Woodland Pharmacy sometimes. Us soda jerks, we all speak a special language."

"What grade are you in?" Cynthia asked.

"Eleventh."

"Do you know Marvin Darby?"

"Of course I do. Everybody knows Marvin Darby."

Cynthia didn't let on that Marvin was the subject of her innermost dreams.

* * *

She left the drug store by the front door and ambled down Glenwood past Harry's. About halfway between Harry's and Moreland Avenue, she had a strange feeling that she was being followed. She looked over her shoulder. A car inched it's way in her direction, keeping pace with her. When she stopped, it stopped. When she went, it went. She thought she recognized the car and the driver.

Chapter Thirteen

Gus Alford

September 28th, 1963

GUS ALFORD CHERISHED MOST SATURDAYS, WHEN HE would rise late, read the sports page without feeling rushed, and enjoy breakfast the way nobody else but his wife, Betty, could make it. He pierced the tender yolk with his fork, sending a gush of yellow across his plate. He sopped it with a forkful of cream gravy-laden biscuit and wolfed it. He was about to top it off with a slice of crisp-fried country ham when the boy came tearing breathlessly into the kitchen.

"Daddy, there's a dead body in the tunnel! A girl."

"What tunnel?"

"At the bottom of Van Vleck."

"The culvert?"

"Yeah, the culvert."

Gus slammed down his coffee in one long gulp and headed toward the hallway. Before he reached the kitchen door, the phone rang. It was headquarters, telling him about the body. He bounded up the stairs.

Gary ran out the front door.

Betty was left alone at the kitchen table.

Gus skipped his usual shower. He squeezed into his trousers and button-down, let out his belt a notch, and tied a half-hearted Windsor. He holstered up and slipped into his blue blazer. Fastened the middle button. His .38 Special bulged through the stretchy poly blend. He held out both hands, fingers spread, and examined his manicured, clear-shellacked nails. The product of his biweekly, early Saturday afternoon visits to Edna's Cut-n-Curl—that's assuming he wasn't tied up on a rubout case. It was his one decidedly unmanly indulgence. Today was manicure Saturday, but it looked like he wouldn't be visiting his favorite nail girl.

In seventeen years on the force, he'd seen his share of stiffs, more than most, and add to those a dozen or so others in '44 at Hürtgen Forest. But the next one, the one today, he supposed, was just as hard to face as the first one he ever encountered. Wait...he liked to say that, but was it really true? On the one hand, it was. But on the other, he got this enormous adrenalin rush every time an 11-44 came through. Hell, truth be told, as repugnant to the "respectable" set as it might be, he got off on it.

All he ever wanted to do was be a cop. And even though he had to supplement his pay with a part-time night job as Atlanta Cabana house detective, keeping the call girls and mack daddies in line and out of sight, he wouldn't trade his badge for anything in the world. Not one damned thing. Did it matter that today was his day off and that he was due back at the Cabana tonight for his weekly vice charade? Of course not. He had a job to do.

* * *

When he arrived at the bottom of Van Vleck, just before the street took an upward course toward Ora Avenue, the place was teeming with four cars and twice as many men. He parked behind the unmarked Newport sedan. One of the officers on the street pointed toward the embankment. Lieutenant Alford inched his way down the slope, stepping carefully onto the juts of hard red clay to avoid slipping. He joined the two other detectives, Sergeant Dan Winstanley and Detective Buford Carpenter at the culvert's entrance. Gnarly vines had grown around its perimeter as if they owned it, their spiderlike tentacles gripping the concrete's edge. Dense weeds—Betty called them ryegrass weeds—two feet high on each side of the opening bracketed the slow trickle of turbid water meandering from inside the tunnel. The rotten branches of a fallen weeping willow lay across the stream about five yards from the entrance, extending up and down the stream and dipping their fingers into the shallow water.

Alford peered into the dank abyss. He saw two uniformed officers about ten feet from the culvert's entrance. They were huddled over what he assumed was the body.

The two men looked up, saw Alford and the other two detectives, and joined them outside the culvert. One of the men, a junior officer whom Alford knew in passing but had never worked with on a case, ran to the edge of the creek bed and promptly gave up his breakfast.

The other one, a veteran of the force named Flannery, avoided eye contact with his partner. "I'm guessing a week at the most."

"White or colored?" Alford asked.

"White."

"Sex? Age?"

"Female. Nude. Looks to be a teenager, maybe, but it's hard to tell since we can't see her face. And we obviously didn't want to turn her over. That's above my pay grade."

Alford and Carpenter were about to go in when they saw the two forensics pull up. They waited for them. Then the four entered the culvert, flashlights in hand. The two detectives led. All four men instinctively reached into their back pockets and retrieved handkerchiefs.

The nude body lay face-down in a shallow pool of standing water. Her arms and legs were splayed in an X. Alford noted the greenish-red to grey skin discoloration and the abundance of flesh flies, burying beetles, maggots. A thin layer of nacreous fluid floated on the surface of the water surrounding the body. There were superficial postmortem scavenger wounds around the back of the neck and on the shoulders. But there didn't appear to be significant soft tissue damage from the wounds.

"Sergeant," Alford said, "based on the subject's post-lividity, the advanced darkening of her skin, the maggots, I believe Flannery's right. If I had to guess, I'd say five to seven days. But we'll see what the ME says."

Carpenter nodded.

They were about to turn the body over when Alford noticed a curious tattoo or something on the deceased's right thigh, just below the buttock. "Look at this, Carpenter."

Alford shined his flashlight on the mark. It wasn't a tattoo. It was a series of crude, deep slashes. It looked like a primitive representation of a person. Like you might see on the wall of a cave. *Appropriate*, Alford thought. It was straight vertical line with an X through it for arms and legs. And a lopsided head.

"Have you ever seen anything like that before?" Alford asked.

"No. It's the damnedest thing. And look at the girl, Lieutenant, her limbs are spread out just like the mark."

The detectives turned the body over. Rigor mortis had fully dissipated, further evidence that the girl had likely been dead more than a couple of days. Otherwise, with her arms and legs splayed the way they were, it would have been difficult, though not impossible, to turn her over. As the officer had surmised, she looked to be a teenager. There were cuts and scratches on her hands and forearms, suggesting a struggle. There were also abrasions on the fronts of her lower legs, ankles, and feet. There appeared to be blood under her fingernails.

One of the crime scene investigators photographed the body, the area surrounding the body, the sides of the culvert. With each flashbulb pop, a momentary bright blue incandescence pierced the dark tunnel, followed by a click-crash as the bulb ejected and hit the culvert's floor. The other forensic took samples—blood, skin scrapings, bodily fluids, hair—and placed them in vials and evidence bags. He took what he could, but there was not much to come by. No hard objects or surfaces to lift prints from. No clothing, shoes, or personal effects. Just a nude body lying in a pool of water in a culvert. With the curious mark etched in her thigh.

The forensics gathered up their equipment, the collected samples, the spent flashbulbs, and exited the culvert along with Alford and Carpenter.

"I'll summon the coroner," Carpenter said, and headed toward the embankment.

"Come on, Winstanley, let's look around." Alford looked over at the forensics. "You guys need to come with us. We've got more work to do."

The four men walked downstream along the creek bed. That's when one of the forensics noticed two parallel lines running from a nearby briar thicket to the tunnel's entrance.

"Looks like drag marks to me," Alford said, and pointed to the thicket. "Perpetrator dragged the body, maybe dead, maybe alive, from over there and into the culvert. That may explain the abrasions on her legs and feet."

"Makes sense to me," Winstanley said.

They continued walking toward the briar patch. They were almost to the thicket's edge when Alford saw his son and two other boys crouched in hiding. He told them to leave. After the third time, they ambled up the street in a pout. *That boy, I swear. I'll deal with him later.* He paused. *But Hell, think I wouldn't have done the same thing at his age?*

The men combed the area around and beyond the thicket, to a point about fifty yards past the culvert where the stream veered forty-five degrees eastward on its course to Sugar Creek. Aside from the suspected drag marks, they found no other evidence. But they knew from years of experience that their task was not over, insofar as searching the surroundings was concerned. It's a matter of triage, a series of concentric circles. Start with the bullseye—the point where the body lay—and work your way out. It might take a few days before you decide you've covered enough ground.

As the body was about to be loaded into the coroner's hearse, a couple hastened from up the street. Officer Pickens, another veteran, said he recognized them as the Dullumses. He had interviewed them in their living room the morning after their daughter went missing. They ran up to the back of the hearse. The morgue worker pulled the sheet from over the girl's face. The father identified Martha Ann, screaming her name to the press, the police, bystanders, and God Almighty himself. The mother's legs gave way, and she collapsed like a marionette onto the pavement. At first, she looked like she had passed out. But then she started hyperventilating, heaving something awful, and wailing, "My baby, my baby." Her husband, the proverbial deer in the headlights, stood over her.

"I think she's having a crack-up," one of the officers said. "Better call Grady."

Fifteen minutes later, an ambulance arrived and took her off. Her husband sat hunched in the back.

* * *

By nightfall, Gus Alford should have been at the Cabana, but he had come straight from the crime scene to Decatur Street. The tail waggers and their tricks would have to make do without him tonight. He stubbed his fourth Lucky into the ashtray stand. "Winstanley, when did the Dullums girl go missing?"

"Two weeks ago yesterday, Lieutenant."

"Two weeks. But unless we're way off base, the girl's been dead no more than a week. Refresh my memory. Where was she last seen?"

"Murphy High. At the end of the school day."

"Any leads since then? About who may have copped her?"

"Not that I know of, sir," Winstanley replied, "but we're checking with Missing Persons."

"We need to bring Dullums and his wife in."

"I agree, but they're in no condition to talk right now."

"Give it a day or two," Alford said. "She's probably still at Grady getting the hysterics drugged out of her."

"Some burrhead probably dragged the poor girl into that tunnel. Raped and killed her like a mad dog in heat," Carpenter chimed in. "Wouldn't be the first time."

"You may not be far from the mark," Alford replied, "But let's give it a while. We don't want to bend the facts to fit the narrative. At least not yet." He smirked and lit another cigarette.

"What do you make of that thing carved into her thigh, Lieutenant?" Carpenter asked.

"I have no idea. Never seen anything like it. They cut right through the skin with a knife or a razor blade or something. I don't think the cuts were old. They looked like they were done the night she was killed. There was no sign of subcutaneous bleeding, bruising, external bleeding from the cuts. That suggests to me that it was done after she was already dead."

"I hadn't thought of that."

"But we really don't know. I guess the ME will tell us all about that, plus how she was killed." Alford took a deep drag. Blew rings. "You know what they say. All good things are worth the wait."

* * *

By the time Gus Alford pulled into his driveway, it was half past midnight. A light shone from the bedroom window, but as soon as he got out of the car, it went dark. He entered the house, easing the door shut. He took off his shoes and, holding them by their collars, ghosted up the stairs. Betty, his wife of sixteen years, lay stone-still in bed. He had gotten used to the routine. He'd come home in the middle of the night, tiptoe up the stairs, play her little game. She'd pretend to be asleep so she wouldn't have to confront him. About what, though? Did she think he was out gallivanting instead of trying to hold down two jobs just to make ends meet? Not that he hadn't dipped his pen in the occasional ink well, but for Christ's sake, she needed to let up a little.

"I know you're awake, Betty."

She didn't move.

"Betty, stop pretending you're asleep. I know you're not."

Finally, she turned over to face him. "Where have you been? I called the Cabana and they said you weren't—"

"Did you think to call the station house?"

"Why would you be there in the middle of the night? On a Saturday night?"

"Betty, think about it. They found a dead body in the culvert halfway down Van Vleck. I assume you knew that. You were sitting at the table when the boy came running in. And then I got the call."

She nodded. "Have you identified the body?"

"It's that Dullums girl. I went straight to the office after they took her away. Been there ever since, sorting things out."

* * *

Early Sunday morning, the phone rang. Gus fumbled for the handset. It was Officer Ingle from Missing Persons.

"Lieutenant, I thought you should know. Another girl's gone missing."

Chapter Fourteen
Billy Tarwater

September 29th, 1963

THE SUNDAY MORNING SERVICE WAS JAM-PACKED. People I hadn't seen since Easter. Even my father joined us, just like he had on the Sunday after Martha Ann went missing. My brother sat next to me instead of in the balcony. Did he do that on his own? Or had Mom forced him to? I assumed everybody was there because of Martha Ann. But I looked around and didn't see her parents. Or Cynthia and her mother. And there was an empty spot in the choir loft where Leonard Seymour usually sat.

I decided I should pay attention to what the reverend had to say. Just like two weeks ago. But his sermon this morning was different. And he was quieter. He preached on the early church—Greeks and Romans. Like he was teaching us, for a change, instead of yelling at us. He made us crack our Bibles to Acts 2:4 and read in unison. "And they were all filled with the Holy Ghost, and began to speak with other tongues, as the Spirit gave them utterance." Then I Corinthians 13:1. "I am become as sounding brass, or a tinkling cymbal." Then Colossians 3:17. He went on and on about Constantine the Great and somebody named Eusebius.

My brother leaned in. "What the hell is he talking about? Is he batty?"

I whispered, "Can it! If somebody hears you, they're gonna grab you by the ear and lead you out the door for an old-fashioned whipping. You know who I mean."

The strange thing is there was no altar call. And not a mention was made of Martha Ann. Toward the end of the sermon, something happened. Something I'd never seen before. The reverend got to prancing back and forth, shaking something crazy, waving his left hand in the air and with his right fist planted in his mouth. Bobbing his head up and down. Until, finally, he collapsed in his green leather throne. The youth minister jumped to the lectern, led us all in a round of three Praise Jesuses, and quickly dismissed us. We filed out of the church, shaking our heads, as the choir sang "Nearer, my God, to Thee."

* * *

No sooner had we knocked off yet another Roman orgy at Granny T's than the doorbell rang. I ran to the door and opened it to Adele Hudspeth's restless hulk.

My grandmother came up behind me. "What is it, Mrs. Hudspeth? You're trembling. And you're white as a flock of sheep."

A big flock of sheep, I thought.

"Can I come in, Jincey?"

I had never heard her call my grandmother by her first name. *And where are her keys? I don't see her keys.*

Mrs. Hudspeth planked down at the end of the sofa. When she did, I swear I thought I saw the legs on the other end rise half an inch off the floor. *Surely not. She's not* that *heavy.*

She took a deep breath before speaking. "Twenty-nine hours."

"Twenty-nine hours what, Adele?"

"Since we've seen her. Twenty-nine hours."

"Seen who?"

"Cynthia."

My heart skipped a beat.

Mrs. Hudspeth explained how she had left the house early yesterday morning. Cynthia was still asleep. She left a note on the kitchen table. When she returned late in the day, Cynthia was gone.

"When midnight came and still no sign of her, Cecil called the police."

"Has she ever run off before, Adele?" my mother asked.

"She didn't run off, Alice. She wouldn't run off. It's just not like her. I'm worried something bad's happened. She's been…" Mrs. Hudspeth looked at me, then at my mother, then at me again.

"Binky, why don't you go play with the shortwave?" my mother said.

I knew my mother well enough to know when I was being politely ordered to leave, but there was no way I was going to miss this. I pretended to head off to the spare bedroom where the shortwave radio was, but as soon as I rounded the corner into the hallway, I made fake footsteps like I was walking down the hall. I lurked just past the doorway. My mother and grandmother were huddled around Mrs. Hudspeth. My father, Uncle Newell and Aunt Lottie, Cousin Loreen, and my brother were on the screened porch. And Dovey Mae was in the kitchen with the door closed. Otherwise, any one of them might have seen me.

"What is it, Adele?" my grandmother asked.

"It's that Leonard Seymour. Cynthia's been undressing in the window. And he watches her."

The window! My head was spinning. I was back and forth between *Oh my God, Cynthia's missing* and *She's been taking her clothes off in front of Launchpad Leonard?*

"Undressing? My heaven's, Adele, is she doing it on purpose?" Granny T asked.

Did my grandmother really ask that?

"I don't know what to make of it. When I asked her about it, she claimed innocence. And when I confronted him—"

"You confronted Leonard Seymour?"

"I did. I had to. He just brushed it off. Blamed her. And then Reverend Kilgallon said—"

"The reverend? You talked to the reverend?"

"Yesterday morning. That's why I left the house early. But he blamed her, too. Says she needs the devil cast out of her."

I sneaked into the kitchen and headed for the back door.

"Where are you going, Binky?" Dovey Mae asked.

"I'll be back. Don't tell them I'm gone." I was halfway up the street before I looked back. Dovey Mae was standing in the doorway with her hands on her hips.

I'll find her. I'll find Cynthia Hudspeth if it's the last thing I do.

* * *

"Don't tell your mama and daddy," Dovey Mae whispered as we stood in the kitchen, "but come next Saturday, if the poor girl still hasn't showed back up, you and me'll go visit somebody that can help."

I had gone all over East Atlanta looking for her, asking anybody I saw. The problem was, almost everything was closed, seeing as it was Sunday. Oscar Morgan was piddling around at the Texaco, even though it wasn't open. He hadn't seen her. I had run into Charlie Averitt, the butcher, walking down Flat Shoals. He hadn't seen her. Nobody knew a thing. I had walked all the way to my school and searched the playground. Behind the library. Behind the A&P. I had asked the firemen at the station. Nothing. I had finally given up and come back to Granny Tarwater's.

"What do you mean, Dovey Mae?" *I trust her, but how can she possibly help?*

"They's a woman I happen to know down Capitol Avenue a piece. She has a way about her. Can see things. Things you and I can't see. I'm not working Saturday. Was supposed to be at Mrs. Hallman's, but she's out of town. We'll go see Madame Ludowici. We'll take the bus."

Just then, Granny T walked in. Dovey Mae got busy stowing pots and pans. Put her finger to her lips and gave me a little wink when my grandmother wasn't looking.

We drove Dovey Mae home, as we did most Sundays. Right before she got out of the car, she slipped me a scribbled note:

Nine o'clock Saturday. Car stop. Martha Brown Church.

* * *

Every morning, for five days, I checked the paper to see if there was anything about Cynthia. And every afternoon, when I got home from school, I grabbed the afternoon paper and scoured every page. Unlike when Martha Ann went missing, there wasn't a thing about Cynthia. I wondered why. Did her parents ask the police to keep it quiet? Did the police keep it out of the papers so it wouldn't scare people? After all, two girls had gone missing in just a couple of weeks, and one of them ended up dead in a tunnel.

I dreamed of Cynthia every night. Bad dreams. One where we were at this park—maybe it was Brownwood Park—and she fell into a deep hole. It was so deep and dark that I couldn't even see her down in the bottom of it. I kept calling her name, but she didn't answer. I woke up bug-eyed and sweaty, fearing the worst. I couldn't wait 'til Saturday, when we would visit Dovey Mae's friend.

* * *

On Saturday, I rode my bike to downtown East Atlanta, leaving the house early enough to make sure I got to Martha Brown Church, the corner of Moreland and Metropolitan Avenues, before nine. I stashed my bike in the bushes at the far end of the parking lot. I waited in front of the church for Dovey Mae, hoping nobody—my mother or father, Granny T, I don't know, whoever—saw me and questioned what I was doing standing there. I wore my Crackers ball cap low on my head and stared at the sidewalk.

I had told my mother I was going to Jimmy's to spend the day. I figured Jimmy was the last person she would worry about me getting in any trouble with. With everything going on with Martha Ann, and now Cynthia missing, she would know I was safe at Jimmy's house. Jimmy's mother and my mother weren't close, and the chances of her calling there were slim. The problem is, I had forgotten to tell Jimmy. I just hoped he didn't take a notion to come visit me. But that was unlikely, seeing as the scaredy-cat was afraid even to venture outside of his yard lately.

A little before nine, I looked up and saw Dovey Mae sashaying up Moreland from the Glenwood corner, her hips swaying back and forth. She had a shopping bag in one hand and a parasol in the other. We waited together for the Number 13 bus. Dovey Mae said it would take us to Butler Street, and from there it was a short walk to Madame What's-her-name's.

I reached deep into my pocket. Took fifteen cents out of my squeeze coin holder. "Dovey Mae, I have carfare."

"You put your money right back where you got it, Binky. This trip's on me."

The bus came to a stop in front of the church. Dovey Mae motioned for me to go ahead of her. I climbed the three steps onto the bus, with her following behind. She plunked coins in the farebox for both of us and motioned for me to take a seat in the third row. "I sit in the back," she said.

"But Dovey Mae, I want to sit with you."

"No, Binky. You'd best sit up here where you belong. I'll tell you when it's our stop."

I watched out the window as we passed Cabbagetown…the cotton mill in the distance…the cemetery. We turned right on Bell Street, not far past the cemetery, then left. The street sign said Decatur Street. I knew we were getting close.

A light tap on my shoulder. "Next stop be ours, Binky."

As we exited the bus, the driver glared at Dovey Mae.

"Why did he look at you like that, Dovey Mae? Didn't you give him enough money?"

"I gave him the right fare, Binky. It's not that. It's just that I'm supposed to go out through the back door. It shouldn't be that way, but like the man says, it is what it is."

I didn't like it when Dovey Mae looked sad.

We walked down Butler Street. I could see the gold dome of the capitol in the distance. We came to Capitol Avenue and turned left. We must have walked a dozen blocks or more—a lot farther than I expected—before we came to a two-story white frame house on the right. There was a purple sign out front with fancy gold letters.

> Madame Ludowici
> Fortune Teller to the Luminaries

Under that, there was a picture of a crystal ball, sort of lit up-like, but not really. Two hands were touching it. And under the picture it said:

> Palm, Tarot, Psychic, Ball Gazing
> Oils, Brews, Charms

There were fancy gold borders along the top and bottom of the sign. In the top right corner was an orange hand—like the policeman on the Slow school zone sign—except this one had a big white eyeball in the middle of it. Across from that was a playing card. But it wasn't like any card I'd ever seen. It had a moon and two howling dogs on it. And in the bottom corners of the sign—a sun and a star. *The strangest sign*, I thought.

"Dovey Mae, what does that mean, fortune teller to the luminaries?"

"It don't mean a thing, Binky. Luminaries is famous people, like movie stars...notabilities...celebrities. She just made that up. She's never fortune told to a luminary in her life. Why, she wouldn't know one if they came up behind her and bit her in the...never mind, Binky. Let's go inside. She's waiting."

We climbed the steps onto the porch. The sun at our backs cast long shadows across the porch planks and part way up the front of the house. A woman threw open the door before we could knock. It had to be Madame Ludowici. She was black—a lot blacker than Dovey Mae. She was in a long red dress that reached all the way down to her ankles. And she had a gold scarf wrapped around her head like Ali Baba. She had these huge earrings that looked like Mom's embroidery hoops. And at least a dozen gold bracelets on each arm. And one of her front teeth was gold and shined when the sun hit it just right. Oh, and she glared at us like she was in some kind of trance. *What are we doing here?* It was downright creepy.

She motioned for us to come in. We entered through a wall of beads into this little room that was so dark you could barely see. It took me a minute to adjust my eyes. The two windows had black velvet curtains that were drawn tight. There was a wooden table with two chairs near the middle of the room. A red velvet loveseat and a side table were up against one wall. There was a lamp with gold tassels hanging from the shade—I called it a gypsy lamp—that put out a faint red glow. That was the only light in the room except for a candle on a little table against a far wall. I could smell it all the way across the room. It smelled like Mom's cedar chest, but a lot stronger.

She told me to sit at the table near the center of the room. She sat across from me. Dovey Mae took the loveseat.

"And what brings you here on this first Saturday in Winterfylleth?"

I shook my head and frowned. "What?"

"October. What brings you here?"

Dovey Mae spoke up. "He's here bec—"

"Sister Walker, I'd like to hear from the boy." Madame Ludowici locked eyes with me.

"I'm…uh…I'm…I'm here because a girl's missing."

"And who is this missing girl?"

"Cynthia Hudspeth."

"Is she a friend of yours?"

"Uh. Yes, ma'am. And I'm scared."

"Tell me more about this girl, Cynthia Hudspeth. How old is she? When did you last see her?"

"Thirteen, ma'am. I saw her…um…a week and a half ago. But she's been gone a week."

"Tell me what she looks like."

"She's the most beautiful girl in the world. She has these brown bangs and brownish-greenish eyes that look like a movie star's. She's a real sweet girl. She talks to me sometimes."

"And you want to know where she is. If she's okay."

I nodded.

Madame Ludowici stood and faced Dovey Mae. She leaned in and whispered, but I could still hear what she said. "You know, I normally don't scry for children. It can be upsetting if I tell them what they don't want to hear. Is he prepared for whatever I have to say?"

I didn't know what scry meant, but I assumed I'd soon find out.

"He's a big boy," Dovey Mae replied. "He can take it."

Madame Ludowici went over to a corner of the room and rummaged through a big wooden box—sort of like a toy box. She came back with a glass ball about the size of a cantaloupe. It was on a little black base. A long, black electrical cord stuck out of the base. She plopped the ball onto the center of the table, plugged the cord into an outlet in the nearest wall, and sat back down. I thought it was strange that she had to go get it out of a box like it was some ordinary everyday object instead of something special. But what did I know?

The ball put out a glow that made the whole room eerie-like. She put both palms on the ball. She fluttered her long black eyelashes and shut her eyes. Her eyelids quivered. She mumbled something I didn't understand. Then she went quiet for what seemed like forever. I wondered if she fell asleep. Then, suddenly, she sprang back to life, her eyes open wide. She stared at the ceiling and rubbed the glass. "I see a girl. Her name is Cynthia. She's drifting down the street."

"She's alive?" I asked.

"She's in the present."

I looked at Dovey Mae and frowned. I didn't know what that meant.

"I see her calling," Madame Ludowici continued. "Calling your name."

I found it weird that Cynthia, wherever she was, would be calling *my* name, but I wasn't going to argue with Madame Ludowici.

"Where is she?" I asked.

She shook her head. "Sad to say, I don't know. It's going all dark on me." She stood and walked across the room again. "I'm afraid I can't help you anymore. Just know she's there."

"But where?"

"I cannot say."

She walked back over to Dovey Mae and whispered, "Sister Walker, I'm sorry, I just can't do this to a boy his age." She held out her hand, palm up. "But you still have to pay me. I gave up another session for this. If you come by next week, I'll give you a free reading."

Dovey Mae gave her some crumpled up money.

I felt betrayed.

On the bus ride back, I asked Dovey Mae how much she had paid Madame Ludowici. She wouldn't tell me, only that she was sorry our trip hadn't worked out.

"Dovey Mae, is Madame Ludowici your sister?"

"What do you mean, Binky?"

"She called you Sister—twice."

"Oh, Binky." Dovey Mae grinned. "That's just what we call each other. She's not my sister. Not my blood sister, anyway."

* * *

When I got home, Mom was at the sink. She had those big yellow gloves on that she always wore when she washed dishes.

"Did you and Jimmy have a nice day?" she asked without turning around.

"We did," It wasn't an out-and-out lie. I figured Jimmy had had a nice day, whatever he was up to. And I had, too, sort of. At least I got to spend some time with Dovey Mae. But I doubted I'd be visiting another fortune teller any time soon.

I went to bed fretting over Cynthia. I didn't know any more than I had when Dovey Mae and I set out on the bus ride. Cynthia had been gone a whole week. I assumed Mr. and Mrs. Hudspeth were ten times more worried than I was.

All I could think of was Cynthia missing and Martha Ann dead. I kept having bad thoughts. I lay under the sheet thinking about what I had heard last Sunday as I hid in the doorway at Granny Tarwater's. Had Leonard Seymour gone and done something to Cynthia? To Martha Ann? I trembled.

Tomorrow, I'll sneak next door to Leonard Seymour's after Sunday dinner. Snoop around. If Leonard Seymour has done something to Cynthia, and maybe Martha, too, I'll never let him get away with it.

Chapter Fifteen

Gus Alford

October 1st, 1963

GUS ALFORD TAPPED THE UNLIT CIGARETTE AGAINST the arm of his chair. Always three taps. He didn't know why three. Creature of habit, he guessed. He struck a match, lit it and took a slow draw. He threw the book of matches onto the desk.

Carpenter reached across the table. Picked up the matchbook with his linebacker hand. "Far from home, Lieutenant."

"What do you mean, Carpenter?"

"The matchbook. Alamo Motor Court. Stewart Avenue, right? Pretty far from home."

Alford glared at Carpenter, then shifted his attention to Winstanley. "Sergeant, what do we have on the Dullums girl?"

"Not much. Autopsy came back this morning. Asphyxia by drowning. No indication of premortem physical trauma, except for the scratches, cuts, abrasions on the body. Suggests some sort of struggle before she died. Medical examiner thinks she flatlined where we found her. Five days ago, plus or minus."

"What about the mark on her thigh?"

"They think she was stone dead when her skin was slashed up," Carpenter chimed in.

"Stone dead before she was slashed up. Medical terminology, Detective?" Alford gibed.

"No sir, those are my words. You knew what I meant, though, didn't you?"

"Do we have any leads, Winstanley?"

"Not yet. But we do have more evidence. We went back to the crime scene, but this time we approached from the other direction. There's a road, really just a dirt path wide enough for a car, that leads from the street to the other side of the creek bed. Do you know it?"

The lieutenant nodded. "My son and his friends play down there all the time."

"We found tire tracks in the dirt. We had forensics check them against tires available on the market."

"And?"

"And the tracks are 6-1/2 inches wide, with about a…a 4-1/2 inch tread width. The most common standard tire at that width is a 6.50-14. But there's also a 6.50-13 and a 6.50-15 on the market."

"And?"

"The tread's a complicated herringbone pattern. A single center groove flanked by two…I don't know…I call them half herringbones but I'm sure that's not the right way to describe them.

Then two regular herringbones. Then two more half herringbones along the outer edge. Forensics checked and said they look like Goodyears."

"Sometimes, Winstanley, you're as hard to make sense of as your partner. But I think I know what you're trying to say. It's a multi-groove symmetrical herringbone tread."

"That's it. Here, Lieutenant. We took pictures." Winstanley pulled an 8x10 out of the case folder and handed it to Alford. "The photo lab just got 'em to us."

Gus Alford briefly studied the photograph and handed it back to Winstanley. "This is good, Sergeant. Get a list of every car make and model that uses a 6.50-13, -14 or -15. Then run it through DMV. Anything else?"

Winstanley shook his head.

"We need to get her parents in here right away." Alford glanced at the flip calendar on his desk. "It's been three days since we found the body. I assume the mother's settled down by now. Unless she's still on the ninth floor of Grady, or wherever she ended up. Carpenter, find out when we can get the mother and father in here. The sooner the better. And I want to be here for that."

* * *

"Cigarette?" Gus Alford extended the pack of Lucky Strikes.

Mr. Dullums declined. Mrs. Dullums' hand shook as she took the one that protruded a half inch from the pack. Alford reached across his desk and lit it. "Have a seat, please."

The Dullumses sat across the desk from Alford. Winstanley and Carpenter sat along the side wall.

"First, let me say..." Gus Alford cleared his throat. "...how sorry we are for your loss. I know how hard it must have been for you to come in today."

"I just can't tell you how...the wife here has had a rough few days. Two-and-a-half weeks, actually. So have I. But we want to do whatever we can to help you find Martha Ann's..." Albert Dullums choked up. "...killer."

Mr. Dullums laid out the sequence of events from the time their daughter left for school the morning of the 13th until they discovered she was missing that evening. There wasn't much to tell. She was at school all day. At least, that's what they were told.

Was she dating anyone? A boy named Marvin Darby. But only off and on. Seems he was more interested in her than she was in him. Close girlfriends? A handful. Can you provide names? Of course. Any ill-wishers that you know of—anybody that might have wanted to do her harm? Martha Ann wasn't the kind of girl to have enemies. She got along with everybody. Any sign of depression? Surely not. She was a happy girl. Always up.

"What else can you tell us about the Friday she went missing?"

Mr. Dullums peered over the rims of his glasses. "You may not know, but we told your people, the Missing Persons people, everything."

Alford looked at Winstanley.

"We have the full Missing Person's file right here." Winstanley waved a quarter-inch-thick file folder in the air. "We've gone through it all. They interviewed a lot of people at the school... principal...bus driver...school patrol captain...the Darby boy...a few other classmates...even the janitor. But there's not much to go on."

"Mr. Dullums," Alford continued. "I know it's hard, but if you don't mind, I'd like to hear it straight from you. About the Friday she went missing."

"She was supposed to go to a football game. At Grady Stadium."

"How was she planning to get there?"

"She'd take the bus home after school, borrow my car and drive there."

"And she never got on the bus," Alford said.

"That's right." Mr. Dullums paused. "And one other thing. Friday morning, as she was heading out the door, I remember her saying something about planning to pick up a girl after school and give her a ride to the game. A couple years younger than Martha Ann. It wasn't anybody we knew."

"Do you remember her name?" Alford asked.

"Cynthia something."

"Hudspeth."

"I think that's it."

"Remember, honey," Mrs. Dullums said. "The girl showed up at the house the Saturday morning after Martha Ann disappeared."

"That's right. I've been so distraught, I completely forgot." Mr. Dullums looked at Gus Alford. "Lieutenant, if you speak with one of the officers who came to the house that morning, you can confirm that's her name. I'm pretty sure he wrote it down. But I don't know whether your people followed up with her. Maybe you can look her up and bring—"

"Missing Persons already interviewed her. It's in here. No need to bring her in again." Winstanley said. He locked eyes with

Alford then looked back at Martha Ann's parents. "Mrs. Dullums, can you confirm what your daughter was wearing when she left for school that morning?"

Martha Ann's mother hesitated. "Let me see. I believe—"

"Mrs. Dullums, I know how hard it is to remember details right now." Winstanley searched the Missing Persons file. "Let me help you out. Here it is. A maroon box pleat skirt, white blouse, black and white saddle oxfords. Is that right, Mrs. Dullums?"

She nodded.

"Tell us more about your daughter. Did she regularly attend church?" Gus Alford felt a little uncomfortable asking the question. He couldn't remember the last time he'd stepped inside a church. Or any of his family, for that matter.

"She goes...went...to Confederate Avenue Baptist. Same as us."

"Was she active there?"

"As active as any sixteen-year-old, I guess. She pretty much hung out in the balcony with the other teenagers on Sundays. She was active in GAs when she was younger."

"GAs?"

"Girls' Auxiliary. It's a program for young ladies. Nine to fifteen, I think. But Martha Ann stopped going when she was around fourteen. She also helped collect the Lottie Moon offering every Christmas. Stopped doing that around the same time. Her interest in church began to wane."

* * *

Winstanley had shown the Dullumses out of the building and returned to Alford's office. He sat back down next to Carpenter. "Anything else we need to over right now, boss?" he asked Alford.

"You know the drill, Sergeant," Alford replied. "We need to interview the people at the school, get affidavits, even if Missing Persons has already talked to them. But don't do it at the school. Bring them in. Even her classmates. Especially that Darby boy. Carpenter, follow up with the father and get the names of the girls she was closest to. Winstanley, arrange the meetings. Reach out to the principal first."

"What about that Alice Tarwater woman? The one that made the call about finding the dead body?" Winstanley asked.

"Interview her. But don't bring her in. Go to her house. I know Alice and Herman. Their boy and my boy are best friends. You can talk to her without getting me involved."

Carpenter and Winstanley got up to leave.

"And one other thing, men." Gus Alford stood and walked around his desk. Lit another Lucky. "We need to take over the Hudspeth case. Take it away from Missing Persons. The fact that the two girls were supposed to be together the day Martha Ann Dullums disappeared and then, two weeks later, just when we find Martha Ann's body, the Hudspeth girl goes missing. That's reasonable grounds for us to grab the case and work it. I just hope we don't end up with another corpse on our hands."

Chapter Sixteen

Marvin Darby

October 2nd, 1963

MARVIN DARBY WAS BORN ON THE WRONG SIDE OF THE fence. The wiregrass side. Screven County. In a tumbledown trailer park between Cooperville and Sylvania. That's where he'd have stayed if his old man hadn't come home one day and, out of the blue, up and said, "Louise, we're movin' to the city. Gonna make it big in retail."

As far as Marvin could tell, his old man didn't know shit about retail. He'd worked his whole life driving trucks for a timber crew just outside of Statesboro. But when he made up his mind to do something, you'd best just go ahead and let him do it. Marvin was sort of the same way; he guessed he'd come by his stubbornness honestly. "Stubborn as a hinny," his mother would say.

When they settled in the city in '57, they first stayed at the Alamo Motor Court on Stewart Avenue, at a weekly rate worked out with the manager. Marvin was ten—almost eleven. His old man said they'd stay at the Alamo 'til they got on their feet. He got a job driving for Williams Brothers Lumber. But he made sure everybody knew that was temporary. He was gonna go big time in the hock trade. Sure enough, in '59, he opened a pawn shop—Pawn de Rosa—not too far from the Alamo. The name was a tribute to *Bonanza,* his favorite TV show. Come hell or high water, when Saturday evenings came, he'd flip the TV to Channel 2 and sit glued to the set for an hour, then on Sunday evenings when they changed the night. Never missed it.

In the middle of '59, they bought a little brick house off of Sylvan Road. It wasn't much bigger than the trailer they'd left behind. They'd been there two years when, in the summer of '61, the old man said, "Pack your things. We're movin' again. Movin' up." They bought a big split level on Liberty Avenue, in East Atlanta. That September, Marvin started his sophomore year at Murphy High. He could walk the six blocks to school rather than take the bus. That was good. He didn't cotton to riding on a bus with a bunch of people he didn't know.

It wasn't until his junior year that Marvin found out how the old man had gotten the cash to open the pawn shop. He'd always wondered. As far as Marvin knew, it took a lot of money to open a place like that—the kind the Darby household sure didn't have. One Saturday afternoon in '62, a stranger showed up at the house. He drove a brand new Lincoln and wore a gangster hat like the guys in *The Asphalt Jungle.* The stranger knocked on the door. He and Marvin's old man stood in the doorway and talked for a minute, then they went around to the backyard—near the toolshed. Marvin's father took out a wad of cash, thumbed off a bunch of bills, and handed them to the stranger. From where

Marvin stood at the dining room window, he couldn't tell how much it was. But it looked like a lot.

Come to find out, the stranger was a silent money man, a loan shark named Backer. But the odd thing was, this guy didn't loan the money to Marvin's father to start the pawn shop, the way a loan shark usually would. Somehow, his father had convinced Backer to go into business with him. That was the other trait the old man had. He could finagle anything out of anybody, given enough time, just like Marvin could. Marvin guessed he had gotten that honestly, too.

Marvin had found out all of this by coming right out and asking the old man. "What were you doing paying that man… what's his name again?"

"Backer."

"Yeah, Backer. What were you doing paying him all that money that day in the backyard?"

"Splittin' the profits boy."

* * *

At first, Marvin had a hard time making friends at Murphy. All he'd ever known before moving to the city was a damned hick life in the middle of nowhere, with the same damned hick friends in the same hick town, from as far back as he could remember 'til the summer of '57 when the Darbys packed up and left. The four years they lived on the west side, it was a little easier to fit in. He was just a kid then. But at Murphy? That was a whole other deal. Teenagers are a lot rougher on outsiders, especially those that don't talk like city folk. They made fun of his accent. The way he dressed. The way he walked. Called him a bumpkin. A clodhopper.

But things started to change once he finagled his way onto the JV team as a running back. It didn't take much finagling, really. He could run like hell. And he had another thing going for him, thanks to his mother's side—she always said she came from a big-boned family. When he was on the field, you'd best get out of his way unless you wanted to end up with a dirt sandwich.

He began to make friends. His way of talking slowly lost its hayseed edge. He dressed better, thanks to the clothes money his mother gave him periodically. He learned to walk like a city boy instead of looking like he'd just gotten off a horse. And he met a girl. Martha Ann Dullums. They started dating. But she never seemed to take to him the way he took to her. No matter how hard he turned on his finagling charm, no matter how much he pushed, she could push back just as hard. He lay awake more than once wondering whether he'd ever get past the fifty-yard line with her. But he'd keep pushing.

* * *

On Wednesday, the 2nd of October, the counselor showed up at the door to Marvin's English class. He stood just outside the threshold and motioned for the teacher. They talked for a minute or two. Then the teacher came over to Marvin's desk and told him to pack up his things. His father was waiting with Admiral Atwood in the front office.

"What is it?" Marvin asked his father.

"They want you at the police station," the old man said. "Something about that Dullums girl."

"They interviewed me already when she went missing," he said to his father. "I don't know that I can go through the whole thing again, with her being gone and all. It's not easy talking about it. About her."

"Marvin, I know it's hard, but somehow you need to deal with it. Don't take it the wrong way. They're talkin' to everybody that was close to her." Mr. Darby stared at his son. A frown swam up his face. "And you two were real close, right?"

Marvin grimaced. Walked to the old man's car.

His father dropped him off in front of the police headquarters on Decatur Street, but not before telling him he was to ask for a Sergeant Winstanley.

"You're not coming in with me?"

"I can't, Marvin. I have to get back to the ranch. See a man about a horse."

By ranch, Marvin knew his old man meant the Pawn de Rosa.

Marvin wasn't sure how he'd get home. He steeled himself and walked through the double glass doors into the lobby.

* * *

"Come with me, son." An officer led Marvin past the elevators to the stairwell. They climbed to the third floor. He led Marvin into a small room off the main hallway.

Two detectives were sitting across the table from where Marvin was told to sit. One of the men extended his hand. "Detective Carpenter." He brushed his hand in the other man's direction. "And this is Sergeant Winstanley. Would you like a Coke? Water?"

Marvin shook his head.

Winstanley did most of the talking. "We want to ask you some questions about Martha Ann Dullums. OK?"

Marvin squirmed. What was he going to do? Not answer their questions? The way he saw it, he didn't have much choice.

"Yes sir. But can I just say one thing before we start. Everybody's been in shock ever since they found Martha Ann's body. I haven't been able to sleep. I just can't believe anyone would have done that to her."

"I understand," Winstanley replied. "But what do you mean 'done that to her?'"

"I mean killed her."

"'Done that to her' sounds like you know more than just that she was killed. What do you mean by 'that,' Marvin? And how do you know she was killed in the first place?"

Marvin wanted to say "Oh, I don't know. Maybe because I'm sitting across the table from two detectives, and the sign on the door says Homicide?" but he decided against it. They probably wouldn't take kindly to his snark. Instead, he said, "I don't know that she was killed, sir. I just know some boys found her in a culvert."

"How well did you know her?"

"We dated some. Went to the movies. Sometimes we'd go to the Nibble Nook for a hamburger afterwards. Sometimes we'd go to Brownwood Park and hang out."

"How long did you know her?"

"Let's see." Marvin paused. Pressed his index finger against his lips as if in deep thought. But he knew full well when he and Martha Ann had first met. "I think it was the first day of class, my junior year. She was in the same homeroom as me. Yeah, that's it."

"When did you last see her?"

"That Friday. The day she went missing."

"The 13th?"

"Yeah, the 13th. It was just after school let out. We had a game that night. At Grady. She said she'd be in the stands watching me. I told her I'd see her after the game. She left—I assume to get on the bus. They always line up along the side entrance. That's the last time I saw her."

"Tell me what she was like. What kind of girl was she?"

"What do you mean?"

"Well, was she the kind of girl that…you know…liked to party a lot? Or was she more…let's say…quieter, more studious?"

"What you're asking me is was she a good girl or a bad girl?"

"Just tell us what she was like."

"She was a good girl. Went to church. Did good in school. Never got into any trouble…as far as I know. She was just real sweet."

"Would you say you were girlfriend and boyfriend? How did you get along?"

"We weren't going steady or anything. Want to know the truth?"

"Of course I want to know the truth."

"I think I liked her more than she liked me. If she'd said yeah, let's go steady, I'd have jumped at it. But she never would. We had our little arguments now and then, but we got along OK."

Winstanley looked at Carpenter, then leveled his eyes on Marvin. "We won't go into your 'little arguments,' as you call them, today. We can discuss that at another time. Let's change the subject. I have to ask you this. Do you know of anybody who would have wanted to do her harm? Who might have wanted to hurt her?"

"Not a soul, as far as I know."

"Was she dating anybody else...while she was dating you?"

"She went out with a few other guys now and then."

"You don't have to do it now, Marvin, but can you give us their names?"

Marvin nodded.

"Are you sure you don't want something to drink?" Carpenter interjected.

Marvin said OK.

Winstanley looked at his watch. "Let's take a five-minute break?"

Both detectives left the room. When they returned, Carpenter handed Marvin a cold Coke and a box of Raisinettes.

"OK. Where were we?" Winstanley said. "How and when did you find out Martha Ann had gone missing?"

"Well, I thought something might be up when I didn't see her anywhere after the game. Some of her friends said she hadn't turned up. I called her house that evening and there was no answer. I didn't find out for sure until Monday morning, at school."

"Marvin, did you go straight to Grady Stadium from school that Friday? Or did you go home first?"

"I went home. Borrowed my old man's car. Drove to the stadium. I had to be there early to get dressed for the game."

"When you went home, between the time you left the school and drove to the game, were your parents there?"

"My mother was."

"And that weekend, after you'd tried Martha Ann's house on Friday and nobody answered, did you follow up any more?"

"I called her house again twice…on Saturday. I let the phone ring and ring, but nobody ever answered."

"Marvin, how many girls have you dated?"

"How many have I dated? A few. Not many. I didn't date anybody 'til my junior year. Before that, I had trouble fitting in, being the new boy in the neighborhood and all."

"Can you give us the names of the other girls you've dated?"

Marvin thought that was an odd request, seeing as that had nothing to do with Martha Ann, but he said OK. He couldn't really say no, could he?

"When and how did you learn they'd found her body?" Winstanley continued.

"This past Saturday evening. One of my buddies called and said look in the paper. Front page. That's how I found out."

"Who called you? What buddy?"

"A boy named Tommy Wright. He's not a close buddy, really. He's a junior. But he knew I had a thing for Martha Ann."

"A thing."

"Yeah, a thing. Meaning I liked her a lot. Like I said, if she'd agreed to go steady, I would've."

Winstanley pulled the newspaper article from a stack of papers on the corner of the table. He slid it across the table to Marvin. "So let's go back to something you said earlier, Marvin. You said… let's see…you said 'I just can't believe anyone would have done that to her.' Marvin, read me what the paper says."

Marvin read the article aloud, word for word.

"Where does it say somebody killed her? Does it say anybody did anything to her? As far as you know, reading that article, she may have drowned by herself in that culvert. Right?"

Marvin nodded.

"Let's go on. Can you tell us your whereabouts between... say...the 20th—that was a Friday—and this past Friday?"

"Well, a week ago Friday, we had another football game. But I didn't play well. I guess I just couldn't get Martha Ann off my mind. I stayed home all that weekend. Didn't feel like going out. My life during the week lately pretty much never changes. Walk to school. Tuesday and Thursday after school is football practice. Walk home. Dinner. Homework. Bed. This past Friday, it was an off week. No game. I went out with some friends, but I was home early."

"Another thing, Marvin," Winstanley continued. "And I want to thank you, by the way, for being so forthright with us. This really helps. Do you know a girl named Cynthia Jane Hudspeth?"

"I can't say I know her. She's two or three years behind me. I've seen her around, though."

"Ever talk to her?"

"Not that I recall."

This went on for two hours. After a while, Marvin caught on to the little game the detectives were playing. The senior one, Winstanley, was all over the map, jumping from one topic to the next and back again. Marvin was pretty sure he was doing that to catch him off guard. Then the other one would be all nice like. At one point, Winstanley left the room again, and Carpenter apologized for how hard his partner was being on him. "I'm here to help you," he said. But by that time, Marvin was on to them. He might have been just a senior in high school, and he might have been from a South Georgia cow town, but he wasn't a knucklehead. Like his sixth grade teacher used to say, "Ain't no flies on Marvin."

They put him through the mill. Ground him down like a sorghum kernel. The only question Marvin could think of that they didn't ask was whether he'd ever gotten to the fifty-yard line with Martha Ann. He was grateful for that. It wouldn't have seemed right, seeing as she was gone and all.

Marvin left the station house wondering whether the police had pinned him as a suspect. It sure seemed that way. Or did they put everybody through what they'd just put him through?

He caught the Number 13 at the corner of Butler and Decatur Streets. Took it as far as he could. Walked the rest of the way home.

Chapter Seventeen

Billy Tarwater

October 6th, 1963

"YEOW!" I WOKE UP TO A CROOKED AND THROBBING left thumb. And another hand-wringing sweat. And wondering what possibly could have happened. Then I remembered the dream. Nightmare, really. I lay in bed, replaying it as I tried to rub the throb away.

I crept next door after Sunday dinner. Placed the toe of one shoe in the space between the chain links in Leonard Seymour's five-foot barricade. Grabbed the top of the fence—I was grateful it didn't have barbed wire or something on it, but it did have those sharp little wire ends that poke up from the top. I lifted myself up. Stepped into another space between the links and hoisted my skinny body to the top. Climbed over. Tore my britches on one of those little wire ends. Plunked to the ground on the other side. Slinked along the concrete trough—I'd heard Daddy call them trench drains—that ran the length of Leonard

Seymour's house. When I neared his front porch, I saw him standing at the foot of the steps. He was holding a girl's blue dress in one hand. And in the other, a can of beer the size of a Pennzoil can, with a big eye on the label. And one of those exploding clown cigars—like you see at the circus—dangled from his lower lip. When he saw me, he let out a thunderous belch, dropped the cigar to the ground, and bared his yellow teeth. That's when I lunged at him. I strangled him with all my might. I buried my thumbs into his neck. I screamed, "Launchpad Leonard, you've gone and done it now."

The only thing I could figure was that I pulled my thumb out of joint and bruised it something awful when I choked him. It must have been some dream for me to do that in my sleep. And damn, it hurt.

My middle-of-the-night incident was enough to keep us from going to church. When my mother saw my thumb, she let out a loud shriek. By then, it had grown to the size and color of one of those figs on Granny Tarwater's backyard tree. Mom called for my father, who came running in from the other room.

"Call Dr. Harper," Dad said. "Maybe he can make a house call today. We need to make sure it isn't broken." He grabbed my hand—way too hard, but I knew he didn't mean to. "Here, let's see if you can move it?"

"Ouch," I screamed, and jerked my hand away.

"I don't think it's broken," he said. "Just dislocated and bruised up. Let's call the doctor."

Mom called the doctor's office, then Granny Tarwater to break the news that we wouldn't be showing up that morning. It wasn't lost on me that I had also managed to relieve my brother of the ordeal of going to church. So he could stay home and read *Mad*

Magazine instead of having to do it in the Brookwood. I told him he owed me big. He just shrugged, strutted down the hall to his room, and shut the door hard. We didn't see him until much later in the day.

My unfortunate thumb incident also kept us from going to Granny Tarwater's after church, which meant I couldn't snoop on Launchpad Leonard for real. It also meant Uncle Newell, Aunt Lottie, and Cousin Loreen would have twice as much food to eat. That's what I assumed, anyway, until my uncle said he would run plates over to us when they were all through chowing down.

"At least we won't go hungry," I said to myself, but within earshot of my mother. Being the excellent Southern cook she claimed to be, she just glowered and walked away.

* * *

At two o'clock on the button, the doorbell rang. I assumed it was Dr. Harper. But when Mom answered it, two men in coats and ties stood in the doorway. The same two men I had seen at the culvert with Gary's father. It was as if they had been sitting in the driveway waiting for the exact time to ring the bell. Was that some kind of detective discipline thing? I wondered.

"Mrs. Tarwater?"

"Yes."

"I'm Sergeant Winstanley." He flipped out his badge. "And this is my partner, Detective Carpenter. We're from the police department. Homicide. May we come in and speak with you?"

"Is this about the Dullums girl?"

"It is. We understand you're the one who made the call…about the body."

"I did, but I'm not the one who found the poor girl. My son Billy, here..." She turned to face me. "...he's the one who discovered her."

"It was Nick," I interjected.

"Nick?" Winstanley asked.

"Nick Papadapoulos. He lives down the street."

Winstanley pulled a spiral notepad from his back pocket, flipped the page. "Can you spell his last name?"

My mother spelled it out. I was glad she did. I wasn't sure I would have been able to.

"Sergeant, they should be home from church by now," she said. "If I call his house, I imagine he can be up here in a few minutes. He lives down the street."

The sergeant said please do that. My mother went into the kitchen. She returned a couple of minutes later. "I spoke with his mother. He'll walk up. It shouldn't take him long to get here."

Ten minutes or so after my mother had hung up, there was a knock on the door. When I opened it, there stood Nick and his mother Norma. Not only was Nick's mother the best cook in the neighborhood—*sorry, Mom*—but I always thought she was the most beautiful grown-up woman I had ever laid eyes on, sort of the way I imagined Cynthia looking when she would become a woman herself. Mrs. Papadapoulos always wore these short pants—my mother called them pedal pushers—and tops that she tied in a knot at her waist. And every time I saw her, she had on bright red lipstick. And smoked these cigarettes called Viceroys. Whenever she put one out in the ashtray, the butt would have her red lips all over it. I thought that was really something.

"Come in, Norma," my mother said. "Hello, Nick. These two nice men are from the police department. They'd like to ask you a few questions about when you found the Dullums girl in the culvert."

"I'm not the only one that found her. Binky...Billy...he found her, too."

I stared at Nick in disbelief. He had made such a big deal before about being the one that found the body. "That's not true, Nick. I was there, but I didn't go inside the cave...the culvert. Only you did that."

Nick told the detectives all about how he, Gary, and I had been playing army. How he had gone inside "The Oven" with the gas mask on. How he had seen Martha Ann's naked body. How he had come running out. How we had run back to my house, but Gary kept going and went to tell his father. The detectives asked a few questions. Sergeant Winstanley wrote everything down.

They thanked us and were about to leave when I piped up. "What about Cynthia?"

"Cynthia?" the sergeant replied.

"Hudspeth. What about Cynthia Hudspeth?"

"Billy," my mother interrupted, "these gentlemen are not here to talk about that. I'm sure Cynthia will turn up soon, and she'll be none the worse for it."

I wondered how she could say something like that. She didn't know. Was she just trying to make me feel better? Cynthia was missing and my mother was making light of it.

She showed the detectives to the door. Then she and Nick's mother went into the kitchen.

"What did you do to your thumb?" Nick asked, after the detectives had left.

"Oh, it's no big deal," I said matter-of-factly. "Threw it out of joint choking a man."

"Choking a man?"

"It's complicated."

Nick and his mother left shortly after that. Nick said he was going to Gary's.

I looked over at the ashtray on the side table. Three cigarette butts, all with bright red lip prints.

* * *

Dr. Harper showed up around three thirty carrying that little black bag he always had with him. He almost killed me when he popped my thumb back in place. He put a splint on it and instructed me and Mom to make sure I kept an ice bag on it.

"Can he go to school?" my mother asked.

"See how he's doing in the morning. If the swelling's gone down, I don't see why he can't." Dr. Harper looked at me. "But whatever you do, don't take the splint off. And keep your hand elevated as much as you can." Then he looked back at my Mom. "Let's see him in my office in a week."

As soon as Dr. Harper had left, my mother filled the ice bag with a full tray of cubes, screwed the metal cap tight, and brought it to me in the living room. With the bag resting ponderously on my thumb and the crook of my hand, I settled into the same chair where Lervene Culpepper, all black and blue and bleeding, had sat two weeks before.

I decided to call it my *convalescent chair*. I was proud of myself, knowing a big word like that. But it was only from when we would visit my Great Granny at the convalescent home in Decatur. Whenever we left there, I would hold my shoulders high, puff out my chest, and keep saying the word over and over again, like some kind of robot, until my brother would tell me to shut up. I must have been insufferable at times.

* * *

Dinner arrived later than I had expected, close to five. I was sure the whole house was starving for Granny Tarwater's food as much as I was. It came in the form of prepared plates covered in tin foil—delivered not by my aunt and uncle, but by my grandmother. I knew she had paid us a visit just to get to the bottom of why we had not been at church that morning. I may have been an innocent eleven-year-old kid, but I wasn't *that* innocent. She just *had* to see my fig of a thumb first-hand. I guess it convinced her, when she saw it, that my mother's claim on the phone early that morning was for real.

Granny Tarwater perched on the sofa. I sat across from her in my convalescent chair.

"Why, Binky, your thumb looks like a damson plum," Granny Tarwater said. "It must hurt like the dickens."

"Fig. And it does," I replied.

She looked at me funny.

"How was the service?" Mom chimed in.

"You picked a good Sunday to miss."

"Why, Jincey?"

"The reverend wasn't there."

"Where was he?"

"He went back to his old church. To take part in a tent revival. What we used to call camp meetings in the country, but I don't know if they call them that anymore. He left right after the Wednesday night supper. He told us he was coming back Sunday, but not in time for the service. The youth minister did the sermon. Alice, that boy can't preach worth a flip. He's just downright tiresome if you ask me."

* * *

Mom sent me to school Monday morning with the splint secured to my hand and thumb, and with strict instructions, whatever I did, not to remove it. One consolation for my infirmity was that I could regale my classmates with the choking story—which I did, to resounding oohs and ahhs. But by Wednesday, they had all gotten wise to the fact that I hadn't really choked a man, that I had somehow pulled it out of joint in my sleep, which they concluded was pretty lame.

At home, I milked my accident for everything I could—another consolation. After all, it isn't every day that a kid gets to be waited on. My convalescent chair became my favorite getting-waited-on spot. I wondered how long I could make that last. Probably no more than a few days. The fig was already beginning to shrink.

Late Wednesday afternoon, I was settled in my chair. My mother had brought the ice pack and rested it on my hand

"Mom, what's for dinner?"

"Pizza."

If there was anything I hated, it was Chef Boyardee cheese pizza from a box. And I was sure that was what she meant by pizza. It was the only kind we ever had. Most kids my age loved it, but as long as I live, I will never get the foul smell out of my nostrils. It wasn't the sauce, which was passable. It was the dough. Something about the smell of that dough baking in the oven always made me gag, unlike Granny Tarwater's biscuits.

Chef Boyardee was Mom's idea of Italian. And Chinese? Chun King Chow Mein. Mexican? El Paso Tortillas in a can. But that didn't come until later—late sixties, I think. Aside from the occasional lamb stew with okra at Nick's house—I always laughed when his mother called it by its Greek name, Arni Kokkinisto—I had no idea what real ethnic food was until I went off to college—unless you call deep-fried Southern ethnic.

* * *

After dinner, I was basking in feigned self-pity when the phone interrupted my thumb gazing.

"It's for you, Binky," my mother called from the kitchen.

I set the ice bag on the table beside the chair and scooted into the kitchen, my socked feet sliding along the hardwood. I looked across the room to the far wall. My mom had cradled the handset on the top of the phone and had gone back to the sink. I grabbed the handset with my good hand.

"Hello?"

"Binky, it's Gary. You need to come up here."

"Where?"

"My house. Nick's here."

I looked over at my Mom. "Gary, I can't. I have to stay here and take care of my thumb."

"Your thumb? You've been to school the past three days with your thumb the way it is. Why can't you come up here?"

"I just can't. You guys come down here."

"But there's something we need to show you. And it's here. We can't bring it down there."

"Gary, I said I can't."

A few minutes later, Gary and Nick showed up at the door. Gary was out of breath. And he was hopping back and forth on one foot, then the other. I swear, I thought he was about to have an accident—of the pee kind. "What is it, Gary?"

"Can we go to your room?" He barely got the words out.

"Sure," I replied. I called out to my mother. "Mom, Gary and Nick are here. We'll be in my room. I'll take the ice pack with me."

"Okay," she replied. "But they can't stay long."

I shut my bedroom door. "Gary. Settle down. What is it?"

Gary plopped onto my bed. I wasn't sure whether he had lost his balance and landed there or he had done it on purpose. Nick pulled the chair out from my desk and sat on it backwards, with his arms folded on the chair back. I stood near the door, ready to run out if Gary got any crazier.

"We snuck into my Daddy's study," Gary said. "Nick showed me how to pick the lock on the desk."

"You what?"

"Know what we found in the drawer? Pictures of Martha Ann. From the culvert. You gotta come see 'em, Binky. She's all grey and green and dead and everything. And her mouth is open. And her tongue is sort of hanging out. And she's—"

"Gary, are you crazy? We know she's dead. We don't need proof. And the last thing I want to do is go looking at pictures of dead people. I think you both are sick. I feel like I'm gonna barf Chef Boyardee all over the floor."

Without lifting his behind off the seat, Nick inched the chair away from where I was standing. Mumbled something about pizza puke.

"Why does your Daddy have pictures like that at home?" I asked.

"He's a detective, Binky. What do you expect him to do? He brings them home so he can study them. You know, like at night when he's trying to solve a case. He's always working, even when he's sleeping. And besides, I'm sure they're extras."

"And how did you manage to sneak into the study anyway?" I asked. "Aren't your mom and dad there?"

"It's my mother's bridge night. She left me home with Daddy. But then he got an urgent call and had to leave. Something about another dead girl."

My stomach tightened like a rock. My heart was going a million beats a minute. "Oh no! Not Cynthia."

"I have no idea who it is. I just know it's a dead girl."

"Where?"

"The only thing he said when he left was he was headed to the Chattahoochee."

Chapter Eighteen

Gus Alford

October 9, 1963

THE CHATTAHOOCHEE RIVER COURSES A CIRCUITOUS route southward from Bull Sluice Lake, making its way down the west side of Atlanta to West Point Lake, near LaGrange. From there, it follows the Georgia-Alabama line to its termination at Lake Seminole. Much of the river is majestic and captivating in its natural beauty. But along the stretch that runs roughly from Peachtree Creek to Carroll County, the water is turbid, the color of milky coffee, and marginally fit for human contact.

It was this stretch, more specifically the Fulton County air field, situated on the eastern edge of the river at the junction of Carroll and Gordon Roads, to which Gus Alford was summoned in the afternoon on October 9th.

When he got there, he was greeted by the air field general manager. Two Atlanta police cars were already at the site, as was the Fulton County sheriff. Winstanley and Carpenter arrived at about the same time. The forensics arrived a few minutes later.

It seems an aircraft mechanic on his mid-afternoon break had wandered down toward the river's edge from the Tee hangar to cop a smoke and take a breather from a tedious engine repair job on a ten-year-old Cessna 170. He was just about to light up when he saw something in the water, stuck in a tangle of limbs growing out of the steep bank and hanging over and into the river. It was a nude body. That's when he ran to get the manager. That's when the manager dialed the operator. That's when the operator patched in headquarters. That's when the police were called to the scene. Then Alford and the other detectives. The Fulton county sheriff had been summoned as well.

"Is there a jurisdictional issue here, Lieutenant?" Winstanley asked. It was a legitimate question, given that the city limits cut a slice through the eastern section of the air field, twenty football fields from where the body had been found.

"Listen, Sergeant," Alford said. "No way I'm giving this up to some goddamned County Brownie. The way I look at it, the air field's on city property, right?"

"Well, a little piece of it, anyway, but—"

"And the body floated from upriver, right?"

"We don't know that."

"For Christ's sake, Winstanley. Think about it. The body's snagged on a tangle of branches in the river. Where else would it have come from? Do you think it just fell from the air? Or swam upstream like a spawning salmon?"

"You're right, Lieutenant."

"And right up the river there, to your right," Alford continued, "the city limit runs along the river. This one's ours. We've got a job to do. Let's get on it. I'll deal with Brownie. Right now, we need to get an extraction crew over here to do a little fishing operation. The bank's too steep to get to the body safely."

The extraction crew arrived and pulled the body out of the water. Carried it away from the river and laid it out, face-up, on the western edge of the tarmac. It was another girl. She looked to be younger than Martha Ann. Perhaps twelve, thirteen. Her palms and the soles of her feet exhibited classic washerwoman features, a telltale sign of prolonged immersion. Alford bent down and shined his flashlight into her nostrils. White edema fluid further suggested death by immersive drowning. He compressed her chest slightly; the same white fluid flowed out of her mouth.

"Winstanley, could it be the Hudspeth girl?" Alford asked.

"She looks to be about the same age. And the same build. Same color hair. Even with corneal clouding, the eye color looks similar. But she doesn't look like the pictures from the MP file. Then again, you know as well as I do how hard it is to identify a bloated, waterlogged corpse."

"Turn her over, Sergeant."

As soon as Winstanley and Carpenter had turned the body over, Alford saw the same mark they had observed on Martha Ann, etched into the girl's thigh, about an inch below her buttock line. Only this time, it seemed a little less crude, like whoever did it was getting better with practice. The head was still connected to a straight vertical line and just as lopsided as before, but it was flat on the left side, like a P. "Gentlemen, I fear we're dealing with a serial killer. And a twisted one at that."

"Aren't all serial killers twisted?" Carpenter asked. "Anyway, how long do you think she's been dead, Lieutenant?"

"Maybe four, five days," Alford said. "If she drowned upriver, she would have sunk to the riverbed pretty quickly, as soon as water replaced the air in her lungs. She would have remained there until the bacteria in her gut and chest cavity produced enough methane, hydrogen sulfide, carbon dioxide to cause her to float to the surface like a balloon. I'm guessing that would have taken three or four days. But I'm probably not telling you anything you don't already know, right Carpenter?" Alford looked upstream. "The question is, how long did she spend floating down the river, and from where. And how long has she been right here where she was found, snagged in that branch tangle?"

After proximate evidence had been gathered and photographs taken, and the coroner had taken the girl away, Alford motioned for the two forensics to join him and the other two detectives. They huddled beside Alford's car door.

"The four of you. Head up Carroll Road. It runs into Bolton Road just north of Bankhead Highway and continues to parallel the river all the way to the Clayton wastewater plant. I doubt she would have drowned north of there. It's too populated. Somebody surely would have seen her in the river. Check out every turnoff, every road, every trail, every footpath—I don't care what it is—that looks like it might lead to the river. I'm going back to headquarters. I want to go through the Hudspeth MP file. Detectives, meet me back there later tonight."

"What about approaches to the river from the other side?" Winstanley asked.

"That's Cobb County," Alford replied. "As much as I'd like you men to go over there, scout the area from that side, I think I'd better get them involved."

"A County Brownie, Lieutenant?" Carpenter piped up.

Gus Alford began to walk away. He swung around. "I'll have the coroner expedite the autopsy."

* * *

Back at headquarters, Gus Alford shuffled through the files on Dan Winstanley's desk until he found the Missing Persons file on Cynthia Hudspeth. He took it back to his office and thumbed through it. There were photographs of the girl, which he assumed had been provided by her parents. And her seventh grade yearbook picture. Murphy picture day was still a few weeks away. He read through the interview notes from when Missing Persons had sat down with the Hudspeths shortly after she disappeared. There wasn't enough there for Alford to sink his teeth into. No indication as to what she may have been wearing. Nothing about what time during the day she may have disappeared, since both parents had left the house early and had not returned until late in the day. There was something about an open peanut butter jar and a nosey next-door neighbor. And notes about a bunch of her friends from school and a soda jerk at the pharmacy where she was known to hang out, but no apparent interviews. That was about it. Nothing in the file indicated that Missing Persons had spoken with nearby neighbors, not even the one next door, a man named Leonard Seymour. There were two follow-up interviews with the Hudspeths. Then a handwritten note at the bottom of the second follow-up page:

VISITED L. SEYMOUR - NO ANSWER AT DOOR - 10/2, 10/3

Alford examined the photos. *Is this the girl we just fished out of the river?* He didn't think so, but like Winstanley said, when a dead girl's body has been underwater for days it's hard to draw any conclusions. And even worse when the bacteria and fish have had their way with her.

He pulled out his notepad and began to write.

DEAD GIRL IN RIVER

CHECK WITH MP - ANY LEADS?

AUTOPSY - MORGUE - BRING HUDSPETHS IN - ID

CYNTHIA HUDSPETH

MISSING 11 DAYS

FOLLOW-UP VISITS:

HUDSPETHS - AT HOME

SEYMOUR

SODA JERK

He drew an arc between BRING HUDSPETHS IN - ID and MISSING 11 DAYS.

What's MP been doing for a week and a half? Sitting with their thumbs up their butts?

He picked up the phone and called Missing Persons. He let the phone ring a dozen times, then slammed the handset onto the cradle. *They can't even answer the phone? Guess I'll have to walk up there.* He climbed the stairs to the fourth floor and walked down the long hallway. He peered through the door window. The office was pitch black. He looked at his watch. It was a quarter to seven Wednesday evening. *Bankers hours. Must be nice. Tomorrow.*

When he returned to Homicide, he found Winstanley and Carpenter waiting for him. "What do you know, men?"

"We found tire tracks and drag marks, just like before," Winstanley said. "We're waiting for photos from the lab."

"Where were the tracks?"

"We headed up Carroll Road. We went down Sandy Creek, but we didn't find anything. So we kept going up Carroll. We turned left on Bankhead Highway and went all the way to the river. Got out and searched all around. Nothing. Then we got back in the car and—"

Alford held up his hand in the Stop position. "Sergeant, I don't need the play-by-play. Just give me the touchdown."

"Sorry. Got a little carried away there. Do you know where Proctor Creek runs into the Chattahoochee?"

"North of Bankhead Highway?"

"Bingo. There's a road that forks to the left off of Bolton. Parrott Avenue. Proctor Creek's right there. We went up Parrott. Just past Proctor Creek, we found tire marks veering off the road in the direction of the river. The tread marks were exactly like the ones near the Van Vleck culvert. Same size. Same herringbone pattern. We followed the tracks about...what do you think, Carpenter...a half a mile?"

The detective nodded.

"Then the car tracks ended," Winstanley continued. "But we saw the same drag marks as before, running from where the tread marks ended all the way down to the river's edge. Right there, at the riverbank, there was a clearing with tall grass, about eight inches high. But it had been disturbed, tamped down, like somebody had been there recently."

"Did you find any other evidence?"

"Not a thing. But I bet that's where she was either drowned or dumped."

Alford walked over to an 8'x8' city wall map. He ran his finger down the Chattahoochee, from Proctor Creek to the air field. "A fairly straight shot. About 2-1/2 miles point-to-point. I'm guessing it could have taken anywhere from 2 to 4 hours for the body to get from A to B once it floated to the surface. Forensics should be able to tell us more about the water flow along there. And we'll know more about the estimated time of death when we get something back from the ME. Sergeant, anything back yet on car makes and models?"

"Not yet, but I'll follow up."

"I've gone through the Hudspeth MP file. We need to talk to them as soon as we can. But I'd like to first know if their daughter's turned up dead in the river. Carpenter, find out from the morgue how quickly we can get the Hudspeths in there. If it's Cynthia, then we've got a second corpse with the same killer's calling card. If not, we've got two corpses *and* a missing person to deal with."

* * *

In the early hours of Thursday morning, Gus Alford sprang to attention. He sat on the side of the bed. *Darby! Louise Darby. Alamo. Why didn't it register before?* He scratched his head and looked over at Betty lying behind him, dead to the world.

"Shit!"

Betty stirred. "What is it, honey?"

"Nothing. Go back to sleep."

It was 4:23. Thanks to the Chattahoochee girl, he hadn't stumbled into bed until well after midnight Wednesday night, and only after the usual *I know you're awake* tea dance with Betty. He'd have to make do with, what, three hours sleep? He'd also make do with a day-old beard and Waffle House coffee. Maybe one of those stale glazed donuts he was sure had been in the glass case for at least a week.

He rolled out of his driveway at 4:45. Pulled into the Waffle House parking lot at 5:15. He sat in his car listening to the news. Dam collapse in Italy, thousands feared dead. President Kennedy going at it with Cuba. Grocer in Albany claims Negro picketers destroyed his business. *Is there no good news anymore?* He turned off the radio. *Fuck the donut, I'm in for the kill. Gonna be a long day.* He left the restaurant full on the works—pork chop and eggs, waffle, hash browns with onions.

* * *

Alford sat at his desk and read through what he'd written on his notepad yesterday. He picked up the phone. Dialed 231.

"Missing Persons, Ingle speaking."

"Pretty chipper this early in the morning for a banker, Ingle."

"What?"

"Never mind. Listen, we found a body yesterday at the Fulton County air field. White female. Looks to be twelve or thirteen. Reddish brown hair. Greenish brown eyes. Five three. Slim."

"Sounds like the Hudspeth girl."

"Could be. We should know later today. But do you have any other missing girls that fit that description?"

"Hold on a second." Officer Ingle set the phone down. He returned in a couple of minutes. "We did have an APB come in from Alabama a few days ago. Girl fits the description. Seems she went missing from somewhere east of Birmingham last Saturday. Want me to alert them that we may have found their MP?"

"Not yet. Let me confirm it isn't Cynthia Hudspeth. We're going to get her parents into the morgue for an ID. Just waiting for the go-ahead."

"Speaking of her parents, we got a call late yesterday from Adele Hudspeth. I'm passing it along since you've taken over the case. Seems she was rummaging through some things in Cynthia's room and found an item of interest."

"Do you know what?"

"A business card or something."

* * *

Winstanley rolled into the office at seven thirty, Carpenter five minutes later.

"Sergeant, you and Carpenter need to pay Adele Hudspeth a visit this morning. Seems she has some new information to share. Go on over there now, before she has a chance to leave the house. Maybe even call her first. Let her know you're coming."

The detectives got up to leave.

"And Carpenter, any word from the morgue?" Alford asked.

"No, but I'll follow up as soon as we get back from the Hudspeths."

Winstanley and Carpenter had been gone no more than thirty minutes when the phone rang. It was Officer Pickens. "We've found the girl."

"What girl?"

"Cynthia Hudspeth."

"How do you know it's her?"

"We're not a hundred percent certain, but she fits the girl's description to a tee."

"OK. I understand, but don't tell me you've found somebody unless it's a hundred percent, Pickens. So you *think* you've found Cynthia Hudspeth."

"Yes sir, we think."

"Is she dead?"

"No. She's alive. Barely. They rushed her to Grady."

"Where did you find her?"

"Next to a construction site near Grove Park. Face down in a shallow spot along the edge of Proctor Creek. Not in the water, really."

"Proctor Creek? Interesting."

"Some concrete pourers arrived at the site early this morning. To pour a foundation in a deep pit. They saw a small car speed off as soon as they got there. Grey or silver, sort of sporty. Then they found the girl. When they realized she was alive, they radioed their supervisor to call Grady. Then us. We're thinking the concrete guys may have scared the perpetrator away before he finished the job."

"So tell me about the girl. You said she's alive, but barely."

"I just checked with the hospital. She's in a coma. Not sure she'll make it."

Alford called Grady and asked to be put through the attending physician.

"Dr. Markham speaking."

"Dr. Markham, this is Lieutenant Alford, Atlanta Homicide. I'm calling about the girl they brought in this morning. I understand she's in a coma?"

"That's correct. She's stable and her vitals are reasonably good, given her condition. She appears to have experienced some degree of cerebral hypoxia. The neurological team is with her now. They'll determine next steps. At this point, I can't tell you much more than that. We're doing everything we can."

"I understand. We believe we may know the girl's identity, but we'll need to bring someone in later today to confirm that. Doctor, I have to ask what will probably seem like a strange question. Was there something carved in her thigh, like a stick man symbol?"

"Normally, Lieutenant, it would be a strange question. But in this case, it isn't. There is a mark on her right thigh, just below her buttock. But it isn't a stick man. It's the letter P. It looks to have been done with a knife. There's subcutaneous bleeding and bruising around the cut, and there was surface bleeding under the bandage the paramedics applied at the scene."

As soon as he hung up, Gus Alford radioed Winstanley. "Are you still at the Hudspeth house?"

"No, we just left. We got a lead, Lieutenant. Mrs. Hudspeth was going through Cynthia's things and found a business card from a man named Jepperson. Sam Jepperson. Goes by Shorty. He's a shoe shiner at the barbershop in East Atlanta, just a couple of blocks from the Hudspeths. There's a handwritten phone number on the back. I checked with the operator. It's the Jepperson residence."

"I know who Sam Jepperson is," Alford said. "I don't know him, though. His wife's the cleanup woman at the Cut-n-Curl."

"Is he colored?"

"Of course he's colored. Do you think a white man would be shining shoes at a barbershop?"

"By the way, Lieutenant," Carpenter, who had been quiet up until now, spoke up, "how do you know about the Cut-n-Curl?"

"Don't worry about it, Carpenter. Sergeant, you need to turn around and go back to the Hudspeths. We think we've found Cynthia. There's a girl in a coma at Grady. They found her near Grove Park this morning. We need to get them to the hospital to ID her. Are they both at home right now?"

"No," Winstanley replied. "He's left for work already."

"Where does he work?"

"The appliance store on Flat Shoals, just north of Glenwood."

"Go there. Tell him we think we may have found his daughter, alive but in a coma."

"But Lieutenant, we've been dealing with Mrs. Hudspeth, not her husband."

"You heard what I said, Sergeant. Go tell the husband. He can break the news to her. Then get back here as soon as you can. We've got a lot of work to do."

"Are we going to just have the Hudspeths go to Grady by themselves? Isn't that a bit insensitive, Lieutenant?"

"You're right, Winstanley. You and Carpenter go with them. But get back here as soon as you can. Do you copy?"

"10-4."

* * *

It was almost noon when Winstanley and Carpenter returned to headquarters.

"We accompanied the Hudspeths to Grady," Winstanley said. "They positively identified their daughter. We didn't hang around long. We left the two of them standing at Cynthia's bedside. Mrs. Hudspeth was holding her daughter's hand. A nurse and a doctor were there. He was explaining everything to them."

"Is she still unresponsive?"

"She was when we left."

"Did the doctor happen to tell you about the P? Not that I would have expected him to."

"The P?"

"There's a P carved in her thigh. Want to know my theory? The perpetrator thought she was dead. Was carving the mark on her thigh when the workers came upon the scene and scared him away."

"She must have bled from the cut. Wouldn't he have known she was alive?"

"Not necessarily. The average person wouldn't know that a corpse doesn't bleed."

"That's a point."

"Sergeant, call the hospital right away. Nobody is to know she's there and alive. She's to be allowed no visitors except her parents. If anybody calls asking about her, no one by that name has been admitted." Alford paused. "In fact, instruct the hospital to give her an alias. Have them change her paperwork. We don't need to take any chances with somebody inadvertently leaking her name. Tell her parents not to let a soul know she's there. There's a killer on the loose. He's killed two girls and likely thinks he's killed a third. If he knows Cynthia is alive, he may try to finish the job. I'm calling Missing Persons about the Chattahoochee girl."

Alford dialed Missing Persons. Ingle answered. "Hold on a minute, Ingle." Alford placed his hand over the mouthpiece. "Winstanley, have an officer sent to Grady to guard her room." He removed his hand. "Ingle, Alford here. Sorry about that. Listen, the body we found yesterday. It isn't Cynthia Hudspeth."

"I have more info on the missing girl from Alabama, Lieutenant. Name's Patsy Boggs. She was at some church event when she disappeared."

"Call the authorities in Alabama. Get them over here to do an ID. But let them know that, until we make headway on this case, I'm not releasing the body into their custody, or anybody's custody for that matter."

"Understood, Lieutenant."

* * *

Gus Alford lit another Lucky. Blew a big smoke ring across his desk.

"Gentlemen, it's been a hell of a day—two days, really. We have an unnamed Chattahoochee girl with a tag on her toe, Cynthia Hudspeth's vegetating at Grady, Martha Ann Dullums is six feet under. Oh, and did I mention that we have a killer running around the city somewhere? You have your work cut out for you."

"We need to bring the Darby boy back in," Winstanley said. "And we need to locate Leonard Seymour. He seems to be missing."

"Sergeant, just because the MP guys paid two visits to his house and nobody came to the door doesn't mean he's missing. Pay him another visit. Adele Hudspeth holds him in high regard." Alford sniggered. "She's actually very suspicious of the man. Thinks he may have been involved somehow in her daughter's disappearance, and now, presumably, her near death. I get that. The man's been getting in a little look-see through the window. Of course, that's not the worst thing in the world. And it certainly doesn't make him a killer. But I know we have to assume otherwise." Alford locked eyes with Winstanley. "Now, about the Darby boy. Let it go. There's no way that boy's guilty. He's just a teenage boy that was trying his best to get in a girl's pants. You can't blame him for that, can you? I guarantee you, there's no way that boy was involved in any of this."

"But, Lieutenant—"

"You heard me, Winstanley, let it go. He's not a suspect. Follow the leads that make sense. We need to get on this bootlips Jepperson ASAP. But I don't want to bring him in. Not yet. We'll pay a visit to where he lives. Check it out. Check out his car."

Carpenter grinned. "And check out his shoes. See if they shine like Shinola."

"Give it a break, Carpenter. Your jokes stopped being funny a long time ago."

"Check out where he lives? His car? Without a warrant?" Winsanley asked.

"He's not a suspect. Until we have PC, we're not to the point of hookem and bookem. We're just snooping around, being the good dix we are. Why, I doubt ole Shorty even knows what a warrant is. I'll tell you what, Winstanley, here, you go see what you can learn about Jepperson. Ask around East Atlanta. But don't be too obvious about it. Check out the barbershop. Get your hair cut if you have to. You need one anyway. Talk to the barber. If you get there early enough, chances are Jepperson won't be there yet. But if he is, get your shoes shined. Carpenter and I will visit his apartment. He lives in the projects. Carver Homes. If he's there, fine. If he's not, we'll work over his wife Ruby a little."

"You said you know her, right?" Winstanley asked.

"I don't really know her. I know her by name. She cleans up the hair and foil and fingernails and shit from the floor at Edna's. She's never there when I'm there. On weekends, Fridays and Saturdays, she goes in real late, when everybody but Edna and one of the hair girls has left. They're the busiest days. Edna doesn't want her there making everybody uncomfortable when it's crowded, if you know what I mean. I only know all this because Edna, bless her heart, doesn't know how to stop running her mouth."

Alford looked at his watch. Then at Carpenter.

"I'm calling it a day. I got three hours of sleep last night. I'll be damned if I'll let that happen tonight. Carpenter, be here at seven sharp in the morning. We're taking a trip to Carver Homes."

Winstanley and Carpenter got up to leave.

Alford called them back. "Gentlemen, better grab your jockstraps and hold real tight. It's gonna be a wild ride."

Chapter Nineteen
Ruby Jepperson

October 11, 1963

THE EIGHT O'CLOCK KNOCK AT THE DOOR BROKE RUBY'S focus on the needle's path, its piercing clackety-clack. She left the makings of Mrs. Hallman's button front shirtdress under the Singer Portable's presser foot. She crossed the room and opened the front door to two hulking men in coats and ties. The bulges beneath their coats told her they weren't here to sell magazines.

One of them flipped his badge. "Ruby Jepperson?"

"Yes?"

"Sam's wife?"

"That's right. May I help you?"

"We're here to talk to you about your husband."

Ruby's first thought was that Shorty had been in an accident or something. Police don't come to your door unless they're bringing bad news—or hauling somebody off to jail. "Has something happened to Sam?"

"He's alright. We just need to talk to you."

"Hold on, please." She straightened the room while the men waited in the doorway. She gathered up Shorty's things: *Daily World*...cigarette pack...matches...butt-filled ashtray. As much as she loved the man, he had a habit of not picking up after himself. Unfortunately, Rufus seemed to have learned his bad ways.

She pointed to the sofa. "You can sit there."

"That's OK. We'll stand. I'm Lieutenant Alford," the badge-flipping one said. "And this is my partner, Detective Carpenter." That one nodded but didn't say anything.

"We need to ask you some questions. I'm assuming Sam's not here."

She found it odd that the lieutenant would ask a question like that, since she had just asked if something had happened to him. Maybe it was just routine. "He left for work already."

"If I'm not mistaken, he works at the barbershop. Shines shoes."

"That's right."

"How long has he worked there?"

"Let's see...eleven years now." She planted her hands on her hips. "Can I ask what this is about?"

"Now Ruby, don't get testy. Like I said, we're just here to ask some questions. Does Sam take the bus to work?"

"No. He drives."

The lieutenant arched his brows. "A car? You're telling me Sam has a car?"

"Yes sir. A Hudson."

"Do you know the year?"

"I believe it's a '51. No, it's a '50."

"Color?"

"Green. I think the man that sold it to him called it peacock green."

"Do you happen to know the model?"

"No."

"Two door, four door?"

"Four door sedan."

"Tell me, does it have those big wide whitewalls? Yea wide?" The lieutenant held his thumb and finger about four inches apart. "You know, the kind you people still like so much, even though they've fallen out of our favor."

"It does."

The lieutenant looked at the silent one and nodded toward the front door. Ruby watched through the window as the silent one walked to where the men's car was parked.

"Has he always driven to work?" the lieutenant continued.

"No. Didn't have a car for years."

"When did he get a car?"

"Four, five years ago."

She looked back out the window. It looked like the silent one was talking to somebody on the radio.

"From where?" the lieutenant asked.

"Used car lot. Out Moreland Avenue."

"Carland?"

"That's the one."

"Now, Ruby." He did the thing with his eyebrows again. "You don't expect me to believe he bought it from Carland. Why, they don't sell cars to coloreds."

"That's where he bought it. There's a salesman there. Sam shines his shoes. Has for years. What's his name? Um...Culpepper. I guess Mr. Culpepper took a liking to Sam or something. Convinced the boss to sell the car to him."

"How could he afford to buy a car, shining shoes for a living?"

"I saved up from my seamstressing. Lord knows, Sam couldn't sa...It took me a while to save up enough, but I knew how much Sam wanted a car, after taking the bus for years."

"What were you about to say? Sam couldn't what?"

"Oh, he's just not much of a saver."

The lieutenant looked over at the sewing machine. The stack of patterns next to it. The half-finished dress under the needle. "Is that your only income, seamstressing?"

"I clean up at Edna's Cut-n-Curl." She stared deep into the lieutenant's eyes. "Haven't I seen you there?"

"Perhaps." Alford held out his hands, palms down. "I visit the nail girl some Saturdays."

"That's it. I saw you when I went in one Saturday morning to pick up my pay. Normally, Edna gives it to me on Friday evenings, but one time she was short on cash and I had to go back to get it."

"What days do you work there?"

"Monday, Wednesday, Friday, Saturday. But I go in late on the weekends. After the ladies have left."

"Ruby, how old is your husband?"

"Forty."

"And you?"

"Twenty-nine."

He did his fingers like he was counting in his head. *There he goes again with his eyebrows. He does it every time I say something he doesn't like.*

Then he pulled a card out of his pocket. Thrust it at her. "Ruby, do you recognize this?"

She took it. Looked at it. "It's Sam's card, from the barbershop."

"Turn it over."

She looked on the back. "It's our phone number."

"Do you know where that card came from. Do you know why we have it?"

"I can't say I do."

"It came from a girl. A teenage girl. A *white* teenage girl. Do you have any idea why she would have had your husband's card?"

Ruby shook her head. "I don't."

"Does your husband make a habit of socializing with white girls?"

"I know Sam. He wouldn't do that." She looked past the lieutenant and out the front window. She thought about her husband sitting on the front stoop night after night, smoking his Old Golds and staring across the Carver Homes commons. In another world. And her sitting at the sewing machine wondering what he could possibly be thinking about for hours on end.

"Are you sure? Because I can't think of any reason she'd have his card, and with his home number written on the back, unless he was socializing with her. Can you?"

She couldn't stop staring at the card.

"I'm going to level with you," Alford continued. "There's a white girl laid up in the hospital because somebody tried to kill her. And she had your husband's card."

Ruby Jepperson felt every ounce of blood drain from her face. Her legs were rubber. She reached out to the sewing table to steady herself. "Who is the girl?"

"Why do you care who she is if, as you say, your husband would have no reason to be hanging around a white girl?" The lieutenant paused. Lit a cigarette. "How do *you* get to work?"

"I take the bus."

"So you take the bus and your husband drives the car you bought with the money you saved up. Is that what you're telling me?"

"It is, but I don't see as that has anything to with anything. And anyway, it's not what it seems. It's a lot easier for me to take the bus than him. He'd have to make a transfer to get to work. Mine's straight there."

"Maybe he needs a car for other reasons. Maybe he needs a car to pick up white girls."

She looked to the floor.

"Does your husband work there every day?"

"Every day they're open. They close on Wednesdays and Sundays."

"What hours does he work?"

"It depends."

"It depends on what?"

"He doesn't have strict hours. Mr. Batson, the owner, he lets Sam come and go some."

"Come and go? So where does he go when, as you say, he comes and goes?"

"I don't really know for sure. Errands I guess."

"Picking-up-white-girl errands, maybe?"

"Sometimes he runs errands for Mr. Batson. And some days he buys groceries before he comes home."

"Does he have another job?"

"No. Just the barbershop."

"What does he do when he's not working and running errands?"

"Mostly, he just sits out there on the stoop and smokes his Old Golds."

The silent one came back in. Nodded to the lieutenant.

"You said Sam's off on Wednesdays. Is that right?"

She nodded.

"But I believe you said you work on Wednesdays. What does Sam do all day when you're at work?"

"I don't know. I suppose he sits right out there on that stoop like he does most every evening."

"Has your husband ever been in trouble with the law?" the lieutenant continued.

"Not as I know. Not as long as I've known him."

"How long is that?"

"Twelve years, almost thirteen."

"I assume, if he'd been in any trouble during that time, you'd know it?"

"I would think so."

"But you don't know for sure, do you?"

"I don't reckon I do."

"Do you have a recent picture of Sam, one we can take with us?"

She went into the bedroom. Returned with a serrated-edged four-by-five black-and-white. "Here, you can take this one." It was a picture of Sam on the stoop.

The lieutenant took the picture and Sam's business card and put them in his pocket. "We need to look around your apartment."

She squared her shoulders, hands on hips. Dug in. "Officer, I've been really good answering your questions, and I want to help you, but I know my rights. Do you have a warrant? Because if you don't, you can't search my home. I don't mean to be disrespectful at all, but—"

"Now Ruby, what do *you* know about rights and warrants, anyway?"

The lieutenant and the silent one locked eyes with each other. Ruby's heart was beating like a snare drum. She knew if they wanted to go through her apartment there was nothing she could do about it, warrant or no warrant. A black woman being stared down by two white men with badges and guns. Inside with the door closed. They could have their way with her, for that matter, and nobody would be the wiser for it. It would be her word against theirs.

For reasons she probably would never know, they relented and left, but not without first letting her know they'd be back.

* * *

As soon as the men had pulled out of the parking space and the car was out of sight, Ruby dialed the barbershop. She asked to speak to Shorty.

"Why Ruby, you know Shorty can't take calls here," the voice on the other end said. She recognized it as Sam's boss.

"I'm sorry, Mr. Batson. Normally I wouldn't ask, but this is an emergency."

"I'll get him, but you'd better make it fast."

Sam came to the phone. "You OK, Baby?"

"Sam, two policemen showed up. Spent over an hour grilling me about you. They had one of your cards with our number handwritten on the back."

"One of *my* cards?"

"They said a girl had it. A white girl. And she's in the hospital now. Somebody tried to kill her. Sam, I'm scared. I think they think you did it."

"I'll come home as soon as I can. Middle of a shine job. I'll leave right after. Mr. Batson, he'll just have to understand."

The tremble in his voice, the labored breathing on the other end, let her know Sam was scared, too. And she suspected he knew something he wasn't telling her.

Chapter Twenty

Dan Winstanley

October 11, 1963

DAN WINSTANLEY WAS ON HIS WAY TO THE BARBERSHOP when the radio cut in. It was Buford Carpenter. "Look for a Hudson. Four door sedan. Nineteen fifty. Green. The woman calls it peacock green, whatever the hell that is. Wide whitewalls, maybe four inches or so. The car's probably in the parking lot behind the shop. Check it out." *How many thirteen-year-old peacock green Hudsons could there be?* Winstanley thought.

He pulled into the lot. At first he didn't see the car. But he found it backed into a space at the far end, under a mimosa. He wondered why Jepperson would have parked so far from the barbershop's rear entrance.

He eased his unmarked Newport sedan beside the Hudson. Got out and walked around it. Peacock green—if that's what it had been when the car rolled off the assembly line—had faded to split pea green. Brown, flaky rust had begun a slow crawl up the sides from the rocker panels. He tried the door handles. The car was locked. He cupped his hands and peered through the driver's side window. That's when the object hanging from the rearview mirror caught his eye. He froze.

He got back in his car and radioed Alford and Carpenter. No response. They were probably still meeting with the Jepperson woman. He left his car parked next to the Hudson. He dashed across the lot toward the barbershop.

The redolence of Clubman and Bay Rum engulfed him as soon as he walked through the door. *Do all clip joints smell the same?* He laughed. He strode to the front of the shop. He scanned the poster on the wall, across from the barber chair nearest the front door. Nine styles in profile encircled: Modern Hair Styling *is a professional art*. The letters were big and bold, as if the artisans at the East Atlanta Barber Shop felt compelled to tout their mastery for all to see. Should he go for the Flattop? He hadn't had one of those in—what—fifteen years? How about a Butch? Or a Forward-combed Boogie? Not today. He picked the one most resembling what he had walked in with. The Executive Contour. *Executive—has a nice ring to it.*

He sat below the poster and waited for the barber to finish working on a teenage boy's pompadour rockabilly—not one of the nine styles encircling Modern Hair Styling. As soon as *Boy Rockabilly* had gotten up from the chair, the barber motioned for Winstanley. The engraved sign on the wall behind the barber's chair said Batson.

"New to these parts?" the barber asked when Winstanley had settled in.

"Not the city," the sergeant replied. "Just the shop."

Batson draped him in a black-and-white tight-checkered cloth cape, wrapped the Sanex strip around his neck, and started snipping away.

Winstanley's arms shot from under the cloth. For some reason, ever since childhood, whenever he got a haircut, he couldn't have his hands hidden under the barber cape. Maybe it was because he always felt like he was hiding something. Maybe it had to do with the fact that, since childhood, he had seen himself he was an interloper—an impostor—in another person's skin. Maybe that's why he always had to do follow the rules. Prove himself—*to* himself.

His thoughts snapped back to the present. At first, the two men made small talk. Winstanley found out Batson was the owner and had run the shop for two decades. When he had gotten comfortable with Batson, he broached the subject. "Tell me about your shoeshine boy there."

"Shorty?" Batson held his chin high. "Best spit shiner in the business. Bar none."

"How long has he worked for you?"

Batson yelled across the room. "Shorty, how long have you been here?"

Sam Jepperson was sitting on a stool, hunched over a pair of wing tips. He looked up.

"About two hours, sir."

"No, Shorty. How long have you *worked* here?"

"Goin' on twelve years, sir."

"Is he dependable?" Winstanley asked.

"Wouldn't have lasted six months if he wasn't."

"Ever give you any trouble?"

"Not a bit."

Winstanley held up his feet from under the edge of the cape. "Seeing as I'm here, and you say he's the best, I think I'll get a shine."

Batson looked down at Winstanley's scuffed lace up oxfords. "Shorty, this good man here needs a buff job."

Sam Jepperson walked over to the barber chair. For the first time, he and Winstanley made eye contact. "If you slip 'em off, sir, I'll take 'em over there and shine 'em up real good."

About halfway through Winstanley's haircut, the phone rang. Batson answered it. "Shorty, it's for you. Make it quick."

Winstanley watched as Jepperson walked over to the phone. When Sam hung up, he was visibly rattled. He went back to his stool. Even from all the way across the room, Winstanley could see his hands shaking.

Batson powdered Winstanley's neck with Clubman talc. The sergeant paid for his haircut and crossed the room in his sock feet to where Jepperson was finishing up his oxfords. "What do I owe you?"

"Fifty cents, sir."

Winstanley pulled out a dollar bill. "Here. The rest is for you." *A big tip throws 'em off guard every time*, he thought.

A big grin formed on Jepperson face, but Winstanley could tell it was strained.

Winstanley slipped on his shoes and stood up. That's when he whipped out his badge—discreetly but in such a way as to dispel any doubt on Jepperson's part. "You and I need to take a walk."

"A walk, sir?"

"That's right. A walk. To your car."

* * *

"Unlock the door."

Jepperson held the key in his hand and did a little nervous two-step with the lock. He was shaking so, it took him three tries. He swung the door open. Winstanley wondered why he had caved without a bit of pushback. The sergeant had expected him to say *What's this all about?* or something. Not a word. Maybe he just didn't know any better. Or maybe he *did* know better—than to resist.

"What's that thing hanging from the mirror, Jepperson?"

"It's a hoodoo haint, sir?"

"A what?"

"A hoodoo haint, sir. Brings good luck. It's Gullah. Them's my people."

"Hand it over."

"Give it to you, sir?"

"That's what I said. Give it to me."

Jepperson untied the stick figure from the mirror mount and handed it to Winstanley.

"I need to search your car."

"Go ahead. I got nothin' to hide."

Winstanley opened the glove box. Dug through the contents. Nothing of note except a tattered Owner's Manual, a registration card made out to Samuel Gibbes Jepperson. A red corded fisherman cap. And slightly withered Red Delicious.

He opened the back door. The back floorboard was empty except for a Fli-Back Bolo paddle. There was nothing in the back seat.

"Pop the trunk."

The trunk was empty except for a spare tire, jack and tire iron, a toolbox, and a raggedy wool blanket. He opened the toolbox. Rummaged through it. He found a slip joint knife. Three-and-a-half-inch blade. The blade was shiny and new looking, unlike the handle. Looked like it may have been cleaned recently. He closed the knife and put it in his pocket.

Winstanley went to his car and returned with a ruler. He got on his hands and knees and measured the tire width.

"Jepperson, come sit in my car with me for a minute."

"Sir, I don't mean no discourtesy, but if I don't get back ins—"

"Don't worry about your boss. I'll explain everything to him. Listen, I can tell you're frightened, but you don't need to be worried about anything. I just need to ask you a few questions."

Winstanley opened the rear driver's-side door of the Newport. He motioned for Jepperson to get in. Sam slid across the seat. Winstanley sat in the front. He placed the stick figure and knife beside him on the front seat. He looked at Jepperson through the rearview mirror. "Sam, tell me what you know about Cynthia Hudspeth." Winstanley realized, as soon as the girl's name passed his lips, that he had to be careful. Alford had given explicit instructions that no one was to know she was laid up in the hospital.

Jepperson scratched his head. "Who?"

"Sam, don't play games with me. How do you know her?"

"I don't know anybody by that name, sir."

"Sam, she had your card, with your home number written on the back. And you're telling me you don't know who she is?"

Winstanley pulled a picture of Cynthia Hudspeth out of his pocket. He passed it across the back of the seat to Jepperson.

Jepperson examined the picture. "I remember her. Picked her up one night. Hitchhiking. Recognized her 'cause I shine her daddy's shoes sometimes. Took her to Grady Stadium. Dropped her off. That's all."

"When was that, Sam?"

"Well, all I remember is it was the second game."

"And why did you give her your card?"

"Cause I was worried about her. Her bein' thirteen and all, and out at night hitchhiking. I told her if she ever needed a ride to call me before she took a notion to thumb. And if you want to know the truth, I kind of felt sorry for her."

"*You* felt sorry for *her*? A *colored* man felt sorry for a white girl? Do you realize what you're saying, Sam?" Winstanley stared at Jepperson in the mirror. "If I were you, I'd be real careful saying things like that. Unless you want trouble. So tell me, after that night, when's the next time you saw her?"

"I didn't, sir."

"So you're saying you never saw her after that."

"That's right, sir. It was the only time."

"Sam, let me ask you another question. When I opened your back door, I smelled bleach. Can you help me understand why I smelled bleach in your car?

"Yes, sir. A few weeks ago, I spilled some polish on the rubber mat. Used water and some bleach to try to clean it up."

"Sam, the last I checked, you don't use bleach to clean up shoe polish. You need to go back to your mulatto home girl and have her teach you a thing or two about cleaning. I would think you, of all people, would know how to clean up shoe polish."

"I understand, sir."

"Sam, explain something else to me. Why did you park way over here, so far from the barbershop?"

"Mr. Batson makes me park here, sir. Says I don't need to be takin' up space where the customers park."

"Listen, Sam. I'm going to let you get back to work. I'll walk back in with you. I'll tell your boss I kept you out here. But I want you to go right home from work and stay there. You understand? We're going to need to talk to you later."

"Yes, sir."

"Listen to me, Sam. You're not in trouble. But if you don't do as I say, you *will* be."

* * *

Alford and Carpenter were waiting for Winstanley when he got back to headquarters. Fast food wrappers were strewn across Alford's desk.

"Nice trim, Sergeant," Alford said. "Here, this is for you." He pushed a Zesto's double cheeseburger and a large order of crinkly fries across the desk. "You know what they say. An army marches on its stomach. So, what did you learn out there in the trenches?"

"Look at this, men." Winstanley pulled out the hoodoo haint. Threw it on the desk. "What does it look like to you?" Still standing, he grabbed the cheeseburger and took a bite out of it. Followed it with two crinkly fries.

Carpenter spoke up. "It looks just like the marks on the girls' thighs. Where'd you get it?"

"It was hanging in Sam Jepperson's car. On the mirror. And he admitted to picking up Cynthia Hudspeth. Seems she was hitchhiking. He took her to Grady Stadium and dropped her off. Said he gave her the card in case she ever needed a ride somewhere."

"So you're telling me she got in his car on her own?"

"That's what he claims."

"A white girl? In his car? On her own?"

Carpenter shook his head in obvious disgust. "I was downtown in front of Davison's a couple of Saturdays ago when—"

"You were shopping at Davison's downtown?" Alford frowned.

"The little lady drug me down there…when I saw this white woman flouncin' down the street with a damned nigger man. I swear to God, I just about gave up my chicken pot pie right there on the sidewalk."

"Now Buford." A smirk came over Alford's face. "You need to be a good boy and call him a Negro, not a nigger. You know Mayor Allen doesn't like us using that word." Then he addressed Winstanley. "What else did you find out, Sergeant?"

"I detected a faint smell of bleach in the car." Winstanley pulled out the knife. "And I found this in his trunk. The blade looks to have been cleaned recently."

Alford lit another Lucky. "Well, gentlemen, I think we have our man."

"What did I tell you," Carpenter chimed in. "A damned burrhead. I knew it."

"Hold on. Lieutenant," Winstanley said. "And you, too, Carpenter. I think that's a little premature, don't you?"

"Why do you say that, Sergeant?" Carpenter replied.

"Well, for one thing. The tires. The Hudson's are 7-1/2 inches, a full inch wider than the tire tracks. And the tread's a zigzag, not a herringbone. There's no way Jepperson's car made those tracks."

"But what about the stick man? The knife? The bleach? The business card? The girl in his goddamned car? Looks pretty damning to me."

"I agree it doesn't look good. But it's just circumstantial at this point."

"Doesn't look *good*? *Who* doesn't it look good for? Jepperson? It looks pretty good for us. I swear, Winstanley, it sounds like you're siding with him."

"I'm not taking anybody's side," Winstanley said. "I'm just trying to be a good detective that's all. That's what you pay me for, isn't it? And one other thing, these girls disappeared a week before they were killed. Do you really think a black shoeshine boy—I don't care how old he is—has the wherewithal to hide those girls somewhere for a week before he killed them? And with nobody finding out? Listen, men. We can't just haul a man in on flimsy evidence just because he's black and he happened to give a white girl a ride."

"Flimsy evidence?"

"Like I said, Lieutenant, it's just circumstantial. Don't you think we have a lot more work to do before we jump to conclusions?"

"A colored man out for fresh white tail. I should have known." Alford ground his cigarette butt into the ashtray like he was twisting its head off. Turned to Carpenter. "You know what, Detective? Everybody knows you're not the brightest bulb in the box. And you're also a royal pain in the butt. But sometimes you're right. You know what they say. A blind hog finds an acorn once in a while. And I think this is one of those *once in a while*s. You've got Jepperson pegged." He looked at the sergeant. "Now Winstanley here, he may have police manual smarts, but he's a straight-ass by-the-book kind of guy. Can't see the obvious if it's three inches in front of him. If you want to know the truth, it's people like him that get in the way. And to think, I went to the trouble of buying him lunch and this is the thanks I get. Sergeant, get an arrest warrant. Haul him in."

"But. Lieut—"

"You heard what I said, Winstanley. Do it. You can live to fight another day."

Chapter Twenty-One

Billy Tarwater

October 13, 1963

BY SUNDAY, THE THIRTEENTH OF OCTOBER, WE WERE back into the *church-followed-by-Sunday-dinner* routine. My thumb was still splinted and probably would be for another week or so, but the fig had shrunk. And I had little excuse for avoiding the Reverend Kilgallon's fevered melodrama. Needless to say, my brother was ticked off that I couldn't milk my infirmity at least one more week.

We filed into the church, assumed our usual pew spots, and waited for the service to begin. Mrs. Simpson, the organist, was playing hymn number 327, "Sweet Hour of Prayer," so loud that I worried the brass organ pipes would shake loose any minute and come tumbling down in front of the tank of water—what did I call it?—oh yeah, that *big, awesome* tank of water.

I occupied myself by taking the stubby yellow excuse for a pencil from the pew rack, placing the hymnal in my lap, hunching over it, and discreetly penciling notations at the tops of the pages, starting with number 327…Go to 493…Go to 122…Go to 270…on and on…to Go to 327. The diversion took my mind off of Cynthia. I was still worried to death that something bad had happened to her. But to this day, I don't know why defacing the hymnal that way engrossed me so. I guess I thought some unknowing soul would obey my handwritten instructions only to find himself all the way back where he started, and maybe even getting stuck in one big wild goose chase that he would never get out of. It never occurred to me that we were the only people who ever sat in that spot—that is, except when a fig of a thumb or something like that kept us away on a given Sunday. God only knows what ill fate would have befallen me if my mother had caught me writing in the hymnal. I knew without her having to tell me that she didn't take kindly to the Lord's property being defaced.

When the youth minister took his position at the pulpit, and the green leather throne was empty, and my grandmother looked at me with that distressed look, just like the constipated woman in the Ex-Lax commercial, I knew the reverend was a no-show again. The youth minister explained that Reverend Kilgallon had taken ill on his trip to his old church last week and was homebound with a spell of fever and chills. We suffered through a yawning sermon, just as Granny Tarwater had predicted. It was one of the few times that I missed the reverend's prancing around, shaking his fists and yelling. I guess outlandish will win out over boring any day.

* * *

When we got to Granny Tarwater's, there was a straight back chair blocking the door to the cellar. Her famous—or infamous in my book—tinned Christmas fruitcakes were stacked five-high in the seat. *Blech.* I assumed they were destined for basement storage to wait out the holidays. But why were they blocking the door like that?

"Binky," my grandmother said, "whatever you do, don't go down to the root cellar today."

"Why not, Granny T?"

"Just don't. Curiosity killed the cat," she replied, and walked away.

After dinner, I went into the kitchen. Dovey Mae was washing dishes. An uneaten plate of food was sitting on the white porcelain table. All the Roman Army had partaken already and were recuperating on the porch. And Dovey Mae had eaten in the kitchen while we were gorging ourselves in the dining room.

"Who's the plate for, Dovey Mae?"

Her eyes got as big as my grandmother's Black Eyed Beauties. "Binky, come fetch some figs with me. I'm goin' to make a tart."

She stuffed the end of a dish towel into her apron pocket. She grabbed a wicker basket. I followed her into the backyard.

"Binky, I'll tell you something, but you have to promise not to tell nobody, not a soul, not even your Mama and Daddy. *Especially* your Mama and Daddy."

"Cross my heart and hope to die, Dovey Mae."

"They's a man in the root cellar."

"A man in the root cellar?" I shouted.

She put her finger to her lips. "What'd I say, Binky? Quiet now."

"Who is it?"

"Do you know Shorty? That shines shoes at the barbershop?"

"Of course, I know Shorty. That's where I get my hair cut. Dovey Mae, how do *you* know Shorty? You don't go there, do you?"

She laughed. "Binky, everybody in East Atlanta knows Shorty. He's my people."

"You're kin?"

"No, not blood kin. But he's my people. Just like Madame Ludowici's my people. We have to stick together. Otherwise... well, we just have to stick together."

"Shorty's in the cellar? How did he get there?"

"I put him down there, yesterday."

"Does Granny Tarwater know?"

"Of course, your grandmother knows, Binky, but she's the only one. And we need to keep it that way."

"What's he doing in the root cellar?"

"Keep pickin' figs, Binky, and I'll tell you."

Dovey Mae left the low-growing ones for me. She plucked the higher-up ones that I couldn't reach.

"He's in some kind of trouble. He needed a place to hide."

"Trouble?"

"With the law, Binky. But he promised me he's cleanhanded."

"What kind of trouble?"

"Let's just say it's not good and leave it be."

"Why did he call *you*?"

"He didn't. I was at Mrs. Hallman's yesterday morning. Remember I told you I work for her most Saturdays?"

I nodded.

"Well, the phone rings. I answer it. 'Hallman residence,' I say. 'Dovey Mae?' the voice on the other end says. 'It's Shorty. Shorty Jepperson. Is Mrs. Hallman there?'"

"How does Shorty know Mrs. Hallman?" I asked.

"Shorty's wife, Ruby. She sews for Mrs. Hallman. So he says, 'Dovey Mae, I'm in a heap a trouble and I need help. Mrs. Hallman got me out of a fix once before.' I say, 'Shorty, she's not here. Where you callin' from?' He says, 'the pay phone at the barbershop.' He tells me what's goin' on. That's when I decided to help him."

Dovey Mae explained that she arranged to meet Shorty in the barbershop parking lot late yesterday afternoon. They sneaked down to Granny Tarwater's. At first, my grandmother said no, that there was no way she was going to let a man, especially a black man, hide in her cellar. But Dovey Mae explained the situation, and Granny Tarwater said OK, if it was just for a day or two. I learned, then and there, standing under the fig tree, that there was a side to my grandmother I hadn't known before, sort of like when I learned about her mischievous streak that afternoon back last summer. Not only was she mischievous, but she had a soft spot for people in trouble, I don't care what color they are. That didn't mean she'd eat at the table with them, but she had a good heart, even if it meant hiding somebody from the law. That's assuming she thought they were innocent and wouldn't get a fair break.

I full well understood why my mother and father were *not* to know.

"Dovey Mae, you didn't tell me what kind of trouble he's in."

"We need to get these figs inside. Your grandmother will get to wondering why we been out here so long." She covered the basket with the towel and headed back inside, with me following behind her.

When we walked into the kitchen, the plate of food was gone.

I joined the Roman Army on the porch. They were talking about something, but I couldn't for the life of me say what it was. I was a thousand miles away. I couldn't get Cynthia off my mind. And now, I couldn't get Shorty off my mind either, down there in the root cellar by himself and all. *What could he have possibly done?*

* * *

Around three thirty, Granny Tarwater, my mother, Cousin Loreen and I had moved to the living room. The rest were still on the porch. A little before four, the doorbell rang—a short ding, like the person barely pushed it. Before anybody could get to the door, Adele Hudspeth threw it open and came lumbering in. Instead of plopping down in a whap like before, she sank slowly into the sofa cushion, assumed a slump and let out a long, deep sigh. There were big bags under her eyes—as big as Davison's shopping bags. She looked worn out. And the flock of sheep hadn't gone away. She rubbed the sofa's rolled arm—back and forth, back and forth—nervous-like. She took her ring of keys off her belt and planted them on the end table. "They found her."

"Cynthia?" Granny Tarwater said.

"They found her. Cecil and I aren't supposed to let anybody know where she is. But I have to talk to somebody about it. I can't just keep it in. It's killing me."

"Where is she?"

"I'll tell you, but you can't tell anybody."

My mother looked at me. "Binky, leave the room."

I headed down the hallway to the spare bedroom. When I reached the bedroom door, I called out to my mother. "OK, Mom, I'm going to listen to the shortwave." I never went into the bedroom, but I shut the door loud, as if I had. Then I assumed my usual snooping spot just around the corner from the living room, out of sight but within easy earshot.

"She's in the hospital," Mrs. Hudspeth said. "Grady. She unconscious. I'm worried sick about her."

Oh my God! Unconscious! My heart leapt out of my throat, all the way to the ceiling, and landed back in my chest.

"What in heaven's name happened?" Granny Tarwater asked.

"Somebody tried to kill her. Left her for dead. Some workers found her. The police are guarding her. Whoever did it, they can't know she's there. Otherwise, they might go there and try to..." I could tell, even from around the corner, that Mrs. Hudspeth was choking up.

My grandmother said something about getting a box of Kleenex from the bathroom. I scurried down the hall and into the spare bedroom before she saw me. I stayed there for a few minutes and then sneaked back out.

Mrs. Hudspeth was still talking. "I asked if what happened to Cynthia was related to the other two...those poor girls that were murdered. But they won't tell me a thing. Just that it's under investigation. And the doctors won't say a word either, except it's touch and go."

Touch and go?

I thought about Leonard Seymour. I wondered if Mrs. Hudspeth suspected him. And then I thought about Shorty in the cellar and his trouble with the law. Could *he* have been involved somehow?

In the hallway, just around the corner from the living room, I was lurking where the telephone sits in its little nook in the wall. I must have accidentally caught the cord on my foot, because the phone went crashing to the floor.

"Binky, is that you?" my mother called out.

My cover was blown. I returned the phone to the nook, composed myself, and came walking around the corner as nonchalant-like as I could.

Mrs. Hudspeth looked at her watch and said, "Oh my, where has the time gone? Cecil and I have to get to the hospital." She leapt to her feet and ran out the door.

"Hospital?" I played dumb.

"Never mind, Binky," my mother said.

I looked over and saw that Mrs. Hudspeth had forgotten the keys to the kingdom. I went running out and gave them to her. I told her I hoped Cynthia was going to be OK, wherever she was. She teared up.

* * *

I had convinced Mom to let me walk to Granny Tarwater's the next day, Monday, after school. My mother would pick me up later that evening. Granny Tarwater said that would be just fine, that she would cook me a big dinner. She never turned down the opportunity to feed somebody. *Especially her favorite grandson*, I imagined.

When I got to Granny Tarwater's, she was in the kitchen. The minute I walked in the door, I smelled the fried apple pies cooking in the skillet. And there were three clean plates on the porcelain table, waiting to be filled out with fried chicken and green beans.

I couldn't keep it in. "Granny T, I know."

"You know what, Binky?"

"I know who's in the cellar."

She turned as white as that flock of sheep that followed Mrs. Hudspeth around. "How do you know about that?"

"Dovey Mae told me. But I promised I wouldn't tell a soul. And I won't."

"Well, when a person's in a pickle, I don't care who they are—"

"What kind of a pickle, Granny T?"

"I don't know, Binky. Dovey Mae didn't tell me. I just know it's not good. And he swears on God's Book that he's an innocent man. And Dovey Mae swears he's innocent. And that's enough for me. The Good Lord teaches us to help people in need. You remember the song, Binky...Red and yellow, Black and white."

I nodded.

"But mind you, he can't stay down there long."

"Granny T, can I take him his food?"

I took the plate down to Shorty. His eyes lit up when he saw me, but he was sheepish-like. I just said Hi, gave him the food, and scurried back upstairs. I didn't want to make him feel bad.

* * *

After dinner, Granny Tarwater and I were sitting in the living room watching *To Tell The Truth,* when I saw the cellar door ease open a crack.

"Miss Jincey, can I come out? I need to use the facilities."

"Come on out, Shorty," Granny Tarwater said.

"Thank you, ma'am." He scooted across the living room in his socked feet, down the hall, and into the bathroom.

Then, a few minutes later, all you-know-what broke loose. Shorty had just come out of the bathroom and was headed to the cellar door. He was halfway across the living room.

The doorbell dinged and Mrs. Hudspeth came barging in before we could get to the door, just like yesterday. I guess she was so distraught about Cynthia that her manners had run away along with her complexion. Anyway, she saw Shorty, did an about-face, and ran out the door.

Chapter Twenty-Two

Adele Hudspeth

October 14, 1963

ADELE HAD BEEN SHAKEN BY THE SIGHT OF A COLORED man in Jincey Tarwater's living room. Even though she had only a fleeting glimpse before she ran out the door, Jincey and the boy didn't seem to be in any kind of trouble. In fact, the expressions on their faces said they were more surprised by *her* than by *him*. Not fear. Not distress. Just surprise that *she* had barged in unannounced. For some reason—*God only knows why*—the Negro was there because they *wanted* him to be there.

* * *

On the way to the hospital, Adele described the man to Cecil. Short—maybe five six. Almost as wide as he was tall. Thick, nappy hair. A big round face, sort of like Andy Hogg Brown. But rounder. And a lot blacker. And, even with the two or three steps he took as she stood there gawking, she could tell he had a gimp.

"Fits Sam Jepperson to a tee," Cecil said. "We need to call the police."

"Let's wait until we get home tonight, honey. We need to tend to our daughter now."

* * *

As it turned out, they didn't leave the hospital until after midnight. They had waited for the neurologist, and Cynthia was at the tail end of his rounds. They had left Cynthia's bedside with some encouragement. There were signs that she may have been easing her way back to consciousness. Adele had wanted to spend the night there, but the doctors had sent them home. They were to return Tuesday morning.

She hoped against hope that, before tomorrow ended, Cynthia would be back to her old self—recounting for all to hear her spiritual journey toward Heaven's threshold, closing in on the bright light, but being told by Saint Peter in no uncertain terms, "Go back. He's not ready for you yet."

Adele had a funny feeling as soon as they pulled into the driveway. For one thing, the trash cans always sat along the driveway's right edge, butted up against Leonard Seymour's chain-link and just across from Cynthia's bedroom window. But now they had been moved toward the far rear of the house. For another, the lilyturf that ran along the side of the house had been disturbed. She got one of those feelings God always sent her when He needed her to know something important.

Cecil stopped near the front door, put the Fairlane in Park and turned off the engine. He left the headlights on. He took a flashlight from the glove box. They walked up the driveway. The lilyturf had been trampled on right under Cynthia's window. Her window was open. Somebody had used a pry bar or something to jimmy the lower sash. Popped it right open like a bottle cap. The gouge marks along the outer sill were about three quarters of an inch wide. A crowbar? A tire iron? She surmised that whoever did it had left the glass intact so as not to alert the neighbors.

They peered through the window into the dark room, which was illuminated only by the beam from Cecil's flashlight, the nightlight beside Cynthia's bed, and what little ambient light made its way through the window from the car headlights. The room had been ransacked. The three drawers on the chest had been left open haphazardly. Cynthia's clothes and personal things were strewn across the floor.

Cecil headed up the front steps. Adele followed. He shined the flashlight at the door. Turned the knob. It was locked. She could tell he was struggling to keep his nerves in check long enough to unlock it. They entered the house. He grabbed the baseball bat he always kept propped just inside the doorway. They searched every room, every closet, every nook and cranny. Under the beds. Behind the shower curtain. In the cellar. There was no one in the house.

It looked as if someone had gone through every room in the house except the kitchen and bathroom, although none of the other rooms had been ransacked like Cynthia's bedroom. Adele Hudspeth's eyes fell on the dining room table. On the corner had been a stock of papers related to Cynthia and Grady Hospital. The papers were gone.

He flipped on the outside lights and they both walked slowly to the toolshed. She carried the flashlight. He carried the bat. There was no one in the toolshed either. Cradling the bat in the crook of his left arm, held tight to his side, he retrieved a handful of ten penny nails, work gloves, and a hammer. He nailed Cynthia's window shut, careful not to disturb any fingerprints that might be on the window frame or glass. Hopefully, the gloves would help.

By the time they got through, it was a quarter to three. They were dead-tired and about to give out. They would call the police first thing in the morning.

* * *

Cecil Hudspeth was out like a rock within ten minutes of hitting the sheets. It had been four before Adele managed to go under, and then only after taking a Sominex with a glass of milk.

But after no more than three hours of sleep, she sprang to wide-awake attention. She rubbed her eyes and stared at the blur of an alarm clock on the bedside table. She could make out five something.

The papers! They know Cynthia's at Grady. They know the name she's registered under. They know her condition.

She reached over and gave The Rock a hard nudge. "Cecil, wake up."

Chapter Twenty-Three

Dan Winstanley

October 15, 1963

IT WAS EARLY TUESDAY MORNING, THE FIFTEENTH. THE sun wouldn't peek above the horizon for another forty minutes.

Sergeant Winstanley replayed the Friday afternoon give-and-take. "You heard what I said. Do it. You can live to fight another day...A straight-ass by-the-book kind of guy. Can't see the obvious if it's three inches in front of him." *And what did Carpenter do the whole time? Not a damned thing. Just sat there bobbing his head up and down like one of those Goofy Drinking Birds.*

Winstanley would do as he was told—but with a pique. His mission was to find Sam Jepperson and haul him in. Once he found Jepperson, he would call for uniformed backup. They'd do the heavy lifting. Throw him in the paddy wagon, take him to the station house and book him.

That was Winstanley's *stated* mission, anyway. But, while he was at it, he had every intention of snooping down some other trails, the lieutenant's protestations be damned. He was grateful that the lieutenant had sent him on the mission alone. Otherwise, Carpenter, or whoever, would have cramped his style—and thwarted his plans.

He sat in the Newport in the barbershop parking lot. This time, he had pulled into the closest empty space to the rear entrance. He flipped his spiral notepad to a blank page. He made two columns, headed A on the left and B on the right. He led off the left column with *Sam Jepperson*. Then he added *Leonard Seymour* and *Marvin Darby*. On the right he wrote *Hudspeths, Dullumses, Darbys, Weldon (last name?) the soda jerk, Tommy Wright*. Then he added a sixth name to the right-hand column: *Boggses*. Just before he had left the station house, the detectives had gotten word that Patsy Boggs' parents had driven over from Alabama and had identified the Chattahoochee girl at the Fulton County morgue as their daughter. They were staying at the Peachtree On Peachtree Hotel, the site of the old Winecoff fire, a stone's throw from the morgue. They had indicated they would remain in town for several days to be of assistance to the police and to make arrangements for the return of their daughter's body as soon as it was released.

Every one of the people in the B column maybe saw something, heard something, knew something. And six of them were the victims of tragedy, with a daughter either six feet under, soon to be, or—what did Alford call her?—*vegetating* at Grady.

But it was the names in the A column that most concerned Winstanley at the moment. One was the target of his stated mission. One was some kind of sex pervert—*alleged* anyway—who was either missing or chose not to come to the door. And

Winstanley had been told in no uncertain terms that Marvin Darby was hands-off as a suspect. As far as the sergeant was concerned, any one of them could have been involved in some way. But Alford seemed dead set on pinning the whole damned thing on Jepperson. So did Carpenter.

Winstanley's first order of business would have to be the *stated* mission. He looked across the lot. There was the green Hudson, in the same place where it had been on Friday.

He walked into the barbershop. Sam's stool and supplies were where Winstanley expected them to be. But he didn't see Sam. Batson was across the room stropping a razor. Winstanley walked over to him. "Mr. Batson, is Sam here?"

Batson stopped stropping and looked up. "I haven't seen him since Saturday afternoon. He walked out of here around three fifteen. Said he was going to smoke a cigarette. Never came back in." He paused and looked across the room at the back door. The groove between his eyebrows deepened. "Funny thing is, his car's been right there in the same spot the whole time. Looks like it never left the lot from the time he parked it there Saturday morning."

"Did you call his house?"

"I did. Ruby said she'd seen neither hide nor hair of him since he drove off that morning." Batson shook his head. "She seemed squirrely on the phone, though. If I had to guess, I'd say she wasn't being straight up with me."

* * *

Dan Winstanley had never met Ruby Jepperson. But he knew where she lived. And he knew from Alford and Carpenter what she looked like. And today was one of her days off from the cut-n-curl place. He'd pay her a visit. His inclination was to drop in on the Hudspeths first, since they were just down the street and around the corner from the barbershop. But he decided against it. He could suffer only so much of Alford's wrath. He'd head over to Carver Homes first.

He pulled out of the parking lot and drove down Gresham. He turned right on Portland Avenue and drove past the Hudspeths' house on the right. Adele Hudspeth was in the front yard. Standing there, with her hands on her hips, gazing down the street toward Moreland Avenue, then up the street toward Gresham, then down the street again. Winstanley had just passed when he looked over his shoulder and saw Cecil come out the door and descend the porch steps. The sergeant hoped the two of them hadn't seen *him*. She had seemed intent on looking at, or for, something far away. Her husband was looking at the ground.

He turned left, heading south, on Moreland Avenue. Two blocks down Moreland, he took a right onto Woodland Avenue. Woodland curved to the left and settled into a south-southwesterly course through Beulah Heights. Eight blocks farther down Woodland, he stopped at the intersection at Confederate Avenue. A church sat at the southeastern corner, ten o'clock from the car's straight-ahead direction. Winstanley recognized the name on the sign, CONFEDERATE AVENUE BAPTIST CHURCH, and below it, REV. VIRLYN KILGALLON, PASTOR. *Martha Ann Dullums' and Cynthia Hudspeth's church. I'll add Kilgallon's name to my list. At some point, I'll pay him a visit, but not today.*

* * *

Winstanley was about to turn onto Confederate Avenue when the radio chimed in. It was Carpenter.

"What is it, Carpenter?"

"Turn around and go back to Portland Avenue. The police are at the Hudspeths'."

Winstanley crossed Confederate and swung into the church parking lot. Pulled out, turned right, and headed back up Woodland.

"What are the police doing at the Hudspeths'?"

"Seems that late yesterday evening, Adele Hudspeth paid a visit to an old lady that lives two doors up, a Mrs. Tarwater, to give her an update on the girl."

"Two doors up toward Gresham or Moreland?"

"Gresham."

"The white frame house on the corner?"

"Yep, on the corner. Anyway, when the Greyhound got to—"

"The greyhound, Carpenter?"

"The Greyhound *bus*, Adele Hudspeth."

Winstanley thought he heard muted snickering on the radio. He shook his head.

Carpenter continued. "When it...she...entered Mrs. Tarwater's house, she encountered a nigger in the lady's living room. The Greyhou...Adele...went running back to her house. She told her husband what she had seen. She described the man to him. Eventually, they put two and two together and decided the man must be Sam Jepperson."

"Why did the Hudspeths wait until this morning to call the police?"

"Your guess is as good as mine, Sergeant. But I'm not through. There's more. After the little living room encounter, Adele and Cecil Hudspeth went to Grady Hospital. They stayed there until past midnight. When they got home, they discovered their house had been broken into."

"So we have an old lady harboring a suspect, allegedly anyway. And we have a burglary."

"You got it, Sergeant. We have two police units out there right now. One at the Hudspeths' and one at the old lady's. And a burglary plainclothesman is on his way to the Hudspeths' as we speak.

"I'm headed to the Tarwater house, Carpenter. Almost there."

* * *

When Winstanley turned the corner off of Moreland onto Portland, he could see the flood of flashing red in front of the Hudspeth house. He drove past. At the corner of Portland and Gresham, not one, not two, but three police cars were parked along the curb—two on Portland and one on Gresham.

He climbed the front steps to the Tarwater house. The door was open. The living room was crowded with three officers and the lady. The other three policemen were searching the property for Jepperson. Winstanley walked into the kitchen. An officer was opening each lower cabinet and peering inside. "He may be short," Winstanley said, "but there's no way he's going to fit in there."

Jepperson was nowhere to be found.

At first the lady said she had no idea what the officers were talking about. She would never allow a colored man to *bed up* in her house—her words. And an intruder had not forced his way inside and held her hostage. Most certainly not.

But after forty-five minutes of questioning, she relented. She admitted she had put Jepperson up, but only for a day or two, and only because she was sure he was innocent of whatever he was accused of. He had been there from sometime late Saturday until yesterday evening. He had up and hightailed it not long after Adele Hudspeth barged into the house unannounced.

* * *

Winstanley jammed the accelerator to the floor, almost ran over a police officer standing near the curb, and sped down Portland. If he hurried, he could get to Carver Homes in fifteen—maybe twelve—minutes.

He had made the decision not to have the uniformed officers accompany him all the way to the Jepperson apartment. A passel of police cars descending on the residence would surely send Sam hotfooting it out the back door, only to fade into the proverbial woodwork. He had, however, instructed the officers to follow sufficiently far behind and wait on Meldon Avenue, outside the grounds of the Carver Homes complex, in case they were needed. His only concern was whether they would do as instructed. He had been a uniformed officer once. There was something irresistible about that goddamned siren and the flashing roof light that seemed to overcome rookies and get in the way of sound judgment. Each of the three police cars was manned by a seasoned officer and a rookie. He was certain that two of the seasoned officers could keep their newby charges in check, but he wasn't so sure about the third.

The sergeant pulled into a space one building up from Jepperson's apartment. He crossed the front scrap of a lawn and approached the door carefully. The Hudson was nowhere in sight, but he had assumed that would be the case, since an hour or so earlier it had been in the barbershop lot where Batson had said it had remained since Saturday morning. If Jepperson had holed up in the Portland Avenue house from Saturday until sometime late yesterday, and the car was still where he left it, chances were he had abandoned it, for the time being anyway.

Winstanley was about to knock on the door when he heard the deadbolt disengage and the knob rattle. Ruby stood in the doorway. She was in a light blue terry bathrobe and open-toed fluff slippers. Winstanley flipped his badge.

She spoke before he could get a word out. "If you're looking for Sam, he's not here. I haven't seen him or spoken to him since he left for work Saturday."

"You haven't seen him. And you haven't spoken to him. But do you know where he is?"

"I wish I did."

"Has he disappeared like this before?"

"Never." She hesitated then corrected herself. "Except that one time in fifty-nine when he ran off to Birmingham without telling me. But that was because his sixteen-year-old son...not *my* son...had gotten in some trouble with the law, and Shorty went to bail him out. I think he was too embarrassed to tell me. But I forgave him for that. If Rufus was in trouble somewhere, not that he would be, I'd do the same thing."

"What kind of trouble was his son in?"

"Something about ogling a white girl. They threw him in jail. He's just lucky he didn't end up like that Till boy."

"So you haven't spoken to your husband since Saturday morning? He hasn't called? You haven't tried to find him?"

"No, sir. Mr. Batson called asking for him, but I told him the same thing I told you. I haven't seen him and I don't know where he is."

"Is there anybody you know...any names you can give me...of somebody who might know where he is?"

She shook her head. "Not that I can think of. Sam just pretty much keeps to himself. Doesn't really have any close friends."

* * *

An APB had gone out for Jepperson. Winstanley had instructed the uniformed police to scour the immediate neighborhood around the Portland-Gresham intersection. "And go through Brownwood Park, across from the Hudspeths', with a fine-toothed comb. I'll circle back later."

Winstanley decided to go back to the barbershop and see if, just maybe, Jepperson had shown his face. Then he would ask around the East Atlanta business district.

The Hudson was still in the lot where it had been that morning. Winstanley radioed Alford.

"Tow it," Gus Alford screamed through the radio.

"Tow it, sir? Are you sure?"

"Of course, I'm sure, Sergeant. What the hell's wrong with you? Radio the goddamned Impound Unit and have them haul it in. We'll give it a once-over like nobody's business."

Neither Batson nor the other barbers had seen Jepperson since Saturday afternoon. "But I'll tell you one thing," Batson bellowed so loud that everyone in the shop, barber and customer alike, looked up. "When...if...he shows up, he can head straight for the back door. I don't care how good his shines are."

Winstanley popped into the pharmacy next door. A kid—looked to be no more than sixteen, seventeen—was washing glasses behind the empty luncheon counter. Winstanley sat on the stool at the center of a bank of seven. "You Weldon?"

The kid looked up. A slight smile formed. "Yes sir, that's me." He extended his hand.

"I was surprised to see you here, Weldon. I assumed you'd be in school."

Weldon the Soda Jerk looked right, then left, put his finger to his lips. "Don't tell anybody. Playing hooky today. Dr. Flanigan, he's the owner, said he needed me here real bad. The lady that normally works today is out sick with the flu." He looked Winstanley up and down. Locked eyes with his. "Wait a minute. You're not a truant officer, are you?"

Winstanley laughed. "No, I'm not a truant officer. You're safe with me. If I were you, though, I'd worry about somebody you know walking in and seeing you behind the counter, questioning what you're doing here on a weekday. Long before I'd worry about a truant officer stopping by."

"What'll you have?"

"Know how to make an egg cream?"

He looked at Winstanley with incredulous eyes. "Of course I know how to make an egg cream. Chocolate or vanilla?"

"Vanilla. Say, Weldon, do you mind if I talk to you while you work?"

"Not at all, just as long as you don't mind talking to my back." Weldon began preparing Winstanley's drink.

"Weldon, do you know Sam Jepperson? Shorty? Shines shoes next door?"

"I get my hair cut there like most everybody around here. I know him."

"Have you seen him lately, say, in the past two or three days?"

"I haven't, but I haven't been looking for him either. Hold on a minute." Weldon yelled across the room to the pharmacist's window, "Dr. Flanigan, have you seen Shorty Jepperson the past few days?"

"Saw him last week when I went in to get my hair cut," Flanigan replied. "That was the last."

"Weldon, while I'm here, I'd like to ask you about something else."

"Sure, Mister—"

"Winstanley. *Detective* Winstanley."

"OK, *Detective* Winstanley."

"What can you tell me about Cynthia Hudspeth?"

"The girl that went missing?"

"That's right. The girl that went missing. I understand she used to hang out here some on weekends."

"She did. Good girl. A little too young for me, but she's a good girl. If she were a little older, I might even—"

"Did you see her the Saturday she went missing?" Winstanley thumbed through his pad. "The twenty-eighth?"

"I saw her. She came in for a milkshake. Perched on the stool right there." Weldon pointed to Winstanley's left. "Struck up a conversation across the stools with Tommy."

"Tommy Wright?"

"Yes sir. Know him?"

"No, I've just heard his name."

"Well, the two of them hit it off, and Tommy ended up buying her a drink. She stayed awhile and then left out the front door. Tommy left right after that. Real quick, without paying. But I knew he was good for the money. He came in the next Saturday and settled up. Even gave me an extra tip for not reporting him to Finnegan."

"So you don't know where he went? Whether he left with Cynthia or not?"

"With Cynthia? I don't know. I just know he left right after her."

"Do you know a boy named Marvin Darby?"

"Doesn't everybody? At least everybody my age. From around here."

"Did Marvin come in that day?"

"Marvin? No way. Marvin never comes in here."

"I assume Tommy and Marvin are both at school."

"I assume so."

"Murphy?"

Weldon nodded. He got a big frown. "Mister, I know you're a detective and all, but you sure are asking a lot of questions."

Winstanley plopped a five on the counter. "Here you go, Weldon. Keep the change. You've been a big help."

* * *

Winstanley sat in his car with the motor running, not quite sure where to turn next. That's when the radio broadcast came through. Jepperson had been found crouching in the two-foot space between the rear wall of the A&P and the Dempster Dumpster. He had a pocketful of figs and was chomping on a cold fried chicken leg. The police apprehended and arrested him, and he was now behind bars on Decatur Street. Winstanley felt a sense of relief, with the *stated* mission accomplished. He was determined not to let Alford's insistence that they had their man get in the way of sound detective work. At the risk of kindling the lieutenant's ire, he would head to Leonard Seymour's first, then to the school to pull Marvin Darby, then Tommy Wright, out of class.

* * *

The police had left the Hudspeth's house. The Fairlane was in the driveway, which surprised him. He had assumed the Hudspeths would be at the hospital.

He opened Leonard Seymour's unlocked front gate and walked up onto the porch. He rang the doorbell. Then he knocked loudly. He walked around the house, peering into the windows. The house was dark inside.

He was about to leave when Adele and Cecil Hudspeth came out their front door. "He isn't there," she said. "Hasn't been for over two weeks."

"Do you know where he is, Mrs. Hudspeth?"

"Word is he went to Sylacauga to visit his sister and brother-in-law."

"Did he tell you that?"

"No. Somebody's come by twice to pick up his mail and newspapers. I didn't recognize them, but they're the ones that told me."

"By the way, Mrs. Hudspeth, they found Sam Jepperson. You'll be pleased to know he's behind bars."

"That's a relief, Sergeant, but I'll be honest with you. We're just really confused right now. And we need to get on over to the hospital to see to our daughter."

"I understand, Mrs. Hudspeth. I hope your daughter pulls through. We're all rooting for a full recovery. And, Mrs. Hudspeth, just so you know, I'm as confused as you are. And I'm supposed to be the one with the answers."

* * *

"Where are you, Winstanley?" Lieutenant Alford's voice was so loud it made the radio housing shake.

"I'm on Memorial Drive, sir, headed eastbound."

"Eastbound where?"

"At Maynard Terrace."

Winstanley could hear Alford's muffled reply. "The son-of-a-bitch is headed to Murphy." He assumed the lieutenant had placed his palm over the radio handset and was speaking to Carpenter.

"Didn't you hear we got our man already?" Alford said.

"Jepperson?"

"Of course Jepperson. Who else would I be talking about?"

"I did, sir."

"Well, then, what are you doing out joyriding? Turn around, get back here as soon as you can. We have some good old-fashioned bright-light interr-O-gatin' to do."

Chapter Twenty-Four

Dan Winstanley

October 16, 1963

"LET ME TELL YOU SOMETHING, IN CASE YOU HAVEN'T figured it out already," said Alford. He cut Winstanley a look. "Do you know what a police interrogator is? Nothing but a thieving and silver-tongued huckster of the worst kind, who could just as soon be selling used cars with rolled-back odometers…or cheap five-year asphalt roofing shingles. But in this case, he's selling long prison sentences to customers who have no real need for the product." He lit a Lucky, gave it a slow drag, and then took in through his nostrils the smoke emanating from his mouth as if to say *I'm going to savor this moment with my every being.* "Now Carpenter here, he gets it, don't you, Buford?"

Lieutenant Alford had called for Sam Jepperson to be transferred from the holding cell on the ground floor of the city jail to the adjacent police headquarters, specifically to the eight-by-eleven interrogation room on the third floor. The one with the two way mirror. The one with the overhead microphones hanging from the low ceiling. The one with the thermostat that could take the room from ninety to forty in less time than it took to brew a pot of coffee.

Winstanley was relieved that he would be the one in the darkened adjoining observation room. He would watch and listen as Alford and Carpenter pounded the poor Negro to oblivion, doing their best to sell him a product that, in the lieutenant's words, he had no real need for. Winstanley didn't have the stomach for leveling the third degree on Jepperson for hours on end. It's not that he wasn't up to the task of forcing confessions. Far from it. But in this instance, it just didn't feel right.

* * *

Winstanley sat in the observation room awaiting Jepperson's arrival. At 9:43, he glanced through the mirror and saw Jepperson shuffle into the empty interrogation room in leg-irons and with handcuffs tethered to a belly chain. He was led in by two uniformed jail attendants. They sat him in the metal chair with its four legs bolted to the floor. Alford and Carpenter would sit across the three-by-six metal table from him. By the time it was all over, the table would be littered with photographs and evidence taken from Jepperson's car. The blinding incandescent light, with its shiny aluminum reflector, had already been turned on and imposed its concentrated beam onto Jepperson's face.

One of the jail attendants walked over to the mirror and gave a thumbs up. The two men then left the room, securing the locked door behind them.

The poor bastard hasn't even been convicted of a crime and they're treating him like a hardened felon, Winstanley thought.

Jepperson stared blankly at the mirror. Winstanley stared at Jepperson. The man's eyes were hollow abysses. His lips were nowhere to be found. His shoulders were slumped in defeat. A far cry from the jovial so-and-so back at the barbershop, shining shoes for a pittance with a big smile.

Alford had jacked the heat up so high that monster beads of perspiration cascaded down Jepperson's forehead and landed on the collar and front panel of his government-issue coveralls. The detectives would leave him there alone, let him sweat it out in solitude until Alford and Carpenter decided it was time to rock and roll. At some point during the interrogation, they would don their jackets and crank the thermostat down so low that his dripping sweat would damned near turn to icicles.

Winstanley had stationed himself in the observation room early in order to watch Jepperson's every move during his forced solitude alone in the interrogation room. Sometimes you can tell a lot about a man by how he behaves when he thinks nobody's watching. But in Jepperson's case, there wasn't much to tell. Just an old black man sitting there looking like every bit of spirit had been sapped out of him.

* * *

At 10:20 it was time for the fun to begin, as Alford put it. The three detectives had agreed that, in the world of good cop bad cop, Alford would start out wearing the white hat. After all, everybody knew Carpenter was an unabashed asshole, and that he felt a visceral animus toward blacks that would surely work in his favor. In Alford's case, on the other hand, it wasn't animus. He just thought they all were shiftless, lazy and disrespectful—and perfect suspects. At some point in the course of the grilling, when a tipping point was reached—they all three would just know when that time came—Alford would then become the asshole and seal the deal. Winstanley had seen the movie so many times he could write the script in his sleep.

Alford swaggered into the interrogation room, shoulders squared and head held high, with the self-confident carriage he'd practiced every day since, as a uniformed officer, he'd first pinned the badge to his shirt. Carpenter followed with a mimicking strut. Alford walked over to Jepperson, removed a key from his pocket, and unlocked the handcuffs and leg-irons. The handcuffs dangled from Jepperson's belly chain. The leg-irons fell helter-skelter to the floor beside his feet.

"You look like shit, man. Want some water?" Alford said.

Jepperson nodded, never making eye contact with the lieutenant.

Alford walked across the room to the small table that abutted the far wall. On the table was a pitcher of water and a stack of Dixie cups. He filled a cup with water, walked back across the room, and set it in front of Jepperson.

The black man's hand trembled as he struggled to navigate the cup's torturous journey from table to mouth. He finished off the cup in three long gulps, spilling a quarter of it down his chin and neck.

"What are you so nervous about, Sam?" Alford asked. "We're just here to ask you some questions. OK?"

Sam nodded. He looked into Alford's eyes and spoke for the first time. "Sir, I don't mean to disrespect you, but I still don't rightly know why I'm here. I haven't done anything wrong. And if I'm just here to answer questions, why was I locked up? Shackled. Shuffled in here like a jailbird?"

"It's standard police procedure, Sam," Alford replied. "I don't make the rules. I don't like it any more than you do. If I had my way, you'd be sitting there in street clothes and we'd just be talking across the table, man-to-man. Look, here's the deal. If you didn't do anything wrong, if you have nothing to hide, and if you cooperate, why, you'll walk out of here a free man and you'll be shining shoes again in no time."

"But if not," Carpenter said under his breath. He rubbed his palms together briskly as if to say *let's get on with it.* He stared into Sam's lifeless eyes. "Listen, Sam. If you don't want to go through with this, if you don't want to answer our questions, if you don't want to cooperate, you don't have to. We'll just end this right now and take you back to your cell and you can stay there forever as far as I'm concerned. It's not like we want to be here any more than you do." He looked over at Alford. "Right, Lieutenant?"

Alford didn't respond.

"Do we continue, Sam?" Carpenter said. "Or do we take you back to the lockup?"

"I'll answer your questions, sir. I got nothin' to hide from you. I promise I don't."

Alford took Sam's Dixie cup, walked across the room and refilled it.

After another fifteen minutes of softening-up banter between Alford and Jepperson, Carpenter was ready to cut to the chase. He slid Cynthia's photograph across the table. Tapped the center of the photo with his index finger. "Sam, do you recognize this female?"

Sam nodded.

"Do you know who she is? Do you know her name?"

"I know who she is. I picked her up one night and took her to Grady Stadium. Dropped her off. That was it. I didn't know her name at the time. I just knew I shine her Daddy's shoes. But then that sergeant man told me her name, that day outside in the parking lot."

"Sergeant Winstanley?"

"Yes, sir. Sergeant Winstanley."

"Her name is Cynthia Jane Hudspeth. Right, Sam? I bet you'll never forget that name, Sam, for as long as you live. So tell me. What do you remember about the night you picked her up?" Carpenter thumbed through his notes. "Let's see, it was Friday, September sixth. Remember that? So you told Sergeant Winstanley, and you just told Lieutenant Alford and me, that all you did was pick her up and take her to Grady Stadium. Is that what you're sticking by?"

"Yes, sir. Picked her up and took her straight to the football game."

"Why would a white girl just up and get in your car, Sam? Why would she do that on her own? A white girl. In a nigger's car." Carpenter shook his head. "It just doesn't make sense, Sam. There's gotta be more to it."

"Well, sir, I can't say, 'cept that she needed a ride. And she recognized me from the barbershop."

"Do you make it a habit of picking up white girls, Sam?"

"No, sir. Just that one time."

"Just that one time. Are you sure? Don't lie to me, do you understand? You lie to me and you'll regret it for the rest of your miserable life."

"I'm not lyin', sir. That's the one and only ti—"

"Sam, you didn't take Miss Hudspeth straight to the game, did you?

"I did, sir. Straight there. Dropped her off. Then I went on my way."

"You didn't take any side trips, stop anywhere along the way or anything?"

"No, sir. Tell you the truth, I was right nervous havin' her in my car, 'cause I know how it looked, bein' with a white girl and all."

"Well, Sam, I guess you should have thought about that before you picked her up. And tell me this. Why would you give her your business card?"

"I told her to call me if she ever needed a ride somewhere. Not to hitchhike. That was the only reason. I didn't mean to cause any trouble by it."

"Why did *you* care whether she hitchhiked or not?"

"'Cause I've got a boy not much younger than her. And a little girl. I wouldn't want them to do it. It's too dangerous."

"You mean dangerous, like she might get accosted by a nigger?"

"I mean somebody might try to do her harm. I never wanted to harm her…or anybody."

"Sam, what time did you pick Miss Hudspeth up that night?"

"Let's see, I think it was close to six o'clock."

"And where were you before you picked her up?"

"I guess I was at the barbershop."

"Right up 'til the time you picked her up?"

"Yes, sir. I guess so."

"You're lying to me, Sam. They told me at the barbershop that you left there around three o'clock on the sixth and didn't come back until the next morning."

Winstanley, observing it all from behind the mirror, scratched his head. *Well, that's bullshit*, he thought. *Nobody at the barbershop said Jepperson left at three that day.*

"Sam," Carpenter continued, "do you know where Murphy High is?"

"I do, sir. It's on Clifton. At Memorial."

"And how long would it take you to drive from the barbershop to Murphy?"

"I guess about five minutes."

Carpenter threw another photograph on the table and pushed it across to Jepperson. "Do you recognize this female?"

Sam shook his head.

"Are you sure, Sam? Look at it, because I think you do."

"I don't recognize her, sir."

"I don't believe you, Sam. Her name's Martha Ann Dullums. She disappeared from in front of Murphy High a few hours before you picked up Cynthia Jane Hudspeth. You know what I think, Sam? I think you picked up Martha Ann first. She told you she was to meet Cynthia later that day. You sought out Cynthia yourself and picked her up. That's what happened. Right, Sam?"

"No, sir. I've never seen that girl."

"Where did you take her, Sam? Martha Ann. Where did you keep her before you killed her in the culvert? Before you carved this..." Carpenter threw the hoodoo haint across the table. "... into her thigh. Before you left her dead body to rot in a filthy pool of water."

Winstanley knew Alford and Carpenter were taking a chance revealing heretofore unpublicized crime details to Jepperson. But he also knew that, as Alford had pounded into his head from the get-go, you never go into an interrogation with any goal other than an out-and-out full confession. Anything less would be a cropper. And if it took planting the details in Jepperson's mind so that, once they beat him down, he would regurgitate it in an admission, so be it. As far as Winstanley was concerned, there was no turning back at this point. They had their man, come hell or high water. And if they got six inches from the goal post and couldn't push the ball over, it wouldn't mean a thing. There's no *almost* for a silver-tongued huckster.

Carpenter pulled one of the Dullums crime scene photos from her file and showed it to Jepperson. "This is the kind of sickening shit people like you do, Sam. You kidnapped this poor girl, took her to the culvert, stripped off her clothes, drowned her, and carved your goddamned nigger voodoo shit into her like she was some kind of sacrificial animal. Didn't you, Sam? Tell me, did you rape her before or after you killed her?"

By this time, Jepperson was trembling like a frightened deer in the woods. Tears mixed with cold sweat drenched his coveralls.

"Are you deaf, man? Answer me, Sam. Did you rape her before or after you killed her? Did you like it, Sam? Did you like that underaged white piece of tail, Sam? Did it feel good?"

Winstanley grimaced.

"I didn't kill her. I didn't. I didn't touch her. I never seen that girl before. I never—"

"Stop right there. You're lying, Sam," Carpenter yelled. "You're a goddamn liar. We know it. And you know it. What did you do with her clothes, Sam? Where did you put her clothes? Did you burn them? Or do you hide them away somewhere as a reminder of what you did? Do you take them out sometimes and smell Martha Ann's scent on them, just to remember what it felt like?"

Jepperson looked to the floor. Shook his head.

Carpenter produced a high school photo of Patsy Boggs. "Recognize this one, Sam? She was from east of Birmingham. We recovered her waterlogged body from the Chattahoochee." He threw a crime scene photo onto the table. "Same carving, Sam. Same voodoo shit. Carved right into her thigh. Sam, you have Birmingham connections, don't you?"

Sam nodded.

"If I'm not mistaken," Carpenter continued, "you have a son and daughter in Birmingham, don't you? Tell me about your son, Sam. They say he got in some trouble with a white girl and ended up in jail. Did he learn from you, Sam? Like father, like son? Tell me, Sam, when were you last in Birmingham? When did you last see your son?"

"It's been a while, sir. I don't get over there much."

Carpenter leaned across the table. "Sam, level with me. Was your son in on this, too? He obviously has a thing for white girls. Is he into the same voodoo shit you're into?"

Jepperson sat military straight and stared into Carpenter's eyes. "Please don't bring my son into this. He didn't have anything to do with any of it."

* * *

Carpenter continued to wear Jepperson down for several hours. First about the discovery of Cynthia at Proctor Creek, comatose and hanging onto life by a thread. "So here's what I think, Sam. You would have killed Cynthia Hudspeth, just like the Dullums and Boggs girls, if somebody hadn't shown up and scared you off. Did you know that some workmen saw you drive off from Proctor Creek right before her body was found? Did you know that, Sam?"

Somebody said they saw a car drive off, Winstanley thought. *But nobody identified Sam in the car. And they said it was grey or silver and sporty. Certainly not a split pea green Hudson.*

Carpenter then brought up the knife in Jepperson's toolbox, the one with the blade that had recently been cleaned to a shine. The boy at the pharmacy who saw Cynthia Hudspeth get in a car on Glenwood Avenue the day she disappeared. The break-in at the Hudspeth house not long after Jepperson had fled Jincey Tarwater's. The tire iron that matched the gouges on the window sash. The smell of bleach in Sam's car.

The only detail Carpenter steered clear of was the nettlesome issue of the mismatched tire tracks. Winstanley thought back to what Alford had said that day in the office. *We don't want to bend the facts to fit the narrative. At least not yet.* At least not yet.

Alford's only role, so far, had been to soften Sam up and to refill his Dixie cup from time to time. His chance to sink his teeth into the black man would come, but not just yet.

Jepperson continued to profess his innocence, but it was obvious that Carpenter was succeeding in slowly breaking him down.

Like a cutter breaks a wild horse, Winstanley thought.

Carpenter looked at his watch. It was almost 3:30. "Sam, do you know what a polygraph is?"

Sam nodded.

"Well if you're as innocent as you say you are, then you'll have no problem taking one, right?"

"It's OK, sir."

Alford gave Winstanley a thumbs up through the mirror. Winstanley picked up the phone and called the Enforcement Division. "Bring the lie box and a technician down to the main interrogation room. Third floor."

A few minutes later, the technician rolled the cart into the room. The Keeler 6338 sat on the cart's top shelf. On the shelf below was a small folding chair. The technician positioned the cart alongside where Jepperson sat. He unfolded the chair, sat in front of the polygraph, and made a few initial adjustments. He then placed the cardio cuff on Jepperson's trembling left arm, the two pneumography bands around his chest and abdomen, and the galvanometers on his fingertips. Once the technician began asking questions, it took twenty-five minutes to administer the test. He then removed the sensors from Jepperson, handed the polygraph printout to Alford, packed up and left.

Carpenter resecured Jepperson's handcuffs and locked the leg-irons to a U-bolt protruding from the floor. He and Alford left the interrogation room, locking the door behind them. They entered the observation room.

"Well, Sergeant, how do you think it's going?" Alford asked after lighting a cigarette.

"About the way I expected, sir."

"We got him just where we want him. The man's sweating like a pig. And he's gonna *squeal* like a pig once I work him over. Seal the deal, right Winstanley?"

The sergeant nodded.

Alford gazed through the mirror. "Look at him sitting there. The motherfucker doesn't even know what's hit him." Then he turned to Winstanley and Carpenter. "Sergeant, call Sally the Stenographer, or whatever the hell her name is. Tell her she'll need to get here fast when we're ready for her. And Carpenter, you stay with Winstanley. I can take it from here."

Alford left and returned to the interrogation room. He left Jepperson's handcuffs and leg-irons secured. He sat directly across from Jefferson, placed his elbows on the table and rested his chin on his interlaced fingers. He stared deep into Jepperson's eyes. "Well, Sam, I have bad news."

At this point, Sam Jepperson was a shell-shocked guise of a man.

"The polygraph says you're not telling the truth," Alford lied. "Listen, Sam, I want to help you, but I can't help you if you don't level with me. Tell me what really happened, Sam."

"I am telling you the truth." Sam could barely get the words out.

"Listen, Sam, I'm going to take you, step by step, through the whole sordid thing. And as I do, I want you to think about it. And I want you to think about the hell you're going to face if you don't go along with what I'm saying. Do you want to end up at Reidsville? Do you want to die in the electric chair? Or do you want me to help you out? I can get you out of this mess, but you have to cooperate."

Alford took Jepperson through his version of what happened, with the kidnapping, imprisonment and murder of Martha Ann Dullums and Patsy Boggs, and the kidnapping and attempted murder of Cynthia Hudspeth.

Then he whipped out a picture of an electric chair. "Sam, do you have any idea what it's like to die in one of these? I've seen it with my own eyes. And I'll tell you something, Sam. I don't ever want to see it again. They'll shave your head and legs and strap you in with belts across your chest, your crotch, your arms and legs. They'll put a wet, salt-soaked sponge on your head—that's to make sure the current flows through your body real good. Then they'll put a metal skullcap over the sponge. That's one electrical connection. Then they'll put the other connection on your shaved leg. They'll blindfold you. Then they'll send two thousand volts through your body. Not once. Not twice. But three, four, five times. However many times it takes. Your body will convulse. You'll shit in your pants. Ever shit in your pants before, Sam?"

Jepperson shook his head, avoiding eye contact with Alford.

"Steam and smoke will rise from your body," Alford continued. "Foam spittle will come out of your mouth. Your eyes will pop out and rest on your cheekbones. Your skin will burn, just like bacon frying in the skillet. It may even catch on fire."

Alford put the electric chair picture away. "I decided right then and there, the one time I witnessed it in Reidsville, that I'd do whatever I had to do to stop it from happening to another man." He walked around to Jepperson's side of the table. He half-sat on the table, with one leg on the floor and the other draped over the table's edge. He hovered over Jepperson. "Sam, we can avoid all this. The evidence is clear. Any jury from here to Biloxi, seeing the evidence and the polygraph results, would find you guilty and send you to the chair. But I can keep you out of the chair. You've just got to work with me, though. You've got to trust me, Sam."

Jepperson was sobbing uncontrollably. "I don't know what to believe anymore. Who to trust anymore."

"Sam, if you don't care about yourself, think about Ruby and the children. Don't you want to live for them? Don't you want to live to see your grandchildren one day?"

* * *

At 5:45, after almost seven-and-a-half hours of interrogation, Sam Jepperson caved.

Alford called for the stenographer.

It took three rounds and an hour and a half before the salient narrative, as recorded in the written confession, suitably conformed to the facts on the ground. Before the stenographer typed out a final version in original and carbon copy. Before Jepperson applied his tremulous signature.

Then Alford made Sam speak the entire confession into a portable reel-to-reel recorder, his voice quivering with every word.

* * *

On his way home that night, Winstanley found himself waiting at the Peters Street crossing as a Southern Railway express barreled past. For the last ten hours, he had sat in a darkened room and witnessed another form of railroading.

Sam Jepperson never exercised his right to ask for an attorney. By the time the jail attendants shuffled him out of the room and back to his cell, and it all had sunk in, he must have realized and regretted the gravity of what he had just done. They all do. But it was too late.

Winstanley had a hard time believing Jepperson was guilty. At the end of the day, he didn't know. But what he did know was that the wheels of justice sometimes wobble, dither, and run off the tracks. Winstanley feared this was one of those times.

* * *

The next morning, Winstanley got to the station house at six thirty, earlier than usual. Two key pieces of information awaited him: the fingerprint analysis from the Hudspeth break-in and the list of makes and models fitting the tire size and tread design from the crime scenes.

He laid the fingerprints from the Hudspeth house side-by-side with those from Jepperson's booking. They weren't a match. Not even close.

He then scanned the list of makes and models that matched the tire tracks. Several stood out: Ford Comet, Chevy Corvair, Plymouth Valiant, AMC Rambler, Studebaker Lark... The standard for most of the Ford Falcon styles was 6.00-13, but Winstanely wasn't inclined to write it off; it wasn't uncommon for wider aftermarket tires to be put on a car. All of the listed models could easily have been outfitted with Goodyear multi-groove symmetrical herringbone treaded tires.

Of one thing Winstanley was certain, however. The tire width on Jepperson's car had come up closer to 7 inches when he got on his hands and knees and measured it in the barbershop parking lot that day. The standard tire on hardtop Hudsons was 7.10-15. Unless he was way off with his ruler, and unless Sam had decided at some point to downsize his tires, there was no way Sam's car made those tracks at the crime scenes. It just didn't make sense.

Then again, maybe there was no connection at all between the tracks and the murders. It was, after all, circumstantial.

Either Jepperson's innocent, another unfortunate casualty...wrong place...wrong time...wrong color. Or he really did do it. And if he's guilty after all, did he have an accomplice? Regardless of his innocence or guilt, the narrative has little regard for the truth.

Chapter Twenty-Five

Ruby Jepperson

October 17, 1963

RUBY JEPPERSON HAD RECEIVED THE CALL FROM SAM late Tuesday night the fifteenth. He told her he had been booked into the city jail but he didn't know any more than that.

"Have you been charged with anything?" she had asked.

"Not that I know of," he said. "They didn't tell me nothing. Just hauled me in and locked me up."

She had taken the bus to the jailhouse on Decatur Street first thing Wednesday morning and demanded to see her husband, but she was told he was not available and likely would not be for the rest of the day. She vowed not to leave until the police told her why he had been locked up but, after several hours of waiting, she finally gave up and went home.

And now it was Thursday morning, a full thirty-seven hours since they had taken her husband in. Ruby walked the nine blocks to the bus stop where Ridge and Milton Avenues intersected. When the Number 11 bus arrived, she dropped her money in the farebox and jostled her way down the aisle to the rear. She spotted the only available window seat, next to a distinguished older gentleman in a three-piece suit, holding a leather satchel. She wondered whether he was perhaps a professor at Morehouse College. The man rose and stepped into the aisle. She settled into her seat and peered out the window, not sure how to strike up a conversation other than the obvious pleasantries—good morning…nice weather we're having…how are you—without seeming out of place. And anyway, she wasn't exactly in the mood for conversation. All she wanted to do was see her husband.

The bus coursed northward on Milton toward downtown. After zigzagging through Peoplestown—right on Capitol, left on Haygood, right on Crew, left on Hatcher—the driver took a right on Washington Street and continued north. As soon as the bus had passed the Hunter Street stop, she reached up and pulled the bell cord. She got off at Decatur Street. The police station and jailhouse were two blocks east, at Decatur and Butler Streets.

She fought a rising disquiet as she dashed toward Butler Street. It was nine thirty when she pushed open the ponderous door and entered the jail lobby. The room was cold and stark. An officer stood behind what looked like a bank teller window at the far end of the room. A row of armless chairs lined the side wall to her left. She approached the officer. She handed him her driver's license and asked to see detainee Sam Gibbes Jepperson. The officer asked whether she had called ahead for an appointment. She said no. But she was determined to not leave this time without seeing him.

"Wait over there," the officer said, and pointed to the row of chairs. He called someone on the phone. She sat and waited. She gripped the handle of her purse so tight that her knuckles blanched.

After a few minutes, the officer entered the reception area through a door to the right of the teller window. He walked over to where she was sitting and thrust a clipboard at her. "Here. Fill this out," he said.

Under the metal clip was a visitor's form. A ballpoint pen dangled from a ball chain attached to the hole in the clip. Her hand trembled as she struggled to put pen to paper, paying careful attention to every stroke, every loop. When she had finished filling out the form, she walked back over to the window and handed the officer the clipboard.

"Go have a seat. I'll call you up here when they're ready for you."

After a few minutes, the officer called her back to the front of the room. She surrendered her purse and watched as the officer rummaged carelessly through its contents.

A jail attendant—a white man who looked to be no more than twenty-five—entered the room. He patted her down nonchalantly before instructing her to follow him through the door and down a long hallway.

* * *

The visitation room smelled of Pinesol and old ashes. Five open-back booths were separated by floor-to-ceiling cinder block walls painted a dull beige with dark brown plastic baseboards. The attendant directed her to a metal armchair at the second booth from the left. The fake leather on both arms was frayed and cracked; the stuffing inside the arms—what little there was of it—protruded through the cracks. A barrier, a thick glass window with a four-inch round sound port, separated her from the inmate room. Ruby rested her purse on the small off-white Formica countertop, chipped along the edges, that projected from the window toward her. She nudged aside the sandbag ashtray, half full of butts, that sat on the countertop. Multiple burn marks in the Formica suggested less than conscientious visitors.

She looked through the window at an empty chair. There she waited for what seemed like an hour before Sam was led, handcuffed and shackled, to the chair. She looked at her watch. It was ten o'clock. That hour had been less than thirty minutes. The guard fastened Sam's ankle cuff to a U-bolt in the floor, walked across the room, and leaned against the far wall. He kept his eyes on Sam and Ruby, but the expression on his face was of boredom rather than vigilance.

Ruby had never seen Sam so hollowed out and bereft. When she stared into his eyes, she saw nothing but dead black holes, sunken deep into an emotionless face. "What happened, Sam?"

"Baby, they think I killed those girls."

"What girls?"

"The ones that went missing. The ones we read about in the newspaper."

"Why, Sam? Why you?"

"I don't know, Baby. I don't know what to believe anymore."

"You don't know what to believe? You didn't do it, Sam. Did you tell them you didn't do it?"

Jepperson hung his head low. Tears cascaded down his cheeks.

"Sam, what did you tell them? What did you say?"

"They beat me down. All day. You just don't know what it was like."

"Answer me, Sam. What did you tell them? You didn't confess, did you?"

Sam nodded slightly, looking at his shoes.

"Sam, how could you? What were you thinking?"

"I don't know what I was thinking. But the lieutenant, he said he'll take care of me. He'll see that everything works out OK."

"See that everything works out OK? How, Sam? How do you think that's going to happen?"

Ruby felt a burning, bilious surge in her throat. For a moment, she thought she would have to make a run for the restroom. "Please tell me you didn't sign anything, Sam."

He looked at her with plaintive, tear-filled eyes. "Baby, I just couldn't help it."

* * *

Sam Jepperson had been booked on three counts of kidnapping, two counts of murder and one count of attempted murder. On Friday morning the eighteenth, he appeared before the Magistrate Court judge. Ruby listened as the judge found probable cause, based on Sam's confession and the testimonies of Alford and Carpenter. And a mixed bag of circumstantial evidence.

That afternoon, a grand jury of twenty-three white men indicted him on all counts.

* * *

How could Sam afford a lawyer? He and Ruby barely got by as it was. And now, Sam's income was gone. She knew she could get on full-time with the National Biscuit Company. They were hiring in the packing department. But the pay still wouldn't be enough to hire a lawyer.

* * *

That evening, Ruby took the bus home. She had arranged for Annie Turner's mother to pick Rufus and Recy up from school and feed them dinner. The sliver of a moon was high in the night sky by the time she got to the Turners' apartment, two buildings down from her own. Rufus and Recy were both sound asleep. They woke just enough to stumble home, each clutching their mother's hand.

She led them inside and put them to bed. Tomorrow morning, Saturday, she would sit both of them down and break the news about Sam. He had been gone almost a week. She had made up a story about a trip to Birmingham to visit his grown children there, but she knew the time had come to tell them the truth. Sam wouldn't be coming home any time soon, if ever. She hoped she would be able to contain herself.

* * *

The next morning the children got up uncharacteristically early for a Saturday, well before sunup. Perhaps they sensed something was wrong. Perhaps her pacing the living room floor for the past hour, rehearsing what she would say, had awakened them.

Ruby told them, still in their pajamas, to sit next to each other on the sofa. She knelt before them. Rufus took Recy's hand. His face did little to conceal his fear. For an eleven-year-old, he had a way about him. He picked up on little things—a gesture, a facial expression—that others his age would miss. He must have gotten that from her. She could read him like a book. And she suspected he could do the same with her.

"Your Daddy won't be coming home for a while." She barely got the words out before she felt her eyes well up.

Eight-year-old Recy spoke first. "Why not?"

"Is he still in Alabama?" Rufus asked.

"He isn't in Alabama." Ruby wiped her tear-salted eyes with the hem of her bathrobe. "Your Daddy's gotten into some trouble and can't be here with us."

"What kind of trouble?" Rufus asked.

"For something he didn't do, Rufus. But please don't worry. I'm going to do whatever it takes to protect him. He'll be OK. We'll all be OK. But he won't be back for a while. Please trust me. I'll take care of him…and you."

* * *

On Friday the twenty-fifth, Sam Jepperson, represented by a court-appointed public defender, was arraigned in the Superior Court in Fulton County. The judge informed him of the charges against him and advised him of his constitutional rights. Upon the advice of counsel, Jepperson entered a guilty plea. Given his confession, a conviction on a plea of not guilty would surely have resulted in a death sentence.

Jepperson was denied bail.

His confession and plea notwithstanding, he would continue to profess his innocence privately, outside the purview of the courts.

Chapter Twenty-Six
Billy Tarwater

October 27, 1963

SUNDAY THE TWENTY-SEVENTH. THE REVEREND Kilgallon was back in the pulpit. He was his same old scurrilous, brawly self that I remembered from before he had visited his old church for the revival and then came home and took ill. But something was different. I couldn't put my finger on it. He seemed, I don't know, even more peevish than he usually was. I nudged Granny Tarwater and whispered, "Granny T, is something wrong with him?"

She put her finger to her lips and said, so softly that I could barely hear her, "He's alright Binky. There's a rumor going about. He may have some news to share."

I heard a big belch from the front of the sanctuary. Even before I looked up at the choir loft, I knew Launchpad Leonard was back too. Sitting in the same spot where he always sat. I couldn't look at him without thinking about how he had seen Cynthia naked, spying on her and all.

It wasn't until the end of the sermon and after the traipsing to the chancel rail by half the congregation that the reverend asked us all to sit stone still on the hard pews and pay heed to what he had to say.

"The Good Lord has delivered justice for those poor little girls." He lifted his arms and searched the ceiling, like he was looking for something up there.

I looked too, wondering what the attraction was. But I saw nothing.

"The killer is behind bars," he continued, "never to lay a hand on an innocent child again." Then he uttered the three words that sent a shock through my body like one of those jellyfish—sea jellies my mother called them—that she used to warn us about on our once-a-year summer trips to Ormond Beach. "Samuel Gibbes Jepperson."

I grabbed my grandmother's hand and squeezed tight. I couldn't believe Sam would have gone and done it. There had to have been a mistake. There was no way he could have done those things to Cynthia and the others.

From that point on, I only half-heard what the reverend had to say. But I was jolted back to attention when he declared, in the booming flurry that I—we—all had become accustomed to, and with a flourish to the holy heavens above, that he would soon be leaving us. "The Lord Almighty, in his infinite wisdom, has called me back to my old flock. Praise Jesus."

I nudged my grandmother and whispered, "Granny T, what in the world is he talking about?"

"He's returning to where he came from, Binky. His Irondale fold as I once heard him call them."

"But why Praise Jesus? It sounds like he *wants* to leave us."

"No, Binky. It's just his way of saying he's a martyr to God's dominion. A sheep following the shepherd's command."

I shook my head. Most of the time, Granny Tarwater made sense. But sometimes, I swear, trying to decipher what she said was more than my mind could handle. I nudged her again, but this time for a Doublemint.

The reverend continued. "I leave you in the capable hands of our youth minister, the Reverend Thomas, until a replacement is called to lead you."

Granny Tarwater put her hand to her mouth, flashed an exaggerated yawn, and then buried her head in her palms. *Outlandish beats boredom any day.*

* * *

After church, back at Granny Tarwater's, I knew I had to get Dovey Mae aside, just the two of us. To talk about Shorty. But how? I couldn't pull off another *drop the jar of preserves on the cellar floor* stunt. My mother was now wise to that little trick. And I doubted a fig-gathering trip to the backyard would work again, seeing as it was the tail end of the season. But there was one thing I'd learned about myself. If I thought about it hard enough, I could always come up with a scheme.

After dinner, as usual, everybody made a beeline from the table through the living room to the screened porch. Everybody, that is, except my brother Chester, who hightailed it out the back door. The procession usually went something like this—Uncle Newell,

Aunt Lottie and Cousin Loreen first, but Uncle Newell would peel off for the bathroom, muttering something about joining us on the porch after he offloaded some freight. Aunt Lottie would snarl at him and he would say something like "Lottie, loosen up, you know I'm just a crusty old Army man." Mom and Dad would follow behind Cousin Loreen. Then Granny Tarwater. Then me.

As soon as I crossed the threshold onto the porch, I said, "Granny T, can I help Dovey Mae with the dishes?"

She swung around and looked at me like I had just touched down from Mars. "Why, Binky, what are you talking about? You've never washed a dish in your life."

"There's always a first, Granny T. And anyway, I'll dry while she washes."

"Well, suit yourself," she said, "but don't go making it harder on her. She has enough to do as it is."

"I won't make it hard on her, Granny T. I'll be the best dish dryer around. You'll see," I said, and scurried off to the kitchen.

When I walked in, Dovey Mae was at the sink with her back to me. She wore her white uniform and that rag thing wrapped around her head and tied in a big knot in the back—sometimes it was red checkered, sometimes it was cream-colored with a light green stripe along the edge like a dish towel, but today it was solid white. From behind, it looked like one of those white turbans Sahara desert people sometimes wear. Like I'd seen in *National Geographic*.

"Can I dry, Dovey Mae?"

She kept doing what she was doing. Didn't even turn around. She pointed to the towel sitting on the counter. "Grab a dishrag," she said. "I'll hand 'em to you one at a time. You wipe 'em dry and put 'em right there in a stack on the counter. Not in the dish rack. And be careful. We don't want no broken china to contend with."

"But Dovey Mae, I'm almost twelve. It's not like I'm a little kid. I won't drop the china."

"I know how old you are, Binky. I also know how you dropped that preserve jar on the cellar floor and I had to clean it up." She turned around to face me, soapy water dripping from the plate she held in her hand. "Have you ever dried a single dish in all of your eleven years?"

"Eleven-and-three-quarters. And of course I have, Dovey Mae. All the time at home," I lied. "I know what I'm doing. And I know how to be careful."

It took eight plates and two serving bowls before I got up the courage to bring up Sam Jepperson. I could tell, as soon as I mentioned his name, that it agitated her.

She stopped what she was doing, put her hands firmly on her hips, and stared out the window over the sink. "Why, that poor man didn't do it, Binky. I know that as sure as I'm standing here."

"Reverend Kilgallon said he did it. At church this morning."

"That preacher don't know nothin'. What does he know? Just that they locked a black man up. And now everybody's sayin' Shorty did it."

"Maybe Madame Ludowici could help."

For some reason, that set Dovey Mae off even more. She glared at me. "Immolene Ludowici? She don't know nothin' either. She just takes your money and tells you a bunch of flapdoodle."

I was shocked. "But Dovey Mae, I thought she was…what did you call her...your people."

"She may be my people, but she takes my people's money. And they don't have nothin' to show for it."

"What made you turn on her, Dovey Mae? What happened?"

She just shook her head. Wouldn't talk about it.

Had she gone back to visit Madame Ludowici? Had the crystal ball told Dovey Mae something she didn't want to hear? Something about Sam Jepperson, maybe?

She changed the subject. "Did you know that Sam and Ruby Jepperson have a little boy, same age as you? And a little girl. And now they's without a Daddy. Might as well be, anyway. Why, if something doesn't happen soon, that poor man's headed to the pen."

"What's his name, Dovey Mae? The boy, I mean."

"Rufus. Rufus Ambrose Jepperson. About the same height. And skinny as a rail. Just like you."

"Can I meet him sometime?"

"You want to meet him, Binky? I suppose I can fix that. But don't tell your Mama."

* * *

"Praise the Lord, she's come to," a voice bellowed from the front of the house.

Mrs. Hudspeth? It sounded like her voice. I bounded into the living room from the kitchen. Just as I did, Granny Tarwater and my mother came running in from the porch. Cousin Loreen stood at the porch door, a look of startlement on her face.

There was Cynthia's mother. Standing just inside the front doorway. The door was half open and swaying slightly on its hinges. I couldn't tell whether it was the wind from outside that was causing it to sway or a trembling from her heavy clumping.

"What do you mean, Adele?" my grandmother asked.

"She's come to. Cynthia's come to. Praise Jesus."

"Come sit a spell on the sofa," Granny Tarwater said, "but close the front door first."

Granny Tarwater sat beside Mrs. Hudspeth. "Why, Adele, are you saying Cynthia is back with us? I mean, that she's conscious again?"

"That's what I mean, Jincey. She's back with us. The Lord wanted her, but he decided it wasn't time. Not just yet. So he said to her 'You turn right around and go back home to your Mama.'" Mrs. Hudspeth took a Kleenex from her bosom and wiped her eyes. "But she can't remember a lick about what happened to her at Proctor Creek. It's like everything from the last month was just wiped away. I've tried and tried to get her to think on it, but she just shakes her head."

My mother looked over at me. "Binky, go play with the shortwave."

"But Mom, please let me stay. Just this once."

"Let him stay, Alice," Mrs. Hudspeth said. "He'll know all about it soon enough. One way or the other. And I know how much he cares about Cynthia. I'm not blind, you know."

I was grateful that my mother relented. Sometimes, usually when I least expected it, she could be alright.

"What did the doctor call it?" Mrs. Hudspeth said, and then squinched her eyes and put her finger to her lips. "Cecil would know. Retro something."

"Retrograde amnesia?" Granny Tarwater chimed in.

How does she know that? Then I remembered. Penny from *As the World Turns.* Next best show after *The Secret Storm,* to hear Granny Tarwater tell it. Penny had been in a coma. Came out of it and had amnesia. *That must be how Granny T knows about all that. It's not like she's a doctor or anything.*

"That's it," Mrs. Hudspeth said. "Retro…what did you call it?"

"Retrograde amnesia, Adele. Is Cynthia home from the hospital?"

"Oh no, Jincey. They wouldn't let her come home in the condition she's in. And I didn't want her at home anyway, what with the break-in. I'm sure the one that jimmied Cynthia's window and tore up her room was the same one that tried to kill her. The one that killed those other girls. He was looking for her. He didn't find her, but he took papers from the dining room table. Hospital papers." She peered through her eyebrows at Granny Tarwater. "You know, don't you, that she's been at Grady under an alias. They've been worried the killer could track her down there. Her made-up name is Patti Black. With an i." She looked at my mother and shook her head. "Who names their daughter Patti with an i? And Black?" Then she looked back at Granny Tarwater. "I don't know why they're still protecting her from the killer, though, what with that colored man Jepperson behind bars. I know he's the one."

It was all I could do not to shout out *No, Mrs. Hudspeth. You're wrong. Shorty didn't do it.* But I kept quiet.

Mrs. Hudspeth searched Granny Tarwater's eyes like she was looking right through her. "Jincey, why was that man Jepperson in your house anyway?"

"Why, I don't know what you're talking about, Adele," my grandmother replied. "He wasn't in my house."

"I know he was, Jincey. I saw him right there." Mrs, Hudspeth pointed to the center of the room. "With my own eyes. And didn't the police come looking—"

"Yes, they came looking. Because somebody called them. Was it you? Are you the one that called the police, Adele?"

"Why, Jincey, I wouldn't do such a thing. But you still haven't told me what he was doing here. My eyes don't deceive."

"I said, Adele..." My grandmother's voice rose. "...that I don't know what you're talking about. And did the police find anybody when they barged in here looking for him? Of course they didn't."

Back in my Binky days, I would occasionally blurt things out without thinking. But most of the time I was pretty good at kicking what I wanted to say around in my head before I uttered something I might regret. What came out of my mouth that day in my grandmother's living room was not a blurt. It was calculated. I wanted to change the subject before the two of them got into a knock-down-and-drag-out brawl right there in the living room. "Mrs. Hudspeth, can I visit Cynthia? I'll even call her Patti if I have to."

My mother glowered at me.

"Why, I think she would enjoy that, Billy," Mrs. Hudspeth replied. "It would probably do her a world of good." She turned to my mother. "Alice, Cecil and I are going to the hospital when I leave here. Could we take Billy with us? We'll take good care of him. We can drop him off at home when we get back. I promise we won't be too late, given that tomorrow's a school day."

What could my mother possibly say except Yes? After all, Mrs. Hudspeth had made the offer. And I was sure my mother didn't want to seem mean-spirited. And what with all the tension in the air, she probably said Yes just to try to settle things down some.

* * *

I didn't really know Mr. Hudspeth that well. He was never in church, except maybe for Easter and Christmas, or when Mrs. Hudspeth dragged him there for some reason. And I never saw him out in the yard, or on the street, or in any of the stores. And he never came around with Mrs. Hudspeth. But what I did learn that day on the way to the hospital was that he drove like a maniac. All the way there, I kept thinking about tomorrow's newspaper headline: THREE PEOPLE PERISH IN A CRUNCHED-UP FAIRLANE. To get my mind off his driving, I rehearsed what I would do, what I would say, when I saw Cynthia. *Patti. Her name's supposed to be Patti. And she may not even know who I am, given her condition. I'll tell her* my *name. Not in an insulting way or anything. I'll just say something like* here I am, your friend Billy. *I'll remind her of that day when I saw her hiding behind the bush. When we talked in the front yard. When she said* You take care of yourself, OK? *For sure she'll remember that. And do I really need to call her Patti when I'm in the room with her? I can call her Cynthia, can't I?*

When we finally parked at Grady and got out of the car, my knees were so wobbly that I wondered whether I would make it across the parking lot. I wasn't sure whether it was from Mr. Hudspeth's driving or my growing fear of seeing Cynthia in a hospital bed. Or a little of both.

* * *

Most of what I knew about hospitals I knew from *Ben Casey* and *Dr. Kildare.* The only time I had ever been inside of one for real was when I had my tonsils taken out. I'll always remember the ether smell when they put the mask over my face and started rolling me away to the operating room. I was out before they got halfway down the hall. *I bet when I walk through the front door that smell will come right back to me.*

* * *

Cynthia was asleep when we got to her room. There was a glass bottle hanging from a pole beside her bed. A long plastic tube ran from the bottle to her right arm. I watched the drip-drip-drip of the liquid as it rippled through the tube and into her arm. I approached the bed slowly, one tiny step at a time. My hands were sweaty. I felt a big lump in my throat. Her eyes were closed. When I touched the bed rail, her eyelids parted. She beamed. "Binky?"

She remembers me.

Mr. and Mrs. Hudspeth left me alone with Cynthia for twenty minutes or so. We talked about school. And church. And East Atlanta. She told me she didn't remember a thing about what happened to her. All she knew was what her mother and the doctors had told her. She said that when she had come out of her deep sleep, all her mother had wanted to talk about, aside from pestering her to recall things that she fought shy of, was did she see a shining light at the end of a long dark tunnel. Cynthia finally had said yes just to stop her mother from asking.

By the time her parents came back into the room, she was dozing off again. Mr. Hudspeth took me to the vending machine to get a Coke while Mrs. Hudspeth stayed in the room with her daughter. When we came back from the vending machine, Mr.

Hudspeth joined Cynthia and Mrs. Hudspeth in the room. I hung around in the hallway while they talked to the doctor.

Then we headed back to the car. All the way home I was over the moon.

She remembered me.

* * *

I tossed and turned all night. Thinking about Cynthia lying in that hospital bed. About what she'd been through. And she didn't even recall any of it. Maybe that was a good thing, seeing as she almost died. When I looked at the alarm clock and saw that it was two thirty and I was still wide awake, I knew I'd be miserable at school tomorrow. But I couldn't help it.

The alarm came way too early Monday morning. I slammed the ten-minute snooze on the Drowse Electric. *Thank you, Grandaddy Parker, for a clock with a snooze button.* I hugged my pillow and drifted back off. When the alarm sounded the second time, I crawled out of bed, wiped the sleep dust from my eyes, and dragged myself to the kitchen. The bowl of Cheerios awaited me. *Thank you, Mom.*

Even though I had to get up in what my body told me was the middle of the night but was really seven o'clock, I guess I was particularly thankful that day. To Grandaddy Parker for a Caravelle watch and a Westclox alarm clock with a snooze button. To Mom for breakfast, although it wasn't the biscuit, bacon and fried eggs I would have gotten from Granny Tarwater. And to Cynthia Hudspeth for being alive and remembering me.

* * *

Monday and Tuesday had come and gone. I'd somehow managed to get through both days without falling asleep at my desk, even though I had been through two toss-and-turn nights.

And now it was Wednesday the thirtieth, the day before Halloween. Come tomorrow evening, I would dress as a hobo, the same thing I went as every year. Chester would claim he was too old for such silliness, but he would still manage to hit every house in the neighborhood with his teenage friends, amassing as much candy as he could stuff in a pillowcase appropriated from the linen closet. And he would still demand half of mine under the threat of an Indian burn.

Wednesday was also the day Dovey Mae would come to our house to clean. I needed to get a message to her. Somehow. Without my mother knowing. I tore a page from the spiral notebook in my schoolbag and scribbled:

Dovey Mae, when can we visit Rufus?

I signed it Binky. I folded the note in a little three-inch square, wrote Dovey Mae's name on the outside, and hid it in the living room, under the porcelain planter with the African violets. She would move the planter to dust, as she always did, and see the note. My mother wouldn't.

I ran out the front door to wait for the arrival of the school bus.

Later that day after school, I rushed home from the bus stop, eager to see whether Dovey Mae had left a note for me under the planter. My mother was in the kitchen. I called out to her from the living room and asked what she was doing.

"Making dinner, Binky," she replied.

I thought I would be safe looking under the African violets. She surely wouldn't come into the living room right in the middle of cooking. I shilly-shallied all the way to the planter, ready to reverse course if she entered the room unexpectedly. I carefully lifted the planter, eager to read the note Dovey Mae would have left for me. But there was nothing there. I was crestfallen.

That night after dinner and homework, I prepared for bed. I got in bed and lay there thinking about Cynthia. And Rufus. And his Daddy stuck in a jail cell. And why Dovey Mae had ignored my message. I reached my hand under my pillow and felt something that shouldn't have been there. When lifted the pillow, there was my note to Dovey Mae, folded just as it had been when I left it for her. But she had crossed out her name and replaced it with mine. I turned on the bedside light and unfolded the note, my heart pounding. Under my message she had written the same words as before, when she had arranged for us to visit Madame Ludowici:

Nine o'clock Saturday. Car stop. Martha Brown Church.

Wednesday brought another night of tossing and turning, but this time it was in anticipation of next Saturday.

* * *

On Saturday morning, I used my tried and true alibi, Jimmy Coleman. But this time, unlike when we visited Madame Ludowici, I had made sure to warn him beforehand. As far as he was concerned, I was spending the day with him. And, just like before, my mother would be none the wiser.

I rode my Schwinn to Martha Brown Church. I stashed it in the bushes at the end of the parking lot. I sat on the stairs in front of the church, my Atlanta Crackers cap pulled down to my eyebrows, and waited.

We missed the transfer downtown and had to wait an extra twenty minutes. I didn't mind, though. I was just glad to get to spend time with Dovey Mae and to soon meet Rufus. Some people who passed by stared at us. They probably wondered what an almost-twelve-year-old white boy was doing downtown with an old black woman, but it didn't bother me in the least. They could think whatever they wanted. I was proud to call Dovey Mae my friend.

We got off the bus at the edge of Carver Homes. As we walked the several blocks to Rufus's apartment, I rehearsed what I would say when we first met. There weren't any black kids at my school. Or in my neighborhood. Even in downtown East Atlanta I didn't see many. Would we have anything in common? Would we find enough to talk about? Did he like playing army? Going to the movies? Baseball? Like me, was he never allowed to be the pitcher?

Come to find out, we had a lot in common. But a lot different too. I learned that Rufus went to a school called T.H. Slater. They didn't have any whites, just like we didn't have any blacks at Nathan Forrest. His favorite subject was science. He played army with his Carver Homes friends, but he hardly ever went to the movies. The few times he had been, he had to sit in the little balcony that wasn't big enough for more than a dozen people or so. The only baseball he got to play was on the dirt lot in the projects. He said he could pitch OK. But when he took hold of the bat, he could hit the ball all the way to Baluthahatchee. I didn't know where that was, but I assumed it was a long way off. He said he had never been to see the Crackers play. *Can you believe it?* I told him we should go together sometime.

The one thing we didn't talk about was his Daddy. I knew, if I brought it up, it would make him sad.

On the ride home, I thanked Dovey Mae for my new friend. I asked her when we could visit Rufus again. She didn't answer. Just smiled.

At Martha Brown, I retrieved my bike from the bushes and pedaled down Glenwood toward home.

How will I tell my parents that I've made a new friend? That we met secretly at his apartment in the projects? That Dovey Mae took me there? That we want to get together again soon? And that he's black?

Chapter Twenty-Seven

Ruby Jepperson

May 4, 1964

WHEN RUBY WAS YOUNG, SHE DREAMED OF TAKING A trip on a train somewhere. But she had nowhere to go and no money to get there. After she married Sam and the children were born, her dreams never waned. Perhaps, one day, they would take the Nancy Hanks to Savannah. Unlike Sam, she and the children had never seen the ocean. Perhaps, one day, they would save up enough money. Take a trip to the beach as a family. Maybe even visit where Sam grew up just outside of Chaseville. One day. But she now feared that day would never come.

* * *

Sam Jepperson would remain in jail for another six months before his trial date of May fourth. But he would never face a jury. He and his court-appointed attorney reached a plea agreement with the prosecution. He would avoid the death penalty and begin serving out a life sentence at the Georgia State Prison in Reidsville—the prison known for housing some of the most dangerous criminals in the state. The prison for lifers and death row cons. The prison where, in the forties and fifties, white volunteers were offered the chance to flip the switch for a mere $25.

Ruby vowed never to give up trying to get Sam off. She knew he was innocent. And she knew in her bones that, if he had been a white man, he never would have been arrested in the first place. And he wouldn't have been blackjacked into confessing. And he wouldn't have been convicted. And he wouldn't have ended up in a five-by-ten-foot cell in South Georgia. But she didn't know where to turn.

The last six months had been hard, but at least Sam had been jailed in Atlanta, close enough that she could visit him regularly. It had taken her two months before she got up the fiber to bring the kids along. Their first trip to visit Sam had been in the dead of winter, the Saturday before Christmas. She had bundled them up and shuffled them off, in their handmade coats, sock caps and mittens, to Ridge and Milton to catch the Number 11. At first they had been standoffish. Seeing their Daddy, handcuffed and shackled, through a thick glass window, they weren't quite sure how to react. When the awkward shock had worn off, the tears flowed.

After a while things had gotten better, and the three of them had visited a half dozen more times. But now Sam had been sent down to Reidsville, two hundred miles away. A four-and-a-half hour ride on the Greyhound. One way.

* * *

Ruby had read in the *Daily World* about a man named Hollowell. Donald Lee Hollowell. Word was he was the best Negro attorney in the city. In 1960, he had gotten Martin Luther King Jr. sprung from the same prison where Sam now found himself.

On Tuesday May fifth, she called in sick at the National Biscuit Company. She'd been on the job only six months and she knew she was taking a chance—she might not even have a job when she went in the next day—but she had to do it. She spent all morning sitting in the reception area at Hollowell's law office.

"I can't afford to hire you," she told him. "I just want you to teach me something about the law. About what I can do for Sam."

"Mrs. Jepperson, your husband agreed to a plea bargain and was sentenced," Hollowell said. "I'm not sure what I could do, short of pursuing remedies if we determined that there has been a miscarriage of justice. Any other time, I'd take on your husband's case pro bono, but I am in the throes of a run for Fulton County Superior Court Judge, and I fear I couldn't do it justice. But I'll do whatever I can to help you better understand the law and what options your husband may have going forward. We have some very good public defenders in this state, but none of them would look out for your husband's interests the way you will. At the end of each day, they set their jobs aside and go home to their own families. Their concerns are not yours. And they're a bunch of white men, with white men's sensibilities and white men's prejudices. The challenges your husband faces are great, especially given the deal he struck. You may think it was a deal with the devil. And it may very well have been. But it's the deal he and his attorney made nevertheless. Perhaps additional, mitigating evidence could be found. Or witnesses might come forward with alibis."

Mr. Batson or one of the other barbers? she thought. *Or Oscar Morgan at the Texaco? Beyond that, Sam doesn't have any friends to vouch for him.*

"Perhaps it can be proven that your husband confessed under duress," Hollowell continued. "I know the shenanigans that go on inside interrogation rooms. I'm sure the detectives lied through their teeth and pulled out everything in their bag of tricks to beat him down. But a reversal wouldn't be easy."

* * *

With Hollowell's guidance, Ruby immersed herself in an effort to better understand the nuances of felony laws in the state, citizens' rights before the law, and false confessions. And the plight of Negro men accused of committing crimes in a white man's world. After all, there was no one else to look after Sam's interests.

Every evening at nine, she would put Rufus and Recy to bed knowing they might never get to see their father again except through glass or, if they were lucky, handcuffed and shackled across the table in a guarded visitation room. After they were tucked in, she would sit at the Singer for two, three, maybe four hours working through her side-hustle piecework, straining through sodden eyes to guide the fabric under the presser foot. When she'd had enough for one day, she would set her work aside, sink into the sofa, and crack open one of the law books Mr. Hollowell had loaned her. At some point in the early morning, her lids would grow heavy and she would fall asleep with an open book in her lap.

Before the break of dawn each morning, after dropping the children off at the Turners'—Annie's mother had been a godsend, offering to get them to school each day—Ruby would take the bus to the National Biscuit Company. She was grateful that they had kept her on. Was it out of pity? Christian compassion? All she knew was that, without the steady income, she and the children would have ended up in the poorhouse.

She vowed never to give up on trying to get Sam off. She knew he was innocent. But every effort she made, every corner she turned, she hit a dead end. The lawyer who had convinced Sam to cop a plea showed no interest in revisiting the case. She sought out several Negro attorneys in the city who had been referred by Mr. Hollowell. But none of them wanted to take it on.

She was heartened when, on July third, she picked up the morning *Constitution* and read the headline: JOHNSON SIGNS CIVIL RIGHTS BILL. A year and two weeks after President Kennedy—God rest his soul—had proposed it. Her heart pounded as she scanned the article. The new law forbid discrimination in voting. In schools. In public establishments. In employment. Might it also apply to a black man in an interrogation room manned by crooked white detectives?

But her hopes were dashed time and time again. Days, weeks, months passed and Sam still sat at Reidsville. Mr. Hollowell was right about it being an uphill battle. She wondered if she would ever find herself at the top of the hill.

* * *

Ruby felt a wave of mixed emotions when, in 1966, the court ruled in Miranda v. Arizona that a suspect must be advised of his Fifth Amendment right against self-incrimination and his Sixth Amendment right to counsel before police could interrogate him. Any admission of guilt prior to such advice couldn't be used against him.

Then, on June 29, 1972, the court struck down all existing state laws allowing capital punishment.

* * *

If only I could have gotten to Sam before those detectives spent the whole day strong-arming him. He might never have signed that paper.

If only Sam's fateful run-in with the law had occurred three years after it did, he might never have confessed to crimes he swore privately that he didn't commit. If the Miranda law had been in place, he might have demanded a lawyer before he spoke.

If only the Supreme Court had already suspended capital punishment, he might not have felt compelled to enter a guilty plea to avoid the electric chair.

If only…

PART TWO

Chapter Twenty-Eight
Billy Tarwater

September 15, 1980

SEVENTEEN SUMMERS HAD COME, AND SEVENTEEN summers had gone, since that day in '63 when Dovey Mae first took me to visit Rufus. Seventeen long, sweltering, sodden summers. And for the duration, Sam Jepperson had languished in a dank, begrimed five-by-ten at Reidsville. And Rufus and Recy had grown up fatherless—at least they may as well have been.

My certainty of Sam's innocence had never waned. And for sixteen years I had wanted to see him somehow exonerated and freed. But life gets in the way. College. Marriage and a career. Children. And the best of intentions become best-laid plans.

As far as the authorities were concerned, the case had been closed long ago. The killer was behind bars. Justice had been served. And that was that.

But I had never forgotten. And I hoped that, one day, a reckoning would occur and Sam would get his due reward—his get out of jail card.

* * *

The call came through to the city desk at 8:25 Monday morning. Nineteen eighty. The fifteenth of September. I took it. A fourteenth child, Darron Glass, had gone missing.

Twelve boys and two girls had disappeared over a fifteen-month period. Most bodies had been recovered. Some had not. A pall hung like a shroud over the city of one-and-a-half million.

Every time a call came in about a missing child—or a body found in an abandoned school building, or a vacant lot, or a briar-covered patch of woodlands—my heart sank. Memories welled up. Of Martha Ann Dullums. Of Patsy Boggs. Of Cynthia Hudspeth. If those construction workers hadn't shown up at Grove Park, Cynthia would probably be dead just like the others. The odd thing was that she had been spared any memory of what happened that day. That was probably good for her. But bad for any hope of finding the one who really did it.

* * *

I hadn't always wanted to be a newspaperman. But it was the experiences when I was an eleven-year-old skinny, spindle-shanked boy—going on twelve, as I was always quick to point out—that set me on my path. Waiting for the paperboy to throw the newspaper into the front yard. Removing the rubber band, unfolding the paper and scouring it, page-by-page, for news of the missing girls. My heart hammering.

Seeing the reporters first-hand, with their notepads and cameras, who gathered at the top of the hill that day when we hid behind the briar thicket at the Van Vleck culvert.

Reading about the Birmingham church bombing. The anti-Castro mob in New York. The Bears upsetting the Packers. Even imagining a reporter composing an article beneath a jaw-dropping headline—Three People Perish in a Fairlane—as Cynthia's father careened down the street.

It was all so exhilarating to this wide-eyed kid from East Atlanta.

In the summer of '74, fresh out of college with a degree in journalism and a minor in pre-law, I had shown up unannounced at the newspaper office. I landed a job, first doing mundane tasks, assisting reporters and junior editors, running errands—hell, I would have scrubbed the bathroom floors if I had to—whatever it took to move the ball forward. After four years, I ended up working the city desk, the job I had wanted all along.

* * *

Four months before I had turned up looking for a job, Reg Murphy, the *Constitution* editor, had been kidnapped. A dread came over me when I first read about it. Murphy embodied the qualities I revered in a newspaperman. Tough but eminently fair-minded. A big city editor who had honed his skills at a small town paper, the *Macon Telegraph*. Willing to speak out for what he believed in, popular opinion be damned. He took a stand against the Vietnam War when others were unwilling to speak out. Jimmy Carter called him one of the city's most distinguished citizens. I feared for his safety. I grieved for his wife. For his two teenage daughters.

The *Constitution* paid a $700,000 ransom. A member of a right-wing militia group was caught, the money was recovered, and Murphy was released. He described it as the most frightening experience of his life, wondering whether he would make it out alive.

* * *

In my mind, a seventeen-year thread coursed through time connecting these disparate events. The '63 kidnapping of the three girls—with two of them ending up dead. The *Constitution* editor's abduction in '74—wondering whether he would live to tell of it. The serial kidnapping and murder of children, all black and between the ages of seven and fourteen—with no end in sight.

The city's a dangerous place. I know that. But damn it, shit like this just shouldn't happen. Not to a thirteen-year-old girl. Not to a black kid from the hood. Not to a grown man. It can't go on. Not in a civilized world.

* * *

Any newshound worth his salt will end up most days at Marnie's Tavern, downing a brewski or two—maybe more—unwinding after a long day of spirited word herding. The West Peachtree route from the newspaper office to The Belmont cuts right by the bar, which makes it easy for me.

The place has been around for damned near as long as I've been kicking. Dovey Mae would have said since Jesus was born. And it hasn't changed a whit since I walked through the front door on my eighteenth birthday and ordered my first legal pint. The thing that hits you when you enter for the first time is the perennial cloud of fuggy blue-grey smoke that cloaks the air, suffocating its quarry like a garotte. You get used to it, though, and before long, it's not even there. The mahogany bar, salvaged from the downtown Cue and Brew Billiard Hall, a favorite among the local Fast Eddy crowd until a midnight vice raid got it shuttered for good, is gently gouged and chafed from decades of use. The wagon wheel chandeliers look like something from a Western movie. Portraits of Franklin Roosevelt, John and Robert Kennedy, and Marnie Ryan—nee ó Dubhghaill—hang on the wall behind the bar. Signed dollar bills are pinned to the other walls. Mine's there somewhere, but for the life of me I couldn't tell you where I pinned it, after one too many, on an evening long ago.

I sit at the same stool every day. At the end of the bar farthest from the front door. Where I can stare up at the portrait of FDR. My Marnie's buddies call it the Billy Roost. I've told Conor Ryan, the owner, on more than one occasion that he may as well put an engraved plaque on the bar rail right there:

> HERE SITS WILLIAM "BILLY" TARWATER. HE DRINKS.
> HE PONTIFICATES. HE GOES ON AND ON ABOUT HIS LADY.

She waits patiently at home. The love of my life. She has this thing she's started doing most Fridays, when the kids go off to spend the night with their grandparents. She calls it our adult play date. She cooks a big ethnic meal. Maybe Indian, Thai, Greek, Mexican—every week is different. She decorates the house with pitch-perfect ornamentations—one time I came home to a living room artfully reconstructed as a Persian hookah lounge. Then she dresses in costume and waits near the door for my arrival. It's the damnedest thing I've ever seen. And hell if I know where she gets all the decorations and getup, or when she has time to do it. But she manages to pull it off. It helps that she's somehow finagled out of having to teach on Fridays.

* * *

Friday, the nineteenth, I was sitting at the Billy Roost when I looked up and saw him walk in. We hadn't seen each other in a year.

"Rufus," I called across the room.

He looked up and headed my way, grinning ear to ear. "Billy, it's been too long."

We embraced right there in the middle of the bar. The stool next to mine was occupied. And anyway, we needed a place where we could talk unbothered by prying eyes and pricked ears. I motioned toward the door leading to the adjacent room—Conor calls it the Sidecar.

* * *

While I had been slogging away toward a degree in journalism at Georgia, Rufus was at Georgia Southern on a United Negro College Fund scholarship. He had chosen to apply there to be close to his father, an hour away by local Greyhound. He was fortunate that the student body had finally been integrated five years before he started there, but a full eleven years after the Supreme Court's *Brown v Board* ruling. The Deep South had never been in a particular hurry to 'amalgamate.'

He had stayed in Statesboro after graduation. But we kept in touch and got together as often as we could. Over the years, I had driven down several times and collected him in Statesboro, and we had gone to Reidsville to see his father. On a couple of occasions, his mother had ridden down with me, and the three of us visited Sam together.

Recy still lived in Atlanta, but not in the projects anymore. She worked as a secretary for Atlanta Life and lived in an apartment on Luckie Street. She had never married.

Ruby remained, alone, in the same Carver Homes apartment, waiting for the day—God willing—that Sam would somehow be back with her. Early on, not long after I came back to Atlanta from Athens, I would occasionally visit her. Take her barbecue from Harold's or a bucket of KFC. "Stay a spell," she'd say. I always would.

* * *

Rufus and I took an unoccupied table in the far rear corner of the Sidecar. The waitress came over. I held my half-full glass in the air. "I have mine," I said, "but my friend here needs a tall one." I looked at Rufus. "What'll it be?"

He ordered a Miller.

I leaned in, elbows on the table. Rested my chin on my interlaced fingers. "How's your Dad, Rufus?"

"He's getting by—one day at a time. But it's my mother I'm worried about now. That's why I'm in town, Billy."

"Your mother? What wrong?"

"She had an accident. At work. Lost a finger. Another one's mangled pretty bad."

"How?"

"Pinch point on a packing line. It was quick. By the time she realized what was happening, it was too late."

"She's still at Nabisco, right?"

"No. She left there a couple of years ago. She's at a small food processor on the southside. Was, I should say. They let her go. Said she was negligent. It was all her fault. They said they'd pay her medical bills, but that's it. They didn't care that somebody had come along and removed the pinch guard. Otherwise it wouldn't have happened."

"Rufus, they can't do that, fire her I mean. Not anymore, anyway. And she's due compensation for what happened. This isn't the thirties."

"I think we have a solid case. We're talking to somebody. Hollowell recommended them. Remember him?"

"I do. He's a legend to black folk. And I remember hearing your mother speak highly of him."

"Listen, Billy, I'm moving back. Recy's here, but my mother's going to need a lot more help than she can provide. You know, with one finger gone and another half-gone, my mother's not going to be able to sew on the side anymore. I'll move in with her for a while. Help her out. Pay the bills. I can teach snot-nosed fourth graders here as well as I can in Statesboro."

"How old is your mom, Rufus? Forty-five?"

He thought a minute. "Close. Forty-six."

"Rufus, I'm here to help any way I can. You know that." I took a big swig before going on. "It may not be the best time to bring this up, with what you're going through with your mother, but I'd like to talk to you about something else."

"Lay it on, Billy. You know you can talk to me about anything."

"For a while, your mother seemed dead set on getting your dad acquitted. But things just sort of died."

"I know. She tried hard. Mighty hard. But everywhere she turned, she hit a brick wall. I helped her as best I could. I'm not saying we've given up. It's just that we got to the point where we didn't know what to do next."

"I understand. But you know that I have always known he didn't do it. You know he didn't do it. I have newspaper connections now, access to information, ways and means that we couldn't even imagine before."

"What are you saying, Billy?"

"I'm saying I'd like to get the case reopened. To try to get him out. Do you remember me talking about a guy named Gary?"

"Sure. His dad's a detective?"

"Was. Gus Alford died over ten years ago. Massive heart attack. Happened right on the sidewalk in front of the Krispy Kreme on Ponce. They rushed him to Georgia Baptist. He never left there. Gary followed in his father's footsteps and is a cop now. Not a homicide detective. Went the larceny route. But I think he might be able to help. I haven't seen him in years, but he's coming over to visit soon."

A big smile came over Rufus. "That would be great, Billy."

Rufus would give anything, do anything, to see his dad freed. I knew that. But I didn't want to give him false hope.

"There's a hitch, though," I said. "You know as well as I, better than I, that a lot of bad shit goes on with the police. *Not on the up and up* shit. The way they railroaded Sam is a case in point. They'll just as soon pin a crime on the next black dude that comes along as do their jobs the way they're supposed to. 'Lock that no-good swinging dick up and book him.' I can hear them saying it right now. 'Done deal. Job done. Case closed.' It was really bad back in the sixties. But how could we have known? We were eleven, for Christ's sake. You would think, in 1980, that we'd be way beyond that. But we're not. Things may never change…at least not in our lifetimes."

"Don't I know it, Billy. My people live it every day."

"Here's my problem. I suspect Gus Alford wasn't the best guy around. I bet he was the ringleader behind Sam's railroad job. I don't know how I'm going to bring Gary along…and convince him to work with me. Gary idolized his father, after all. I've got to be careful how I frame things. Gus can't be the bad guy."

* * *

I left Marnie's more convinced than ever that I had to do something to get Sam out. Clear his name. And Rufus was behind it a hundred percent. Said he'd do whatever he could to help me.

I swung out of the parking lot and hung a left onto West Peachtree. I sat at the red light at Ponce, eager to get home. I turned right on Fifth and then left into The Belmont courtyard. I parked and headed to the entrance. Mrs. Haywood, our neighbor one floor down, entered just ahead of me. We got on the elevator together. She got off at 3. I continued to 4.

I inserted the key in the lock in anticipation. I turned the key and eased the door open.

Cynthia was standing just inside in a bright green Pa'u, Mai Tai in hand.

Chapter Twenty-Nine

Billy Tarwater

September 20, 1980

I HEARD THE ELEVATOR DOORS OPEN. K'CHAKA. AND close. Scrrr. Several seconds passed. There was a tapping against the marble floor in the elevator lobby. Like a metronome. It grew louder. And then it stopped.

The knock on the door was light. So light that I couldn't be sure it wasn't at the apartment next door. It was followed by a more assertive rapping. It sounded like metal hitting against the wooden door rail. Perhaps a large ring. Or maybe it wasn't metal—just an aggressive knuckle.

I opened the door slowly.

He stood imperious at the threshold. He was a big man. Not particularly tall. But stout. His open-collar shirt pulled away at the buttons. He wore a blue windbreaker. And a Braves cap, slightly frayed along the visor edge. He held a wooden walking stick—it looked like birds eye maple—with a brass wolf's head. At first I didn't recognize him through his salt-and-pepper beard. His eyes were hidden behind horn-rimmed glasses with dark brown, almost opaque, lenses. *Is he blind?* I thought. But his cane wasn't white. He had a blue sapphire Murphy High class ring on his right hand.

"Gary?" He was thirty minutes early. But that was OK. "Come in." I motioned to one of the two armchairs near the window.

He halted across the room and sank into the seat cushion. He leaned his cane against the chair, with the handle end wedged between the cushion and the arm. The other end projected at an angle at least two feet across the floor.

"Would you like coffee?" I asked. "Tea?"

"Coffee. Black. That would be great, Billy."

"You got it. Back in a second," I said. I was careful not to trip over the cane on my way to the kitchen.

I poured two mugs of fresh-brewed dark brown arabica. The tiny pools of oil floating on the surface were a sure sign of dark roast perfection. If there's one thing I know, it's my coffee. I took in the aroma of nuts roasting on a campfire on a cool autumn day. I wished I could be anywhere at the moment except in midtown Atlanta. Some conversations are easier than others.

I returned to the living room, careful again not to trip over Gary's cane. I placed the mugs on the table between the chairs and sat down. "How long has it been, Gary?"

"I don't think we've seen each other since we went off to college. What was that, seventy?"

"That sounds about right. It's funny how people can be so close in high school and then after graduation they just drift apart. It's great to see you after all these years."

"Same here." Gary took a big gulp of coffee. Wiped his mouth with his shirt sleeve.

"I could have predicted you'd follow in your dad's footsteps," I said. "I know you always looked up to him."

"He was a good man." Gary stared out the window as if he were miles away. Then he looked back at me. "Billy, you were the smart one, going off to the university and all. Becoming a big newspaperman. I see your name in the paper. But me? I never was the studying type. You know that. Two years of community college. Associate's degree. That was it. Then off to the police academy. Krispy Kreme school." He sniggered. "And the rest is history, like the man says."

His Krispy Kreme joke surprised me, seeing as his dad—his hero—had given up the ghost right in front of the one on Ponce de Leon. Best not to bring that up, though. "But you had street smarts. That counted for something. I'm sure that helps you be a better cop."

"Yeah. Without that, I doubt I'd have made it."

I looked down at the cane. At his left leg, slightly smaller than the right. "Gary, what happened?"

"What do you mean?"

"The limp. The cane."

"Oh, that." He acted as if it was nothing. "Let's just say I had a little run-in with a coupla semi-wadcutter hollowpoints. Line of duty. Got me in the upper leg. Chest." He unfastened the top two buttons of his shirt. Pulled his shirt panel to the side to reveal a five-inch scar across his left pec. "Still have some dead lead in there that they couldn't get out. They tried, but it was too close to my ticker. I'm surprised you didn't hear all about that, being a city desk man."

"When did it happen?"

"Late '76. Almost four years to the day after they first pinned the silver badge to my chest."

"Somehow I missed it. I was a lowly grunt back then. I was probably fetching coffee for the boss when you were out there putting your life on the line. I didn't join the city desk until '78. Anyway, I'm so sorry you had to go through what you did."

"It's OK, Billy. I'm here, aren't I?" A slight grin came over him. "And about the leg. At least I didn't get my gimp on the Siegfried Line like you that time."

"That was Jimmy Coleman, not me," I replied.

"Oh, that's right. Chickenheart Jimmy. I swear, his own shadow could set him off. And that Nick, he used to give Jimmy so much shit about it. Chicken*shit* Jimmy."

"Hell, Gary, Nick used to give us *all* shit."

"You're right. Now, where was I? Oh, yeah. When I took the pops in my leg and chest, I fell to the pavement. Cracked my head open." He grabbed the temples of his glasses and pulled the frame down the bridge of his nose. He peered over the rims. "Somehow, that blow to the head messed up my eyes. Can't stand the bright light anymore. Gives me migraines."

I considered bringing up Jimmy and Nick again but I thought better of it. Jimmy had come up short in the Nam lottery. They called only ninety-five numbers when our year came up, and his was one of them. Shipped out of Fort Ord in '72. Died at the

Battle of An Lộc in April of that year. Poor sucker. And Nick? Last I heard, he'd fallen in love with an Indiana girl, married her, and was selling aluminum siding in Terre Haute.

Gary and I made small talk. He told me he'd married a girl he met at the community college. "A nice Southern lady from Rome," he said. "Georgia, that is." She was an assistant manager at Payless. They were working on having a kid, but things hadn't panned out yet. His mother had stayed in the same house in East Atlanta after his father died, even though white flight had damned near driven all the old owners out of the neighborhood.

I told him about my dad dying in a car wreck three years ago. He said he'd heard about it. That he was sorry. My mom had remained in our old house, too, steadfastly refusing to leave "just because the whole damned east side's going to the dogs." Her words.

"I heard you got hitched to that girl Cynthia Hudspeth," Gary said.

I nodded.

"An older woman." Gary's grin grew. "Good catch, Billy."

"I'm a lucky man, Gary."

"Any rug rats?"

"Two. Billy Junior's three. Adelaide's two."

I had contacted Gary by phone the week before and asked him to drop by, but I didn't tell him why. Now, I figured it was time to go ahead and broach the subject. "Speaking of Cynthia, do you remember when those girls were killed back in '63?"

"Do I remember? Of *course* I remember. How could I forget? We were there right after they found the first body. And my Dad was all over the case. They ended up catching that black guy and sending him off to the pen. No-good son of a bitch."

I tensed. Braced myself. Watched Gary's body language for what I thought might be the right opening. But I couldn't wait. I blurted out, "He didn't do it."

"What do you mean?"

"The black man. Sam Jepperson. I'm convinced he didn't do it."

I explained to Gary how I'd gotten to know Rufus. How we'd spent time together. How we'd visited his father at Reidsville together. How I'd gone over all the whys and wherefores of the case with his mother.

Gary removed his glasses. Stared at me with steel eyes. "What are you saying, Billy? That was my father's case. Are you accusing him of sending the wrong man to the pen?"

"I'm not accusing your father of anything, Gary. Your father was a good cop." *Dissembling isn't my strong suit, but I can do a pretty good job of it when I have to.* "It's just that, when I look at all the evidence, at least what I've been told—what I've been privy to—it just doesn't add up. I'm not saying anybody did anything wrong, at least not intentionally. And anyway, your father didn't send him to prison. A judge and jury did that."

"So why are you telling me this, Billy?"

"I'm telling you this because I'm planning to get the case reopened."

"Wait a minute. Your own wife was almost killed by Jepperson, wasn't she? And now you're telling me you want to get him off? After all this time? Man, are you crazy?"

"I'm telling you that I owe it to Sam Jepperson if he's innocent, as I believe he is. To Cynthia and those two dead girls. To their families. To Rufus and his sister and mother. I owe it to all of them to see justice done."

"Why you, Billy? Why do you owe anybody anything?"

"Because if I don't do it, nobody will. And I'm in a position as a newspaperman to do what others might not be able to, even if they tried. I know how to dig. I know how to get people to talk. I can get to the bottom of things. But I need inside help."

"Billy, I'm larceny. Not homicide. And anyway, I'm swamped right now. I've got three break-ins from last night alone. It's like the whole town got liquored up at once and went crazy. As soon as I leave here, I'm heading over to West End to interview a package store owner with a shattered, boarded-up plate glass window and a shortage of gin. Surely you're not asking me to help. Hell, you're the newspaperman. You know the guys in homicide as well as I do."

"I know, Gary. That's not what I'm asking for. I know who to talk to in homicide. I know who'll work with me. Who'll help me sort through the evidence. The police reports. Interview people who are still around. That's not the kind of help I need from you."

"OK. What do you need from me, then?"

"Remember when you and Nick went to your house back when the girls were killed and looked at those crime scene photos? And you wanted me to join you, but I said I couldn't?"

"I remember that."

"Well, do you think those photos are still around? Maybe in your mother's attic? Or in a closet somewhere? And another thing. I know detectives back then used to keep all kinds of records at home. Do you think there's any paperwork stored away somewhere that might help me build a case? I need to put my hands on anything and everything I can find. If I can put a good enough story together, I'll turn it over to the D.A."

"A good enough *story*? Are you serious, Billy? You want to cobble together a *story*?"

"You know what I mean, Gary. We go way back. Will you help me? As a friend?"

* * *

I hadn't said a word to Cynthia about my plan. But I knew I had to. Sooner rather than later. I looked at my watch. It was noon. She should be home from Agnes Scott by one. The weekend to ourselves was half over.

I'll sit her down. Lay it all out for her. Tomorrow.

I poured myself another coffee.

I walked to the window and gazed across the courtyard. Three girls—maybe nine or ten years old—were playing hopscotch on the sidewalk.

Chapter Thirty

Cynthia Tarwater

September 20, 1980

THE ODYSSEY JOUNCED ACROSS THE TRACKS AT THE McDonough Street crossing. Cynthia took a left onto West Howard Avenue. There were faster routes home. But she preferred the cutover through Lake Claire and the drive westward down Ponce de Leon and through the succession of verdant parks. Dellwood. Shadyside. Virgilee. Springdale. For as long as she could remember, she had heard people speak reverently about Atlanta's love affair with her trees. Her parks. Her abundant swaths of green. Cynthia's near-daily drive from Agnes Scott to Midtown embodied this devotion as clearly, as succinctly, as any other. The bounteous oaks, which would soon be showering the city with reds and oranges and yellows, lived in solidarity with stately American colonial homes and majestic granite and marble churches. Just past Springdale, outside the Hare Krishna Temple on the left, men and women in salmon dhotis and saris chanted their call-and-response kirtan.

But it wasn't just the idyllic stretch of Ponce from East Lake to Moreland Avenue that appealed to Cynthia. At Highland, two blocks past Moreland, the backdrop underwent an abrupt change. The proud oaks and august homes, the manicured lawns and tree-lined byways, the trappings of grace and class, gave way to another world. Gritty. Coarse. Hard-boiled. Street-corner vendors hawking porn mags and cheap thrills. The twenty-four-hour Majestic Diner, serving up corned beef hash at three in the morning to hustlers and pimps and all-night partiers. The Plaza Theater, serving up a different kind of fare, X-rated flicks with names like *Teeny Buns* and *Smoke and Flesh*. The Clermont Lounge titty bar. The Ponce Krispy Kreme, dishing out midnight sugar fixes to cops and crooks alike, sitting side-by-side on two-foot-high swivel stools. What used to respectable homes and storefronts had given way to flophouses and head shops.

My god, Billy's rubbed off on me. I'm thinking like a city desk man now.

Cynthia found intrigue in the transition—she called it her Highland Passage—from one foot there to one foot here. Light to dark. Yin to yang. And she liked it.

* * *

Just after the right onto Peachtree, she glanced up at the Fox Theater marquee to her left:

> ALVIN AILEY DANCE THEATER - LAST PERFORMANCE TONIGHT
>
> JIMMY BUFFETT - COMING SOON - SEPT 27.

She never got the Buffett mania. Sure, more days than not, she wouldn't mind escaping to Margaritaville. Who *would* mind? But he was just a little too glib for her taste. Now, Alvin Ailey, on the other hand—she had been enthralled by his dance company ever since she and Billy went to see him at the Civic Center back in February of '75. Billy was fresh out of college. She was two-and-a-half years into grad school. It was their first date, of sorts, but for reasons that she still didn't completely understand, he had invited Rufus along. He said it was because he thought Rufus would enjoy the black dancers. Perhaps. But she wondered at the time whether it was really because Billy was shy and needed emotional support. *Who knows? But on a first date?*

As soon as Billy had gotten to Athens in '70, he had sought her out. Pursued her relentlessly. She was a junior at the time and would go on to Emory graduate school two years later. At first, she couldn't countenance dating Binky from the neighborhood. But he persisted until, finally, she gave in and agreed to go out with him.

Less than two years after that first date, they were married. She was wrapping up grad school. And pregnant.

* * *

She pulled into The Belmont and parked. As she walked across the courtyard, she saw Billy looking out the window. He waved. She waved back.

Billy Jr. and Addie were staying over the weekend with her parents, which always gave her an unnerving mix of elation and angst. On the one hand, she and Billy had the weekend to themselves. On the other, her mother would, true to form, do her best to indoctrinate both kids with crazy evangelical apocalyptic

BS. It would take at least two days to detox them when they came home. Addie had even taken to prancing around the apartment with a ring of plastic toy keys hanging from a length of yarn tied around her waist. She would shake them and gabble, "Tees ta da teendun." Cynthia had, on more than a few occasions, implored her mother to dispense with the preachifying around the kids. But to no avail.

Cynthia took the elevator to the fourth floor. The door to the apartment was ajar. Just past the threshold, she scanned the living room but didn't see Billy.

He strode around the corner out of the kitchen. He had somehow managed to slip into her green Pa'u. He had an ear-to-ear grin and a Mai Tai in each hand. He extended one of them, the one with the cocktail umbrella, in her direction. "Here, beautiful. This one's for you. Now, where did we leave off?"

* * *

Sunday morning, she awoke to the aroma of fresh coffee wafting through the apartment. And the nutty scent that butter gives off when it melts in the pan and turns to a golden brown. Did she like these smells? Usually. Did they call forth a hankering? Not this morning. She'd just as soon go back to sleep.

She stumbled into the bathroom and popped a couple of Extra Strength Tylenols with tepid tap water before shambling to the kitchen.

The table was decked out with an ambrosial array of buttermilk pancakes, strawberries, fresh-whipped cream, bacon. Her stomach churned. *That's my Billy.* She sat in her usual spot. The *New York Times* sat undisturbed on the corner of the table. Billy preferred the Sunday *Times* over his own newspaper. He said it was his weekly chance to see what the big guys were doing. He would read it like a newshound, sizing up every word, every jot and tittle. Professional judging professional. Like she imagined a deadheading airline pilot would do.

He sat across from her. He unfolded the paper, pulled out the Book Review section and handed it to her. *He knows me well.* He took the Main section, held it with both hands and joggled it the way he always did, as if he were shaking the ply out of it.

* * *

They had finished breakfast—she had managed to make a respectable dent in the repast he'd heaped on her plate—and were on their second cup of coffee when he double-folded the paper, set it aside, and said, "We need to talk."

The tone of his voice startled her. "Is something the matter?"

"Nothing's wrong, Cynthia. It's just that I've been meaning to bring something up."

He ushered her into the living room. They sat in the armchairs by the window. He fidgeted with the edge of his bathrobe. Finally, after two or three minutes of dithering and throat clearing, squirming and shifting, he spoke. "Cynthia, it's about what happened back in '63."

She suspected as much, what with all the time Billy had spent with Rufus. His past trips to visit Rufus's father. His conversations with Rufus's mother. But Cynthia wasn't in any mood to dredge up the distant past. "Billy, you know how hard it is for me to talk about it. I wish I *knew* what happened in '63. It's a pitch-black abyss. I can't tell you how many times I've tried to remember something...anything...but it never comes."

"I know. I wish you could, but the most important thing is that you're here. If it hadn't been for those workers—"

"Billy, this is so hard for me to think about. I could have died like the others. I almost did. But I can't recall a thing. It's as if, in a twisted way, it never happened. Seventeen years is a long time. I've put it behind me."

"But Sam Jepperson hasn't been able to put it behind *him.*"

She explored Billy's misty eyes. The downturned corners of his lips. "You're convinced he didn't do it, aren't you?"

"One hundred percent," he said. "I've been convinced from the day Virlyn Kilgallon uttered his name from the pulpit. Actually from the day I saw Sam cowering in my grandmother's cellar. Although at that time I had no idea why he was on the lam. All I knew was what Dovey Mae told me, that he was running from the man for something he didn't do."

"And you believed Dovey Mae? Your grandmother's maid?"

"I just knew. But I can't tell you how I knew. How could an eleven-year-old kid figure something like that out?"

"You just knew. What you're really saying is you had a hunch. That's what it really was, right? A hunch."

"OK. Perhaps it was just a hunch."

"And it's more than a hunch now? More than loyalty to your friend Rufus? To Ruby?"

"A lot more than that, Cynthia. You know that I've spent at least half of these seventeen years trying to make sense of it all. Poring over the evidence. The facts on the ground…at least as I understand them. And I just can't give it up. I lie awake at night thinking about Sam wasting away in a grimy cell in a godforsaken hellhole of a town for something I'm convinced he didn't do."

"And now you want to be the hero. His redeemer."

"I want to do what's right."

"And out of a million and a half people in this city, the burden falls on *you* to do what's right."

"Gary Alford came by today, and I'll tell you what I tol—"

"Gary Alford came by? He just happened to be in the neighborhood?"

"I called him last week. Said I'd like to meet with him. I didn't say why. So he dropped by. We talked for almost two hours. I'll tell you what I told him. I know how to dig. To get to the bottom of things. To ferret out the truth. That's my stock in trade. That's why I'm a newspaperman."

"You're also a husband. And the father of a toddler and a preschooler. And the son of a widowed mother who needs you more than ever...God knows your brother Chester won't be there for her. How much time do you think there is in a day?"

He reached across the table. Took her hand in his. "Cynthia, this is something I have to do. And I need your help. I can't go it alone."

* * *

Cynthia went to bed that night knowing she couldn't stop him. It wasn't even worth trying. He was dead set on dredging up something she had long since put behind her.

There was really nothing for her to put behind, though. The last thing she remembered from before the erasure, as she'd taken to calling it, was leaving the drug store by the front door. Heading down Glenwood past Harry's. A car following her. When she stopped, it stopped. When she went, it went. What kind of car? She couldn't recall. Just a car. *Car. It may as well just be a word plucked out of the dictionary. Without form or substance. Nothing more.*

The fact that she could remember that little detail, but no more, puzzled her. She knew it had a name. Localized psychogenic amnesia. She had spent hours in the college library reading about it. Reading expert opinions. Case studies. A robbery victim has no memory of being held at gunpoint but can recall other details preceding the event. An adolescent has no recollection of the abuse inflicted on her by a relative but has a vague notion of something happening. A teenage girl almost loses her life and ends up in a coma but can't remember a damned thing.

Cynthia had racked her brain on more than one occasion, trying to reconstruct the events of that day. What had happened before the erasure? Before she headed down Glenwood and then saw the car—the car without form or substance? She recalled something about peanut butter. And that potbellied Seymour man ogling her as he huffed and puffed at the helm of his mower—that pathetic perv who used to watch her in the window. And the ambulance hurling toward Flat Shoals. Lights flashing. Siren blaring.

Then the car.

Then everything went blank.

The next thing she could recall was waking up at Grady.

Chapter Thirty-One

Billy Tarwater

October 10, 1980

I FOUND HIS AW-SHUCKS GRIN ENDEARING, IN A WAY. But, at the same time, it bothered me. It seemed a little too pat. It wasn't until we'd talked for a while that I realized there wasn't a calculating bone in his body. What you see is what you get.

We had agreed to meet at Marnie's. We sat at the same table in the far corner of the Sidecar where Rufus and I had sat three weeks earlier.

"Tommy, thanks for coming."

"No problem, man. But call me Tom now. I grew out of Tommy when I left high school. Sounds more grown-up, don't cha think? Tommy's probably still back at Murphy tryin' to stuff little Dewey Purvis in a locker." His big, open-mouth hee-haw exposed a gap where his right canine should have been. "What can I do you for?"

"Do you remember a girl named Cynthia Hudspeth? Went missing back in '63?"

"Of course, I remember her. How could I ever forget that? The police brought me in once. Grilled me about her going missing and all. I told them everything I knew, which wasn't much. Then they never contacted me again."

I had run across Tommy Wright's name in the police files, which one of the detectives, Captain Nickerson, had given me full and unfettered access to. Full and unfettered. No need for FOIA. No 'investigatory records exemption' pushback. No slogging off to the chief inspector in the DA's office to plead my case. A newspaperman's cumshaw. It seems a boy named Weldon, a soda jerk at the East Atlanta Pharmacy, had seen Tommy leave the drug store with Cynthia right around the time she went missing.

"Am I correct that you left with Cynthia the day she disappeared?"

"It's not like I left *with* her," Tommy said. "I left right after her."

"Were you friends?"

"I wouldn't say *friends*. She was three years younger than me. But I bought her a shake that day." He squinched his brow. "Whatever happened to her?"

"I hear she's still around."

There was that big callow grin again—missing canine and all. "Damn, I'm glad of that. At least she didn't kick the bucket like that Martha Ann girl. That was awful."

"Did you know Martha Ann?"

"Not really. I knew who she was. A friend of mine had the hots for her."

"Marvin Darby?"

"Yeah, Marvin. Know him?"

I shook my head. "So what happened then? After you bought Cynthia the drink."

"Well, we talked some. She seemed like a real nice girl. A little flirty-like though, especially for a thirteen-year-old girl. She finished her drink and headed for the front door. I followed her out."

"And then?"

"She headed down Glenwood toward Moreland. That's when I noticed the car."

"The car?"

"Yeah. The car that was following her real slow."

"Did you tell the police anything about a car?"

"No. It wasn't until a lot later that I even remembered seeing it. I was headed to McKnight's. That's where I work. Junior grease monkey." The open-mouthed grin. "Anyway, just as I was about to hang a left at Gresham, I looked down Glenwood one last time. The car had stopped just before Moreland. Cynthia was leaning against the car. Talking to the driver. I assumed they knew each other."

"Do you remember what kind of car it was?"

"Now we're cookin'." His eyes lit up. "I know my cars."

"So you know what kind of car it was."

"No. I didn't say that. We're talkin' about a long time ago. I can tell you this, though. It was sporty. Fastback. And light grey. Maybe silver."

"Did you consider going back to the police when you remembered about the car?"

"No. Maybe I should've."

"Think hard, Tommy."

"Tom."

"Tom. Think hard. Are you sure you can't remember the make and model?"

"Late model. I know that. But I just can't remember what it was. I can tell you this, though. It wasn't a real fancy sportscar like a Cobra or a 'Vette. Or one of them foreign cars. It was sporty, but I wouldn't call it a sportscar."

"This may be a strange question. But I have to ask. Could the car have been a Hudson?"

"A Hudson! You gotta be kidding me? It wasn't no Hudson. That's for sure. I'm talkin' a small car. Low to the ground. Hudsons ain't small. And they sure as hell ain't sporty."

"I know. But I had to ask. Is there anything else you can remember about that day? Did she talk to anybody except you and the soda jerk…what's his name…Weldon?"

"Yeah, Weldon. No, she didn't talk to anybody else."

"What was she wearing?"

"You're askin' me hard questions after all these years. Let me think. I believe she had on jeans. Real tight jeans. And I think a sweatshirt. Yeah, I remember now. It was a Murphy sweatshirt."

"Did she seem like she was planning to go somewhere after the drug store? To meet somebody?"

"No. She seemed real nonchalant. Just hanging out at the fountain."

"Anything else about her? About that day?"

"Not as I can remember."

"Tom, I may need to talk to you again later. That OK?"

"No sweat, man." He looked around. "I'll come back here anytime."

I found it odd that it never occurred to Tommy—Tom—to question who I was. Why I was asking so much about Cynthia. I think he was just happy to get a couple of free PBRs.

* * *

I pulled out of the Marnie's lot with my first new clue—a late-model fastback. Grey or silver. Low to the ground. Sporty but not a sportscar. The last thing Cynthia had said she remembered, before everything went dark, was a car of some kind approaching her from behind.

The tire tracks.

I hadn't gotten more than a couple of blocks down West Peachtree. I swung right onto Linden. Then double backed onto Peachtree. I did a big loop back onto West Peachtree and pulled into Marnie's lot. I parked in the same spot I had vacated a few minutes earlier. I sat for a minute with the motor running. The radio was on WSB. Another boy had gone missing the day before. Twelve years old. They found his body in a wooded area near his home. He had been suffocated.

I turned off the ignition. Got out of the car. Opened the trunk. My notes from the police files were in my cardboard bankers box. I sifted through the papers and stuffed a few select ones into my leather satchel, the same satchel I'd carried since my first day on the city desk.

I jostled my way through Marnie's—the Friday crowd was already growing—and back to the Sidecar. The crowd had not yet spilled out from the main room. I headed straight for the table where Rufus and I, then Tom and I, had sat.

I thumbed through my notes from the police file until I came to the DMV report. The possible makes and models from the crime scenes were there: Ford Comet, Chevy Corvair, Plymouth Valiant, AMC Rambler, Studebaker Lark, Ford Falcon.

Just then, the waiter approached the table. "The usual, Billy?"

I gave him a thumbs-up. I'd taken to drinking boilermakers—my new usual—the bane of the newspaperman, I've been told. But I was always careful not to cross over the fine line between *I know what the hell I'm doing* and *somebody please hide my car keys.* Especially on Fridays.

For the time being, I ruled out the Comet and the Falcon. Neither of them had what I would call a fastback model. The Falcon did have a funny-looking fastback cousin in Europe, but I'd never seen one on the streets of Atlanta. A long shot.

I also ruled out the Rambler. I had seen pictures of a Rambler fastback concept car in *Motor Trend*, but nothing on the street.

Studebaker had a Lark two door that, if you used a little imagination, looked like a fastback. They also had an Avanti honest-to-god fastback. I had no idea about the Avanti tire size, but it was possible that the DMV report had missed it. After all, it wasn't the most popular car in the city. The Corvair and the Valiant were both possibilities.

So I was left with the Corvair, the Valiant, the Lark, and maybe the Avanti. All of this was assuming, of course, that the car Tommy saw had any connection at all to the one that made the crime scene tracks. It also assumed that Tommy was correct when he said the car following Cynthia was a fastback. And maybe there were other models that matched the crime-scene tire size; there was no reason to assume the DMV report was exhaustive, especially considering that some underpaid soul in a windowless room somewhere had gone through a comprehensive list by hand and pulled the matches. I was sure some computer somewhere hadn't done it, based on the typewritten list, with its blue-pen corrections, that I had seen in the police file.

* * *

I scanned my To Do list. Marvin Darby was on it. And I'd heard Winstanley was still alive. I'd look him up. And Carpenter. And it wouldn't hurt to try to find *Weldon (no last name) the Soda Jerk*. I found it strange that he was referenced in Winstanley's report, but there was no indication he had ever been brought in for questioning. He and Tommy may have been the last ones to see Cynthia before she was abducted. And then there were the Grove Park construction workers. The ones who saw a car drive off just when they came upon Cynthia face-down in a shallow spot beside Proctor Creek. I needed to locate them.

The Darby boy. *What would he be now? Thirty-three? Thirty-four? Not a boy anymore.* He was the next on my list after Tommy/Tom. He and Martha Ann Dullums had been close. He was likely the last person, aside from the killer, to see her alive. And I couldn't say that he hadn't done it. The detectives had questioned him for a long time. And their notes suggested he was a suspect. But, for some reason, they never followed up.

The oak-trimmed booth in the back of Marnie's was not your typical phone booth. Conor called it the Alibi Booth. He was a tinkerer and knew more about electronics that I could ever hope to know. He had soundproofed the booth and rigged it up with a continuous-loop tape player device so you could play different backgrounds. An office with typewriters clickety-clacking away. Downtown traffic. Even The Varsity, with the guy behind the counter taking and barking orders—whaddya have, two naked dogs walking, onion rings, big frosted orange on three—that sort of thing. I never quite understood that background option. Using a fast food joint as cover from your wife's suspicions, when you should be home for dinner, didn't make a lot of sense.

I shut the phone booth's accordion door. Just for grins, I started The Varsity. I ran my finger down the list of Darbys in the white pages. There was a Marvin Darby on Ormewood. I dropped in the quarter and dialed the number.

"Hello," the voice on the other end said.

"Marvin Darby?"

"Yes."

"The Marvin Darby who went to Murphy High?"

"Yes. Who is this?"

I explained why I was calling. We agreed to meet the next day at the Pawn de Rosa.

* * *

I crammed all of the papers back into my satchel, downed the last of my boilermaker, threw a five on the table, and headed back out the rear door to the parking lot. This time, I was determined to go straight home with no diversions or double-backs.

It was Friday.

Cynthia was waiting.

Chapter Thirty-Two

Billy Tarwater

October 11, 1980

WHEN I WAS A SENIOR AT MURPHY, A HIGH SCHOOL buddy of mine, Jeff Tanaka, died of acute leukemia. He was the second smartest guy in my class. During the war, his parents had endured four years at Tule Lake, an internment camp for Japanese Americans in Northern California. In '46 when they were released, they got the hell out of Dodge. They packed up the few belongings they had and headed to Virginia. That's where Jeff was born. When he was fourteen, they moved to Georgia. I've often wondered how different Tule Lake was from Camp 16. Was it better? Was it any more humane, with its barbed wire and squalor? I can't imagine my parents having to endure something like that. I can't imagine myself having to endure something like that. I hate to think about Sam Jepperson languishing in a modern-day, South Georgia version of concertina wire and misery.

On my drive to the pawn shop, I thought about the many Saturday mornings that Gary, Nick, Jimmy, and I would raid the Jap camp and free the desperate American POWs. We were always fighting somebody from far away. The filthy Japs. Or the lowdown Krauts. People who didn't look like us, four white boys from East Atlanta, with white boys' sensibilities and white boys' worldviews. White boys who had learned their ways from their parents. I was glad Jeff Tanaka hadn't been around to play army with us back then. What would he have thought about Kwai? Saito? The Oven?

Back in grade school, there was one thing I didn't have in common with my classmates. Or with my parents. Even though we trash-talked people who weren't like us, I didn't see myself as being any better than the handful of black people I knew. Dovey Mae saw to that. She was the best grown-up friend I had. She taught me right.

Dovey Mae and I never talked about my Army excursions along the creek bank, but if we had, I'm sure she would not have approved of the way we put those people down. I don't care how far away they were. They were still people. Just like us.

* * *

I passed the Alamo Motor Court on my left, styled and stuccoed to look like the *Misión de Álamo* in San Antonio, where two hundred Texians and Tejanos were slain by invading Mexicans in 1836. I wondered why, in our East Atlanta Army escapades, we had never fought the Mexicans. What would we have called them? Beaners? Spics? Would we have disparaged them the way we disparaged the Japs and the Krauts? I wondered.

I swung into the lot at the corner of Stewart Avenue and Pegg Road, less than a block past the Alamo. I put the car in Park. A streetwalker in black fishnet stockings, torn at one knee, stalked up and down the sidewalk, looking for her next trick. She eyed me. I looked away.

For as long as I could remember, the motor courts and back alleys along Stewart Avenue had been legendary for crime and vice—a quickie for a few bucks in a dingy hovel of a room, a blow job behind a dumpster. Rumor had it that a man had been running a child porn ring out of the Alamo. Mainly early teenagers. I thought about the missing and murdered children. A connection? Perhaps.

Was the Pawn de Rosa at 2871 or 2891? I couldn't remember. I had scribbled the street number on a three-by-five and placed it in my shirt pocket. I checked it. Neither number was correct. But I was close. I pulled out of the lot and continued down Stewart Avenue.

The pawn shop loomed on the right. The plate glass windows were fitted out with steel burglar bars. The glass door was protected by a hinged folding door gate, the kind I was accustomed to seeing on liquor stores in the worst downtown neighborhoods. The big neon wagon wheel, encircling a bright green dollar sign above the words Buy-Sell-Loan, screamed out to anyone passing by. Above the wagon wheel, in huge neon letters fashioned to look like logs: Pawn de Rosa. You couldn't miss it even if you tried. I parked under the R.

Marvin was waiting for me just inside the door. He was in a black and white bowling shirt with two red stripes down the front. He took a draw from a half-smoked cigarillo and swept his other arm toward the center of the room. "Make yourself at home.

Need a guitar? I got all kinds. How 'bout a watch? I got Accutron. Timex. Bulova. Got kids? Maybe an Atari Pong?"

"Sorry, Marvin. Not in the buying market today. Maybe another time."

"That's OK. I get it. You're here to talk about Martha Ann, aren't you. Here, let me make a place so you can set yourself down." He removed a stack of dust-covered cardboard boxes from a metal folding chair. "Here, you sit here."

I sat in the chair. I took out a small spiral notepad from my pocket.

When he turned around to stub the rest of his cigarillo into an ashtray on the display case, I saw what was on the back of his shirt: BOWL-A-RAMA. And in smaller letters below three tumbling tenpins: HOSS'S HEAD PINS. He grabbed another chair, which was leaning against the display case, unfolded it, and sprawled with his feet spread wide. He hunched forward and placed his palms on his knees. "I saw your name in the paper."

I explained that I worked on the *Constitution* city desk.

But he knew that already. "Tell me what you want to know."

"I'd like to hear about Martha Ann. From your perspective. What was she like? When did you last see her? Before she disappeared."

He sat up. "Look, the police brought me in and ripped me a new one for damned near half the day. I'd already met with them once before and told them everything I knew about Martha Ann going missing and all. That was a long time ago. I'm sure a good newspaperman like you can get your hands on what I told them."

I didn't tell him I'd already read every page, every word, in the police report. "I'd just like to hear it from you, if that's OK."

"Why don't we do this?" he said. "You ask me what you want to ask me." He looked at his watch. "I got twenty minutes. But if a customer comes in, I gotta stop. OK. Twenty minutes. Go."

I asked the questions. His answers were terse, clipped. He talked about his relationship with Martha Ann. About how he'd had a thing for her since junior year. More than she'd had for him. About the day she disappeared. They had parted ways—she headed for the school bus, he headed home. They agreed to meet after the football game. That was the last time he saw her. Then he got the call from Tommy Wright. "Look at the paper, front page," Tommy had said.

Marvin said there was nothing to add beyond that.

I thanked him and got up as if to leave. But I had decided to hang around. "Mind if I shop some?" I said.

"Make yourself at home. Maybe you'll find something you can't live without."

I looked around the pawn shop. On the wall behind the front display case, there was a framed black-and-white photograph of a man standing in front of the shop with a big fat cigar in his hand. It looked to have been taken in the late fifties. "This your dad?"

He walked over to where I was standing. "Yep. That's from right after he opened the shop."

"So he's had the place for—what—twenty-five years or so?"

"Almost," Marvin said. "But he's not around anymore. He died last year. It's my store now."

"I'm sorry to hear that, Marvin. Your mother still alive?"

He nodded. Looked away.

"If it's OK, I'll look around some more. You've got a lot of interesting things here."

"People bring shit in here all the time and I ask myself, are they so damned hard up they gotta give it up for dimes on the dollar? But that's not my problem."

I walked to the back of the shop. I saw two blue and white leather books sitting on the far end of the rearmost display case—the one that held all the expensive jewelry—presumably positioned in the far innards of the shop so as not to attract the attention of ne'er-do-well drop-ins. The book on top was the '63 Azuwur. I picked it up. The one below it was '64. I opened the '63 to the bookmarked page. There was Martha Ann's junior year picture. As soon as I laid eyes on her, I remembered the day in '63 when I had snuck into my brother's room and looked at the same photograph.

When Marvin saw what I was up to, he hastened to where I stood. "You found her," he said. "Ain't she a beaut?"

"I'll say. She was quite the attractive young lady. I can see why you liked her. Mind if I look through the other one?"

"Suit yourself." Marvin stayed by my side

I opened the '64 to the first of two bookmarked pages, the one with Martha Ann's senior headshot. I then turned to the other bookmark. The page was filled with a montage of photographs, including one in the lower right that appeared to have been taken from the school's side entrance, based on what I remembered from my time there. A row of six school buses were lined up in the picture's right foreground. A portion of the parking lot, to the left of the buses, could be seen in the background. Students milled about in the left foreground. None of them looked like Martha

Ann. Several large trees—oaks?—lined the sidewalk where the students gathered.

Marvin jabbed his finger at the picture. "That's where she would have caught the bus home. But that day she didn't."

I studied the picture. The yearbook would have been issued in the spring of '64. But based on the trees' foliage, the student's attire, the clear skies and absence of cumulus clouds, I guessed the photograph had been taken in the fall of '63. Could it have been around the time Martha Ann disappeared? I tried to imagine her walking out the side door. Looking around. Seeing someone she knew. Or perhaps she didn't know. Leaving with them voluntarily. Or perhaps under duress. There was only a handful of cars in the parking lot. One of them looked to fit Tommy Wright's description of the car that had approached Cynthia on Glenwood. And the car the Grove Park workers had seen speeding away. But I couldn't be sure. The photograph was small. And a little out of focus.

"Marvin, who would have taken this picture?"

"Beats me. Probably somebody from the yearbook staff. I remember there was this one student who was really into taking pictures. His dad was a professional photographer. Had a darkroom at home."

"Do you remember his name?"

"Why do you need to know that?"

"Just curious." I thumbed through the '64 yearbook until I found the page with the Azuwur staff. Off to the side of the group portrait, there were several pictures of individuals. One was of a student named Petey Samples. Beneath his name, it said Photographer. "Marvin, is this the guy you were talking about?"

Marvin nodded. "That's him."

A couple of people had entered the shop during the course of our conversation. I could tell Marvin was trying hard to attend to what I was doing and watch them at the same time. But my opportunity to keep his attention was waning. I decided a little provocation might jolt him a bit. Pull him back into my world. "Hey Marvin. What did you say the police did? Oh, yeah. I remember. They ripped you a new one for damned near half the day. Tell me something, Marvin. Did they have reason to suspect *you*?"

He glared at me. "Why would they?"

"Why would they rip you a new one for half the day if you *weren't* a suspect?"

"They dropped it. OK? That's all you need to know."

I could tell I had hit a nerve. Had thrown him off guard. *Do I push him more? Or do I let it slide for another day?* I was on a roll. I decided to go for it. "I don't think you're being straight up with me, Marvin. What are you holding back?"

By now, the two visitors had left. Marvin walked to the front, flipped the Open/Closed sign to Closed, and locked the door. "There's a room in back. We can talk there."

I followed him to the rear of the shop, wondering each step of the way whether I was walking into a trap. We entered the back room. He shut the door and fired up a cigarillo. We sat across from each other.

"Off the record. Understand?"

I nodded. "Of course, Marvin. Anything you tell me, off the record, stays off the record. But just so you know, I have no intention of getting press out of this. My mission is personal. Not as a reporter."

He got up. Walked across the room. Stood with his back to me for a minute or so. Swung around and walked toward me. Sat back down. "You don't know anything about me. About my family. About what we went through when I was a kid. Do you?"

"I don't know anything about you, Marvin. Except what you've told me."

"Well, how about I tell you what my life was like? When I was a kid, for the first ten years, I lived in a fuckin' trailer park in the middle of goddamn nowhere. My old man drove a lumber truck—a timber truck, really. He barely made enough to put food on the table. Mama was…is…a half-breed. Her own daddy was from Guadalajara. Her mama was from just outside Sylvania. Her mama stayed home. Couldn't have gotten a job if she tried, except cleaning houses. Even then, there wasn't much available our side of Cooperville. And she didn't have a car. We didn't have a pot to piss in. Then one day, the old man up and says, 'Pack your bags, Louise'—that's my mother's name—'we're leavin' this shithole.' We moved to Atlanta. My old man drove a lumber truck here for a while, before he opened the pawn shop. At first we lived at the Alamo, just up the road. Know it?"

I nodded.

"It's another shithole," he continued. "We cooked on a fuckin' hot plate. Kept food in a picnic cooler." He took a draw. "Well, here's where things get complicated. The old man was working long hours. I was in school. Mama was at the Alamo all day by herself. Every day. Bored shitless. And the old man was stingy with his money. Gave her just enough for groceries. But no more. Well, let's just say some of the people that hung around the motor court were bad news. It's a lot worse today, but some were around back then, too. Anyway, she decides to make some extra money. Pleasuring men on the side. Do you understand what I'm saying?"

Again, I nodded. But I wasn't quite sure how to respond.

"Anyway, fast forward to…what was it…'69…I think that's right…and she was reading the paper. Ran across an obituary for a man named Gus Alford. Know him?"

"I know who he was. Homicide detective. His son and I were best friends growing up."

"Well, what I didn't know at the time was that he was seeing my mother. Even after we moved away from the Alamo, they would still meet there. Get a room."

"How did you learn this?"

"Well, that day when she was reading the paper, she came across the obituary. She broke down bawling. I was twenty-two at the time and had dropped by to visit. The old man was at the Pawn de Rosa. I asked her what was wrong. That's when she told me the whole thing. Made me swear not to tell the old man. Which I never did."

"Why was she so distraught?"

"All I can figure is she cared a lot about him. Anyway, back in '63, I'm pretty sure he told the other detectives not to come after me. That's why the whole thing was dropped all of a sudden. Not that they would have had any reason to come after me anyway. I didn't do anything wrong. Except fall in love with a girl that got murdered. I wish they hadn't have dropped it, though. As hard as it was to put up with their bullshit, at least I could have gotten off fair and square. Anyway, they got the guy that did it. That's all that matters, isn't it?"

* * *

I walked back to my car. As I placed the key in the ignition, I looked up. Marvin was standing in the doorway. Then he turned and walked away. I sat in the car with the motor running, wondering why Marvin had spilled his guts. Was it to garner sympathy? Attention? To shift the focus away from Martha Ann? He didn't have to tell me what he did.

I pulled out onto Stewart Avenue and turned south. I decided to take an immediate right onto the side street that bordered the Pawn de Rosa. The back yard of the pawn shop was bounded by a six-foot-high chain-link fence with a padlocked gate. I scanned the yard as I drove past. There were a couple of old camping trailers. What looked like a rundown Ford pickup, maybe '49, '50. A dilapidated shed.

That's when I saw the car. It was parked at the far rear of the property and partially obscured by the shed. I slammed on the brakes.

It fit the description.

But it was the wrong color. A faded navy blue.

Chapter Thirty-Three

Billy Tarwater

October 13, 1980

IT WAS LATE MONDAY. THE ALIBI BOOTH WAS OCCUPIED. I waited. I could hear the clickety-clack through the closed door. It reminded me of the song, "The Typewriter," performed by Jerry Lewis in that movie that came out the same year Cynthia almost died. The one about the department store heiress and the dog walker. But for the life of me, I couldn't remember the movie's name. I wondered whether Conor Ryan had perhaps lifted the alibi soundtrack from the song. A few minutes later, a bleary-eyed patron—I didn't recognize him—stumbled out of the booth, staggered back to the bar, and crash-landed onto a bar stool midway down the counter's length.

I entered the booth and closed the door. I found three entries with the name Peter Samples in the phone book. One lived in Kirkwood, not far from Murphy High. The other two were all the way across town, one on Bolton Road and the other in Brookhaven. I took a chance on the first one. I inserted the quarter and dialed the number. He answered "Petey." Pay dirt. I explained why I was calling. We agreed to meet at his place after work on Friday. We'd go down to his darkroom in the basement. Root around. He said he'd kept the negative from every picture he'd ever taken. "Like daddy like son," he said. I hung up the phone. *What must he be? Thirty-two? Thirty-three? And he still calls himself Petey?* But then again, at twenty-eight, I've never seen fit to graduate to William or Bill.

I then dialed Gary.

"Meet me at my mother's house," Gary said. "Tomorrow after work. I'll show you what I found."

* * *

Gary's mother greeted me at the door. I hadn't seen her in fifteen years. I guessed she was pushing sixty. But she looked young for her age, especially for someone who had spent the past decade-plus as a widow. She ushered me into the living room. Three dust-covered cardboard boxes—each measuring about a foot square by six inches tall—sat in the center of the room.

She pointed to a captain's chair in the corner of the room. "Make yourself at home," she said. "Gary'll be in shortly."

I chose to stand.

In a moment, I heard a rapping coming from the hallway just off the living room. I assumed it was Gary's walking stick hitting the wood floor. He entered the room and, with his free hand, dragged the captain's chair over to where the boxes sat. "Take a load off, Billy. It's good to see you again."

I sat in it.

"This is what I found in the attic," he continued. "They're labeled. Have at it."

Each box had been marked with what appeared to have been a broad-tipped Magic Marker:

Hudspeth, C.J. 1963

Dullums, M.A. 1963

Boggs, P.M. 1963

I pictured Gary reluctantly—begrudgingly?—lugging the boxes from the attic. He hadn't even bothered to open them, judging from the dust on the packing tape. He said I could rummage through them, but none of the contents were to leave the room. Judging from his pursed lips, the jigging of his pocket change with his free hand, it was obvious to me that he didn't really want to remain nearby while I sorted through the boxes. *Fine with me.*

After Gary had left the room, I bent over and opened the box labeled Dullums. It was full of 8x10s. Handwritten notes, some of which appeared to have been from interviews with persons of interest, including Marvin Darby. Crude hand drawings of the area around the Van Vleck culvert, including one with parallel lines running across the sheet of paper—I assumed to represent the drag marks referenced in the police report. An outline drawing of Martha Ann's splayed body inside the culvert. I shuffled through the photographs. Most of them I had already seen from my inspection of the files in Captain Nickerson's office. But some were new to me. My eyes fell on a photograph that I had not seen. It was a close up of the back of Martha Ann's thigh. A stick figure looked to have been carved into her skin, its head flopped over like a rag doll. I wondered why this 8x10 had not been in the police file. Surely, I wouldn't have missed something like that. I sifted through the photos until I came to one of her full body, face down in the shallow water. I had seen it in the captain's office. But now, alone and unhurried in the privacy of Mrs. Alford's living room, I examined it more closely. The image was there, on her thigh, albeit small and somewhat indistinct in this photo. I had somehow missed it when I went through the files with Nickerson. Perhaps I had felt a bit rushed, with him looking over my shoulder most of the time. Full and unfettered? Perhaps. Free and unrushed? Not really.

I found the photograph showing the tread marks near where Martha Ann's body had been discovered. I had seen it before, but I had not had the benefit of being able to take measurements. This time, I came prepared. I took a small metal ruler, the kind engineers use, from my shirt pocket. I knew the tire width had been recorded in the police file as 6-1/2 inches. I measured the width of the tire imprint in the photograph. I then measured the center-to-center distance between the two tire marks. I'm halfway decent at mental math, but I relied on my pencil and pad, and some long division, to calculate the track width. I got 56 inches.

I moved on to the Boggs box. In it I found a close-up of a mark on the girl's thigh, similar to the one on Martha Ann Dullums, but less crude. It didn't have a flopped-over rag doll head. The body and head looked more like a P. As with the Dullums close-up, I realized that I had not seen this photograph in the police file.

A wave of disquiet came over me when I reached for the box labeled Hudspeth, C.J. I slowly removed the packing tape and opened the top flaps. I leafed through its contents. The first photograph I came to was the 8x10 of Cynthia lying unconscious.

Proctor Creek cut a diagonal across the upper right-hand corner of the photo. She was naked. Her head was face-down at the water's edge. I had seen the photo in the police file, but at the time I had not made out the faintest image of the P on her thigh. The same P that I had gotten to know over the years. The same P that Cynthia went out of her way to avoid discussing. Had the Grove Park workmen perhaps scared the knife-wielding, murderous would-be tattoo artist away before he finished the job? I wondered.

I carefully examined a photo of the surrounding crime scene. I scanned the shoreline along the shallow creek bed. A stand of trees—white oaks?—lined the far edge of the creek. Scattered among the trees was what looked like Chinese privet. A foreign object seemed to be suspended from one of the privet branches, but I couldn't make it out.

I looked around the room to make sure Gary wasn't nearby. Then I quickly slipped three photograph into my satchel. The Dullums and Boggs close-ups. And the one with the foreign object in the privet.

* * *

I didn't see Cynthia's car when I pulled into the Belmont lot. I hurried to the lobby and bounded up the stairs to the fourth floor. I opened the door to the apartment and called out for her. No answer. I closed and locked the door behind me. I engaged the security chain. I removed the Proctor Creek photo from my satchel. Photograph in hand, I searched for the magnifying glass that I knew had to be somewhere in the apartment. I found it in the top drawer of the bedside table. The one on Cynthia's side. The foreign object hanging from the privet branch came into clear focus through the lens. It was a pair of girl's panties. Not unlike the ones I had found along the Van Vleck creek. The ones I had kept in the pocket of Uncle Newell's field jacket ever since. The field jacket that was now somewhere in a trunk in my own mother's attic.

My first thought was that the panties in the photo had belonged to Cynthia. That whoever tried to kill her had removed them, or forced *her* to remove them, before he buried her face into the creek bed's edge. Before she struggled to breathe. Before she lost consciousness. Before he was scared away.

But what of the panties I had found back in '63? Had they belonged to Martha Ann Dullums? Her body had been discovered near where I found them hanging from the briar thicket. But that was two weeks later. And the police report said she had been dead only a few days when they found her. The timing didn't add up.

And why, after the three girls had been found—two dead and Cynthia half-dead—hadn't I had the presence of mind to turn the panties over to the police? Perhaps I was too infatuated with my find to even consider such a thing. Or perhaps I was scared to let on that I was carrying around girls' underwear. Or maybe I was just scared. Period. After all, I was eleven.

I heard a rattling of the doorknob. *Cynthia.* I returned the magnifying glass to the drawer, stuffed the photo back into my satchel, and hurried to the front door.

"What's with the chain lock?" she said, as she breezed past me with Addie in her arms and Billy Jr. following close behind.

* * *

I would spend the rest of the week focusing on my day job. The body of another black boy, 10-year-old Charles Stephens, had been found on Norman Berry Drive on a grassy hill near the entrance to a trailer park. He had been suffocated. Charles was last seen at home watching TV. He was reportedly going to visit a friend in Carver Homes.

The number of missing or dead children now had reached fifteen. My job was to stay on top of breaking developments, to thread the needle as best I could between a deliberate and meticulous police department and an up-in-arms, *I want answers now* citizenry, and to await news of the next victim.

I had a hard time concentrating on my job, a condition I attributed to three things. First was the inhumanity of the senseless killing of innocent children. Compounding this was the angst I continued to feel over what had befallen Martha Ann, Patsy, and Cynthia seventeen years earlier. And then there was the inescapable conflation I made of what happened then and what was happening now, even though I realized there was no substantive connection between the two.

* * *

Friday afternoon came. And not a minute too soon. I left the newspaper office and headed across town to Petey Samples' house. I had warned Cynthia earlier in the week that, for the first time in what, four years?, I likely wouldn't make it home in time for our Friday night fling. I didn't tell her why. Just that I was on a mission, and she had agreed to back me up. I hoped she understood.

Petey lived in one of those Craftsman bricks characteristic of Kirkwood. White flight had color-washed the neighborhood back in the mid- to late-sixties. But apparently Petey had decided to remain, as had my mother—and Gary's mother—just down the road in East Atlanta.

Petey was a small guy—short and reedy. He reminded me a little of Wally Cox, except for his full head of ginger hair—rather, two heads of ginger hair bisected by a meddlesome shock of white.

"You just come raht on in," he said through his nose and with a sweep of his hand. "What's that thing they say south of the border? Me cawsa es su cawsa."

He led me down the creaky unrailed stairs to his subterranean darkroom. He shut the door. "Now, when that ray-ed laht's on…" He pointed to the bare bulb over the door, then to the door itself. "…we caint open it. OK?"

I nodded.

Prior to my arrival, he had pulled the negatives—all 35 mm—from the '63 Azuwur yearbook photograph collection. They were stored in faded yellow sleeves. "Now. Lahk the man says, you git what you git, and don't throw a fit." He showed an ear-to-ear grin. He took the negative strips out of their sleeves and laid them out in tracks on a light table.

I studied them one by one. I picked out three for starters. One was the photograph of the school buses and parking lot outside the Murphy side entrance—the picture I had seen in the yearbook at the Pawn de Rosa. Another was of the same location, but this time it showed the football players and cheerleaders lined up alongside a school bus, presumably waiting to board the bus for an away game somewhere. The third was of a dozen or so students, mostly girls, in the cafeteria line. "Can you enlarge these three into positives?" I asked.

"I can. But mah trays can't hold but two at the time. Which two do you want to do first?"

I picked out the two from outside the entrance to the school.

He placed the first negative in the Beseler enlarger and projected it onto the photographic paper. Then he did the same with the second negative.

I watched as the two images came to life in the photography trays. I saw no sign of Martha Ann or Cynthia in either picture. But the same sporty car was in both. Sitting by itself in a largely empty parking lot.

Petey clipped the positives onto a wire that was strung from one wall to its opposite.

I examined each picture while he processed the third one. I had assumed, from the blurry yearbook photo, that the car was a grey or silver two door. And I was right. In both positives, the way the car was positioned, I could see the driver's side and part of the front grill. The side had one large window and two small triangular windows, one in front of and one behind the large window. The front had an egg-crate grill and two sets of double headlights. I could make out a man sitting in the driver's seat. He wore glasses. His looked vaguely familiar, but the image was too blurry for me to go beyond that.

The third photograph was of little benefit. None of the girls in the cafeteria line turned out to be Martha Ann or Cynthia, and there was nothing in the background that jumped out at me.

"Can I take these with me?" I asked.

"I think I see your name on 'em."

I examined the negative strips again but decided that, at least for now, I had what I had come for. I thanked Petey and asked if I could return if I decided I needed more enlargements. He replied with the "mi casa es su casa" thing again. And then the grin.

* * *

Cynthia greeted me at the door with a plaintive pout. Plaintive but playful. I could tell she was doing her best to make light of the fact that we had forgone what would otherwise have been an evening of costumed frolic on the island of Mykonos. But the night wasn't over. And she had, after all, gone ahead and prepared a spread of dolmas, tzatziki, and melitzanosalata just in case I got home in time to eat.

I bought some time—just fifteen minutes, I had said—to retire to my closet of a home office and pore through back issues of *Motor Trend.*

It didn't take long for me to pin down the car in the photograph. It was clearly a Valiant. Sixty-one. Or maybe sixty.

Chapter Thirty-Four

Cynthia Tarwater

October 18, 1980

THE P. SHE HAD NEVER BEEN ABLE TO GET SHED OF IT, a phrase her mother was so fond of using. Fortunately, it was on the back of her thigh and not front and center. She could manage to put it out of her mind for short stretches. But then something would happen. An over-the-shoulder glance in the mirror when she was drying off. The protrusive snag of scarred flesh when she ran her hand down her leg. The unsettling feeling that Billy was staring at it when they were intimate.

The erasure. Localized psychogenic amnesia. An entire block of time evaporates into thin air. Headlong. Gone. Likely never to resurface. She considered herself a reasonably intelligent person. A little quirky. Flirty. But intelligent nonetheless. With a penchant for recall. Without it, she wouldn't be able to do her job with the deftness that had become a trademark. So why couldn't she remember something so vital to her existence? So proximate to her near demise? The riddle would forever haunt her, no matter how hard she tried to escape it.

The God thing. She was not a religious person. Her mother had seen to that, with her incessant prancing, spouting her "reborned again" blather, her "keys to the kingdom." Dragging Cynthia to church and making her listen to that dreadful man rail from the pulpit. Imploring her at the hospital, when she came to, to produce some absurd story about having seen the bright light at the end of the tunnel. No, Cynthia wasn't religious. But at times she wondered why she had been spared and the others hadn't.

She abhorred her mother's missionary zeal. So how did Cynthia ever end up teaching Contemporary Theology to college seniors? How many times had she asked herself that simple question? And how many times had she come up short of an answer? Perhaps it was a twisted variant of the Stockholm syndrome. Her mother, the captor of her spirit. She, the hostage. Her attraction to religious studies, the emotional bond she couldn't shake. Perhaps.

* * *

"I have something I want to show you." That's how Billy started the morning. It was Saturday. This time, the kids were with their other grandmother—Alice—the *sane* grandmother.

Cynthia had taken to cringing lately whenever Billy said he had something he wanted to show her. Or something he wanted to talk about. Or something preying upon his mind. It always seemed to pertain to '63. And his determination to get to the bottom of what happened and see Sam Jepperson freed.

"What is it this time?" she replied.

"I have some photographs."

"Billy, trust me. If it's pictures of dead bodies, that's the last thing I want to see."

"They're close-ups, Cynthia. You can't see anything except the backs of the girls' thighs. And I have a couple other pictures. Of a car in the Murphy parking lot. You need to look at them."

"Why do I need to look at them?"

"For starters, maybe you can make sense of what's on the girl's thighs. What it means. And the car in the parking lot? Maybe it'll ring a bell."

"Ring a bell? After seventeen years? I doubt it. But go ahead. I'll humor you."

He pulled the two close-ups from a manila folder and laid them side-by-side, facing her, on the breakfast table. He pointed to the one on her left. "That's what was carved into Martha Ann's thigh." Then to the other one. "Patsy Boggs."

The one on the right was more refined. It was as if whoever did it was getting better as he went along. And if the construction workers hadn't come upon the perpetrator in the act, or so Cynthia had been told, she would likely be six feet underground with a fully-inscribed image on her own thigh.

She studied the Boggs photograph. The P. The extended vertical leg. The X through it. She was not ready to reveal to Billy that she recognized what it was—at least she was ninety percent sure of it. But she needed to think it through—perhaps talk to a colleague. "Billy, I don't know what to say, except that I could have—."

"I know," he said. "It could have been you. If only." He searched her anxious eyes. "Some twisted, fucked-up soul did this, Cynthia.

And I've got to get to the bottom of it. Does it look like anything you've ever seen before?"

"It looks familiar. That's all I can tell you now. Go ahead. Show me the others."

He placed the photographs back into the manila folder. He pulled out the other two pictures and placed them in front of her.

Her eyes locked on the image in the parking lot. A foggy sense of having been there came over her. "I know the car, Billy. Sort of."

He reacted with a start. "You know the car?"

"I know it. But I *don't* know it."

'What do you mean, Cynthia? Either you know it or you don't. It can't be both."

"What I mean is I've seen that car. I know the car. But I just can't place it. Do you know what lethonomia is?"

"It sounds like a disease."

"Ha." She threw her head back and smirked. "Some might call it that. It's that *on the tip of your tongue* feeling when you can't find the right word. You know it. But it just doesn't come. It's named for Lethe, the river in the underworld of Hades. The source of forgetfulness of the past. Erasure, Billy. That's what it is. Erasure. That's what I feel as I gaze at your photographs. But in this case, it isn't a word or a phrase that doesn't come. It's reality itself. I know the car. Somewhere, rattling around in a part of my brain I can't get to, it has a name. A character. A singularity. But it just won't surface."

"Would it help if I told you I'm pretty sure it's a Valiant? Early sixties, I think. Probably grey or silver."

"It might help. Give me some time. Maybe it will come to me. But not now. Not today."

* * *

Lethe. The River of Forgetfulness. One of the five rivers in Hades, the others being Acheron, Cocytus, Phlegethon, and Styx. Everybody knew Styx. The others were lost to all but serious students of Greek mythology.

As the story goes, the dead had to drink Lethe's waters in order to forget their life on Earth.

Only then could they be reincarnated.

Only then could they carry on.

Chapter Thirty-Five

Billy Tarwater

October 20, 1980

PAGE A16 OF THE MONDAY ***NEW YORK TIMES*****. DATELINE:** Atlanta. October 19. Skeleton of Missing Child is Identified. I knew that already. I had learned on Saturday that seven-year-old Latonya Wilson's skeletonized body had been found not far from a railroad track near her Verbena Street home. And the *Constitution* had run the story on Sunday. Page 1. Above the fold. But reading it in the *Times* two days after I'd found out about it still evoked a chill. Perhaps it was the word skeleton that I couldn't shake. Not just a dead body, but one so decomposed, down to the bone, that authorities had no hope of determining the cause of death. Or perhaps it was that the news of another dead child in The City Too Busy to Hate wasn't just a local story. Its shock circled the globe.

Latonya had disappeared in June. A witness claimed to have seen a man climb into her apartment window, carry her out, and hold her in his arms as he spoke to another man in the apartment parking lot.

When will it end?

But the kidnapping and murder, or near-murder in Cynthia's case, of the girls in '63 *had* ended. Just like that. Why had it stopped? Why not six? Or ten? Or fifteen? The police had said it was because Sam Jepperson had been arrested, convicted, and incarcerated. *An easy answer. But the wrong one.*

Perhaps almost getting caught in Grove Park had caused Cynthia's would-be killer to flee the scene. To lay low. To cease his fiendish ways. Perhaps he had moved on to other nefarious deeds, ones that were not so deadly, obvious, or newsworthy. Or perhaps there was meaning in the number three. Perhaps he had never intended for there to be more.

* * *

The downtown library was on Carnegie Way. The Brutalist monstrosity of a building had opened earlier in the year. It replaced on site the old one, a classic structure with marble façade and Corinthian columns. With its massive door and windows. Its seven bibliostones dedicated to great writers. I understood that the city had outgrown the old library but, for the life of me, I couldn't understand why Atlanta had a penchant for tearing down historic buildings and replacing them with steel and concrete.

I found the Edmunds used car guide in the Reference section. I looked up car specs from '60, '61. The Corvair had a 54.8" average track width. The Lark, 53.0. The Avanti, 57.0. The Valiant, 55.8.

It jibed.

And another thing made sense. Unlike with the Corvair, Avanti, and Valiant, the difference between the Lark's front and rear track widths was almost nine inches. That would have left four distinct tracks at the crime scene, not two.

I left the library and walked the four blocks to Rich's. I popped in to the Crystal Bridge. I ordered date nut bread and cream cheese. And a Coke. Just like back in the day. It brought a brief smile. But then I remembered the time the black waitress's arm had brushed against mine. My mother had freaked out. Rushed me to the restroom to wash up. A lot of things have changed since then. But some things stay the same.

* * *

I went back to the Pawn de Rosa. I wanted to show Marvin Darby the enlarged photographs of the Murphy parking lot. And I wanted to get a better look at the faded navy blue car parked behind the shop. Beyond the chain-link fence. Beyond the padlocked gate.

Marvin met me at the door. In the same black, white, and red bowling shirt as before. Half-smoked cigarillo between his yellow-tinged fingers.

I showed him the pictures. "Marvin, think back to the day you left Martha Ann at the side entrance to the school. Where the buses parked. She was to take the bus home. Right? She was to meet you at Grady that evening after the football game. That was the last time you saw her. She never showed up for the game."

"That's right. I've been over this a dozen times. With the police. With my father. With you."

"I understand, Marvin." I pointed to the car in the photos. "But what I want you to try to recall is this. Do you remember seeing a sporty car in the lot the day Cynthia disappeared? Like the one here? Maybe grey? Maybe silver?"

Marvin pondered the photographs. Lit another cigarillo. Swirls of smoke clouded his face. "It was a long time ago, you know."

"I know, Marvin. But this is important. Look at the car. Think about that day. You walked Martha Ann to the parking lot. You said goodbye. Then you left her there. Do you remember a car? Perhaps a car that looked out of place? A car that didn't fit in with what the students or teachers would have been driving at the time?"

"All my friends drove souped-up '55 Chevys. Fords. Hot rods. And the teachers? They were mainly old ladies and geezer types. They didn't drive sporty cars."

"That's my point, Marvin."

"I'm sorry, man. I'm drawing a blank. I don't remember seeing a car like that."

I waited for an acknowledgment from Marvin that yes, he had seen the car. But it never came. I stuffed the photos back into my satchel and headed for the door. I swung around. "One other thing, Marvin. When I left here the other day, I happened to see an old Ford pickup truck in your backyard. Maybe a '49. My granddaddy had a '49 pickup." I lied. "Is yours for sale?"

"Everything has a price around here."

"Can I see it?"

Marvin bolted the front door. I followed him to the back of the shop. He unbolted the steel rear door and ushered me outside. I scanned the property. Past the pickup truck. Past the old camping trailers. Past the dilapidated shed.

The faded blue car was gone.

* * *

"Lieutenant Alford. What a piece of work he was."

Dan Winstanley, gravel-voiced and leather-skinned, looked like his better days were long gone. I had sought him out. Found him living alone in a rundown trailer park on Stewart Avenue. He said he'd retired early on a disability pension. But he didn't let on why. And I didn't ask.

"You know, no matter how hard I tried, Alford and I just couldn't see eye to eye."

"What do you mean, Sergeant?"

"He was always quick to jump to an answer. And when he made up his mind about something. It didn't matter what. A murder case. Who was gonna win the next mayor's race. Hell, the color of the sky, for that matter. That was that. You couldn't get him to budge. When it came to work, all he cared about was getting somebody behind bars. Screw the facts."

"Tell me about the Sam Jepperson case."

"Sam Jepperson? Do I have to? What a mess. The problem with that case, as I saw it, was that Alford stubbed his toe on a detail."

"What do you mean?"

"I didn't think Jepperson did it. But I also knew if I bucked the lieutenant, he'd serve my ass up on a platter. Alford had worked it all out in his mind. Jepperson was the one, and that was that. Problem is, the details didn't square with the lieutenant's plan.

Especially the car. The tire tracks. There's no way those tracks came from Jepperson's car. And we never found one piece of solid evidence that tied Jepperson to the murders. Not one."

"So why Jepperson?"

"You have to understand something. Alford didn't give a rat's ass about solving the case. I mean *really* solving the case. If he could put a damned nigger…his words…away for life and score another point with the higher-ups, he'd do it in a heartbeat. On the surface, Alford fit the bill of a stand-up guy. That was all that mattered. And Jepperson? He was an easy target. A simpleton of a black man still shining shoes at forty. With his backwater way of speaking. Driving around with a voodoo doll hanging from his rearview mirror. He was collateral damage."

"Sounds like it."

"And you gotta admit. The murders *did* end after we locked Jepperson up, didn't they? That went a long way toward supporting the lieutenant's sham."

"Did you have any suspicions about who really did it?"

"I always wondered about that Darby boy. But I didn't really have any solid reason to believe he was involved. We brought him in. Questioned him. Then there was the Hudspeths' next-door neighbor. The peeper, I called him. But we didn't have anything on him either."

"Tell me about the Darby boy. Based on what I read in the police file, you seemed to be on to him as a person of interest. And then you just dropped it."

"The lieutenant ordered me to."

"Any idea why?"

Winstanley rubbed his hand across his face and down his neck. "I'd rather not get into it. Let's just say we were getting a little too close to home, if you know what I mean, for the lieutenant's comfort. You're a newspaper reporter. You can figure it out. Read between the lines."

"What about...what did you call him...the peeper?"

"Leonard Seymour. We interviewed him. But we ruled him out. The way we saw it, he was just a rake that got off on watching a pubescent white girl undress. Hell, you can't blame a man for that, can you?"

I was glad I had chosen not to tell the sergeant that Cynthia and I were married.

"Any others? Suspects, I mean."

"Not really. As soon as Jepperson was put away..." Winstanley brushed his hands together like he was wiping the dust off. "...we closed the case. Moved on."

* * *

I headed east on Georgia Avenue past the Atlanta Stadium. Then left on Martin Street and left on Crumley.

How long has it been? I hadn't seen Dovey Mae since '76, when she showed up at Granny Tarwater's funeral in her finest black mourning crape. I thought back to that day. My family eased into the same pew where we had always sat for Sunday service. Cynthia was next to me. My mother sat to her right. Then my dad. Then Chester. But this time, Dovey Mae occupied the spot to my left where Granny Tarwater would have sat. Uncle Newell, Aunt Lottie, and Cousin Loreen occupied the pew behind us.

"Dovey Mae, do you have any chewing gum?" I asked with the slightest grin.

She looked at me quizzically and shook her head.

Granny Tarwater would have been amused.

I sat on that cold, hard pew and thought about the many Sundays when I had endured Virlyn Kilgallon's histrionics. Telling us our sins were as heavy as lead. That without salvation, we would perish in the great furnace of wrath. A sulfuric, Stygian hell.

I remember looking up at the baptismal font behind the choir loft. I thought back to '65, when I had finally seen fit to suffer the water dunk in the arms of the Reverend Thomas, who had graduated from youth minister to stand-in, then to Kilgallon's permanent replacement. It was supposed to be the ritual purification I would never forget. I'd never forgotten it, alright. The water went up my nose, and I thought I was going to die right there in front of the entire congregation.

As I sat in the pew, sandwiched between Dovey Mae and my mother, and thought back to those dreadful days when Kilgallon would order the teenagers in the balcony to repent, I felt the same electric charge run down my spine as I had back then.

A year after Granny Tarwater died, my dad would be gone as well, having succumbed to injuries from the car wreck. Dovey Mae, laid up with diverticulitis, had been unable to attend his funeral.

On Monday afternoon, October twentieth, I pulled as close to the curb in front of her tiny Mechanicsville bungalow as I could. Crumley Street was narrow, barely wide enough for two cars to pass. But there was already a sedan in the short driveway and no room for another. The street would have to do. I put the car in Park and walked to the front door.

I hadn't told her I was dropping by. My decision to visit had been a spur-of-the-moment one. I likely wouldn't have thought of it had I not just left Dan Winstanley's place on Stewart Avenue, a mile and a half away.

I barely recognized the woman who greeted me at the door. Dovey Mae had aged a lot since that day at Granny Tarwater's funeral. She was weak and frail. Her eyes were vacant and grey. Her wrinkled skin hung precariously on her bony arms and hands. In the mere four years, her hair had gone from matronly silver to ghostly white. She must have been pushing eighty.

We sat on her sofa and talked for upwards of an hour. About Sundays at Granny Tarwater's. About the broken jar of fig preserves in the root cellar. About her having to ride in the back of the bus to visit Madame Ludowici, that "quack of a woman." About the Woolworth sit-ins, something I hadn't been aware of at the time, given that I was only eight. About the low spirits she felt in '68 when, as she described it, "two fine young men were mowed down by an Arab and a racist." We talked about the fifteen children who had gone missing since July of '79. Most of them found dead. All of them black.

She told me her husband had passed away around the same time as my father. The car in the driveway belonged to her nephew, who had moved in with her shortly after Perlie—that's what she called her husband—had "crossed over." But I didn't meet her nephew. Either he was away or had chosen not to leave his room.

Was it by design that she had refrained from mentioning Sam Jepperson? Had she avoided bringing him up because the thought of his incarceration was too intolerable? After all, she had been the first person to avow, at least to me, that Jepperson was being railroaded. Finally, I mentioned him and my mission to clear his name.

"Goin' against the man," she said. "Ain't gonna be easy. I'm just sayin'."

I asked her whether she recalled anything—anything at all—that might help me see Sam freed. She hesitated. But then she said she remembered one little thing. Something that, at the time, hadn't seemed that important.

"Remember back when I hid Shorty in your grandmother's cellar?" she said. "When the man was after him?"

"Of course, I remember, Dovey Mae. How could I forget that?"

"Well, when he was hidin' down there, we talked a lot. Seems Cynthia had kept his shoeshine card with his phone number on it. She called him again. For a ride."

"My *wife* Cynthia? When?"

"Three days before she went missing. Late in the day. He picked her up at a phone booth."

"Where?"

"Where Confederate Avenue runs into Moreland. She told him she had come from the church. He tried to talk to her about why she was so het up, but she said she just wanted to go home. He dropped her off a block from her house."

I had seen nothing in the police records about Jepperson's second encounter with Cynthia. I assumed he hadn't told them for fear that it would further implicate him. Might she remember the second ride if I mentioned it? Perhaps.

* * *

I had spent the better part of Monday dealing with what Cynthia had started calling "your damned obsession." But I still had a day job. I left Dovey Mae's and went straight to the newspaper office. I reviewed the front-page article for the next morning's paper, along with its headline: City Orders Curfew For Children.

I would stay at the office until late into the evening. Marnie's would have to wait until Tuesday.

* * *

It was ten thirty before I finally pulled into my parking space at The Belmont.

Cynthia was still awake—and hyped. I had considered bringing up the second ride with Sam Jepperson but, before I had a chance to, she said she had something she needed to talk about. And it couldn't wait.

Chapter Thirty-Six

Sam Jepperson

October 20, 1980

"OLD SPARKY" SAT IDLE ON THE FIFTH FLOOR. IT WAS A quiet reminder of the past. It occupied the highest point of the building. A testament to the outsized role it had played in the prison's history. For almost sixty years, it had been a not-so-silent witness to the deaths of too many poor souls to count. But it had been more than just a witness. It was the executioner's henchman. Some of its victims were surely innocent. Sam supposed that most were guilty as hell.

News had traveled fast through the cellblocks when, in June of 1980, the chair, with its bright white enamel finish, was moved from Reidsville to the new Death House at the state prison in Butts County. But later that year, "The Man" decided it was time to put Old Sparky out to pasture. So it came back to Reidsville, where Sam imagined it would spend its remaining years up there on the fifth floor, on display for people to gawk and gasp—and thank the Lord Almighty that they, unlike the hundreds who had sat in it, were a fortunate lot.

Sam had never laid eyes on Old Sparky. Didn't want to. Not in the least. Some things are better left unseen. He didn't like to think too much about where he'd be if they'd given him the death penalty. Then again, the prospect of spending the rest of his life, twenty-three hours a day in a five-by-ten, plus thirty minutes in a chain-link-and-razor-wire exercise cage and ten minutes in a cold shower, might as well be a death sentence.

They say when you die at Reidsville, you die alone.

* * *

Sam had received the letter from Billy two days earlier. How many times had he unfolded it, read it, refolded it? Surely half a dozen.

> October 14th
>
> Dear Shorty (I hope you don't mind my calling you Shorty),
> I'm writing this late in the evening. Cynthia and the kids are sound asleep. I'll mail it first thing in the morning. If we're lucky and the Reidsville Mail Nazis don't hold it back, you should have this within a couple of days. (Note to the Mail Nazi's: if you're reading this, I'm talking to you.)
>
> How are things there? On second thought, don't answer that. I know they're not good. I'm doing everything I can to spring you. Soon, I hope. Gary

Alford, Gus's son, has been a big help. Unlike his father (may he rest in peace, wherever he is). I met with Gary earlier today. He shared Gus's files with me, at least the ones he found in his mother's attic. A lot of useful material there, including crime scene photos.

I'm hoping to meet with Sergeant Winstanley next week. Surely you remember him. Based on what I know so far, he seems like the only one in Homicide back then with a sympathetic bone in his body. We'll see how that goes.

Shorty, don't lose hope. Okay?

Billy

* * *

Ruby and the kids had visited last week.

The kids. They're sure not kids anymore. But they're still my *kids. That Rufus. He's become such a strapper. And a school teacher, even. Who would have thought? And Recy? Looks and talks just like her mother. But Ruby doesn't look so good these days, since she messed up her hand at the food factory.*

Ruby had told Sam all about the work Billy was doing to get him out. But it was good hearing it firsthand in Billy's letter. Early on, Ruby had tried to free him. That man Hollowell was a big help, she said. But it never came to anything.

Sam hoped things would be different now, with Billy on it, being that he was a big ole paperman.

Sam hadn't seen any of his Alabama family face-to-face since that time back in '59 when he had gone to Birmingham to bail the boy out. And they hadn't picked up the phone and called, or written a word, since he'd been hauled off to jail back in '63. He doubted he'd ever see them or hear from them again.

* * *

Sam was sitting at the foot of his cot-of-a-bed in deep thought when he looked up and saw the prison guard standing just outside his cell. It was shower time. Sam folded the letter and placed it in his shirt pocket. The guard opened the cell door, handcuffed Sam's wrists behind his back, and led him down the narrow corridor.

They passed the window that looked out onto the prison yard. Sam gazed down at the empty playing field. At the dry Georgia red clay, crusted and cracked by the autumn sun. At the guard tower in the distance. At the town beyond the tower.

Back in '73—or was it '74—the high-muck-a-mucks from Hollywood had filmed *The Longest Yard* out on that playing field. Sam had gotten a glimpse of Burt Reynolds one day. But for the most part, the guards had kept the prisoners as far away as they could.

The guard led Sam into the tiny shower cell, unhandcuffed him, and slammed the steel door shut.

Sam removed his shoes and socks, trousers and underwear. Then his shirt. The letter fell out of his shirt pocket. He placed it, still folded, atop the pile of clothes on the floor and stepped into the shower.

The ice-cold water cascaded down his face.

Chapter Thirty-Seven

Cynthia Tarwater

October 20, 1980

ΧΡΙΣΤΟΣ.

What Cynthia had learned from her colleague, an expert in Early Christian and Byzantine History, confirmed what she thought.

She read over her notes. Meticulous. Handwritten. Verbatim. Taken from the book he had loaned her.

> In ancient Gaul, in 312 AD, before the Battle of the Milvian Bridge, a vision came to the emperor Constantine the Great. At the noon hour, he saw a cross of light in the sky. Below it were the Greek words Τούτῳ Νίκα! In this sign you will conquer! [*Why didn't I ever bother to learn Greek?*]

> That night, Christ visited Constantine in his sleep. Christ told the emperor to make a replica of what he had seen in the sky. A labarum with the Chi-Rho. An imperial standard to the honor of the Lord. [*I've heard they had psychedelic sacraments back then. Could it have been?*]
>
> Constantine formally converted to Christianity that same year. Historians were clear on that. But when had he informally begun to convert? Had he adopted his mother Helena's faith in his youth? Or, as Eusebius of Caesarea had claimed, was it the other way around? Did Constantine encourage Helena to convert to Christianity? The truth would be lost to history. [*What was his relationship with his mother like? Surely better than mine.*]
>
> Another thing was clear to historians. Constantine had been baptized on his deathbed, not long after the Feast of Easter, 337 AD. At Constantine's request, he was christened by another Eusebius, the Arian bishop of Nicomedia. An acolyte likely was at Constantine's side, holding the labarum above the dying man's head. [*The Chi-Rho.*]

A war totem. That's what it was.

She thought of that dreadful hymn, "Onward Christian Soldiers." Of the Confederate Avenue Baptist Church choir bellowing it out—between belches in Leonard Seymour's case. Of Reverend Kilgallon pumping his fist in the air to the music—like a drum major. Of her having sat in the pew mouthing the words. *Marching as to war.*

* * *

That night, Cynthia and Billy sat across from each other at the breakfast table. She nudged the cup of fresh, piping hot coffee, black the way he liked it, across the table toward him.

"Let me see the close-ups again," Cynthia said. "Of the girls' thighs."

"It's ten forty-five and I've been at it all day. I'm dead tired. Are you sure this can't wait?"

"I'm sure, Billy. Drink your coffee. It'll keep you awake."

He retrieved the photos from his satchel and placed them on the table, facing her.

She examined the image carved into the Boggs girl's skin. "I know what it is, Billy. I thought I did when you first showed me the pictures. But I'm certain now."

Billy drew back in his chair. "What do you mean, you know what it is?"

"I met with a colleague this morning. He confirmed what I thought."

"And that is?"

"Have you ever heard of a Chi-Rho cross?"

"Sounds familiar. I'm sure you'll fill me in."

"It's one of the earliest forms of Christogram. Dating all the way back before Constantine the Great. It's a P with an X through it." She pointed to the Boggs photograph. "Look at the girl's thigh, Billy. See the P. That's the rho. And the X is the chi."

"So what does it mean?"

"It's the first two letters of the Greek word for Christ. Christos. It represents Jesus Christ, the embodiment of God in the flesh."

"In the flesh?" He held up the Boggs photo facing her. "Do you see the irony in that, Cynthia?"

"Honestly, Billy, I see irony in everything these days."

"So the carvings don't have anything to do with Sam's hoodoo haint after all?"

"Is that a rhetorical question?"

"Perhaps."

"Of course they don't. But I suspect you knew that already. After all, you're the one who's been convinced from the start that Sam Jepperson wasn't involved in any of this."

Cynthia looked across the table at Billy's heavy lids—unmoved by what was probably the strongest coffee she had ever made. "Go get some sleep. We can talk about this in the morning. Who knows? Maybe you'll come up with an REM epiphany."

* * *

The next morning, well before sunup, she awoke to Billy standing beside her. He was holding the wooden bed tray with foldable legs. The one his parents had given them way back before Billy Jr. was born. The one they rarely used. On the tray was a cup of coffee, a cloud of steam rising from its brim. And a china plate. On the plate were two eggs sunny-side up, whole wheat toast, strawberry jam. For a moment, she thought it must be the weekend. But then she remembered it was only Tuesday. And even if it had been the weekend, breakfast in bed? What was that about? She wasn't complaining, though.

"Billy. You're something else. And on a weekday, no less."

Billy sat at the foot of the bed as she dug into her Tuesday-morning surprise. "I figured you've been through a lot. You deserve it. And if it weren't for you, I'd still be scratching my head, trying to make sense of the thigh marks."

"Don't give me too much credit. We know what they are now. But that's just the start. We don't know who put them there. Or why."

"That's what I've been pondering."

"So. Come up with any overnight breakthroughs?"

"Not exactly."

"Not *exactly*? What does that mean? You sound like you may have an idea."

"Cynthia, you remember Sam Jepperson giving you a ride to the football game, right?"

"Of course. I've told you that. That's one of the few details from around that time that I *do* remember."

"Do you recall getting a ride with him a second time? A few days before you disappeared?"

She looked past Billy as if she were far away. Shook her head.

"Think, Cynthia. Sam said you called him from a pay phone on Moreland Avenue. You were distraught. You said you had come from the church. All you wanted to do was go home."

"The church? I told him I'd come from the church? Why would I have been there? What day of the week was it?"

Billy shuffled through his notes. "I don't know exactly, but Dovey Mae—"

"Dovey Mae? What does she have to do with this?"

"Sam told her about it. When he was hiding in Granny Tarwater's cellar. Here it is. Sam said it was three days before you went missing. You disappeared on a Saturday. That would make it Wednesday when he gave you the second ride."

"How could Dovey Mae remember a detail like that? After all this time?"

"Cynthia, I've learned over the years that Dovey Mae has a really good memory when things matter to her. And this mattered a lot."

"I'm drawing a blank, Billy. But that shouldn't surprise you."

"Cynthia, I remember Granny Tarwater going to supper at church every Wednesday night without fail. Could you have been there for that?"

"As crazy religious as my mother is, Billy, I don't recall her ever going to Wednesday night supper. When it comes to her holier-than-thou piety, she's above mixing socially with the unredeemed hoi polloi. And I certainly don't think I would have gone on my own."

"Is there some other reason you would have been there? Maybe to meet with Kilgallon?"

"Billy, the very mention of that dreadful man sends an icy chill through me."

"I understand, but might you have gone there to meet with him anyway? Because your mother told you to? Or perhaps out of a sense of duty?"

"A sense of duty? To whom?"

"To God, perhaps? After all, you were a good girl back then. Weren't you?"

"Back then? And I'm not a good girl now?"

"I'm just saying—"

"Billy, you're treading on thin ice."

"There was a little girl…who had a little curl…right in the middle of her forehead—"

"I know. I know. When she was good…she was very, very good…and when she was bad…she was fantastic. You've shared that little ditty with me before. Thanks for the levity. I needed that."

Just then, she heard stirring outside the bedroom door. The kids were up.

* * *

It wasn't until that evening, when the dinner table had been cleared, the dishes washed, and Billy Jr. and Addie were safe and sound in bed, that Cynthia and Billy were able to resume their conversation.

"Cynthia, I've been thinking about something. Do you think there's a connection between the Chi-Rho and the shit that was going on at church back then? I know you were getting a lot of pressure from your mother and the-man-whose-name-shall-remain-unsaid."

"It doesn't make sense to me, Billy. Confederate Avenue Baptist was evangelical Protestant. Insanely so. As far as I know, evangelicals, the Protestant variety anyway, stay as far away from Greek and Latin iconography as they can. Lily-white Jesus hanging from an old wooden cross, his head hung low, blood trickling from the holes—that's all the symbolism they care about."

"I hear you. But I just wonder...perhaps we should talk to your mother about it. She's the quintessential evangelical, isn't she?"

"Are you kidding? She'd be clueless. She wouldn't know the difference between the Chi-Rho symbol and Karo corn syrup."

"Funny, Cynthia. But I still think we should talk to her. It can't hurt."

"You bring it up if you wish. I'd rather stay out of it."

Chapter Thirty-Eight
Billy Tarwater

October 25, 1980

IT HAD BEEN SIXTEEN DAYS SINCE THE LAST BLACK child went missing. While there had been longer stretches between disappearances, everyone on the city desk was optimistic that maybe—just maybe—we'd seen the last of it. But the killer was still on the loose. And the city's nerves were frayed—raggedy-edge frayed.

A psychic from New Jersey named Dorothy Allison had arrived in Atlanta at the request of the police. She claimed there would be no more slain children as long as she was in town. Her arrival brought back memories of the time Binky—my eleven-year-old self—visited Immolene Ludowici. What had Dovey Mae, years later, called the self-styled Fortune Teller to the Luminaries? *That quack of a woman*. As an adult, I had about as much faith in Dorothy Allison's prognostications as Binky should have had in the Ali-Baba-turbaned, gold-toothed diviner with the plug-in, cantaloupe-of-a-crystal-ball. How had Binky, and Dovey Mae for that matter, fallen for such bilge?

But what if it wasn't bilge? Could Madame Ludowici have been on to something? What had she said as I sat across from her at the table, the glass ball glowing between us? *She's alive. In the present. I see her calling your name.* But then, as soon as she had gotten my hopes up, what did she do? She walked across the room and said something to Dovey Mae. In a whisper, but loud enough that I could hear her. *Sister Walker, I just can't do this to a boy his age.* What had she meant by that? Had she known about Cynthia's whereabouts at the time?

I shook my head. *Get real, Billy. She was a charlatan. Even Dovey Mae finally figured that out.*

A lot of shit seemed to be going down in the city. That added to the tension that already held damned near one-and-a-half million people in its thrall because of the child murders, and it had occupied much of my time all week.

The past Monday, an inmate at the Fulton County Jail had escaped by removing an exhaust fan in the jail kitchen wall and crawling through the opening. And another escapee from the same jail was discovered in a sewer pipe after having lowered himself through a manhole in the inmate exercise yard.

And then on Tuesday, a chain of seven runaway locomotives pushed an unmanned train across six miles of downtown track, injuring two workers and crashing into two other trains before derailing on the west side of town. Authorities weren't ruling out foul play.

And on Wednesday, a 23-year-old expectant mother and her unborn child died at Northside Hospital from injuries suffered in a hit-and-run. Police were looking for the driver of a light-colored Ford—model unknown.

* * *

By the time Saturday came along, I was ready for a break from work—and the chance to refocus on freeing Sam Jepperson.

The kids were at my mother's house for the weekend. I was sure that, right about then, they were enjoying hot bowls of oatmeal—Quaker Old Fashioned—heaped with brown sugar and walnuts and puddled with whole cream. How did I know that? Because, two decades earlier, that's what Binky would have been doing—and grinning ear to ear between mouthfuls. *Like mother, like grandmother.* I was grateful that they were safe and sound in their grandmother's care. Innocent. Carefree. And shielded from iniquity.

Cynthia and I headed out that morning to visit her parents. In adulthood, I found Adele and Cecil to be tedious at best. But Cecil wasn't the problem, really. Most of the time when we visited, he was either in the toolshed or up at McKnight's shooting craps or doing the parlay thing—mainly, no doubt, to get away from Adele's missionizing. On more than one occasion, Cynthia had commented on the fact that old habits die hard. Her father's penchant for hanging out gambling at McKnight's. And Adele's obsession with doing the Lord's bidding.

The traffic eastbound on I-20 was unusually heavy for a Saturday. I wondered why. As we neared the Boulevard exit, I realized it was because of a wreck just before the off-ramp. It looked like an F150 had decided to annihilate a Chevrolet Vega.

No match, I thought. The right lane was blocked. That lane and the shoulder were awash with flashing blue and red. Several police cars. A fire truck. A Grady ambulance. Paramedics were attending to an injured party off to the side. Firemen were hosing down what I assumed to be a gasoline spill. My years on the city desk hadn't eased the sick feeling I got in the pit of my stomach whenever I saw a bad accident, especially one with a casualty lying on the side of the road. I thought of the trip to Grady one night seventeen years earlier. To visit Cynthia. With the madman Cecil at the wheel. And Binky wondering whether we'd get there alive.

Past the stop-and-go, the stretch between Boulevard and Moreland Avenue was typical for a weekend. Smooth sailing at fifty-five. We exited at Moreland. When we passed Martha Brown Church on the left, I thought of Binky standing near the corner of Moreland and Metropolitan waiting for Dovey Mae. Of my bike stashed in the bushes. Of my cap pulled low, lest someone recognized me.

We pulled into Cynthia's parents' driveway. We were on a mission to pump Adele for information. Actually, it was me. I was on a mission. Cynthia had made it clear that this was my brief, not hers. She was the one teaching contemporary religion at Agnes Scott, but I was the one insisting that we consult her batshit crazy mother about a possible connection between Protestant evangelicals and Chi-Rho. *It doesn't make sense to me*, Cynthia had said. *You bring it up if you wish. I'd rather stay out of it.*

Cecil was away. No surprise there. Adele greeted us at the door in a gingham blouse and her trademark dungarees. Keys dangling. She asked if we'd like coffee. Tea? Cynthia and I both passed on the offer. We sat on the sofa. Adele sat across from us.

It became clear after about five minutes that Cynthia had not been far from the mark with her Karo joke. Her mother didn't have the foggiest notion what a Chi-Rho cross was, except that she thought it was "one of them Catholic graven images." I came close to asking Adele whether she thought her "keys to the kingdom" hanging at her side might just be her own form of graven image. But I backed off. Not for her sake, but for Cynthia's.

* * *

We pulled out of the driveway and headed back to The Belmont.

"She's some piece of work, isn't she?" Cynthia said.

"That's for sure. Would your mother have let you marry me if I'd been Catholic?"

Her smirk spoke volumes. "Hell, Billy, that's not the half of it. She'd have done everything she could to stop it even if you'd been Methodist or Presbyterian. And god forbid you'd been Lutheran. They're as bad as Catholics in her eyes."

"How did she let you get away with everything you did? Given that she's so…what's the word?"

"Sanctimonious? Pharisaical?"

"I've told you not to use those big words around me, Cynthia." I laughed. "I'm just a lowly newspaperman, not a college professor."

"What do you mean get away with everything? I was a good girl. You implied as much the other morning. As I was polishing off my breakfast in bed."

"I believe I said 'You were a good girl back then. Weren't you?' It was a question."

"I see. Well I *was* a good girl. Still am."

"Yeah, right. But just so you know. I'm not saying I don't like you just the way you are…and were. You used to drive me nuts in those Daisy Dukes. And your flouncing around and all."

"I never flounced."

"OK. Parading around, then. Whatever it was, it worked. I'm surprised your mother let you dress like that. Act like that."

"Believe it or not, I set boundaries early on. Boundaries that I wouldn't let her cross. Daddy used to say I popped out headstrong. It took my mother a little longer…maybe 'til I was five or so…to figure out that I was a force to be reckoned with."

* * *

We had just walked through the apartment door when the phone rang. Cynthia answered. It was Gary. She handed me the phone.

"I found something," he said. "You need to come over."

"What is it?"

"Just come over."

"Come over where?"

"To my mother's house."

Chapter Thirty-Nine
Billy Tarwater

October 25, 1980

HE MET ME AT HIS MOTHER'S FRONT DOOR. I COULD tell he was anxious—uncharacteristically so for the knockabout-kid-from-East-Atlanta-turned-detective Gary I knew. He was fidgeting. And rocking up and down, cockeyed-like, on the ball of his foot—the one at the end of his good leg. He had a large manila envelope in one hand. His walking stick in the other. "Come in, Billy. Have a seat."

I eased into the same captain's chair as before. Well, not eased, really. I sat on its edge waiting for Gary to tell me what he had discovered.

"I found this tucked away in a corner of the attic." He thrust the envelope toward me. It said Hudspeth in Magic Marker. And below it, CONFIDENTIAL in all caps. "I can't believe I missed it before. It was under a stack of dusty paperwork. You need to look at it."

I unfastened the metal clasp, rusted around the edges, and opened the seal flap. Inside were five photographs. Three were the close-ups of the marks on the backs of the three girls' thighs. But unlike in the photos I had purloined from Mrs. Alford's living room on my last visit, someone had taken what appeared to have been a red wax pencil and had drawn circles around each girl's incision. Martha Ann Dullums' was labeled with a big red 1. Beside Patsy Boggs' was a 2. Cynthia's was labeled 3. I didn't know what to make of the wax-pencil markings, except for the obvious conclusion that Gary's father had considered the thigh carvings to be prime evidence. Of course. Anybody would. Nothing new there.

It was the two other photographs that gave me pause. The first was a wide shot of a creek bed. Paramedics huddled over a body near the leading edge of the creek. A stand of trees ran along its far bank. Shrubby overgrowth obscured the trunks of the trees and the space between them. Someone, presumably Gus Alford, had also marked that photograph. With a big wax-pencil arrow pointing to a spot in the overgrowth. I looked at the other photograph. It was a close-up of the area indicated by the arrow in the first picture. A section was circled in red. I could see an image inside the circle. It was a face. I could barely make it out but, from what I could tell, it looked like a man's face.

In the white margins at the bottoms of both photographs were the words: HUDSPETH CRIME SCENE. The body was Cynthia's. I froze. Could her attempted killer have sped off in his car, returned to the scene along a back street, and lurked behind the bushes as the detectives swarmed the area and the paramedics attended to his prey? Was he deriving perverse pleasure from watching everything that was going on? Would he—could he—have known that Cynthia was still alive when they placed her on a stretcher, loaded her into the ambulance, and sped away toward Grady, lights flashing, siren blaring? Or did he think he had consummated the deed?

I had been so engrossed in studying the photographs that I failed to notice a page of typed notes stuck to the inside edge of the envelope. I removed the sheet of onionskin paper, discolored and brittle from a decade and a half of attic heat and humidity. It was a shortened list from the DMV report that I had studied as I sat at the table at Marnie's two weeks earlier. But this time, the only cars listed were Valiants. And unlike the typewritten list in the police report, the owner's name was handwritten beside each vehicle. I wondered why names had been missing from the report in the police file. Had DMV provided the list without owners' names? Or had the list been retyped by the police with names missing? And if so, why? To protect somebody? To conform the narrative to a foregone conclusion?

Two thirds of the way down the page, my eyes fixed on one name. Circled in blue ink.

Seymour, Leonard.

Launchpad Leonard. Cynthia's next-door peeper creeper. Was he the killer after all? Had he managed somehow to evade scrutiny by the detectives—through omission or commission on their part? He had spent seventeen years walking free while Sam wasted away in a prison cell. Had Gus Alford sat on critical information that could have sent Seymour up for life and exonerated Jepperson? It looked that way to me.

It took me a solid five minutes before I finally found my tongue. But I needed to play it cool with Gary—at least for the time being. The last thing I wanted to do was betray what I felt at the moment. I knew I couldn't leave without the photographs and the typed list. But I couldn't sneak out with them in my satchel like before. I needed to be nonchalant about the whole thing. It was poker face time. "Gary, got a question."

"Shoot."

"Can I borrow these. I'll return them in good order."

Gary stared across the room. He replied without looking at me. "Take 'em. But bring 'em back."

I walked to my car. I wondered why Gary had gone back into the attic. Had he suspected something was missing from the original box of evidence? Or did he just happen to be up there and ran across the envelope? Whatever the reason, I was glad he had gone back.

* * *

I knew Leonard Seymour still lived next door to Cynthia's parents. I could have gone straight to his house. But I decided against it. The last thing I wanted was to have Adele Hudspeth see me visiting next door and start asking questions. Plus, I needed to gather any additional evidence I could before confronting him.

I hadn't been able to shake the thought of the faded navy blue car in the back lot at the Pawn de Rosa. The fact that I saw it there. And the fact that it went missing between the first time I visited Marvin Darby and when I went back the second time. I decided to call on Marvin a third time. I would quiz him about the car. Ask him where he got it and where it went. Point out that it looked a lot like the car in the Murphy parking lot, the one caught on Kodacolor by Petey Samples. Except in Petey's pictures it was grey or silver—I couldn't tell which—not navy blue.

Marvin was behind the counter, arguing with a prospective pawner over a wristwatch. Marvin held the watch to his ear. "Buddy, this ain't no Accutron," I heard him say to the man.

"It most certainly is," the man said. "I got it from my daddy. It was a birthday present. He bought it fair and square. From Davison's jewelry department. Downtown."

"Accutron's don't tick. Now go ahead on and get the hell out of my store."

The man snatched the watch from Marvin's hand and hightailed it to the front door, brushing against me as he passed.

"People got a lot of nerve trying to pull a fast one on me," Marvin said to the room after the man had walked out. "What they don't realize is you never try to bullshit a bullshitter. You'll always lose." He turned to me. Looked me up and down. "Back again, I see."

I asked Marvin about the car. Where did he get it?

"I didn't get it from anywhere. My old man got it. Back in the sixties. I happened to be hanging out here after school the day the guy came in—the one that pawned it off. Said he needed to get rid of it in a hurry. Said he didn't have a title. Lost it or something. I don't know." Marvin lit a cigarillo and dragged a lungful. "My old man thought the car might have been stolen, with no title and all. And it looked fresh painted. But he took it anyway. Didn't give the man much money for it. But the funny thing is, the man didn't seem to care."

"What kind of car was it?"

"Valiant. I think it was a '61."

"The car's gone now. What happened to it?"

"It sat out there for years. But then a fellow came in the other day and paid cash for it. Said he planned to restore it to its original…what was the word…splendor, that's it. Whatever that was supposed to mean. Damned thing was faded like hell. Rusted along the bottom. Didn't run. The man had to have it towed away."

"Do you recall who the guy was? The pawner, I mean. Not the one who bought it."

"It was a long time ago. I don't remember his name. Just that he was a big man. Sloppy. Beer gut hung over his belt. Belched a lot. Loudest I've ever heard. Damned near shook the rafters. I'll never forget that."

* * *

As I walked through the door and into the apartment, I asked Cynthia, "Do you remember Leonard Seymour ever driving a late-model Valiant…fastback…in the early sixties?"

"Are you kidding? That man was so cheap he wouldn't have thought of spending money on a new car. And certainly not a sporty one. The only thing I remember him ever driving was an old clunker. Why do you ask?"

I pulled the typewritten list from the manila envelope and showed it to Cynthia. "What do you make of this?"

"I have no idea, Billy. I don't believe I ever saw him driving a car like that. But you know there's a lot that I can't recall."

"Do you think your mother might remember him ever having a Valiant fastback?

"She might. Why don't you ask her?"

"Another thing. Do you think Seymour still sings in the choir?"

"How would I know?"

"Your mother would. Want to go to church tomorrow? We could kill two birds with one stone. We could ask your mother. And we could confront Seymour."

"Billy, are you out of your mind? A wave of panic would come over me just walking through the door."

"Because of Kilgallon? He's long gone. Or because your mother will be there?"

"I've told you before. Hearing Kilgallon's name sends an icy chill through me. Like just now. But you're right, he's long gone. It's not that. And as for my mother, she wouldn't be there, if we were to go."

"Why not?"

"She stopped going not long after the new preacher took over. The old youth minister. She claims he's a misbeliever of the worst kind. A reborn pretender. Her words."

"What is it, then? What's the panic about?"

"It's just that I find the whole idea of that church to be repugnant. Horrid, really. And just thinking of being there instills fear in me. I'd just as soon strip naked and parade down Peachtree."

"That's a titillating thought. Can I join you?"

"Right, Billy. Dream on."

I decided not to show Cynthia the photographs. Not yet, anyway. If being in the Confederate Avenue sanctuary instilled fear, I could only imagine what seeing a picture of paramedics huddled over her body would do to her.

* * *

Sunday morning, I decided I would pay a visit to Adele Hudspeth first. With her daughter's blessing, of course. Cynthia was more than happy to let me go by myself. Then I would head over to Confederate Avenue Baptist, timing my arrival for toward the end of the service so I wouldn't have to sit through the Reverend Thomas's blather. I would seek out Leonard Seymour after it was over, assuming he was there. I would ask him about the car.

I had considered waiting to confront him until I had more information. The Department of Revenue—GDR in insiders' parlance—could run a check on the VIN and tell me all the prior owners. And the current owner. It was easier to get a VIN check from GDR than DMV, in part because I had solid contacts there. But it was the weekend, and the office was closed. Getting to Leonard Seymour took precedence.

The church was neutral grounds. It seemed like a safer place to confront him than on his own home turf. Then again, there was always the possibility that lightning would fell me to the ground for defiling the Lord's house with discord.

* * *

When her daughter wasn't present, Adele Hudspeth was always different around me. Standoffish. Downright rude. I always wondered whether she thought I was a bad influence on Cynthia. She didn't understand that there was a wild side to her daughter. One she had never seen—and probably never would.

She greeted me on the front porch with her hands on her hips. She flipped her middle finger back and forth against the keys dangling from her waist, making a noisome jinglejangle. I wondered whether this was the result of a nervous tic or an attempt to let me know that she, not I, held the Keys to the Kingdom. Or perhaps it was her subliminal way of saying Fuck You. It was, after all, her middle finger.

She never invited me inside, so we sat on the front porch. That was fine with me. I asked her about Leonard Seymour. Did he ever drive a '61 silver or grey Valiant fastback. She said she couldn't recall anything like that. If he had, she'd surely know about it, being that he always parked his car right out front.

"Why are you so all-fired curious about a Valiant, anyway?" she hissed.

"Just trying to track something down. That's all."

She stood, stared at me, and jingled her keys some more.

I thanked her and got up to leave. I was halfway between the porch and the curb when she called out to me. "The reverend drove a silver Valiant."

I swung around. "Which reverend?" I asked.

"Virlyn Kilgallon. He used to drive one. Before he moved back to Alabama. I saw it once or twice in the church parking lot."

"Are you certain, Mrs. Hudspeth? Memories can deceive after seventeen years."

"Your memory may deceive, Billy, but mine doesn't. The Lord's seen to that."

Chapter Forty

Billy Tarwater

October 26, 1980

I ENTERED THE SANCTUARY AT THE TAIL END OF Reverend Thomas's sermon—something about everybody being somebody and the Son being everything. At least, that's what I surmised, although I had missed most of it. I stood in the back until the exhortation ended. As abhorrent as I found the whole affair, something from my childhood days—I guess it was the memory of sitting quietly in the hallowed hall with Granny Tarwater—prevented me from interrupting the flow of things by my presence. I was certain that, had I headed down the center aisle before the reverend had finished, all eyes would have been frozen on me. I waited until the choir began to let loose with "Jesus Is Tenderly Calling." I padded silently down the aisle until I came to an empty seat at the end of a pew halfway to the front of the sanctuary.

I eased in. But just as I had gotten settled, I looked up to see Leonard Seymour in the choir loft staring at me. Our eyes locked. Had he recognized me from so many years back? Perhaps he had seen Cynthia and me on one of our visits to her parents' house.

Then, about midway through the song—at the part about bringing Him your burden and being blest—Seymour stood, straightened the front of his beer-belly-bulging robe, and scooted out the side door that led from the choir loft to the rear hall. Had he gotten wind that I was on his trail? Had somebody tipped him off? Or maybe he had overheard my conversation with Adele on her front porch. Launchpad Leonard, after all, *was* a snooper.

I couldn't run after him down the aisle. Surely that would have created a scene. Like the time back in the sixties when the mouse had run across the room, causing Mrs. Hunnicutt, sitting on the front pew, to collapse into a faint. I got up and fast-walked to the rear of the sanctuary, at a good pace but not so fast as to attract undue attention. It was not until I had passed through the doors to the outside that I took off in a sprint. Just as I rounded the corner of the building and headed toward the parking lot, I saw Seymour shed his robe, throw it into his car, and heave himself into the driver's seat.

I ran to my car and cranked the ignition. By the time I drove out of the lot, he was already half a block up Woodland Avenue. I followed him, racing to reduce the distance between us. But he must have been going 65, maybe faster, in a 30 speed zone, and I couldn't gain on him. He slowed down a little along the near-ninety-degree curve just past Beulah Heights. He turned left on Moreland and then sped up again. I turned left fifty or so yards behind him. But just as I did, a large delivery truck pulled onto

Moreland in front of me, slowing me down and blocking my view ahead. I tried to go around it, but there was too much traffic.

I assumed Seymour was headed home, but by then he had managed to lose me. I turned right on Portland and full-throttled down the street toward his house. I saw his car parked in the driveway, inside the chain-link fence. But he wasn't in it. I parked along the curb and cut the engine. I grabbed the manila envelope that Gary had given me. I removed the handwritten vehicle list, folded it, and placed it in my shirt pocket. I headed to Seymour's front gate. Not the one at the driveway, but the smaller one at the walkway that led to his front porch. I disengaged the fork latch—fortunately it wasn't padlocked—and entered his yard. I looked to my right. Granny Tarwater's place had gone to seed since she had passed away. Paint was peeling. Shrubs were overgrown. I didn't know the people who currently lived there. But I was sure I wouldn't like them. I looked to my left. No sign of Cynthia's parents. *Please don't come out now, Adele. I don't have time for your madness.*

I was almost to the steps leading up to Seymour's porch when his front door swung open. "What do you want, Tarwater?" he called from inside the screen door.

"You remember me," I said. "After all these years."

"I knew who you were as soon as you came through the gate. I see you in the paper all the time. And I saw you in church this morning." He squared his shoulders. Sucked in his ample gut as best he could. "I'll ask again. What do you want with me?"

"I just need a few minutes of your time," I said.

"For what?"

"It's about a car."

"What car?"

"A Valiant."

"I don't know what you're talking about."

"You never owned a '61 Valiant? Fastback?" I pulled the list from my pocket. Unfolded it. "It says here—"

"I said I don't know what you're talking about."

"I have paperwork with your name on it. It indicates that you owned a Valiant. Back in the sixties."

"Indicates? Listen, Tarwater. What would you do if some swingin' dick showed up at your house, came to your *church* even, and accused you of something you didn't know anything about? Why should I give you the time of day?"

"Maybe because the paperwork is from the police?"

"The police? I don't believe you. Let me see."

I climbed the steps onto the porch. Showed Seymour the vehicle list through the screen. I wasn't about to let him get his turgid hands on it.

"A handwritten list? You've gotta be joking." he said. "You want me to believe that's official? And anyway, I don't know anything about any Valiant. Maybe there's another *Seymour, Leonard* out there somewhere. That's not me."

I shuddered at the thought of two Seymour, Leonards. I considered ending the conversation there. I obviously wasn't getting anywhere. And absent an official VIN run, I didn't have much to back me up. But I decided to carry our little tête-à-tête one step further. "Take a good look at the description of the car beside your name," I said. "Sorry, by *Seymour, Leonard*'s name." I took a deep breath. "I think I found that car. Funny thing is..."

I looked down at his now-relaxed beer belly. His shirttail half hanging out. A grease stain on the front. I thought of his incessant belching and what Marvin Darby had said. "…the fellow with the car said his daddy bought it from a guy fitting your description to a tee. Only problem is it was a different color from what it says on the paperwork here. It was blue. The man said it looked fresh painted when his daddy bought it."

I could have sworn I saw Leonard Seymour's face blanch a shade. He ran his eyes from my shoes to my head and back again. Without looking up, he placed his hand on the door latch. I thought he was about to step out onto the porch. But then I realized he was locking the screen door. He slammed the front door shut. I heard the deadbolt engage.

Leonard Seymour wasn't on the up-and-up. That was obvious. But I was clueless as to what the deal was with the car. And whether he was mixed up at all in what happened back in '63.

* * *

Monday turned out to be another slow news day, slow enough for me to break away in the afternoon from my day job to take care of two pieces of personal business.

First, I would call one of my buddies at GDR. Have him run the Valiant VIN check that I hadn't been able to get my hands on over the weekend. Then I would drop in on Petey Samples. See if he could blow up the photograph. The one with the face peering through the overgrowth where Cynthia's body had been found. The face that someone—I assumed Alford—had encircled with red wax.

It didn't take long for me to get through to the one person at GDR I knew I could count on to come through in a pinch—and in a hurry. At least I thought in a hurry. He told me he'd get back to me soon. But when three o'clock came and still no word, I headed to Kirkwood to pay Petey a visit. I probably should have called ahead of time, but I took a chance.

* * *

"This is eeyit?" Petey said as soon as I had pulled the photograph and shown it to him. "No nehgative?"

"This is all I have, Petey. Can you blow up the part circled in red?"

"I can. But it'd be a lot easier with a nehgative."

"Sorry Petey. I don't have the negative."

"Well, like the man says. That's all she wrote. Ah'll make do. Wanna come watch?"

I followed Petey down the stairs and into the darkroom.

"What we're gonna have to do," he said, "is take this camera here." He pointed to a Nikon sitting on the table. "Ah'll take a picture of the picture, if you know what I mean. Ah'll zoom in real close. Cain't do it any other way." He swung around and stared at me. "You know, Billy, they have these things called magnifyin' glasses." He chuckled under his breath. "Did you try that?"

"I should have."

"Mighta worked," he said.

"Oh, well." He reached for a lens sitting on the table. "This here's a macro, 105mm. Kinda like a magnifyin' glass." He popped the lens onto the Nikon with a click.

There was a closet at the far end of the room. He opened the closet door and took out two tripods. He mounted the camera onto one. A studio lamp onto the other. He taped the photograph to the wall. He shined the bright light onto the picture at an oblique angle, I assumed to cut down on the glare. He positioned the Nikon close to the wall. He then took three or four shots, adjusting the lens between each take.

"Ah'll need to do the nehgatives. Then make prints. Wanna watch that too?"

"I'd like to, Petey, but if you don't mind, could I use your phone while you're doing it?"

"Sure. There's one upstairs in the living room. Make yourself at home. You can just wait there 'til ah'm through. You cain't come in when the red light's on."

I headed out of the darkroom and for the stairs.

Petey called out to me. "Hey, you're not makin' any long distance are you. 'Cause if you do, you gotta pay me back."

"No, Petey. Just local. I promise."

I rang the city desk. Any messages? Someone had called from the Department of Revenue. I hung up and dialed my GDR buddy. His secretary said he had stepped out. It was pushing five. I gave her Petey's number and asked her to have him call me there before he left for the day. She said she'd relay the message if he returned. But no guarantees.

I sat in the living room and waited. For a callback. And for Petey to ascend the stairs with what I hoped would be a clean blowup.

A few minutes later, I heard his footsteps.

Petey walked into the room. He was carrying a stack of photographs. He handed them to me.

The first enlargement I looked at was a blur. All I could make out was a gaunt face with sunken cheeks and two dark eyes behind what looked like wire-rimmed glasses. I found it oddly evocative. Unsettling. But I couldn't quite put my finger on why. The other photographs were no better.

When six thirty rolled around, I assumed GDR Buddy had left his office without calling me. I thanked Petey, stuffed the enlargements and the original into my satchel, and turned to leave. I was about to the front door when the phone rang.

Petey answered. He extended the handset toward me. "It's for you."

I walked across the room to where he was standing.

He handed me the phone.

It was GDR Buddy. "Got the goods on the car," he said. "Only two owners. Purchased new in '61 by a Virlyn Jephthah Kilgallon."

That's when it hit me. Was Kilgallon the blurred face in the photograph? Maybe. But I couldn't be certain. I hadn't seen him in over a decade and a half.

"Who was the other owner?" I asked.

"Kilgallon transferred the title in '63. October 15th to be exact. To a Leonard No Middle Name Seymour."

Chapter Forty-One

Cynthia Tarwater

October 27, 1980

CYNTHIA HAD PUT BILLY JR. AND ADDIE TO BED AND was watching them venture off to neverland when she heard the front door open then close. It was nine o'clock. She looked up to see Billy slouching in the bedroom doorway. His tweed sport coat was slung over his shoulder, hanging tenuously from his index finger. His satchel dangled from his other hand. His face was drawn. His eyes were bankrupt.

"Billy, you look like you've lost your best friend. Where have you been? I've been worried about you."

"Marnie's. Driving around. *First* Marnie's. *Then* driving around."

"Driving around where?"

"Woodland Avenue. East Atlanta. Grove Park. Stewart Avenue."

"You covered a lot of ground. Can I ask what you were doing driving all over town?"

"Cynthia, we need to talk."

He took her hand and led her from the children's bedroom to the kitchen table, the same place they always seemed to end up for serious discussions. He pulled out the chair and motioned her to sit. He hung his sport coat on the seat back across the table from her and sat down. "I have something I need to show you," he said. "A photo."

"I've heard *that* before."

He pulled the enlargement from his satchel. He eased it across the table to her. "Recognize this face?"

She studied the blurred close-up of a man peering through a tangle of brambles. "It looks a little like that revolting preacher. My scourge from a past life."

"That's what I thought too."

"Where was it taken?"

"Alongside the creek where you were found," Billy said. "This is hard, I know."

"It's not easy, that's for sure. When you say it was taken where I was found, do you also mean it was taken *when* I was found?

He nodded. "The police took it. And they saw the face, too. At least one of them did. Because he circled it. I suspect Gus Alford did that. I had it blown up so I could get a better look at it."

He retrieved the other photograph. The one she'd seen before. Of the car in the Murphy parking lot. "Remember this picture? That's where Martha Ann Dullums was last seen before she—"

"Was swept away to her death. I know."

He pointed to the car in the picture. "That car. Right there. It fits the descriptions of the ones at the Dullums and Boggs crime scenes, based on the tire tracks. And the one the Grove Park workers saw speeding away from where you were almost…" He looked away.

"Go ahead and say it, Billy. Killed."

"That make and model car, a '61 Valiant fastback. Do you know who owned one in '63?"

"No, I don't." *Jump in feet first, Cynthia. Say what you're really thinking.* She narrowed her eyes. "Billy, I know how important all of this is to you. It's important to me too. But sometimes you talk to me like you're that guy on *Dragnet* instead of my husband. Just the facts, ma'am. What's his name?"

"Joe Friday. I'm sorry, honey. I don't even realize I'm doing it. I guess it's just the investigative reporter coming out."

"I get that. Just thought I should let you know." She half smiled. "Where would you be if you didn't have me to keep you in line?" Her half-smile retreated. "So are you going to tell me?"

"Tell you what?"

"Who owned a car like that?"

"Virlyn Kilgallon. And in mid-October of that year, sometime after you were attacked, he transferred the title to…want to hazard a guess who?"

"I have no idea, Billy."

"Leonard Seymour. Your next-door peeper."

"What? Leonard Seymour? The other scourge from my past?"

"The one and only. Then what does Kilgallon do after he transfers the title? He pulls up stakes and leaves town."

She felt a numbness come over her.

* * *

Cynthia did something out of character that night.

Billy had fallen asleep around ten thirty. She tossed and turned.

It was nearing midnight when Cynthia finally got up and crept into the bathroom. She stood barefoot on the cold, hard tile. Staring at the medicine cabinet. At the dark spots along the edges of the mirror where the silver had fallen away, no doubt due to moisture buildup behind the glass. She opened the cabinet. She fumbled through the bottles—some prescription, some over-the-counter—until she came upon the one she was looking for. The name on the bottle said Adele Hudspeth. How had it ended up in *her* bathroom? She remembered. Her mother had given it to her when she was pregnant with Billy Jr. and having trouble sleeping. "Try these," her mother had said. She never did.

She carried the bottle into the kitchen. Took a Ball jelly jar glass from the cabinet. Turned on the faucet marked Cold. Ran her hand under the water. Half-filled the glass. Downed the water with two benzodiazepines. Chased them with a double shot of Billy's Jim Beam.

She sat at the kitchen table. Replayed the conversation from three hours earlier. She buried her head in her folded arms. Nodded off.

* * *

She awoke to a throbbing headache. She rubbed her eyes, struggling to read the clock over the sink. It was four thirty. She staggered back to the bathroom. Stood before the mirror.

She stared at the black spot along the mirror's bottom edge. It was creeping up the surface of the glass, like an amorphous blob. She bent over the washbasin and splashed cold water on her face. When she looked up, that's when she saw the stranger peering back at her through the glass. She swung around. There was no one behind her. *Am I awake?* She ran her fingers across her nose bridge. Her cheekbones. Her mouth. Down her neck. It felt real. Not like a dream. But was it? *Is it a mirror I'm looking into? Or a window I'm looking through?*

The stranger stared back at her, tracking her eyes with a penetrating gaze. She looked to her left, the stranger looked right. She looked right, the stranger looked left. She lifted her right hand. The stranger lifted her left. She touched her right cheek. The stranger touched her left. But then, when Cynthia managed to pull off an ever so slight smile, the stranger's lips curled down in a sad frown. A chill ran through Cynthia's body from the cold tile below.

She explored the face in the mirror. A young girl, fifteen years her junior. Maybe twenty. She was wearing a Murphy High sweatshirt. That's when Cynthia realized the girl was no stranger at all. It was her own self. In another time. Another place.

I'll play along. Until Billy shakes me awake and kills this little charade. "What do you have for me, Cynthia Jane?" she said to the girl in the mirror. *Why not call her for who she is, Cynthia Jane Hudspeth, the force to be reckoned with.*

The girl spun in a flirtatious pirouette and bounded into the mirror's depths. But as she did, she looked back at Cynthia with a *follow me* wave. Cynthia passed through the mirror's plane and shadowed her temptress.

Cynthia Jane landed flat-footed on the edge of the Glenwood Avenue sidewalk and strolled down the street toward Moreland. A lanky rube of a boy with a Cheshire Cat grin stood outside the pharmacy and watched as she ambled away.

Cynthia Jane looked over her shoulder. A car was easing along Glenwood, following her. It was a dark gray fastback. Sort of sporty. She stopped. It stopped. She went. It went. She stopped again, turned around, and walked over to the car. The faceless driver rolled down his window. She placed her hand on the door's chrome trim.

Cynthia heard a faint *Get in, missy*. Cynthia Jane circled to the other side of the car and slid into the front passenger's seat. The car drove off.

Cynthia's eyes fell on the dark spot on the mirror. It had now crept halfway to the top. She watched as the blob morphed, filling the mirror with an onyx question mark.

The question mark faded. The car was back again, stopped on Glenwood. Cynthia zeroed in on the driver and passenger. The driver stared through thick, wire-rimmed glasses into the plane of the mirror. Bared his teeth in a wide grin.

The car drove off, this time at a clip.

Cynthia rubbed her eyes again. Waited for the focus to come back. She stared into the mirror. The car came into view a third time. But now it was parked at the end of a long driveway. Beside a house that sat back from the street. A canary yellow clapboard bungalow—with russet shutters and a matching front door. A broad porch, flanked by four tapered Craftsman columns. A front-pitched roof with gable windows in a threesome. A little cupola at the crest of the pitched roof. With a rooster weather vane.

The lights were off in the house.

The car was unoccupied—at least as far as she could tell.

The vane remained still, pointing to Cynthia's left. But the rooster turned its head in her direction and winked.

Cynthia's mother appeared in the foreground. "Cynthia," she said. "Bless your heart. You fell out of a difficult tree, hit every branch, then got stuck on the last one for a little while."

* * *

When Cynthia was young, around the time her mother came to the realization that she was a force to be reckoned with, Adele started playing a mind game with her—one of many that would follow. "Where did that good little girl go?" her mother would say whenever Cynthia did something she didn't approve of. "That good little girl went away. And then *you* showed up."

Years later, with the benefit of hindsight and Psychology 101, Cynthia had come to appreciate the horror that lies in the grey areas of identity. And the seed sown by her mother—intentional or otherwise. *Where did that good little girl go?*

On the one hand, Cynthia's sense of self was secure. A happy marriage. Two wonderful children. A rewarding career. And finally, her mother's ministrations notwithstanding, she had come to strike a healthy balance between wholesome and puckish. She wore it well.

But then there was that one nagging fixation, the black abyss, the chasm in her memory that she couldn't avoid. No matter how hard she tried. She wondered whether her *real* identity, the identity she could never quite finger, lay somewhere in a fight-or-flight mindset, a product of life-threatening trauma.

Sometimes, when she was alone and broody, a vexing thought would well up inside her. Whatever had happened to her in '63—was it somehow her fault?

That little girl went away, and then you showed up.

* * *

"Wake up." For a moment, she wasn't sure whether it was her sleep speaking. "You're going to be late to class." The voice, and the hand joggling her shoulder, belonged to Billy.

She pulled the covers from over her face. Rolled over to see him standing beside the bed. "I'm not going in today, Billy. Please do me a favor. Call the college. Tell them I'm under the weather."

She drifted back to sleep.

* * *

She awoke again, this time to Billy standing over her with the wooden tray. Coffee. Eggs. Toast. Just like before. She looked over at the clock. It was 10:15. "Where are the children?"

"I drove them to preschool. Here. I made you a little something. I thought you would be hungry."

"That's so like you, Billy." She sat up and arranged the pillows behind her. "What are you doing at home? At this hour?"

He unfolded the tray legs and placed it across her lap. "Cynthia, I called my office too. I told them something had come up. A family issue. Said I needed to take a few days off. They understood."

"Billy, you shouldn't have."

He sat on the edge of the bed. "I had to."

She told Billy about her episode with the bathroom mirror. Her younger self—her Cynthia Jane self—riding off in the car.

The bungalow with the gable windows and the rooster weather vane (absent the winking part). Her mother and that strange thing she said about falling out of the tree and getting stuck on the last branch for a while.

"The man in the car," he said. "It was Kilgallon, wasn't it?"

"I think so, but I'm not posit—"

"It's coming back, Cynthia. Isn't it?"

She stared into a void. "Perhaps."

* * *

Cynthia stepped out of the shower, grabbed the terry bath towel and dried herself off. She had decided that thirty minutes under the steady cascade of hot water would do her a world of good. Might even help her begin to make sense of it all. It did. And it didn't.

Billy was gazing out the window when she walked back into the bedroom. "Have you wondered at all," he said without diverting his gaze, "what happened during those twelve days?"

"What twelve days?"

He turned to face her. "The twelve days you were unaccounted for. You disappeared on September 28th. But you didn't turn up in Grove Park until October 10th. I don't recall the exact dates with the other girls, but they went missing at least a week before their bodies were found. Based on the police reports—and the autopsies—they hadn't been dead nearly that long."

"Where was I? All that time?"

"I wish we knew." He sat on the edge of the bed. "Sit with me?"

She joined him on the bed.

"Tell me again about the house," he said. "The one in your dream."

"Did I say it was a dream? Billy, the encounter with the mirror was as real to me as you are right now. Maybe it *was* a dream. But maybe it *wasn't.* Maybe it was the diaz..." She caught herself. "Who knows what it was?"

He put his arm around her. "I understand."

After she had recounted every detail she could remember, he said, "How would you like to take a little ride? Across town?"

* * *

As soon as they neared the house, she recognized it. The canary yellow that had jumped in living color from the mirror had faded to a dull pastel. And the russet had turned drab. And the car in the driveway was different. But the porch columns, the gable windows, the cupola and weather vane. They were dead ringers.

"This is the house I saw in the mirror, Billy. Who lives here?"

"Have you been here before?"

Just then, the front door opened. A man walked out the door, locking it behind him. He climbed into the car and cranked the engine.

"Who is it, Billy?"

Billy eased past the house and turned around in the driveway next door. The man pulled onto the street and headed toward Bouldercrest. Billy followed, but far enough behind so as not to draw attention. He turned right onto Bouldercrest and then drove a mile or so before taking a left at Eastland.

"Where is he going, Billy?

"If my hunch is right, you'll find out soon."

She began to get a knot in the pit of her stomach when he crossed Moreland and turned right onto Woodland Avenue toward the church.

The man drove into the church lot and parked near the side door. He got out of the car and walked toward the door. Billy pulled close to the curb on Woodland Avenue.

"Recognize him, Cynthia?"

She shook her head.

"It's Reverend Thomas."

"That's his house? Where we were?"

"It's the parsonage. Been part of the church as long as I can remember. I went there once with my mother. To visit Kilgallon. But for the life of me, I can't remember why." He turned to her. "Have *you* ever been there?"

"You mean other than last night? In the mirror?"

He cut the engine. "Cynthia, what I'm about to ask...you have every right to say no. I'm flying blind here, but I have another hunch. Will you go back to the house with me?"

"You mean break in?"

"No. Not break in. Just snoop around."

"You mean go back now?"

"Tomorrow night. Thomas will be at the Wednesday night supper. It'll be the best time to do it. I know we're taking a chance. But there's a reason the house came to you last night. What if that's where you spent twelve days of your life...twelve days that you can't remember? Inside that house? Do you think that maybe, just maybe, being there might help bring it back?"

"Do I *want* to bring it back?"

"Do you want to get to the bottom of what happened? Once and for all?"

"I do. It's just that—"

"I don't want to force you to do something you don't want to do."

She paused. "I'll do it, Billy. I just hope we both don't end up regretting it."

* * *

The next day, after they dropped the kids off to spend the night with Billy's mother, they drove past the church just before sunset. Thomas's car was there.

They drove to the parsonage. They parked in the cul-de-sac down the street. Billy took a flashlight from the glove box. "I know this isn't easy for you," he said, squeezing her hand.

They slid out of the car. They crept, hunched low to the ground, along the shrubs that lined the left side of the house. They rounded the rear corner. Two windows flanked the back door. They peered through the first window into what seemed to be Thomas's bedroom. On the other side of the door was the kitchen window.

They turned the corner to the other side of the house. On that side, about halfway to the front, there was a bulkhead cellar entrance. There was a padlock on the hasp that secured the two large doors. But the padlock's shank was disengaged. Billy looked at Cynthia. "Should we?"

She half-nodded.

Billy removed the lock and opened the doors. A flight of cinder block steps led to a partially excavated basement. They descended the steps. He handed her the flashlight. He went first. She followed, flashlight in hand. The first thing that hit her, halfway down the steps, was the pungent smell of must and mold.

When Cynthia's feet landed on the cellar's dirt floor, a rush of frigid air swept over her. The hairs on her arms stood at attention. "I'm not feeling good about this, Billy. Not at all."

Billy took her hand. "I understand. We can turn around now, walk up those steps, and drive away. And we won't say another word about it. I don't want you to—"

"We're here. We might as well go through with it."

Billy swept the room with the flashlight. The exposed floor joists above were supported by two sagging crossbeams running the length of the cellar. Four wooden posts held the beams in place. The right and far walls, and the wall behind Billy and Cynthia, were crude whitewashed stone. A foot-high brown band of moisture stain ran along their bases. There was a small window, high on the wall straight ahead and, Cynthia assumed, near grade level on the outside. She figured the window had been obscured by the shrubs—otherwise, they would have noticed it. Both of its panes were broken out. A torn curtain, partially covering the window, flailed as the wind whipped past it. A rusted set of free-standing metal shelves stood against the right wall, straining under the weight of cardboard boxes, old tools, a hand-crank ice cream churn, what looked like a dehumidifier, assorted junk. One of the legs on the metal shelves was bent near the foot. The whole thing looked like it could collapse any minute.

To Billy and Cynthia's left, toward the front of the house, a foundation of unexcavated red-clay earth ran the length of the cellar. It was held in place by a wall-like barricade of unpainted lath. About three quarters of the way across the barricade, the run of lath ended. There was a wooden stud—two 2x4s nailed together—where the strips stopped.

A large metal cabinet, the kind with two side-by-side doors, was jammed up against the dirt foundation at the double-stud's far edge. Billy opened the cabinet. It was empty. He went around to its right side. "Look at this," he said. He pointed to another double-stud, just like the one to the cabinet's left. "There's something behind here." He wobble-walked the cabinet out of the way. Behind it was a wooden door. It was secured with a 2x4 barricade held in place by two metal brackets nailed partway into the double-studs, the rusty nails bent over and lying flat against the bracket plates. *Billy Jr. could have done a better job*, she thought.

Billy removed the barricade and opened the door.

Inside was a small cell. Barely large enough for one person.

A dryer duct through the outside wall. A dirty rag stuffed into its open end.

A mattress lying on the floor. Twin-bed size. A large yellowish-brown stain in the center.

A tattered wool blanket.

A 5-gallon plastic pail in one corner.

A small table—maybe a foot square—in the other. Several empty glass vials—they looked like medicine bottles—on the table and strewn around its base.

Billy asked her for a Kleenex. He picked up one of the vials with it, careful not to leave his prints on the glass, and put the bottle in his pocket.

Taped to the wall was a picture of Jesus, standing tall in all his fair-haired splendor. Bearded. Sandaled. Robed in white. His arms outstretched.

Little children gathered at his feet. Angelic. Smiling. In glorious rapture.

Cynthia froze.

Chapter Forty-Two
Billy Tarwater

October 30, 1980

THE PREDICTIONS OF DOROTHY ALLISON, THE PSYCHIC from New Jersey, had panned out. She had said there would be no more slain children as long as she was in town. Three weeks had gone by without another missing child. It was now Thursday, the thirtieth. *Dumb luck*, I thought.

Sometime between her no more slain children prognostication and now, she had left town without fanfare. The next I heard of her, she had turned up on a radio call-in show in St. Louis. She predicted that the body of a store clerk named Bruce Lindsey, who had been missing for four months, would show up on a dead-end road near a lake, a pond, creek. His skeleton was found on the twenty-eighth in the Busch Wildlife Area. On a dead-end road. Near August A. Busch Lake Number 1. The *Constitution* ran the story on Page 5-C of the Thursday paper. Another lucky break?

* * *

I had more pressing things on my mind that morning than the so-called prophecies of a so-called psychic. Namely, Virlyn Kilgallon and Leonard Seymour.

Had Cynthia and I stumbled upon the prison cell where she had been locked up for ten days, as well as the other girls before they met their untimely ends? Had Kilgallon been involved? Had Seymour played a role? Could it be that the latter was the consigliere to the former's brute? His aider and abettor? Or was it the other way around? Or perhaps there was no connection between the two of them at all, except for the fact that, for years, one of them had sung in the other's choir. And had procured a car from him.

Or was I headed down a dead-end shunpike?

I had made sure to leave everything as we had found it in the prison cell, except for the vial I had pocketed. I had resecured the cellar doors with the padlock, left its shank open. We had retreated from the neighborhood before Thomas returned.

* * *

Back in '63, the detectives had been unsuccessful in lifting fingerprints from the crime scenes. At least, according to the police files. There was no apparent murder weapon. And no blood. No other bodily fluids—semen, sweat, saliva—and even if there had been, they couldn't have used it to pin the crime on anybody.

And here I was, seventeen years later, trying to fit the pieces together. Make sense of it all. Find who did it. Free Jepperson.

But circumstantial evidence wouldn't get me very far. There was a possibility that Cynthia's or one of the other girls' fingerprints could be lifted from something in the cellar dungeon: the plastic pail, the table, the medicine vials. The vial I'd pilfered?

But I wanted to keep that option for myself, at least for the time being. I needed more evidence before I could credibly convince the detectives to reopen a decade-and-a-half-old, seemingly settled case. And besides, why should I trust them in '80 to care more than their '63 compeers had about finding the real killer?

* * *

I would first pay another visit to Leonard Seymour. With the official GDR report in hand. With solid evidence that he had acquired the car from Kilgallon, maybe—just maybe—I could convince the man to talk.

It was just before dusk when I pulled alongside the curb in front of his house. He was standing on his front stoop. In a too-small Braves T-shirt and holding a PBR can. He made an abrupt turn toward the door when he saw me.

"Hold on," I called out from the car. "I know you don't want to talk to me. But I have something you should see."

He was halfway through the door.

"Before I share it with anyone else," I said.

He swung around. Walked down the steps, through the front gate, and onto the sidewalk where I now stood. "What is it, Tarwater?"

I showed him the official report that my GDR buddy had sent me.

> '61 Valiant V-200 Fury
>
> VIN 1311100083

June 30th, 1961. Purchased new by Virlyn Jephthah Kilgallon.

From Harry Sommers Chrysler-Plymouth.

October 15th, 1963. Title transferred to Leonard Seymour.

He tried to grab it from me.

I jerked it away. "No, Leonard. Look but don't touch."

His demeanor took an abrupt change. "OK, Tarwater. Let's talk. Want a cold one?"

Did he have a change of heart because he realized the futility of denying he owned the car? Did he think he could sway me with a couple of cold beers? Perhaps he thought he could convince me to let sleeping dogs lie.

I followed him into the backyard.

He crushed his empty beer can and tossed it to the ground next to the back stoop. It landed with a clank on top of three other empties.

I sat in one of the two turquoise-and-white-webbed folding lawn chairs. The one with three of the webbing strips frayed to the point of imminent riving. I figured, since he was now proffering magnanimity by claiming me as his newfound drinking chum, I should let him take the good chair.

He went inside.

He came out with two unopened PBRs. He popped the top on one and handed it to me. Then he sat in the good chair, popped the other top, took a deep slug, and wiped his mouth with the back of his hand. "I don't know what you're up to, Tarwater. But

I'll tell you everything I know about that goddamned car. You're right, I owned it," he said. "But not for long."

I didn't say anything. As a newspaperman, I had learned years ago that sometimes silence is best. There was so much I wanted to ask. Why did Kilgallon sell you the car? What happened to it, if you didn't keep it long? Was the car I had seen in the back of the pawn shop—and then not—the same car? But I just stared at him. Waited for him to talk.

After a few minutes, he opened up. "Kilgallon came to me. Asked me to take it off his hands. He titled it over to me. For a dollar. All he asked was that I make it go away."

"What do you mean, make it go away?"

"He said get rid of it. But don't just get rid of it like, you know, sell it legit. *Really* get rid of it." He put the can to his mouth, bent his head back and cocked the can in the air, shook it a little bit, crushed it, and threw it across the yard and onto the pile. "Want another?"

"I'm good," I said. "Still nursing this one."

"Don't go anywhere." He lumbered back inside and returned with another PBR. He sat down. When he did, I thought I heard a faint rip in the good chair's webbing.

"So anyway," he said, "I took the car off his hands like he asked me to. I didn't ask questions. After all, he was the pastor. And a friend."

I remained silent.

"So you're probably wondering," he continued, "what I did with the car."

"That thought crossed my mind."

"Well, the first thing I did was take it up to McKnight's. Mac's a good man. Solid as they come. Must be pushing seventy-five now. But he's still up at the garage every day. Rain or shine. Know him?"

"I know *of* him."

"Well, I called in a favor. I said 'Mac, can you get this car painted for me? In a hurry?' And by god, he had it painted and back in my hands in two days. That's Mac McKnight for you."

I didn't ask what he meant by calling in a favor. Maybe it had something to do with craps or parlay, although I didn't know whether Seymour was involved in the wagering at the garage—that was Cecil Hudspeth's purview for sure. The thought even crossed my mind that, when the good old boys were huddled in McKnight's service bay doing whatever they did, perhaps Leonard had shared stories of his exploits at the window. Maybe even shared Polaroids. Maybe that's what the favor was about. But I put that thought out of my mind quickly. Before the bile in my stomach got the best of me. That scenario didn't make sense anyway. Cecil Hudspeth was a regular at McKnight's. Even if he hadn't been around to witness first-hand a recounting of Leonard's mischief, surely word would have gotten back to him.

Seymour was on a roll. Why break his momentum?

"A nice blue color," he said.

"So that was your way of making it go away?"

"Of course not. I couldn't stop there." He extended his right arm toward the ground with his palm pointed upward. Wagged his index finger back and forth as if pointing to an imaginary orb weaver swaying in its web. "Right down inside the left front door. On the hinge pillar. That's where the VIN plate is. At least on a

'61Valiant." He looked up at me. "Do you know how easy it is to pop a VIN plate?"

"No idea. I've never considered doing anything like that."

"Not as easy as popping a beer tab. But pretty damned easy. All you gotta do is take a drill. Get a good, strong bit." He poked his index finger toward me, back and forth in a piercing motion. "Drill the rivets right out. Child's play."

I was about to ask how he disposed of the car, when he rose from the chair. He heaved the can through the air like he was making a twenty-yard pass. It landed next to the pile. He put his hands on his hips. "That's about it, Tarwater. I have no idea why the reverend was so dead set on getting rid of the car. But whatever it was, I had nothing to do with it, except taking it off his hands. Now, if you'll excuse me, I have things to do. I'll walk you to your car."

When we reached the sidewalk, I looked over at Cynthia's parent's house. At the one-inch crack between two Venetian blind slats in the front window. At a pair of eyes staring through the crack. Partially illuminated by the porch light. Cecil's eyes? I couldn't tell for sure, but I thought so.

My attention shifted back to Leonard. "I appreciate your time," I said. "And your candor. Can I ask you a couple more questions?"

"Depends on what they are. Try me."

"Where did the car end up?"

"Unloaded it with some Shylock down on Stewart Avenue. I bought it for a dollar and sold it for a C-note. Can you believe that? Pretty good markup."

I didn't need to ask who the Stewart Avenue Shylock was.

"And the other question?" he said.

"Did the police ever approach you about the car? Back in the '60s?"

He kicked the dirt patch between the sidewalk and the curb. Scrubbed the palm of his hand across his face. Glared straight through me. "Police? Why would the police get involved?"

"I'm just asking did they talk to you?"

"Look, I had that car for three days—maybe four—before I got rid of it. Whatever interest the police had in the car, Kilgallon was the one they needed to talk to."

"They *did* talk to you, didn't they, Leonard?"

"OK, they talked to me. So what? That doesn't mean a thing. I told them they needed to go see Kilgallon."

"Did you tell them about Kilgallon asking you to make the car go away? And about how you did it?"

"Of course not."

"Surely they bothered to ask where the car was, if it wasn't in your possession anymore."

"I told them someone had stolen it. From the barber shop parking lot. While I was getting my hair cut."

"And they believed you."

"I guess they did."

"Did they ask whether you filed a police report?"

"I *did* file a police report."

"So you're telling me you filed a police report about a car that was supposedly stolen. But it wasn't stolen. You knew exactly where the car was."

"No I didn't." Seymour was defiant. "I knew where *a* car was, but not *that* car. The car I knew about didn't even have a VIN number. And it was the wrong color."

I changed the subject, knowing I'd get nowhere trying to argue with his twisted illogic. "What about Kilgallon? Did the detectives go see him?"

He looked at his watch. "I thought you said two questions. You've asked me about a dozen already."

"Just one more. What about Kilgallon? Did they visit him?"

"How would I know that?"

"Well, for starters, it's not as if you two were strangers, right? You and Kilgallon must have been pretty close for him to have trusted you the way he did. He passed the car on to you and asked you to 'make it go away.' So hear me out. Let's assume the police *did* visit him. Don't you think he would have come back to you *after* that to make sure you had disposed of the car?"

"Sounds reasonable."

"I'm not asking if it sounds reasonable. I'm asking if that's what he did. Came back to you. Told you the police had paid him a visit. Asked you if you had made the car go away. And how you'd done it. That's what Kilgallon did, isn't it?"

"OK. That's what he did. You're trying to make me out to be some kind of bad guy, when all I did was help out a friend in need."

"Did you tell Kilgallon you had the car painted? Took off the VIN plate?"

"Of course I did. I'm not the lying type, Tarwater."

"But you didn't tell the *police* that."

"They didn't ask."

* * *

I stopped in at Marnie's. Went straight to the Alibi Booth. Dialed Winstanley. He answered on the first ring. He agreed to meet me that evening at his place at the Stewart Avenue trailer park.

I downed a beer, dropped a single on the bar rail, and headed out the door on my way to the southside.

Winstanley was waiting outside his trailer when I pulled up.

We went inside. He had brewed a fresh pot of mud-for-coffee. Just for me, he said.

I had a lot of questions for the detective. About the car. The handwritten vehicle list—with Leonard Seymour's name circled in blue ink. The official GDR list—with both Kilgallon's and Seymour's names. The face peering from the shrubs—this time circled in red wax pencil. A dead ringer for Kilgallon—surely they would have noticed that if they interviewed him. What Seymour had said—that the police had talked to Kilgallon in '63. Why there was no reference to an interview with Kilgallon in any of the police records from that time. Had Virlyn Kilgallon been a suspect?

He proceeded to lay it all out for me—with the caveat that memory fades with age.

Winstanley said Kilgallon never became a suspect. At least not officially. I asked him why, when we had spoken a week and a half earlier, Kilgallon's name hadn't even come up.

"Because I was given clear instructions—*your-job's-on-the-line* instructions—not to discuss Kilgallon as a possible suspect. Or even that we talked to him, for that matter."

"By whom?"

"By Gus Alford. Who else?"

"But Gus Alford's been dead for years. And you're not on the force anymore."

"I know. I should have told you. But I just didn't see any benefit to rehashing it all. Look, Tarwater. I'm an old man. I probably don't have many more years in me. I just couldn't bring myself to relive something that happened so long ago. You didn't bring his name up. And I wasn't about to. The case is long closed."

According to Winstanley, based on the crime scene evidence, the detectives had a '61 Valiant in their sights. Then the GDR report came in. There were several owners in the area. The detectives followed up with most, but not all, of them.

I wondered why not all of them, but I didn't ask. I was focused more on Seymour and Kilgallon. I knew things Winstanley didn't know—at least that was my assumption. The tortured relationship between Kilgallon and Cynthia. Between Seymour and Cynthia. The prison cell. The *make it go away* instructions.

The detectives had narrowed the field down to a couple of Valiant Furys. Why a couple? Again, I didn't ask. At least not yet. One of the cars was owned by Kilgallon, then Seymour. Carpenter and Alford interviewed Seymour. He said talk to Kilgallon. Did they ask where the car was, if not in Seymour's possession at the time? Seymour told them it had been stolen. They checked with larceny. It hadn't turned up.

The detectives had seen the face in the photograph—the one across the creek from where Cynthia had been found. Alford drew the red circle. They didn't have a clue as to whose face it was. Until they met Kilgallon. That's when they picked up on the resemblance.

I asked Winstanley what they had learned from the interview with Kilgallon.

"I didn't meet with him," he said. "Alford and Carpenter did. They came back with nothing of substance to report."

It was Carpenter who took the official GDR list and transcribed it by hand, leaving off a lot of the detail, including Kilgallon's name. It was Carpenter who circled Seymour's name in blue ink.

By then, Sam Jepperson had been arrested and was in jail.

Alford said there was no way a man of the cloth, an upstanding member of the community, could have been involved. He said drop it. He said to leave everything about Virlyn Kilgallon out of the police files. Even including Leonard Seymour's mention of Kilgallon's name.

Winstanley gazed out the trailer window. "Memory may be failing me. But I recall, all these years later, the exact words out of Alford's mouth. He wagged his finger in my face and said, 'Winstanley, I don't want to hear Kilgallon's name again. Period.'"

Carpenter had backed Alford up. Said everybody with any sense at all knew *that damned nigra* did it.

Jepperson was convicted. The case was closed.

I asked Winstanley whether he ever thought about the fact that an innocent man may have been sent to Reidsville.

He looked at his lap. "All the time."

I wondered why, if what he said was true, he "didn't see any benefit to rehashing it all." To reopening an old case and perhaps seeing Jepperson exonerated.

"I'm going to visit Carpenter," I said. "Do you think he'll talk to me?"

Winstanley paled. "You haven't heard?"

"Haven't heard what?"

"Buford Carpenter died last week. Throat cancer."

Chapter Forty-Three

Billy Tarwater

October 31, 1980

I THOUGHT BACK TO MY HOBO HALLOWEEN DAYS. EVERY year, my mother would smear charcoal on my face and paint one of my front teeth black with God knows what. It would take three days to get my tooth pearly white again. She filled a cloth bag with old rags and tied it to the end of a long hickory stick. She dressed me in a pair of my brother's old overalls rolled up at my ankles and scrunched around my waist with a two-and-a-half-foot length of sisal rope—tied in the front in a big knot with the frayed ends hanging down. She gave me a pillowcase to carry my stash.

My favorite Halloween visits as a kid were to Mrs. Knopp's house. I didn't know it at the time, but she was an incorrigible tosspot. I just thought she was the jolly type. Every Halloween, she would dress as Santa Claus, get hopelessly crocked, and greet us at her door with bright red candy apples—prepared, no doubt, before she crossed the point of no return. She would continue this practice until sometime in the '60s, when the *New York Times* reported a story about twenty children biting into Halloween apples only to encounter implanted razor blades. After that article hit the local paper, no East Atlanta mother with any sense would let her child walk up Mrs. Knopp's front steps and ring the doorbell. I don't know what happened to Mrs. Knopp after that. We never saw her as Santa Claus again. Perhaps she was forced to retreat to the solitude of her house, despondent that she could no longer derive pie-eyed joy from the grins on our faces.

We were never allowed to take our trick-or-treating next door. My mother said Ben Culpepper was a drunkard and too volatile. And I'm sure she didn't want to risk my seeing Lervene's bruises up close. Ben Culpepper was off-limits, but the tosspot up the street wasn't, at least until the razor blade scare.

The Halloween of my eleventh year had been bittersweet. On the one hand, Binky the Hobo got an apple from Santa Claus. And I managed to garner a substantial cache of candy—notwithstanding the fact that Chester, as usual, invoked the Indian burn threat to take half of it.

But it had been a sad year too. Cynthia had almost died and was in the hospital, hanging on. Two girls were gone. Sam Jepperson was locked up. And the perpetrator was on the loose.

* * *

Now, seventeen years later, Cynthia and I were taking Billy Jr. and Addie out for Halloween. He as Batman. She as a black cat. No hobos. Cynthia wouldn't hear of that, understandably. No candy apples. No Santa Claus. Only prepackaged goods. Delivered by temperate adults.

It did Cynthia good to see the smiles on the kids' faces. And it took her mind off other things.

After an evening of trick-or-treating in and around The Belmont, we decided to drive to East Atlanta to visit my mother, then Adele and Cecil. We would have caught hell from both grandmothers had the children not been given the opportunity to show off their costumes, endure the *ooh*s and *aah*s and *aren't you something*s, and load up with even more sugar.

We visited my mother first. Then we piled back into the car and drove to Portland Avenue. When we pulled into Adele and Cecil's driveway, I noticed Leonard Seymour's house was pitch black. Was he hiding inside in the dark to avoid the annoyance of the begging children? I didn't think so—his car was gone.

Cecil greeted us at the door. "What did you do, scare him off?" he said to me.

"I don't know what you're talking about, Cecil."

"I saw you yesterday. Next door."

"I had some things I needed to talk to your friend Leonard about," I said.

"Don't ever call him that. He's not my friend."

"OK. He's not your friend. What do you mean, did I scare him off?"

"As soon as you left, he started loading up his car. He was about to take off when I went outside. Asked him where he was going."

"I thought you said he wasn't your friend."

"He's not. But I still wanted to know where he was off to. Especially after the two of you had your little beer drinking party in his backyard."

"Where *was* he off to?"

"Sylacauga. To his sister's. Said he didn't know when he'd be back."

"Alabama."

"Of course Alabama. What other Sylacauga is there?"

* * *

On the way home that evening, Billy Jr. and Addie had fallen asleep in the back seat.

Cynthia turned to me. "You didn't tell me you visited Leonard yesterday."

"I'm sorry," I said. "I was planning to. But it was late when I got home. And you were sound asleep. You looked so content. I didn't want to wake you."

"A beer drinking party, huh?"

"That'd be a stretch. I paid him a visit because I wanted to confront him about the Valiant."

"What did he say?"

"He didn't deny owning it. But just for a few days, he said. Claims he got rid of it for Kilgallon."

"Do you believe him?"

"I don't believe anything anymore until I can back it up."

"You must have been there for a long time. You got home so late."

"After I left Seymour's, I stopped by Marnie's for a drink. I called Sergeant Winstanley from the bar."

I told her about my visit with the sergeant at the trailer park. And what he had shared with me. About the car. The GDR list. Virlyn Kilgallon. Gus Alford's order not to pursue Kilgallon as a suspect. Not even to say his name.

"I never wanted to hear his name either," she said. "But now I'll say it. What if Kilgallon did it?"

"Exactly. What if he was the one all along? And Alford sat on it? And an innocent man went to prison. And by the way, Buford Carpenter at that time backed Alford up. Went along with the whole thing."

"Are you going to talk to Carpenter?"

"I wish I could. Unfortunately, I'm a week too late."

"A week too late?"

"He's dead."

* * *

When we were back at the apartment, and Billy Jr. and Addie were tucked in, I asked Cynthia if we could talk for a few more minutes.

We sat at the kitchen table. I reached across and held her hands. "I want to take a trip," I said.

"Where are we going?"

"I don't think this is a trip you want to be a part of."

"Where are *you* going?"

"Alabama."

"Why Alabama?"

"I want to find Kilgallon."

"You know that's dangerous."

"I understand. But if I'm ever…if *we're* ever going to get to the bottom of this, I have to find him."

"What will you do when you find him?"

"I'm still thinking that through."

"It doesn't give me a good feeling."

"I know. I don't feel great about it either. But I don't see another option at this point. If I went to the police with what little evidence I have, they'd do nothing. It's a seventeen-year-old closed case. The police hate it when they have to admit a mistake, even if it was years ago and the ones involved aren't around anymore. Winstanley's helped some, but he can take me only so far. And Seymour? I'm still not sure about his involvement in the whole thing. Gus Alford and Buford Carpenter are no longer with us. The best evidence we have so far is from Gary's mother's attic and Reverend Thomas's cellar."

"And you can't approach Thomas about the cellar," Cynthia said. "What would you say? We were trespassing in your basement and happened upon a jail cell?"

"That wouldn't go over well, would it? And besides, even if I could come up with a plausible story, he and Kilgallon were close. May still be. If I confronted Thomas now, I might end up blowing the whole thing."

"Why do you think you won't blow it by confronting Kilgallon? If he was involved, do you think he's just going to come right out and confess?"

"No. I won't confront him right away. I'd like to go to Irondale and snoop around first. See what I can dig up."

"Irondale," Cynthia said. "That's where the church is, right? The one where he pastored before he came to Atlanta."

"And the one he went back to in '63."

"I wonder why he left Irondale the first time. Did something happen to make him leave? Or was he just ready to move on?"

"I don't know. Maybe I'll find out."

"You know, don't you, that I won't be able to sleep at all from the time you leave until you walk right back through that door."

"I know. But if it helps ease your mind, even a little, I'm going to see if Gary will take a couple of days off and tag along. I wouldn't mind having a cop as a sidekick."

"One other thing, Billy. Didn't Cecil say Leonard had gone to Sylacauga?"

"That's what he said Leonard told him."

"Sylacauga's right down the road from Irondale," Cynthia said. "Do you find that oddly coincidental?"

* * *

Saturday morning, November 1st, I called Gary.

Ain't no way I'm gonna lean into a left hook. Those were the first words out of his mouth, or something to that effect.

But the more we talked—the more I pleaded—he finally came around to the idea of going with me.

"I'll go for two days," he said. "Tops. And just so you know, my badge doesn't mean a damned thing in Alabama. You know that, don't you?"

"Of course," I said, knowing full well that Gary's badge *would* make a difference. Assuming we should need to make use of it. Police have some pull with other police, wherever they are. The camaraderie of the badge knows no boundaries. But I didn't bring that up.

We agreed to meet at Marnie's later that day to hammer out a plan. Two o'clock sharp.

* * *

I arrived at one forty-five and got the usual table in the rear corner of the Sidecar. I ordered a Miller and waited for Gary.

Two ten came and went. Still no sign of him. *So much for two o'clock sharp.*

At two fifteen, I looked up. Here he came, hobbling across the room. I stared at my watch. Then at him.

"Hey, cut me some slack, man," Gary said. "Last I checked, *I'm* the one doing *you* a favor." He leaned his cane against the chair across the table from me, its brass wolf's head hanging over the chair's top rail, staring at me like a specter. He sat down.

"You're right," I said. "You're doing me a huge favor. What can I get you?"

Gary said he'd have whatever I was drinking. I ordered a Miller draft for him and another for me.

"Gary," I said, "Cynthia mentioned something last night that got me thinking. She asked abou—"

"I assume you've kept the missus up to speed about what you're doing."

"Of course."

"That's good. The last thing you want to do, trust me, is piss off the wife. You were saying?"

"I was saying she asked me about Kilgallon's time in Irondale before he came to Atlanta. I know next to nothing about his past."

"Maybe there's somebody in the church that'll remember him from the first time. When did he leave there?"

"December of '42."

"That's a long time ago," he said.

"But there should be adults still around who'd remember him. They'd be in their late sixties, seventies now…maybe some in their eighties."

"But how are you going to pull off asking around without it getting back to Kilgallon?"

"That's a challenge. I've thought about it. I'll have to finesse it."

Gary raised an eyebrow. "Finesse it. You're going to finesse it."

"Yes. Like any good newshound. But I have an idea about where to go first, before we visit Irondale."

"Where?" Gary said.

"Into Birmingham. See what old records we can find there. Before we show up in Kilgallon's neck of the woods."

"What kind of old records?"

"Think about it, Gary. What do I do for a living?"

"Well, until recently I thought you were a newspaperman. But now I'm thinking you switched jobs without telling me. Billy Tarwater, Private Dick." He laughed.

"There's a daily in Birmingham called the *Post-Herald.* Covers Irondale too. I know a guy there. Let's look him up. Pay him a visit. Search their archives from the late '30s, early '40s. See if we can find anything. If nothing else, we can read the weekly sermon listings...see what bullshit Kilgallon was peddling from on high back then."

We settled on a game plan. We would set out for Alabama early Monday morning, the 3rd. Me behind the wheel. Gary shotgun.

* * *

Gary and I hadn't spent much time together since our *bones and butterball* days. You really get to know a guy when you spend two-and-a-half hours together in a cramped car, watching a sliver of light peek over the horizon as you barrel down the highway in the dark. Halfway to Birmingham, I had begun to have second thoughts about having brought Gary.

It had all started with the radio. It didn't matter to me what kind of music we listened to, or whether we listened to anything at all. But Gary had an annoying habit of twirling the knob incessantly—to one staticky station after another—and commenting along the way about how my antenna was too inferior to render anything worth listening to.

And then there was the matter of speed. "Slow down, man," he would say. "Don't expect me to whip my badge out when smokey bear nails your ass. You're on your own, buddy." Then when I let up on the gas for a stretch, mainly to get him to pipe down, he'd let out with, "Hell, at the rate you're going, we *might* get there in time for lunch."

Dawn had broken when we finally rolled into Birmingham. The foundry furnaces had been shut down for almost a decade, but the city was still dog-eared and dingy. Like a washed-up rummy who had sworn off the drink but hadn't quite found his footing. Vacant industrial sites dotted the landscape. Run-down neighborhoods spoke to the Jim Crow legacy that the city still hadn't been able to shake.

I thought of the four girls killed in the 16th Street Baptist Church bombing. I remembered what Dovey Mae had said as she stood in Granny Tarwater's cellar, soap and purple smeared across her apron. *Pure evil. That's all it is. Pure evil.*

I thought of Sam Jepperson's family—his *first* family—somewhere in Birmingham. I wouldn't go out of my way to try to find them. For seventeen years Sam had been in a five-by-ten in Reidsville, and they hadn't bothered to call or write.

* * *

"Know Bogue's?" Gary said.

"What?"

"Bogue's. The diner."

"Can't say I do."

"Friend told me about it. Best breakfast in these parts."

"Where is it?"

"Hell if I know."

I swung into the Amoco.

Gary ran inside and asked for directions while I filled up.

We headed down 40th Street toward the southside.

Bogue's was in an old fire station at the corner of Clairmont and 32nd.

Gary had a blueberry fat stack, two eggs scrambled, cheese grits and two sausage patties. I went light—two over easy, wheat toast and a large OJ.

Gary was finishing up when I excused myself and located the pay phone. I dropped a quarter in the slot and dialed my *Post-Herald* friend. He said come on over. Park in the lot across the street.

The newspaper office was less than ten minutes away.

We parked in the lot as instructed.

We walked toward the newspaper entrance. Well, I walked. Gary limped.

Halfway across the lot, Gary said, "Here goes nothing."

"Thanks a lot," I said. "Talk about inspiring confidence."

My *Post-Herald* friend Craig beamed when he saw me. He and I had been in J-school together at UGA. We hadn't seen each other in years.

After fifteen minutes of small talk, and evident boredom on Gary's part, Craig led us to a work room on the second floor. Two 3M microfilm readers and a Xerox lined the wall farthest from the door. There was a long table in the middle of the room. Gary and I took seats next to each other. Craig sat across from us.

An attractive young woman—I guessed she was in her late twenties—entered. She had a Dorothy Hamill wedge, but blonder. She wore a floral knee-length dress tied at the waist. Craig introduced her as Bonnie Jean Pitman, archivist, researcher and coffee girl.

Craig got up and walked to the door. He turned to face us. "You're in good hands with Bonnie Jean here. Whatever you need, she'll do it for you."

After Craig's unfortunate *coffee girl* comment, I was determined not to ask for a cup. And when Gary did, I kicked him under the table.

"We have about a month's worth of newspapers on each reel," she said.

Miss Pitman gave us a brief microfilm machine tutorial, solely for Gary's benefit—the *Post-Herald* had the same kind of readers we had back at the *Constitution.*

"Could you get the January and February reels?" I said. "1942. Please."

She returned with two reels and handed them to me.

I gave January to Gary and told him to scan the pages, looking for news about Kilgallon, Irondale, the church, anything else that jumped out. And to zoom in and hit the Print button whenever he found something of interest.

When we had finished with January and February, which had revealed nothing of note except for sermon notices, which weren't worth printing, Miss Pitman took them away.

She returned with March and April.

It had taken us almost two hours to work through January and February. My mental math told me that, at that rate, we'd be well into the night before we finished one year. And even then, we were having to go so fast that we ran the risk of missing something important. I told Gary to start skimming lightly through the less important pages: full-page ads, classifieds, national and international news. By my calculation, we could shave maybe thirty minutes off each reel and still allow more time to concentrate on the pages that mattered.

March and April turned up nothing.

Same with May and June.

I looked at the clock on the wall. It was a quarter to three.

"Soldier on?" I said to Gary.

"Fine with me," he said. "But you owe me a ribeye when we're done."

We still had a lot to get through before the end of the day. I asked Miss Pitman to bring four months this time. She came back with July through October. I took September and October.

I was halfway through September when the Page 1 headline blindsided me. Monday the 14th. MISSING GIRL FOUND DEAD. A fifteen-year-old's body had been found on the eastern bank of the Coosa River where it flows under I-20. She had been drowned. The marks on her neck showed signs of a struggle. I read through the article. No mention of a carving on her thigh or anywhere else on her body. But I knew that a detail like that would not have ended up in the newspaper unless, for some reason, the authorities wanted it to.

I had to steady my right index finger with my left hand to hit Print.

Gary had obviously seen that I was agitated. "What is it, Billy?"

I told him what I had found.

My hand did a little quiver as I advanced the film to the next screen. Then the next. And the next.

On October 1st, another girl's body had been found. This one twelve years old. This time at Fourmile Creek near Bon Air. Same cause of death. Same neck marks.

I had reached the end of September and two girls were dead.

I loaded October onto the machine. For the first two weeks of the month, the police had searched frantically for the killer but had turned up nothing. Not even a suspect. Birmingham was on edge.

It brought back memories.

October 19th. A third body. This time a fifteen-year-old black girl. Along the shoreline of Drummond Lake. Drowned after a struggle.

For the remainder of the month, the police had accelerated their search.

I handed September and October to Miss Pitman. Gary had already completed July and August. He said he hadn't found anything worth printing.

It was almost seven. Craig was standing in the doorway, fidgeting.

I told him what we had found. But I didn't elaborate on why it mattered. I asked him if he could call his contacts in the police department, maybe the Alabama SBI. Find out whether the killer was ever identified. He said that was a long time ago, but he'd see what he could do. I asked him for one more favor. Could Miss Pitman scour November, December, and into '43, and print anything she could find about the murders. Were there more? Were suspects identified? Were the crimes ever solved?

"Anything for you, Billy," Craig said. "Like I told you, whatever you need, Bonnie Jean can get it for you."

I thanked Craig. Told him I'd call him tomorrow.

It was seven thirty by the time we took the elevator to the lobby. The front door was locked. The night guard let us out.

We headed across the parking lot.

I was exhausted. We had a long, stressful day ahead of us. A solid night's sleep would do us both a world of good.

I looked at Gary. "We passed a little motel between here and Irondale. No great shakes. But as long as the sheets are clean and the cockroaches are in hiding, and assuming they have a phone for me to call home, I'm OK with it. That work for you?"

"Sure," Gary said. "But what about that ribeye?"

Chapter Forty-Four

Cynthia Tarwater

November 3, 1980

AT HALF PAST NINE, THE PHONE RANG. SHE PICKED UP quickly. It was Billy.

"It's late," she said. "I've been worried."

He apologized for not calling earlier. Said something about Gary and a ribeye. It didn't make sense, but she let it go. He told her they had just checked into a dive between Birmingham and Irondale.

What did they used to call them? Motor courts.

"How did it go today?" she asked.

He told her about his and Gary's research at the newspaper office. About the Alabama girls. Same ages—give or take—as Martha Ann, Patsy and her. Same narrative. Same cause of death.

Only difference—it happened in '42, not '63. And three girls were killed, not two.

Her eyes welled without warning.

She asked who did it.

"Not sure," he said. "Maybe they don't know."

"Were there scars?"

There was a pause. "Cynthia, I'm sorry you have to go through this."

"I know. But it has to be done…so were there?"

"The paper didn't say. But I wouldn't expect it to. And I haven't seen the police report."

He told her that he and Gary planned to go to the church tomorrow morning.

She asked when he'd be home.

"Gary said he'd give me two days, tops," he said. "We'll see."

"Take care of yourself, Billy."

She hung up.

Popped a benzodiazepine.

Chapter Forty-Five

Billy Tarwater

November 4, 1980

I AWOKE TO GARY PROPPED UP IN THE TWIN BED NEXT to mine. He was watching the local news on what was a dead ringer for the twelve-inch black-and-white from my Binky days. And chomping on a day-old glazed cruller he'd picked up from the EZ Mart on the way home from dinner.

"Gary," I said. "You do realize what today is, don't you?"

"The day we meet our end?"

"Well, maybe. But that's not what I mean. It's Election Day." I knew there was no way we'd get back before the polls closed. But I also had pretty much figured out Gary's politics. Even if we *could* make it back, we'd surely cancel each other out. I decided to have some fun with him. A little levity couldn't hurt. "Here we are in a roadside fleabag of a motel a hundred fifty miles from home. If we don't get back in time, we won't be able to get our votes in for Jimmy."

"What's with the *we*?" Gary groused. "Do you think I'd vote for that communist? Reagan all the way for me."

"Reagan? That washed-out B actor? Bedtime for Bonzo. Are you kidding?"

"Hell, I'd choose the other one...what's his name...over a damned communist any day."

"You mean Anderson?"

"Yeah, Anderson."

"Well," I said. "It doesn't matter. There's no way we're getting back before tomorrow at the earliest."

I hit an intended nerve. "Tomorrow!" he howled. "What did I tell you, Billy? Two days max."

"Well. If you're gonna hold me to two days, we'd better get our asses out of here." I looked at the clock beside the bed. It was 7:23.

Gary was about to turn off the TV when a breaking news story came on from Atlanta. Another body had been found face-up on a river bank. Black. Nine years old. Strangled. The three-and-a-half-week respite in the Atlanta child murders had ended. The total count was now sixteen.

I sat on the edge of the bed. Part of me wanted to be back at the city desk doing my day job. But I had to stay the course.

We headed out the door at 7:35.

* * *

"Billy, do you think Kilgallon'll recognize you?" Gary asked.

"After seventeen years? I doubt it. But who knows? Maybe he's seen my picture in the paper."

"Does he know you ended up marrying Cynthia?"

"That's a damned good question. He may not even be aware she survived, unless somebody told him. They kept everything hush-hush when she was in the hospital. Admitted her under an alias. Guarded her around the clock."

Halfway between the motel and the church, I ducked into a phone booth at the 7-Eleven. I called Craig about the '42 killings. Thirty-eight years later and still a cold case, he said. Shortly after the girls were murdered, the police tried to pin it on a couple of black guys. Hauled them in. Worked them over. But it didn't pan out, and they were let go.

* * *

The marquee sign read:

IRONDALE MISSIONARY BAPTIST CHURCH

REV. VIRLYN KILGALLON, PASTOR

and under that in changeable black-on-white reader-board letters:

LET JESUS BE THE TREAT. HE IS NOT A TRICK.

I pulled into the parking lot, into the space nearest the street. I cut the engine. There were four other cars, all parked near the building. One, a late-model Datsun 280Z, was in the space marked Pastor.

The building looked like something thrown together on a tight budget in the mid to late fifties. Lifeless brick—the plain orange-red kind—set off by blindingly white mortar. Windowless front.

Three concrete steps leading to a small covered parvis flanked by two posts—you'd be hard-pressed to call them columns. Double glass-and-metal door. Spindly prefab steeple.

A sun-leathered man was pushing a mower. A woman was trimming what little shrubbery there was along the front of the church. They might have been seventy. Or they might have been eighty. Too old to be hired hands. They had to be church members.

Gary held back at the edge of the parking lot.

I walked over to the man. I shouted over the steady drone of the mower. "Sorry to bother you."

He looked up, startled. "The reverend's inside."

"Can I have a minute or two with you?"

He reached down and shut off the motor.

I extended my hand. "Name's Buddy Baxter. New to the area. Looking for a church home. You go here?"

He looked over at Gary. Then back to me. "Where you from?"

"Valdosta. Georgia." I had a passing acquaintance with the town. But if he started asking a lot of questions, I was screwed. Then again, I'm pretty good at talking myself out of a bind. I changed the subject. "What did you say your name was?"

"I didn't. But it's Braswell. Warren Braswell." He pointed to the woman with the hedge trimmer. "That's Eunice. The wife."

"Been going here long?"

"My whole life. Mama and Daddy went here. They're buried out back. God willing, I'll be too. Baptized here. Got married here." He glowered at the building. "But not in that eyesore. For the longest, we worshiped in a little three-room church right about where I'm standing. There's pictures of it inside."

"What happened? Did you outgrow it?"

"Heck no. That wasn't it. We'd still be in that building if the reverend hadn't up and left."

"Who was that?"

"Reverend Kilgallon."

I pointed to the sign. "*That* Reverend Kilgallon?"

He nodded. "He was here before. But then he moved on. A new man came in. It took a few years for folks to start takin' a likin' to him. And then, before we knew it, he was raisin' money for a new church. What did he call it? Movin' up in the world. Movin' up my..." He pointed to the spindly-steepled building. "And that thing's what we ended up with."

"When did the reverend come back?"

"Oh, around...let me think." He called across the yard to Eunice-with-the-hedge-trimmers. "When did the reverend come back to Irondale?"

She swung around. "Nineteen and sixty-three. Remember? It was the year Pee Wee was born."

"Pee Wee's the grandson," he said to me.

"You must know the reverend well, then."

"Probably as good as anybody."

I happened to look over at the building. I saw a shadow of a figure lurking behind the glass door, peering out at me. I could tell it was Kilgallon. Then the shadow disappeared. I saw him scurry out the side door and make his way to the Datsun.

"I lost track of time, Mr. Braswell," I said. "Need to be on my way. I'll try to come back Sunday."

I motioned for Gary. We fast-walked back to my car. We pulled out of the lot and tailed the Datsun, maintaining enough distance so as not to attract attention. But I was pretty sure Kilgallon knew we were following him. Unlike with Leonard Seymour a week earlier, I didn't have to pull a Dale Earnhardt. Kilgallon was going about thirty-five.

We headed southeast. We crossed over the interstate and turned left. We entered a quiet neighborhood of oak-shaded streets lined with mid-century bungalows and Craftsmans. The sign said East Irondale Acres.

He stopped in front of a house not that different from the parsonage in Atlanta.

I slowed to a crawl and hugged the curb half a block behind.

He pulled into the driveway and went inside.

I stopped on the opposite side of the street, one door down from the house he had entered. I assumed it was his house. I turned off the ignition.

The front door suddenly swung open. Kilgallon stood in the darkened doorway, hands on hips, and stared in our direction. Then he disappeared into the house, leaving the door wide open.

We waited for a few minutes. The door remained open, but he didn't return.

I looked at Gary. "What do you think?"

"He's on to us. The fact that he drove so slow. Stood there at the door staring at us. Then went inside and left it open. Like he's expecting us to follow him."

"A trap, right? It's a trap."

"Maybe."

"Do we take the bait?"

"You came here to confront him, didn't you? This is your chance if there ever was one. You gonna give up now?"

"I'm not comfortable just sauntering up to an open door. What if he's hanging back with a shotgun?"

"I'll protect us," Gary said.

"You'll protect us. With what?"

"I'm packing, man. I always pack. Just like American Express says. Don't leave home without it."

"Where is it?"

"In my bag. In the trunk. You aren't packing?"

"Are you kidding? I don't even *own* a gun."

Gary looked at me like I had just arrived on an *Invaders from Mars* spaceship. "Does that mean I'm your honor guard?" He laughed.

We got out of the car.

"Not taking your cane?" I said.

"Ain't no place for a man with a walking stick." He grimaced. "I'll get by."

I walked around to the passenger side and opened the door. I took a small flashlight and two pairs of disposable gloves out of the glove box. I put the gloves in my pocket.

Gary retrieved his gun from the trunk and holstered up. He rolled his shoulders back, puffed out his chest, and placed his right palm on the pistol handle. "Let's go see what's up, pardner."

"OK, John Wayne," I said with a half-laugh. "Or is it Barney Fife?"

"Go to hell, Tarwater."

The curtains were drawn tight. The house looked pitch black inside.

We crossed the street and into the yard next door. There was no car in that driveway. It was mid-morning on a weekday. Probably no one was home. We hugged the front of the house and crossed into Kilgallon's yard. We crouched low along the pyracanthas that lined the front of his house. Halfway to the front steps, Gary let out a grunt.

I could tell he was struggling with his bad leg. "You OK, man?" I said.

"Never mind me," he replied. "Let's soldier on."

We inched our way up the steps. Gary shadowed beside and slightly behind me, his gun drawn. We climbed the steps in a half-hunch. When we reached the threshold, I called Kilgallon's name twice. No response.

Gary entered first, sweeping his pistol from side to side into the black. I followed. We were in a living room that looked to be about twelve-by-twelve. A strong scent of must permeated the room.

I called out again. Nothing.

I panned the room with the flashlight.

To the left was a dining room/kitchen combo.

A darkened hallway led down the center of the house. There were two doors along its left wall. Two along its right. Three of the doors were closed. The second door on the right was slightly ajar. A sliver of light shown through its crack. At the end of the hallway was what appeared to be a door to the backyard.

We checked the closed-door rooms—two bedrooms and a bathroom. They were empty.

We approached the sliver of light. Gary eased the door open with his foot, his gun drawn. We walked into a ten-by-ten unkempt den. The sunlight shone into the room through the open rear window to my left. There was a four-shelf bookcase on the wall across from where we entered. Newspapers and magazines were strewn on the floor. A cheap Naugahyde chair sat in the corner to the right of the window, a crocheted afghan draped haphazardly across its back. Beside the chair was a small round table. On the table was a lamp. And a half-eaten Snickers. On the wall behind the chair was a wooden crucifix with INRE across its center. On the floor to the window's left was a one-foot-high concrete cherub fountain with recirculating water. The kind you'd see in a garden, not a den.

"You got me covered?" I said to Gary.

"You bet." He kept his gun drawn, switching back and forth between the door and the window.

I gloved up.

I scanned the bookcase. At eye level, religious books. *A History of the Evangelical Lutheran Church in the United States. The Biblical Bases, the Meaning, the Necessity, & the Joy in Baptismal Dedication. The Early Christian Fathers (Studies in Theology).*

One shelf down, four books by Flannery O'Connor. Three by C.S. Lewis. A Chesterton. Peale's *Sin, Sex and Self-Control.*

I was about to go to the next shelf when I glanced down and noticed something under the chair, shoved back toward the wall. I got on my hands and knees and pulled it out. It was not one object, but three. Hard cardboard file boxes, two-inch grey-green, with clasped lids. Each box had a handwritten paper label taped to the spine.

My eyes fixed on the one labeled YEAR 43. I opened it. It was jammed with notes and newspaper articles chronicling the '63 East Atlanta abductions and killings. I rifled through the papers, scattering them across the floor. At the bottom of the stack were color Polaroids of the bodies of the Dullums and Boggs girls. Taken from the crime scenes. Full-body and close-ups of their thighs. There were no pictures of Cynthia.

Beneath the photographs was a manila envelope labeled Louise Darby. I bent back the metal prongs and removed the contents. There were notes from what appeared to have been a series of one-on-one sessions between Kilgallon and Marvin Darby's mother. She had come to him distraught over a shadow life she had been living. It all started because she needed money. Pin money, she called it, but grocery money was more like it. There was a reference to the Alamo Motor Court. One of her johns was a senior detective. A man named Gus Alford. And now Alford had her son in his crosshairs. She was seeking guidance. God's forgiveness. And protection for her son.

Beneath the notes was an onionskin carbon copy of a letter. It was addressed to Gus Alford. My eyes rushed down the page. The gist: Come after me and I'll blow your little secret. I know where you live. I know who your wife is. I know who your son is. Would Betty and little Gary want to know your secret? Would the department want to know? Would Chief Jenkins want to know? Lay off me, Alford. And lay off the Darby boy. The last line of the letter said V.J. Kilgallon.

Gary, looking over my shoulder as I read the letter, pulled back. Crossed to the other side of the room. Stared at nothing.

"Gary, I'm sorry," I said.

"It's OK, man," he said. He puffed his chest back out. "Doesn't surprise me, really."

The second file box I opened was labeled YEAR 22. It contained details of the three girls killed in '42. Beneath the notes and articles were black-and-white Polaroids. And hand-drawn maps of the three areas where the Alabama girls were found.

What did the file box labels mean? I did some quick mental math. Year 0 would have been 1920. Was there something special about that date? I guessed Kilgallon would have been twelve or thirteen then. The age of believer's profession?

The label on the third box said YEAR 61. *Next year. Two months away.* I frantically opened the box. It was empty except for a single sheet of paper with three girls' names. Ages eleven to fourteen. And below their names, January 1981. My heart sank. *He's about to do it again.*

"Gary, look at this."

No sooner had the words left my lips than we heard a click-click coming from the backyard. I looked out the window. I saw a dark figure staring at us from the doorway of a weather-beaten outbuilding that could have been a cowshed, but there were no cows anywhere. It was Kilgallon. How long had he been watching us? Listening to us? He was holding a rifle. He raised it to firing position. Pointed it in the direction of the open window. Fired through the window. I ducked. He just missed my right ear. The bullet lodged in the wall at the other end of the room.

Gary shoved me aside, assumed a Weaver stance, and aimed at Kilgallon.

Kilgallon fired another shot in our direction, this time high.

Gary unloaded two rounds, one just over Kilgallon's head and the other at his feet.

Kilgallon retreated into the outbuilding and slammed the door.

We waited. Dead silence.

Kilgallon was probably expecting us to approach so he could ambush us. The whole thing was a trap to lure us onto his playing field, away from passersby. To stack the deck in his favor.

We heard another shot, this time from inside the shed.

We went out the front door. We circled around the house next door, through the backyard and into Kilgallon's yard. We approached the shed from the rear.

Gary circled around to the front of the shed, with me close behind him. With his gun drawn, Gary kicked the door open. "Freeze," he yelled.

Kilgallon was on his back. On a wooden chair that had fallen backwards onto the ground. Blood gushed from his mouth. The ground beneath his head was puddled with blood. The rifle lay on his chest. The bloody barrel pointed toward his face.

"Twenty-two bolt action Rimfire," Gary said. "Remington."

I rushed back to the house and phoned for help.

* * *

The police arrived first. Then the ambulance.

The paramedics estimated Kilgallon had died instantly.

Gary and I spent four hours with the police. Telling them everything we knew. Going over the evidence, both proximate and from afar. Signing handwritten affidavits.

The police wanted us to remain in Birmingham, but they finally relented. They let us return to Atlanta as long as we agreed to stay close to home and to come back when requested. It helped that Gary was a cop.

* * *

"Another day in paradise," Gary said as we walked to the car.

I found it odd that he could be so nonchalant about what had just happened. I pointed out that we had witnessed a suicide first hand, in case he'd forgotten that little detail.

"That's the way us hard-ass cops have to be, Tarwater. Otherwise, it'd drive us crazy."

We got into the car. I was about to put the key into the ignition when Gary turned to me. "You plan to put this in the paper?"

"I can't, Gary. I'm part of the story."

"You and me both."

We headed out of the subdivision.

We had just passed the East Irondale Acres sign when I glanced over and saw a car parked on the side of the road. I didn't think much of it at first. But then, half a block past, the image of the driver flashed before me. I swung onto a side street and idled.

"That parked car," I said. "Did you see it?"

"I saw it, but I wasn't paying any attention."

"The man in the car. He looked a little like Leonard Seymour."

I doubled back and headed toward where the car had been parked. It was gone. We drove all over the neighborhood but couldn't find it.

"Did the car look like his?" Gary asked.

"No. At least not the one I remember."

"Probably nothing. Just a coincidence."

"Yeah. I've been so wound up over all this, I think I'm starting to see things."

* * *

I stopped at the first phone booth I saw. I called the Birmingham PD. Told them about the sighting on the side of the road. Like Gary said, probably just a coincidence. But better safe than sorry.

* * *

We didn't speak again until we were on the highway.

"You're a damned good shot," I said to break the silence.

"Shut the fuck up, Tarwater. Some mess you got us into." Gary slapped my shoulder. "That's OK, though. I still like you, man."

The sun was making a slow descent behind us as we barreled toward Atlanta.

Chapter Forty-Six

Billy Tarwater

November 4, 1980

CYNTHIA BEAMED WHEN I WALKED THROUGH THE DOOR. "You're back." She wrapped her arms around me and squeezed tight. She led me by the hand to the sofa.

But her smile became more pinched by the minute as I chronicled everything that had happened in Alabama.

"It looks like Kilgallon did it," I said. "But his day in court will never come. Our opportunity to see justice done will never come."

She collapsed into my lap. "What do we do now?" she said through tears.

"We get on with our lives, that's what we do. But we still need to get an innocent man out of Reidsville. And I'm certain the Birmingham PD and I will end up bosom buddies by the time this is all over."

She gripped my hand hard. "Billy, how does somebody get on with their life…with everything that's happened? This isn't closure."

I put my arm around her. "I know. I can only imagine what you've been through. What you're going through now. I'm here for you. I love you, Cynthia. More than anything."

* * *

The next day, I put the wheels in motion to get Sam freed. It would be a long, hard slog. Stifling red tape. A judicial machine that, even in '80, didn't abide setting black men free. And an aversion to admitting that the system could have screwed up.

I knew I'd have to deal with the expected BS from almost everybody I talked to—the Fulton County DA's office, the Superior Court, even skeptical defense attorneys.

How do we know Jepperson wasn't involved somehow?

Because there is no evidence whatsoever that he had anything to do with it—that he even knew *Kilgallon, for that matter.*

But we have no direct evidence that Kilgallon did it either. No weapon. No prints. No blood. Nothing. Just some pictures and paperwork. Can you convict a man on that alone?

But you do *have a wealth of circumstantial evidence that Kilgallon is your man. And there may be prints for the taking, if someone bothers to look for them. And you have what sure looks like a blackmail letter to me. On the other hand, you have* nothing *on Jepperson.*

But blackmail isn't murder. And shouldn't we trust the justice system? After all, a jury of twelve men heard the evidence and decided Jepperson did it.

But the jury didn't have the benefit of knowing what we know now. And twelve white men. C'mon, really?

This would surely go on for weeks, probably months.

I needed to find a lawyer with a sympathetic ear. And the energy and wherewithal to get the job done.

I stumbled upon just the man I was looking for. A sharp-as-a-brass-tack old guard veteran with a resume to match his pugilistic sensibilities. And I didn't find him in Atlanta. Or Macon. Or Augusta. The man worked out of a gabled Victorian in Tallapoosa, an hour west of Atlanta and a stone's throw from the Alabama state line. I had called up a friend from UGA who was clerking at the Georgia Supreme Court. He said, "Go see the old codger. You won't regret it."

* * *

It was Thursday morning, the 6th. My first visit ever to Tallapoosa. The "old codger" had reluctantly agreed to meet me early, before things got busy. He said he had a full day of meetings, but he'd fit me in.

I left the apartment at 5:30. The Majestic Diner was in the wrong direction, but my choices were limited that early in the morning. Waffle House, Huddle House, Krispy Kreme—I'd take the Majestic over those places any day. I popped in for an order of dry wheat toast, a couple of scrambled eggs, a spritz of Tabasco, and a pitch-black caffeine pick-me-up. I skimmed through the morning *Constitution* before hitting the road. It felt odd reading the paper—*my* paper—after having been away from the city desk for a week.

* * *

And now I sat waiting in the front parlor—aka reception room—on Bowdon Street in Tallapoosa, wondering whether I had made a mistake. *Surely there are better options than in this godforsaken town.*

After waiting for upwards of thirty minutes, I was close to leaving when I heard a shuffling down the hall. *Hunchback foot-dragging?* I looked up expecting to see Quasimodo in the flesh. But instead, I saw an old man, no more than five-foot-six, who couldn't—or didn't bother to—lift his feet off the floor. His face was ruddy-red. His hands trembled like a juicehead's. The waistband of his suspendered suit trousers rode a foot and a half below his chin. His three-inch-wide repp tie hung to his crotch.

For a moment, I regretted not having walked out when I had the chance.

He apologized for the shuffle. Said he was a "martyr to the frostbite" in the war. I was reluctant to ask *which* war, but from the looks of the man, I assumed The Great War. The War to End All Wars.

He led me to his office just off of the parlor.

I sat across the massive mahogany partners desk from him. He was so slight and sat so low that the desk practically swallowed him up.

He reached for his briar pipe. "Mind if I smoke?" But before I could answer, he had taken a wooden match to the bowl and was puffing billows of grey-blue smoke into the air, filling the room with cloyingly sweet notes of cherry and vanilla. "Have you asked yourself Why yet?" he said.

"Why what?"

"Why me?"

"I was told you're the best."

"Damned lies. Or the musings of the delusional." He laughed. "But seriously..." He shared his backstory—he called it the "CliffNotes" version. Born in McDuffie County. Joined the 106th Field Signal Batallion at the age of eighteen. Mercer Law School after the war. Georgia Supreme Court clerk. Fifty years as a trial lawyer.

CliffNotes or not, I was suitably impressed. When he spoke, he did so with an air of confidence and authority not befitting his bearing. I retained him on the spot.

I laid out the whys and wherefores of Sam Jepperson's arrest, conviction and imprisonment. I told him about Kilgallon. The jail cell in the parsonage. The trip to Irondale. About the file boxes in Kilgallon's back room. Finding him in the barn with a bullet through his head.

I retrieved the plastic bag from my satchel and pushed it across the desk.

"What's this?" he said.

I told him it was the medicine vial I'd taken from the parsonage. Evidence tampering wouldn't be a stretch, although at the time, there was no open case to tamper with. That I'd debated turning it over to the authorities, but there was plenty more where it came from. If the detectives cared to go looking for evidence, they'd find it.

"Did you tell the police about the room in the cellar?" he said.

"The Birmingham police, yes. All about it. I'm sure the Atlanta police have been fully briefed by now."

"Did you tell them you had walked away with the vial?"

"Of course not."

"Here. I'll take it. I'll keep it under lock and key. As far as you and I are concerned, it doesn't exist. OK?"

I nodded. "It may have Kilgallon's prints on it. I used a tissue when I handled it."

He locked the bag in his desk drawer. He stood and shuffled across the room. Stared out the window. Relit his pipe. Swung around to face me. "Jepperson'll walk free," he said. "I'll see to it. I just need some time."

"His kids are growing up without even knowing him."

He leaned in. Lowered his voice to a raspy near-whisper. "Tarwater, just so you know. If you want him out fast, it'll cost you. I've got friends in high places. DAs. Judges. But they don't come cheap."

* * *

I drove back to Atlanta hoping to spend some time alone with Cynthia. She had the day off from Agnes Scott, and the kids were away.

But before I went home, I needed to stop by the office. I was grateful for the time off. But the higher-ups at the paper had agreed to only a few days. And it had been a week. I didn't want to push my luck.

Chapter Forty-Seven

Cynthia Tarwater

November 6, 1980

CYNTHIA AWOKE TO AN EMPTY BED. SHE LOOKED AT the clock. It was 5:42. She ran her hand across the depression in Billy's pillow. It was still warm. She buried her face in the sheets, breathed deep, and took in the woody aroma of Aramis.

She called his name but there was no answer. She wiped her eyes with her knuckles. Stumbled into the kitchen. On the table was a note:

> Sorry I left without a word, but you looked so content. I couldn't bring myself to wake you. Have gone to Tallapoosa for an early-morning meeting. Long story. I'll fill you in later. Hope to be home early. Up for a badly needed play date? Love, Billy

* * *

How long had it been since Billy met her at the door in her green Pa'u and holding two Mai Tais? She still remembered his words. *Here, beautiful. This one's for you. Now, where did we leave off?*

That next morning, after breakfast, he had sat her down and broken the news. *It's about what happened back in '63.* He told her of his plans to make sense of it all. To get to the bottom of it. To find the killer. To free Sam. *Cynthia, this is something I have to do. And I need your help. I can't go it alone.*

That was forty-six days ago. How did she know it was forty-six days? Because not a day had gone by since then that she didn't think about it. Daily, in her mind, she marked a bold, black slash through each square on an imaginary calendar.

In twelve hours, her life had gone from *where did we leave off* to *I can't go it alone*. From putting the past behind her to reliving it daily.

Now Kilgallon was dead. And the lives of three girls, roughly the same age she had been in '63, had likely been saved. But five were dead.

She would continue to harbor a degree of guilt. Why had she lived when five girls died? Was it providential or mere coincidence that the workers showed up at Grove Park when they did? She didn't buy into providence, but a little part of her wondered.

Why did it all have to happen in the first place? She had never gained comfort with a Manichean, good-and-evil worldview. But when she thought about Kilgallon, about the senseless drowning of those poor girls, she realized that she had come face-to-face with evil of the worst kind.

Maybe now, with Kilgallon gone, she really could put the past behind her. She and Billy could move on with their lives. They owed it to Billy Jr. and Addie. They owed it to each other.

She took her imaginary marker and, on her imaginary calendar, she wrote a big Live Life diagonally across the Nov. 6 square.

She walked into the bathroom. Opened the medicine cabinet. Took the half-full bottle of benzodiazepine off the shelf. Emptied it into the toilet. Pushed down the handle and watched the swirl of blue Mother's Little Helpers disappear. A profound sense of relief came over her.

She was ready for that play date. Past ready. She would prepare for Billy's arrival.

Some people say you only live once. That's not true. We live anew every day. We only die *once.*

Chapter Forty-Eight

Leonard Seymour

November 7, 1980

FRIDAY MORNING, LEONARD SEYMOUR WAS ABOUT TO plump himself down into the driver's seat when the patrol car pulled up. Two men got out. They approached him.

The stout one with the ruddy face did the talking. "Leonard Seymour?"

"Yes?"

"Mr. Seymour, we'd like you to come to the station for questioning."

"About what?"

"Just come with us, please."

"Am I under arrest?"

"Why would you think that? We just want to ask you some questions."

It was his first time riding in the back seat of a police car. And he hoped it would be his last. But he had willingly gone along with the officer's request. He could have resisted. But where would that have gotten him?

They raced up Memorial Drive toward downtown.

The car's interior smelled of sweat and cigarettes. The inside handles had been removed from the rear doors. He ran his hand across the tear in the thick heavy-grade plastic that covered the rear seat. A heavy wire mesh partition separated him from the officers. The men in the front seat seemed oblivious to the car radio's constant crackle. Seymour could barely make out what they were saying, but it was something about a landslide and a B-grade actor.

* * *

The ruddy-faced one led him to a small, windowless room on the third floor of the Decatur Street station and directed him to sit at the steel table in the center of the room. Ruddy-face left the room, shutting the door behind him. The table's linoleum mist green top was spotted with cigarette burns and coffee rings. There was a half-filled ashtray on the table, but it obviously didn't get enough use. He looked around. The room was bare except for the table, the chair he was sitting in and the two across from him, and a Mister Coffee on a matching side table in the far corner of the room.

After about fifteen minutes, two plainclothes anal-retentive types—*tight-assed Joe Fridays*—entered the room. They were affable enough, going out of their way to assure him that he had nothing to worry about. Then they proceeded to grill him.

"Did you know Virlyn Kilgallon?"

"*Did*? What do you mean *did*? Has something happened to him?"

Neither answered. They peppered him with questions. How long had he known Kilgallon? How did they meet? *When* did they meet?

Seymour told them he had moved from Sylacauga to Atlanta in early '44. Said he was twenty-five at the time, fresh out of the Seabees and eager to get away from his deranged sister. He had considered Birmingham, but it wasn't far enough away. He moved to Atlanta. Rented a garage apartment. Got a job at the East Atlanta ice house. Started looking for a church right away and stumbled upon Confederate Avenue Baptist. Kilgallon was the pastor.

"What about your wife?"

"What *about* my wife?" He frowned. "I thought this was about Kilgallon."

"It is. But did your wife move to Atlanta with you?"

"Yeah. She came with me. Then three sprats later and she takes off."

"Takes off?"

"With a brush salesman. Can you believe it? A goddamn brush salesman."

"When was that?"

"Nineteen years ago. Almost to the day."

"Did your wife know Kilgallon too?"

"Of course. She went to the church with me. Until she up and left."

"And you didn't know him until you started going to his church. When did you say that was?

"Early '44."

"How well did you know him?"

"Well enough. I sang in the choir. Helped him out with things around the church."

They asked him how he had come to obtain a Valiant from Kilgallon? On what terms? And what happened to it?

He told them Kilgallon had approached him in '63 about getting rid of the car. Turned the title over to him. At that time, Seymour didn't ask questions. Didn't need to know more. After all, it was the reverend. You can't blame a guy for doing his pastor a favor, can you?

"What happened to the car?"

"It was stolen. Out of the East Atlanta Barber Shop parking lot. Surely you can go look at your files from back then. I told the police all about it when it happened."

"Did they ever recover it?"

"You tell me. I'm not the police."

Had he known the two girls who were killed back in '63? Plus the one who survived?

"I knew two of them. They went to Kilgallon's church. The other one…what was her name?"

"Boggs."

"Yeah. That's it. Boggs. She didn't go there. I think she was from Alabama. The one that survived…Cynthia Hudspeth…her parents lived next door to me. Still do. It's so tragic what happened to those poor girls."

"When was the last time you saw Kilgallon?"

"When he left Atlanta to go back to Irondale."

"When was that?"

"Late '63. You already knew that though, right?"

"So you never visited him in Alabama?

"No."

"Were you in Alabama three days ago?"

Seymour wondered how the detectives could have known that. "I visited my sister for a long weekend. Decided to stay over a couple extra days."

"The deranged sister?"

"Yeah, my only sister," Seymour replied. "She's not really deranged. Just a little crackbrained. Her husband's worse." He smirked. But his smirk quickly faded. "Has something happened to the reverend?"

The detectives ignored his question—again.

Had he ever visited the parsonage in Atlanta when Kilgallon lived there?

He told them he hadn't.

"After Kilgallon had left Atlanta?"

"Nope. Never did."

"By the way, what happened to your hand, Seymour?"

"I had a run-in with a cinder block wall."

"A cinder block wall?"

"I was carrying a crate…you know, one of those wooden produce crates…full of jars of canned something…to my sister's basement. Halfway down the stairs, I lost my footing. I caught my fall, but I rammed the crate into the wall. My hand wedged between the crate and the cinder block. It still hurts like hell, if you want to know the truth."

By the time one o'clock rolled around, the detectives said they were through with him. He wasn't sure whether they were *really* through with him or, more likely, it was past lunchtime. He agreed to come back if they had more questions.

The detectives offered to have somebody drive him home. *Mighty thoughtful for tight-asses*, he thought. He declined. Said he'd rather take the bus.

* * *

When Leonard Seymour got home, he locked the deadbolt. He drew the curtains tight. He settled into his La-Z-Boy. Shotgunned a PBR, taking in the cold, citrusy drag as it cleared his bone-dry throat.

Had the police believed him? Would they be back?

He would wait until early evening to build the fire.

* * *

Four tall boys and as many hours later, he carried the papers and photographs under his arm to the backyard. In his right hand, a pocket-size box of Diamond safety matches. In his left, a gasoline canister. Draped over his left forearm and around the canister—the bomber jacket, the khaki trousers, the denim work shirt.

He approached the half-rusted-out 55-gallon drum in the corner of the backyard farthest from the Hudspeths. He placed the canister, the clothes, the matches on the ground. He thumbed through the papers, reading each page before tossing it into the drum's belly. He reached into his pants pocket and retrieved the three-inch pocket knife he had been carrying since his Alabama visit. Tossed it in with the papers. Threw in the bomber jacket, the trousers, the shirt.

He glanced over at Cynthia Hudspeth's old bedroom window. Someone was watching him from inside the darkened room.

He doused the drum's contents with gasoline. Lit a match and flicked it into the drum. The glowing cinders, rising into the dusk like a million tiny fireflies, held him spellbound. Took him back to another time and place.

Leonard thought back to a warm and muggy summer night in Mobile.

> It was 1930.
>
> A twelve-year-old boy, Mason jar in hand, coursed through the long grasses, reeds, and marshy fens along the edge of Wragg Swamp. He headed home with a jar full of flickering light. When he got to the house, he unscrewed the lid, opened it ever so slightly, and slipped an apple slice into the jar. He sealed the lid tight. He took an ice pick and poked a dozen holes in the lid. He placed the jar on his nightstand. He sat staring at it.
>
> Leonard was that boy.
>
> The country was in the throes of an economic downturn the likes of which no one had ever seen. Leonard's family had not been spared. His father had lost his job as a shipyard pipefitter and had sunk into a bog of despondence. His mother,

true to her strong German stock and determined to provide nourishment for the four of them, scraped together whatever food she could get her hands on. His father and the others stood in bread lines for hours. He did odd jobs for a nickel here, a dime there.

Before the depression set in, they had been active in the local church, Grace Lutheran. Not just active, but avidly so. His father was a diaconal minister, a member of the Lutheran Laymen's League. His mother sang in the choir. But by 1930 his father had stopped going—the old man could no longer buy into the notion of a just God. Soon after that, the other three stopped going too.

In July of '30, the family took in a young boarder to make ends meet. The man was twenty-two. He said he had been called by the Almighty Himself to spread the Word. Seymour never saw him without a well-worn bible in his hand. But when he wasn't spouting the scripture all over the place, he mostly kept to himself. He took his meals in his room. He never let on where he had come from. Where he was headed.

Leonard was twelve and infatuated with the odd man who had showed up with a Room To Let want ad in his hand. He sometimes wondered how the renter managed to pay the rent. But he never asked.

A year later, Virlyn Kilgallon moved on.

By the time '37 rolled around, *dire straits* had slowly turned into *barely getting by*. At least they had survived the worst of it, but Leonard came out on the back end of the depression with a chip on his shoulder the size of the *S.S. Mobile City*, named for the goddamn town he'd do anything to leave.

That spring, Leonard's sister took a secretarial job with Sylacauga Fertilizer. Leonard, nineteen years old and past ready to bolt, decided to move with her. He'd heard the marble company was hiring, and he could stay rent free with her until he was able to stand on his own two feet. They bought two bus tickets for $3.45 each at the Greyhound station on Government Street, boarded the Super Coach, and headed northward, suffering eight hours and three hundred miles of patches and potholes, lurches and lunges.

Why is it that some memories are vague, but Leonard Seymour remembered the reverend's words as if they had been spoken yesterday? Did the man have that much sway over him, like some Svengali?

Irondale. January. 1942.

Leonard stood on the muddy river bank. At the shallows where the Cahaba makes a hundred-eighty-degree turn and wends its way southward on its circuitous journey to the Alabama River. It was early in the month and bitter cold.

He waded into the river's edge with the others. The bone-chilling water saturated his white robe. His body trembled. He stood in line awaiting his turn.

Virlyn Kilgallon, all of thirty-three and clad in a dark grey suit and tie, stood waist-deep in the water. He cradled Leonard's back with his right arm. Placed his hand over the young man's nose. Lowered him into the water.

Leonard struggled to make out the reverend's fevered utterances through the water's muffle.

"I now baptize you in the name of the Father and the Son and the Holy Ghost," Kilgallon said. "Buried with Him in the likeness of His death, raised with Him in the likeness of His resurrection to walk in the newness of life."

The bright morning sun, broken into fragments by the water's ripples, shone through his partially-open eyes like dancing points of light.

When I came up, I let out a gasp. Kilgallon thought I was moved by the Holy Spirit. I didn't have it in me to tell him that what moved me was not the spirit but the ice-cold water.

Three weeks prior to that, Japanese bombers had attacked the naval base at Pearl Harbor. Twenty-three and prime war material, Leonard Seymour needed good asylum. He remembered having read in the *Birmingham News* that Virlyn

> Kilgallon had landed a pulpit in Irondale. He sought him out.
>
> "I can make you a man of the cloth," Kilgallon had said. "Just like that."
>
> "Just like that?"
>
> "Just like that. But first you need to be cleansed by the water."

Leonard's attention briefly returned to the conversation he had with the detectives. *Seabees my ass.* He stifled a chortle. *I would have done just about anything to keep from getting killed in that damnable war.* A hot cinder rose from the drum and found his cheek. His smile became a wince. *But a price was paid.*

> East Atlanta. September. 1963.
>
> The phone rang three times before Leonard picked up.
>
> It was Kilgallon. "How soon can you get to the Zesto's on Moreland?" he said.
>
> Leonard asked if he meant the one in Little Five Points or the one at Confederate Avenue, near the church.
>
> He said Confederate Avenue.
>
> "Fifteen minutes, tops," Leonard said. "Where are you? You sound like you're in a tunnel."
>
> "At the Texaco."
>
> "What's up?"
>
> He said don't ask questions. Just meet him behind the Zesto's. Near the dumpster. There was

a long pause on the line. "You got the goods?" he said.

Leonard knew what he meant, but he asked anyway. "The goods?"

"The goods. Bingo Barbie."

"I got the goods, Reverend."

Leonard drove down Moreland. Just past Confederate, he turned into the Zesto's lot. He pulled behind the building. He parked past the dumpster, out of sight of passersby. He cut the engine. He waited for Kilgallon.

Less than five minutes later, the Valiant eased into the lot and pulled up beside him. He recognized the girl sitting in the passenger seat in her well-worn Murphy High sweatshirt. He jumped out of his car and approached the Valiant.

She reached for the door handle. Kilgallon grabbed her wrist. She struggled to break free. His grip tightened. So hard that her hand began to turn plum. She buried her teeth into his hand. He jerked away.

She reached for the door handle again. She pulled the handle down and pushed hard, but the door wouldn't open. She looked up and saw Leonard standing outside the Valiant, his hand clenching the outside handle.

He swung the door open with one hand and grabbed her arm with the other. He pulled her out of the car and onto the pavement.

Kilgallon reached into the back seat and threw a roll of duct tape out the open door.

Leonard bound her hands behind her back. He rolled up her Murphy sleeve. He retrieved the vial and syringe from his pocket and removed the cap from the syringe. He held the vial upside down. Pierced the rubber septum with the needle. Filled the syringe with liquid. Injected it into her vein even though she struggled mightily to pull away.

He heaved her into the back seat and got in the front with Kilgallon. They headed for the parsonage, leaving Leonard's car in the Zesto's rear lot.

"Where'd you find her?" Leonard said.

"Her mother visited me at the church this morning. I left when she did. She told me she was heading to McKnight's to have her car looked at. I had a hunch I might find the girl hanging around downtown East Atlanta somewhere."

Leonard said he had been driving down Flat Shoals when there she was. Parading down the street. He followed close behind her. When she stopped, he stopped. When she went, he went. She looked over her shoulder. They made eye contact. He pulled over. She walked up to the car. He concocted a story about needing her to come to the church. That her mother was meeting them there. "Get in, missy."

When they arrived at the parsonage, Cynthia was out like a light. Leonard carried her around the side of the house and into the basement.

They entered the cell. She awakened partially. She wobbled. Leonard held her up by her arms, tied behind her back at her wrists with the duct tape.

Kilgallon cupped his palms over the top of her head. Gazed into her glassed-over eyes. A drop of spittle coursed from the corner of her half-open mouth and down her chin.

Leonard stood over the girl. "In the name of the Lord Jesus, drive these wicked demons from this poor girl's soul. Release her. Come out of her." He pushed hard against her forehead.

She fell backwards and onto the mattress.

Kilgallon's body convulsed. His eyelid began its restive twitch. "…neema gash monavah solema golah…" He staggered backwards. His knees began to buckle. He let the cellar wall take his weight.

Leonard thought back to that September seventeen years ago. He and Kilgallon had kept her in the cellar for twelve days. About the same as the Dullums girl. *Five days longer than the ones in '42-—the first ones—and the other one from Alabama. The Boggs girl.* He remembered the day Kilgallon told him the time had come.

East Atlanta. October. 1963.

Day 11. They had seen to it that, once a day, Cynthia awakened long enough to eat, to use the bucket, to receive Kilgallon's ministrations.

Kilgallon lifted his hands in the orans pose. "I have made a watchman for the house of Israel. Whenever you hear a word from my mouth, you shall give them warning from me. If I say to the wicked, O wicked one, you shall surely die, and you do not speak to warn the wicked to turn from his way, that wicked person shall die in his iniquity, but his blood I will require at your hand. But if you warn the wicked to turn from his way, and he does not turn from his way, that person shall die in his iniquity, but you will have delivered your soul."

Leonard injected her with another dose of phenobarbital.

She drifted off.

Kilgallon nodded to Leonard. "It's time. Tomorrow morning." Then to Cynthia. "Poor wretch."

Well before daybreak the following morning, Leonard was jarred out of a deep sleep by the phone.

"How quick can you get here?" Kilgallon said.

"Where?"

"The parsonage."

"I'll be there in twenty minutes."

At the parsonage, Leonard gave her another shot of phennies. He carried her to Kilgallon's car and loaded her into the back seat.

"Where are we headed?" Leonard said.

"You know Grove Park?"

Until that day in October, Leonard had never been to Grove Park.

Grove Park. October. 1963.

Leonard would have completed the job if the construction workers hadn't shown up. But they did.

When they arrived at Grove Park, Leonard disrobed her and threw her clothes into the back seat of Kilgallon's car. He carried her to the creek's edge. The reverend held her head face-down in the water while Leonard grasped her thigh with one hand, held the knife in the other.

"This is for you, Father," Kilgallon said.

Leonard's own father, the diaconal minister, the Lutheran Layman from Mobile, appeared before his mind's eye.

He opened the pen knife.

But Kilgallon raised his palm. "Wait." He placed his open hands on the back of Cynthia's head. "Go therefore and make disciples of all nations, baptizing them in the name of the Father and the Son and the Holy Spirit." Kilgallon pushed her face hard into the water.

She lay dead still.

"Okay, now," he said.

Leonard felt the pen knife handle's subtle tension against his thumb and fingers as he ran the blade across Cynthia's skin. "This is for you, Father," he said.

The workers arrived before he could finish. He closed the pen knife and stuffed it into his pants pocket.

He and Kilgallon ran back to the car and took off. Kilgallon crossed Proctor Creek and pulled up alongside the curb directly across from where they had just been. Leonard stayed with the car while Kilgallon watched the workers from behind the bushes.

It wasn't long before they heard sirens.

Leonard stood over the drum and watched as the last flame died. He crossed the yard and went back into the house. He grabbed another tall boy from the refrigerator and popped the top. He took a couple of swigs and ambled into the living room. He sank into the La-Z-Boy. Took in another big gulp.

He held out the back of his right hand. The swelling had gone down, but the bruises were turning a hideous purple-black. His knuckles were raw. A catching pang radiated down his right side.

His drive back to Atlanta three days ago had been fraught.

He wouldn't have even ended up in Irondale in the first place had it not been for the conversation he and Billy Tarwater had had in his backyard five days before that. He had a hunch Tarwater would end up seeking out Kilgallon. And on that hunch, Leonard had loaded up the car, made up a story about visiting his sister in Sylacauga, and took off for Birmingham.

Birmingham. October 30th, 1980.

A little before ten in the evening, Leonard checked into the Quality Inn near the Birmingham airport. He would wait until morning to call Kilgallon.

Early the next day, he called. "He's on your tail," he said. "It wouldn't surprise me if he turned up on your doorstep." Leonard told Kilgallon where he was. "Call me first thing if he shows up. If I'm not here, leave a message with the desk clerk. I'm in Room 106. Or try my sister. I may end up paying her a weekend visit. That's assuming all's quiet on the western front."

Leonard holed up in the darkened room that evening. *No interest in a bunch of damned street urchins begging for candy. Not that they'd show up at my motel door anyway. But why chance it?*

The following day, Saturday, he did end up visiting his sister after all. He spent one night with her and her husband, watching her flit around the house like a tsetse fly and listening to her husband blather on about the differences between whole and universal life.

On Sunday, he returned to Birmingham and to his room at the Quality Inn, which he had kept. He had convinced his sister to let him drive her car back to Birmingham on the pretense that his engine had started misfiring periodically and he was worried about driving it back and forth. She didn't need to drive more than a few miles a day and, anyway, they could take her husband's Cadillac if they had far to go. She relented. *What if she drives my car and realizes it's fine?* he thought. *Hell, she's so crackbrained, she wouldn't know the difference between a misfire, a backfire and a dumpster fire. And Mister Insurance Man? He's even dumber.* Leonard promised to return to Sylacauga in a week to switch out the cars. Said he'd have his own car checked out at the Sylacauga Auto Repair before heading back to Atlanta.

Two more days passed before he got the call from Kilgallon. He picked up on the first ring this time.

"He's here," Kilgallon said.

"Where?"

"The church."

"What do you plan to do?"

"I'm heading home. They'll follow me there. I'll lure them into the house somehow. Once they're inside, they're mine. You can't blame a man for doing whatever it takes to protect his castle, can you?"

"Them? Who's *them*?"

"Tarwater has somebody with him. A big guy. With a gimp."

"Need me to meet you there?"

"Not yet. Sit tight. I'll call you if I need you."

Seymour knew there was shit in Kilgallon's house. Shit that could implicate both him and Kilgallon. Shit that he needed to get rid of before Kilgallon and the others got there. If Billy Tarwater and the other one found it, and if Kilgallon didn't end up killing them, he and the reverend would both be dead men walking.

He threw his bomber jacket into the passenger seat of his car. He jumped in and sped off. He could be at East Irondale Acres in ten minutes if he floored it.

He parked one street over, in front of the house that backed up to Kilgallon's. He had little time to spare. He put on his jacket. He crossed through the neighbor's yard and into Kilgallon's backyard. He ran past the barn—*or whatever you call it*—to the house. The back door was locked. He checked the window to the right of the door. It was locked. But the window to the left, the one into Kilgallon's den, was not. Seymour opened the window and managed to squeeze his ample frame through it.

He knew exactly where the shit was. Kilgallon had shown it to him more than once. He was bending down to pull the boxes out from under the Naugahyde chair when he happened to notice the books on the shelf, including the one he had given Kilgallon. The Lutheran one. It had once belonged to his diaconal minister father. But his attention quickly shifted back to the boxes under the chair. *Time's wasting. Task at hand.*

He opened the first box. The YEAR 22 box. He rifled through the contents. Near the bottom of the stack of papers and photographs were notes penned in Kilgallon's handwriting. They implicated Seymour. Said Seymour had done it alone. Killed those girls in Alabama by his own hand. Then came to Kilgallon begging for atonement.

Seymour stuffed the notes in his jacket pocket. *The low-down son of a bitch.*

He went through everything again. Nothing else in the box connected him to the murders.

Seymour opened YEAR 43. He found a similar note in the bottom of the stack. He also found a Polaroid picture of him holding his pen knife over the Dullums girl's thigh. And another of him dragging her body out of the Valiant. *How did Kilgallon manage to take them without my noticing?* Halfway through the stack were detailed notes from Kilgallon's meeting in his office with Adele Hudspeth—the meeting where Adele had revealed that Seymour had been spying on her daughter through the bedroom window.

He took the notes and the Polaroids out of the box and added them to the papers already in his jacket pocket.

He checked the third box. There was nothing in it except some girls' names. Names he didn't recognize.

He slid all three boxes back under the chair.

He had to act fast. Kilgallon and the others could show up any minute. He ran out the back door. He hid in the barn. He waited.

His mind reeled. Kilgallon had hatched a plan to lure Billy Tarwater and the other one into his house. To kill them in apparent self-defense. What had he said? *You can't blame a man for protecting his castle.* Seymour wasn't sure what he would do when Kilgallon and the others showed up.

Twenty minutes passed before he heard scurrying outside the barn. He peered through the crack in the barn door. Kilgallon was in the backyard. He had a gun. A rifle. He raised the rifle. Took aim at the house.

A single shot rang out. Then another.

A third shot, this time coming from the house. Then a fourth.

Seymour saw Kilgallon heading to the barn door. He ran and hid behind a large wooden chest in the far corner of the barn.

Kilgallon entered the barn and slammed the door behind him. He reloaded his rifle.

Time's wasting. Task at hand.

Leonard leaped from behind the chest. "You're trying to pin it all on me, you son of a bitch."

Kilgallon leveled the rifle at Leonard's head.

Leonard charged him. Grabbed the rifle barrel with his right hand. Torqued it toward the wall of the barn.

Kilgallon drove Leonard into the wall, jamming his right hand between the barrel and the rough-hewn planks.

Leonard pushed Kilgallon hard with his left hand.

Kilgallon let go of the gun. Leonard shoved him to the ground. Knocked the wind out of him.

Leonard pulled a wooden chair over to where Kilgallon lay. "Get up, Virlyn," he said. He pointed to the chair. "Sit in it."

Kilgallon whimpered as Leonard stood over him with the barrel trained between his eyes. He begged Leonard to back off. "I didn't mean to," he cried. "We're in this together, you and me."

"Shut the fuck up, Virlyn. We're not in this together. From this point forward, it's all on you."

Leonard thrust the barrel into Kilgallon's mouth. Pulled the trigger before he could react. The bullet's impact propelled Kilgallon and the chair backwards and onto the ground. Leonard placed the rifle on Kilgallon's chest, with the barrel's end near his mouth and his hand near the trigger.

Spattered blood spotted Leonard Seymour's open bomber jacket, the front panel of his shirt, his right trouser leg. His knuckles were bleeding. He grabbed an oily rag and wrapped it around his hand.

He ran out the rear door of the barn. His first inclination was to take off immediately, but he heard footfalls outside the front of the barn. He hunched behind the barn and peered through the crack between the door and the frame. Billy and the other one entered the barn. Then Billy left. Soon, the police arrived. Then the ambulance. The police took pictures. The paramedics covered Kilgallon with a sheet and carried him off on a stretcher. Leonard heard the siren blare as the ambulance sped away. Then the police, Billy, and the other one left the barn.

Leonard lingered behind the bushes that separated Kilgallon's backyard from the neighbor's and watched them enter the house through the back door. He could see them in Kilgallon's den. He watched them as they went through the contents of the file boxes. Had he removed everything from the boxes that he needed to? Might there be something else in Kilgallon's den that he had missed?

They left the den but, as far as Leonard could tell, they didn't leave the house.

Leonard waited. Then Billy and his sidekick came outside through the backdoor and walked around toward the front of the house.

Leonard crossed through the neighbor's yard. He removed his jacket and threw it into the back seat. He got in his sister's car and took off.

He had just left East Irondale Acres when he pulled over to the side of the road. He took the pen knife and tore off part of the arm of his work shirt. He removed the blood-soaked oily rag from his hand. He threw it out the window and into the brush along the side of the road. He was in the process of wrapping the cloth from his shirt around his hand when he looked up and saw the car pass. Billy Tarwater was driving. The other one was in the passenger's seat.

Chapter Forty-Nine

Billy Tarwater

November 26, 1981

THE ATLANTA CHILD MURDERS HAD CONTINUED through '80 and into '81. Then, in June, the police arrested a man named Wayne Williams. Despite Dorothy Allison's proclamations, thirty people had been killed, all but six under the age of twenty. One as young as seven. Allison had given the Atlanta police a list of forty-two names of murder suspects derived from her supposed clairvoyant gift. Williams was not on the list.

I was reminded of Madame Ludowici, who never provided a whit of insight back in '63. But I have to admit, she did add a bit of excitement to an eleven-year-old's day. *Thank you, Dovey Mae.*

Williams was charged and indicted for first-degree murder in the deaths of only two of the victims. A jury would likely not be convened until sometime in late December and a verdict not reached until '82.

The killings ended with Williams' arrest.

The city breathed a collective sigh of relief.

* * *

While my own relief paled in the grand scheme of things, bringing what happened in '63 to a close and seeing Sam Jepperson freed meant everything to Cynthia. To Sam. To Sam's family. To me. And even to Gary.

I remembered what my UGA friend had said. "Go see the old codger. You won't regret it."

The old codger did, indeed, have friends in high places. And they didn't come cheap. But I never for one second regretted it.

Based on the evidence found in Kilgallon's Irondale house and in the basement dungeon in Atlanta, and thanks to the old codger's schmoozing, arm-twisting, and deal-making, the '63 case had been reopened. Kilgallon was found guilty of kidnapping the three girls and killing two of them. And the stage had been set for reopening the '42 case in Alabama. And three girls' lives had likely been saved. But Kilgallon didn't live to pay, or to atone, for his transgressions.

He had the last say. Killed by his own hand in a rundown backyard shed.

It had taken damned near nine more months to free Sam Jepperson. To clear his name. To reunite him with his family.

And now it was Thanksgiving Day. Cynthia and I were headed to Carver Homes. Ruby had prepared a midday feast "fit for my king," as she had said on the phone. We would celebrate with Sam, Ruby, Rufus, and Recy. And Rufus's wife Theda, whom we had never met.

But first, we would drop off Billy Jr. and Addie at Cynthia's parents' house. We would return there in the evening for yet another Thanksgiving meal. My mother and Chester would join us.

We pulled into Adele and Cecil's driveway. I cut the ignition. I reached over and hugged Cynthia. "It's been a long journey, babe. But we got through it. We can finally put it behind us."

She nodded and smiled. She squeezed my hand. The painful uncertainty in her eyes that I had grown so accustomed to had disappeared.

As we walked the kids to the house, I looked next door. Leonard Seymour was sitting in a lounge chair in the front yard drinking a tall one.

He waved.

Acknowledgments

I AM FOREVER INDEBTED TO MY FELLOW WRITERS GLEN Heefner, Julia Sennette, Dru Sumner, and John Ripma. They guided me through every chapter, every page, and every word of *The Devil You Knew*, and they continue to inspire me every day. For that I am grateful.

I am also indebted to Laura Sadri, who helped edit the book in its entirety and provided valuable feedback, and to Kian Sadri, Mandy Rahiya and Laura Sadri for cover conceptualization and design.

Caren, my wife of forty-four years, stood by my side and provided encouragement every step of the way. She continues to give me the support I need to pursue my passion for writing. She is my soulmate in every sense.

In short, I had a lot of help writing this book. I could not have done it alone.

About The Author

MIKE COBB'S body of literary work includes both fiction and nonfiction, short-form and long-form, as well as articles and blogs. While he is comfortable playing across a broad range of topics, much of his focus is on true crime, crime fiction and historical fiction. Rigorous research is foundational to his writing. He gets that honestly, having spent much of his professional career as a scientist. He vehemently refuses to box his work into a specific genre.

Mike splits his time between Atlanta and Blue Ridge, Georgia.

MGCOBB.COM

MGCobbWriter

@mgcobb

cobbmg

About The Type

This book is set in Adobe Caslon, a typeface designed by Carol Twombly and based on William Caslon I's original design dating to the mid 1700s. Caslon, a trained London engraver and typefounder, is widely credited for creating the first original typeface of English origin and establishing a national typographic style. Caslon's self-titled typeface is know for its enduring style and legibility.

In the late 19th century the Caslon typeface was adapted for hot metal typesetting with the gaining popularity of mass-market printing.

CPSIA information can be obtained
at www.ICGtesting.com
Printed in the USA
BVHW040852230922
647453BV00003BA/8

9 780578 371436